PRAISE FOR
CHARLES RYAN
AND HIS THRILLERS

"Electrifying, action-packed."
—W.E.B. Griffin

"Charles Ryan is the real deal."
—Stephen Coonts

"Ryan knows how to spin a pulse-tingler."
—*New York Times Book Review*

"Charles Ryan is a true master of adventure."
—Clive Cussler

"A page turner . . ."
—*New York Daily News*

"Fast-paced and crisp."
—*Publishers Weekly*

BOOK YOUR PLACE ON OUR WEBSITE AND MAKE THE READING CONNECTION!

We've created a customized website just for our very special readers, where you can get the inside scoop on everything that's going on with Zebra, Pinnacle and Kensington books.

When you come online, you'll have the exciting opportunity to:

- View covers of upcoming books
- Read sample chapters
- Learn about our future publishing schedule (listed by publication month *and author*)
- Find out when your favorite authors will be visiting a city near you
- Search for and order backlist books from our online catalog
- Check out author bios and background information
- Send e-mail to your favorite authors
- Meet the Kensington staff online
- Join us in weekly chats with authors, readers and other guests
- Get writing guidelines
- AND MUCH MORE!

**Visit our website at
http://www.kensingtonbooks.com**

RECON FORCE STORM FRONT

CHARLES RYAN

PINNACLE BOOKS
Kensington Publishing Corp.
http://www.kensingtonbooks.com

To Charlie, Danika, and Little Ryan

Like bees innumerable from ships down to the
Deep foreshore streamed those regiments toward
The assembly grounds—
And Zeus commanded Strife down to the beachhead,
Hardbitten goddess, bearing in her hands the
    stormfront,
Sign of war. . . .

                                        —*The Illiad,* Homer

DECISION

Southwick House,
Portsmouth, England
4 June 1944
2132 hours British double summer time

Supreme Allied Commander General Dwight D. Eisenhower eased back his heavy chair from the long, green baize-covered conference table, rose, and walked to a series of tall windows across the room. He stood there a moment, then eased the thick blackout curtain aside slightly and silently gazed out.

In the darkness he couldn't see the long stretch of neatly groomed lawn that went down to steep chalk cliffs, which then sloped to the densely packed homes and buildings of the city of Portsmouth. Yet even if it had been day, everything would have appeared misty as rain, hurled by forty-five-knot winds, slammed against the French crystal panes.

He was in the library of Southwick House, his D day headquarters. Seated behind him at the table were six of his senior commanders. On one side were his fellow Americans, Generals Omar Bradley and Walter Biddel-Smith, along with British Admiral Sir Bertram Ramsey. Across the table were British Air Chief Marshall Sir Arthur Tedder, Ike's deputy commander,

Deputy Air Chief Marshall Sir Trafford Leigh-Mallory, and General Bernard Montgomery in his usual corduroy trousers and roll-neck sweater.

Since the first of June, these men had met here twice a day, primarily to receive weather updates from their chief meteorologist, Group Captain J.M. Stagg, a dour but brilliant Scotsman who was already two minutes late for this meeting.

Ever since March of 1943, the massive preparations for the invasion of western Europe and the opening of the Second Front against Nazi Germany had been under way. Nearly a quarter million soldiers, sailors, airmen, and merchant seamen, with millions of tons of equipment and over seven thousand ships in assembly ports from Felixstowe on the North Sea to Milford Haven, Wales, were on hold, waiting for the word to cross the English Channel.

D day had originally been scheduled for 4 June. But then a violent low front, designated L5, had swept across the British Isles. Strong winds and drenching rain quickly turned the Channel into a cauldron. Eisenhower was forced to order the invasion postponed for at least forty-eight hours.

A light tap sounded at the library door and a young major came in to inform Eisenhower that Captain Stagg had arrived. The Scotsman swept in briskly, snapped to attention, and curtly apologized for his tardiness. He waited for Ike to return to his chair, then moved to a large weather map on an easel in front of a wall of books.

He quickly went over the latest weather reports from the three primary stations in Britain: the BCF office at Dunstable, the USAAF station in the Thames Valley, and the British Admiralty, London. Things didn't look good.

He then moved on to his own team's analysis of the situation. "Although it is admittedly quite dicey at this point," he said in his heavy accent, "I do believe we have a window. L-Five has reached its dissipation cycle and another low front is behind it, coded L-Six. However, I believe this one will issue from the north, off the Greenland coast. L-Five originated off Norway in the east." He indicated the areas on the map. "This difference will allow us a break during four and five June. It should last for at least eighteen hours."

Montgomery interrupted in his piping, squeaky voice, "How firm is your forecast of this break, Captain?"

"I believe it is *very* firm, sir," Stagg answered. "There *is* disagreement, I must admit. Both the Admiralty and Dunstable believe it will come in from the east. The Americans, however, agree with my analysis."

Eisenhower asked, "Is eighteen hours optimistic or a stretch?"

"I believe it would represent the median, General. A bit less, a bit more."

For the next twenty minutes, the commanders worked Stagg over with sharp, blunt questions. Tedder, Leigh-Mallory, and Admiral Ramsey were particularly concerned over ocean conditions as well as cloud cover above the French coast, which could badly hamper air strikes. Montgomery challenged the meteorologist's conclusions, asked when the next opening would come. Stagg said 15 to 17 June. Eisenhower listened quietly while the captain tenaciously held his ground.

At last, Ike dismissed him and he and the others spent the next half hour discussing probabilities, options, and the feasibility of postponing until the next solid weather window. Opinions seemed evenly divided.

Eisenhower finally took a table vote. Tedder, Leigh-Mallory, and Ramsey were hesitant and called for continued postponement. Bradley, Bidell-Smith, and, surprisingly,

Montgomery, considering the harsh way he had gone after Stagg, voted to utilize the forecast break and launch the invasion immediately.

Eisenhower again rose from his chair and went to the window. No one spoke. The final decision was now on his shoulders alone. Afterward, these men would recall how terribly lonely he seemed there at the window, the fury of L-Five lashing right at his face.

At last, he turned. In his quiet, midwestern voice, he said simply, "Okay, let's go."

NORMANDY
D day

Chapter One

2358 hours
5 June 1944

They were volunteers, Pathfinders from the 501st Parachute Infantry Regiment of the 101st Airborne Division. Except for Blue Team and three noncoms transferred from the 82nd, which had already seen combat in Sicily and Salerno, they were all green and untested.

Standing forward of the open door, the stick jumpmaster, Lieutenant John "Red" Parnell, gave the men lined along both sides of the Douglas C-47 *Airtrain* a close study. He wasn't a part of the 501st. Instead he was leader of a five-man unit designated Blue Team, which was part of an elite recon force called the Mohawkers.

All the team members were combat veterans from North Africa, Sicily, and Italy. Two of the original team had been lost at Monte Cassino: one killed, the other badly wounded. Now, besides Parnell, the unit consisted of Sergeant Wyatt Bird and three corporals: Cowboy Fountain, Weesay Laguna, and Smoker Wineberg.

Once on the ground with the drop zone secured for the main force of paratroopers scheduled to come in at 0130 hours, Blue Team's Task Mission required it to immediately leave the other Pathfinders to move inland and rendezvous with a unit, or circuit, of the French Resistance.

Together they'd assault a small German garrison guarding a farmer's bridge across the river Pointe, a small tributary of the Douve. The bridge could be used by the Germans to rush in reinforcements against the main elements of the 101st and also into the coastal area designated Utah Beach, two miles away. The Resistance members, known as Maquis, a word meaning *underbrush*, had not been told the main assault of western Europe was only hours away.

Next they would proceed northwest to recover a cache of heavy weapons and explosives dropped the previous night. Then the force would split, the Maquis moving on to destroy the Cherbourg–Volognes–St-Lô rail line, while Blue Team, bolstered by more Resistance fighters, would turn due east and assault a three-gun battery of German 105mm field howitzers emplaced near coastal cliffs just beyond the tiny village of Ravenouville. If the assault was successful, Parnell would send up an orange signal flare. If, however, no flare was spotted by 0540 hours, the heavy cruisers USS *Tuscaloosa* would commence battery fire againt the German position in an effort to neutralize it.

Parnell deliberately scattered his own men and the three 501st noncoms among the jumpers on the chance somebody might freeze during the drop. As he scanned the troopers, everybody with their faces smeared with camo grease, which accentuated the whites of their eyes, it was easy to spot the combat vets. They sat quietly, some even dozing. In contrast, the new men kept shifting uneasily in their seats, stared a bit too long at the deck, or continuously fidgeted with their equipment.

Each man carried nearly 150 pounds of gear: T-7 chutes—no emergencies now since they would be jumping from only three hundred feet—weapons, bandoleers, and clip pouches of spare ammo, grenades, Hawkins mines, blocks of TNT, three days of K- and D-rations, smoke grenades, and signal flares. In addition, several had small bags roped to their legs, which contained Eureka radar sets to mark out the three drop zones, A, B, and C, assigned to the 101st. Farther southeast, the 82nd Airborne Division was also deploying their own Pathfinder teams to light up *their* three DZs.

Parnell checked his watch. It was four minutes after midnight. They'd be over their jump point in six minutes.

Three-quarters of an hour earlier, they'd taken off from the RAF base at Greenham Common, England, a flight of six aircraft from IX Troop Carrier Command. At first, they'd gone southwest, then turned due south and headed straight for the Cherbourg Peninsula. Below them, the ocean was momentarily calm and sparkled in brilliant moonlight, while the plane's airstream hurtled past the open door filled with the roaring sound and smell of hot metal from the starboard 895-kW Pratt and Whitney engine.

Holding on to the static line cable overhead, Parnell shrugged his big shoulders boxer-style and settled into his bulky chute harness. Right then he felt the first tension begin, combat coming, down in his belly and chest, the adrenaline starting, the sensation not particularly unpleasant and somewhat like the butterflies he remembered before a football game: that anticipatory eagerness, joy even, to get on with the damned thing. Only now his feelings were controlled, quieted by the knowledge of his own deliberate professionalism, which had come after having been in similar situations so many times before.

The red light behind his head flicked on.

Parnell bellowed, "Stand up."

Everyone rose, their boots shuffling on the aluminum deck as they lined up in the center of the aircraft, facing him. He gave the order to hook up. There were sharp metallic clicks as the men clipped their static lines to the overhead cable. He waited a moment, then called out, "Run your equipment check." Each man quickly checked the equipment of the man in front of him. Finally Red shouted, "Count off." The response was rapid, each trooper calling back in sequence: "Seventeen okay," "Sixteen okay," "Fifteen okay. . . ."

He glanced out the door, saw land suddenly appear, first a narrow strip of bright white beach and then the dark of earth, everything flashing past just below them. Now lights began to appear on the ground, bright flashes as flak and multicolored tracer rounds came up toward them, moving so slowly, arching like Roman candles. He caught the faint clatter of explosions over the roar of the engines.

The aircraft veered sharply to the left, held for a moment, then jinked back to the right, the pilots nervously dodging flak bursts. All the men swayed back and forth, grabbing for support. Parnell leaned forward slightly, looked straight down. The ground was now a sheet of white fog down there, only the tops of trees showing, jetting past. Shrapnel began to hit the outside of the aircraft. It sounded like heavy rain and made the C-47 jostle and buck.

He glanced at his watch: 12:09. "Coming up on one," he called out.

There was a *bang* and a heavy jolt, then the hiss of incoming air. A hole the size of a basketball had been punched into the right side of the aircraft's fuselage, back near the tail. The C-47 shook violently. Men cursed, frantically tried to remain upright.

Red turned, looked up at the red light. *Come on, you son of a bitch*, he thought, *we're gonna overfly*. He could vaguely hear the radioman shouting time and position reports to the pilots through his intercom.

The red light snapped off and a green one came on. Parnell bellowed, "Go! Go!"

The first two out were Bird and Wineberg, point men, the most dangerous position in a drop. Behind them came the others, moving forward hurriedly, shuffling, and then going out, their bodies twisting to face the tail as the slipstream hit them, their static lines whipping back.

There was a sudden loud crack and a bright burst just outside the door. Shrapnel flew in, slammed into the other side of the fuselage. Red felt the concussion wave hit him and the body of the trooper who had been in the doorway crashed into him and knocked him to his knees. He realized he was covered with blood and bits of clothing and bone and unfired cartridges. The trooper had taken the full force of a German 3.46-inch Pak/Flak shell. It had blown his head and right shoulder completely away.

For one miniscule moment, Parnell went nearly motionless under him, only his head swiveling. He saw the faces of the others glowing green in the jump light, everybody else frozen too as the C-47 rocked and rolled crazily. Little flecks of fire leaped and twisted on the fuselage bulkhead.

Then he moved, his mind pounding at himself, *Get them out!* He bodily lifted the trooper's corpse and hurled it through the doorway, letting its weight pull him fully to his feet. The man's static line snapped back. He turned, saw a young face staring at him. He reached out to grab a handful of battle tunic and screamed, "Jump, goddammit, *jump!*"

Slowly the aircraft leveled. By now, the line of men was moving again. He heard Weesay's voice and that of two of the noncoms cursing them on. They came past Parnell, some slipping on the bloody deck but going out and away until finally Laguna appeared and was instantly gone.

Red slammed his own static line buckle over the cable, braced his hands on the doorway. It was slimy, the metal ripped and jagged. He lunged forward and out, his arms automatically snapping against his chest, his head down. He turned himself in the air as the blast of the slipstream hit him like a hurricane.

Cowboy Fountain had been glad to get out of that C-47, leaving it before the flak hit. He'd always hated getting shot at up there. Like most paratroopers, he was terrified of getting struck in the testicles, gelded with his boots on aircraft aluminum. The T-7 chute gave him its usual crotch-crunching jolt as its Ramtex cotton panels blossomed open, the chute a canopy-first deployment unit made for low jumps. This one *damn* low, only time enough for two oscillations before he hit the ground.

Coming down, it had looked like the Fourth of July, fireworks going off everywhere, except out over the swampland to the east that shone in the moonlight like a huge lake. He landed in an open, grassy field, fog-layered and mushy. *Well,* he thought, *at least I missed them damn swamps.* In their premission briefing, they'd been told that Rommel had flooded the swampland in nearly fifteen feet of water. Any paratrooper going down there with so much gear on would drown, sure as hell.

He was halfway out of his harness when he saw one of the C-47s take a solid flak strike. He stiffened. God-dammit, it was *his!* He stood there, saw men dropping, their chutes looking like mushrooms in the moonlight.

How many out? He'd lost count. Then the aircraft was on fire. It moved off to the left, banked steeply, and plunged down into the ground. It exploded in a huge ball of flame.

He felt a frozen chill ripple through his body, thinking, Jesus Christ, the lieutenant and Weesay were the last ones in line. He cursed, then forced that thought from his mind. Hurriedly recovering his chute, he unbagged his Thompson submachine gun, charged it, and moved off stealthily, scanning the misty ground and horizon. A line of trees was visible on his right and a solid, dark line, a hedgerow, in the other direction.

The firing stopped abruptly and the drone of the remaining planes faded off into silence. Around him the night seemed suddenly remote. His boots made slushy sounds. The air smelled of grass and field flowers, lilac and hyacinth, old lady odors. He continued back along the line of the jump, searching for the rest of the stick.

After leaving Naples, Italy, Blue Team had been flown straight to England, to what would be their primary training base, a onetime cricket pavilion outside Nottingham that was now used by the British Special Air Service, the SAS.

But first they were given a four-day leave. Fountain spent most of his time with a girl named Edie Fowler, blond and buxom, a spotter-predictor with the town's Auxiliary Territorial Service. She talked a mile a minute, fucked like a mink, and raved about his western drawl, said he "sounded like Wyatt bloody Earp."

Afterward, in quick succession, he and the team trained at several bases. First, at Nottingham where the SAS gave them a rush course in French, taught them updated demo techniques using the new PE 808 RDX plastic explosives and supplied them with captured German small and medium field arms to strip and test-fire. Next, they were sent to F-Section of the British Special Operations Executive in Maidstone for classes on the French Resistance and its operational systems. Finally, they spent three weeks making ultralow insertion jumps with the Second Battalion of the 501st at Chilton Foliat. . . .

Three minutes later, Fountain was challenged, the tiny chirp of a metal "cricket." Each trooper of the 101st and 82nd had been issued one of these toy clickers just before takeoff so they could identify each other on the ground. Cowboy stopped instantly, frantically searched for his own. It was gone. The cricket chirped again, the clicks ominously faster this time.

A thought occurred to Cowboy. He called "Jimminy." There was a pause, then a voice came back: "Cricket." A shadow rose from the grass and approached. It was one of the 501 noncoms, Sergeant Glenn Briggs. He barked, "Where the fuck's your clicker, soldier?"

"I lost it."

Briggs dug one from his battle tunic, handed it over. "Here. Was that our transport got hit?"

"Yeah, I think so."

"Shit! . . . Okay, let's go."

Soon they encountered Bird, Wineberg, and two other 501st troopers, one with a Eureka unit. Briggs sent one man back along their track to see if he could find any other members of their stick while he and the radar man began setting up the unit and their signal lights.

Bird, Smoker, and Cowboy silently moved off to reconnoiter the entire DZ, the three of them going without words. Far off, the blaze from the C-47 crash had died down until it was now merely a faint glow like that of the firepit of a near-dead volcano.

* * *

Weesay Laguna had crashed through a tree and then into swamp, rocketing straight to the mud-thick bottom in ten feet of water. All the way down with his gear like a lead anchor, he was thinking, *Jesus y Maria, I'm gonna fuckin' drown!*

As soon as he had left the C-47, he knew he was in big trouble. Below him, the ground was *glistening*, for God's sake, moonlit water in all directions. The damn pilot's jerking around back there and the flak hit had put them beyond the DZ, right out over the flooded swampland.

Still, he didn't have too much time to think about it before that tree sitting on a bank loomed up at him, its leaves etched with moonlight. He went through it like a cannonball and into the water. It wasn't particularly cold and was alive with shafts of moonlight all shattered and distorted by his plunge. He reached the bottom and sank into two feet of slushy mud.

Frantically, he drew his boot knife and began cutting harness. He felt tension on his risers and realized the chute had caught in the tree's branches. Getting more desperate by the second, with his cheeks puffed and straining to hold in every tiny whisper of air, he started to climb hand over hand back up the risers. God, getting himself up through the water was like lifting a car, his body weight doubled. The risers jerked, started to slip. Moaning in his throat, he sped up: *reach, pull, reach, pull . . .*

He broke the surface and kept right on going until he was up among leaves, everything dripping, the folds of his chute and the risers entangled all over him. Panting, he listened, heard screams and violent splashes. He looked out, tried to pinpoint where the screams were coming from, but couldn't. The water's surface was covered with scattered patches of thin fog.

The screams stopped.

He cut himself loose and climbed down out of the tree, dropped to the bank. The tree was on the side of a narrow berm. Thickets of pussy willow and swamp grass covered the ground except for a narrow foot trail along the top of the berm. He quickly unbagged his weapon and lay with his head just below the trail, scanning.

Something moved way off to his left. It was a man running. He stiffened. The figure came on. He put his muzzle right on the center of it, worked the clicker with his left hand. The figure stopped. There was an answering clicking. The man came up. It was Lieutenant Parnell. They squatted beside the tree. He could smell the cloying odor of fresh blood on Parnell's tunic.

Red asked, "How many landed out here?"

"I heard at least three, Lieutenant."

They listened. Total silence. "Damnit!" Parnell hissed.

They waited several minutes. Another figure came along the causeway. He was limping, hobbling along like a gnome. Both men challenged, got an answering click. The man was a private from the 501st. Parnell asked him about the others.

"I know they was at least three ahead of me, sir," he said, breathing hard. "And Sergeant Meisell. But I couldn't find *nobody*."

"How bad you hurt?"

"Ankle sprain, sir. I can move okay."

"All right, you two wait here. I don't get back in five minutes, head out." Parnell rose, glanced up at the tree. "Get that chute outta there. Shows up like a fucking neon sign." He went sprinting off along the causeway, going low, back in the direction from which the private had come.

They cut down the remnants of Laguna's chute and buried it in the bank mud. Then they waited, their eyes constantly sweeping the landscape. It was eerie how still the night was, no breeze, no night birds. Yet they did spot a crane flying across the moon, way up, a stick figure struggling on long wings.

Weesay said, "What chu name, *meng?*"

"Foley." The private sighed, his shoulders shuddering as if he were cold. "Shit, I heard them poor bastards drowning out there. You know?"

"Yeah," Laguna said.

Parnell returned, shaking his head. "They're all gone. Let's move."

They headed back along the jump line, going as fast as Foley could manage.

Captain Joe Lightfine, the name translated from Norwegian, put his tiny vest light onto the rubber terrain map spread on the wet grass. Lightfine was chief jumpmaster for the two Pathfinder sticks assigned to Zone A.

He and Parnell had trained together back at Chilton Foliat. As part of the training, they had studied sand tables made from aerial photos of the jump area. Someone eventually got the brilliant idea of molding out rubber terrain maps from the sand tables, which the unit officers could take along to quickly orient themselves once they were on the ground. Lightfine's map looked like a tiny landscape, the flashlight casting its hillocks and hedgerows into shadow relief.

"We're right here," he said to Parnell, pointing. "Just south of those hedgerows."

A few feet away were two troopers. One was setting up a Eureka unit from which he would transmit a homing frequency to a so-called Rebecca unit aboard three of the lead aircraft of the 101st's main contingent of paratroopers. The other soldier carried an S phone pack, a new invention that would allow Lightfine to communicate directly with the troop carrier pilots.

"Is your perimeter secure?" Parnell asked.

"Yeah. There hasn't been any enemy response yet." He grunted. "Looks like we fooled the bastards." After dropping their sticks, the C-47s had headed inland to give the impression they were on a bombing run.

"You lose any?" Red inquired.

"Nobody dead, but four injured." The captain shook his head. "I'm sorry about your guys, John. Thank Christ *we* didn't come down in those goddamned swamps."

Red made no comment. He leaned in, ran his eyes along a series of low berms on the rubber map that indicated three hedgerows two hundred yards south of their position. Good cover for rapid movement, he thought. He followed the hedgerows northwestward, the land rising slightly, here and there patches of crinkled rubber indicating woodland. To the east toward the coast were the squares marking the hamlets of St. Germainde Varreville and Ravenouville. The Pointe River bridge was due west.

Their DZ, code-named Zone A, was the northernmost of the three 101st's main jump sites. Zone B was four miles to the south outside Ste. Marie-du-Mont, and Zone C was near the key rail junction of Carentan. To the east were the three DZs of the 82nd, the first of which was between the smaller junction town of Ste. Mere Eglise and the Merderet River.

Both men consulted their watches: 12:43 A.M. The main drop was now only forty-seven minutes away.

"Well, I guess you'd best head on out, John," Lightfine said.

Like Parnell, Lightfine had been an outstanding football player in college, at Michigan State, where both he and his twin brother, Jerry, had made All-American mention. Red had twice received All-American honors at the University of Colorado and then gone on to play pro ball with the Detroit Lions.

Jerry Lightfine was now a pilot with the Ninth Air Force, flying B-26 Marauder tactical bombers on night strikes over France. Twice he'd come up to Chilton Foliat with his brother and the three of them had gotten drunk in the local pubs, debating the ability of Colorado to whip Michigan, the two Lightfine brothers identical-looking, big men with the broad, open features and the faintly Norwegian-tanged speech of their Minnesota farmer rootstock.

"Watch yourself," Joe added. He smiled. "I got a bottle of Crown Royal stashed back in England. I'd hate to drink it alone."

"I'll be there," Red said.

They shook hands. Parnell signaled his four men who had been patiently squatted down a few yards away. Together they quickly, silently moved off toward the hedgerows.

There were three Maquis at the rendezvous, the place chosen a quarter mile downstream of the Pointe bridge near a farmhouse where three haystacks had been set out to form a triangle as a signal.

Parnell had flashed his recognition signal, three groups of three quick Morse flashes from his vest flashlight, S . . . S . . . S. They were quickly countersigned. He and Wyatt went in while the others maintained cover.

The leader was a tall man whose code name was Lucas. His real name, Parnell would later learn, was Vaillant Duboudin, a famous French Grand Prix driver. He, like the other two, was dressed in black leather jacket, dark trousers, and a fishermen's cap. Each carried a British Sten Mk III machine pistol and bandoleers of spare rounds.

Duboudin shook Parnell's hand, grinning. "*J'ai Lucas, Lieutenant. N'hesitez pas a France.*"

"*Merci.*"

The French Resistance movement was composed of over 300,000 members. The two main groups were De-Gaulle's BCRA, or Free French, and the French Forces of the Interior, the FFI. In between these were numerous, independently acting circuits and cells, some with as few as two members. Many were violently opposed to each other, yet they had momentarily banded together to fight the greater enemy, the Nazis.

Lucas immediately launched off into a rapid appraisal of the situation, speaking in French. Red listened for a few moments, getting about half of it, then held up his hand. "Whoa, hold it," he said in English, then in French, "My French is no that good."

The leader tilted his head, surprised. "I was told you spoke it well."

"No well. *Un petit.* If you are speaking slow, I am possibly to understand."

Lucas shook his head, grunted. One of the other Maquis quickly stepped forward and said in pure American, "Actually, your French rather stinks, Lieutenant." It was a woman.

Parnell turned to her, surprised. "You're American?"

"Of course." She laughed, a soft, merry, tinkling sound. "Anabel O'Keefe Sinclair, Chicago born and raised. Look, fella, let's just use English, okay? It'll be a damn side simpler."

She explained the layout: "The bridge has a single pillbox on the eastern side. Usually four men, two MG-

34s. Their bivouac's two hundred yards farther on in some trees. All told, there're about twenty men and a radio unit."

Parnell listened. Anabel Sinclair had a nice way of gesturing, very feminine. He couldn't see her face clearly in the moonlight and her hair was tucked up under her hat. But now that he knew, he could see the obvious curve of female hip in her trousers.

"We have fourteen men here," Sinclair went on. "Armed mostly with Stens, handguns, and a few captured German MP-40s." She nodded toward one of the haystacks. "There's a Kraut antitank rifle for you in there—a 7.92 Panzerbuchse 38. You take out the pillbox, we'll handle the bivouac. I suggest you do it quickly. As soon as our weapons fire off, the Jerries'll dispatch troops from Ste. Mere Eglise, posthaste."

He said, "You're Flapper, aren't you?" Back at the SOE briefings at F Section in Maidstone, agents' names had never been mentioned. But in the final, premission data he'd received, there were the code names of the three agents he'd be meeting in France: Lucas, Alain, and Flapper.

Except for a handful of key leaders, none of the rank and file of the Resistance Movement knew the specifics of the coming invasion. This also included Sinclair. As far as she and the others were concerned, this American team of elite specialists was here simply to conduct specific sabotage raids.

"That's me," Anabel said perkily. She pushed back the cuff of her jacket to look at her watch, then turned to Duboudin and the other man and rattled off something in French that was way too fast for Red to follow. She came back to Parnell. "Any questions, Lieutenant?"

"No."

"Till later, then." The three moved away quickly and were soon gone from sight beyond the farmhouse.

Wyatt chuckled quietly. "I guess we got our orders, ain't we, Lieutenant?"

Red chortled. "Sure as hell sounds like it, don't it?"

They were able to approach to within sixty yards of the bridge's German pillbox, crawling through a field of spring wheat almost ready for harvest. The spickletts smelled strongly of germ-oil. Bird, who would be firing the Panzerbuchse rifle, carried it in the crook of his arms, the telescoped barrel of polished carbon steel freshly oiled. Weesay brought the two-legged mount and Cowboy had the saddle magazine that fitted directly onto the weapon's breech.

The pillbox was an old-fashioned Type 630 modified by emplacing a tank turret over a sandbagged pit. One machine gun was visible through a square embrasure that faced the bridge. The other was higher, open, with a steel plate welded to the turret. It was camouflaged with tree branches and tufts of river grass. A German soldier was standing beside it, smoking.

The Pointe bridge itself looked old, formed of stones and double arches with no railing. It looked to be wide enough for two horse carts to pass abreast. The river was narrow, perhaps thirty yards across. It appeared languid, yet in the moonlight small ripple lines were visible in its center, indicating a current and a decent depth to it.

By signal, Parnell deployed his men. He gave Wyatt a clear line of fire to the machine gun's embrasure while the others took up positions along the riverbank so as to shoot around the steel shield on the second gun. Quietly, Bird assembled the antitank rifle, affixing the mount and clipping on the magazine. Then he stretched out, fitted the padded butt stock to his shoulder, and took a bead on the target through the weapon's big O-ring sight.

They waited, Parnell lying beside Bird. It was 0121 hours. The ground seemed alive with tiny bugs, mosquitoes droned about their heads. High up, the moon had passed its zenith. In the clear night air it appeared flat-round, bright as a vanilla-colored balloon caught in a spotlight. Across the river, the German soldier had finished his cigarette and returned to the pillbox.

It came as a low drone at first, so faint it might have been a distant wind. It grew in volume until it was a roaring of many, isolated engines. The night began to light up, flare clusters and the pink and green and white tracer streams arching upward, while the staccato chatter of machine guns and the deeper booms of flak cannon rumbled across the landscape. The motionless brightness of the moon seemed suddenly diminished.

Parnell's hand tapped Wyatt's shoulder. A second later, the Panzerbuchse fired off with a deafening slam. Again and still again, the rounds rocketing across the river and shattering the air. The small pillbox exploded in a shower of white-hot metal fragments as Thompsons came into action, their low, throaty, slow-steady raps sounding hollow beside the antitank gun's muzzle blasts.

Parnell's ears rang. He looked over at Bird. The sharp smell of cordite smoke drifted among the wheat stalks. They smiled icily at each other. Wyatt had just fired the first round in the American sector to begin the invasion of western Europe. Ironically, it had come from a German weapon.

Chapter Two

At precisely 0130 hours, British double summer time, which was one hour behind German summer time, the first massive thrust against the Germans in France began. Inland of what would be the American landing beaches, 13,400 paratroopers from the U.S. 82nd and 101st Airborne Divisions dropped onto the soil of western Europe. A few minutes earlier, 6,255 British and Canadians of the British 6th Airborne Division had jumped forty miles to the east.

The Americans' task, like the Brits', was to secure the flanks of the main assault force, clear out beach exits, and attack specific rail and highway junction points through which the Germans could pour in armor and troop reinforcements after the main invasion began at 0630 hours.

During the planning stages for Operation Overlord, there had been strong objections to the use of airborne troops as the spearhead of the invasion. Even some of the senior commanders of Supreme Headquarters Allied Expeditionary Force openly considered it suicidal. Tactically, they further claimed, the entire operation would be compromised, and the Allies would lose their powerful advantage of surprise. But Eisenhower disagreed. He had great faith in paratrooper operations and gave the plan the green light.

Although it was an overall success, the initial stages of the paratrooper drops turned into a massive, confused mess. Strong winds and fog hampered the British and Canadian sectors. Some of their DZs were missed entirely. Men drowned in swampy areas, others were scattered miles from their assembly points.

It was even worse in the American zones. Inexperienced pilots, panicked by the heavy German flak, became totally disoriented. Many unloaded their sticks of troopers right down into the areas Rommel had flooded. Some were so far off course their jumpers actually went into the sea. Since each man carried so much equipment, few survived in the water. The rest were scattered all over hell, most of them in small groups or totally alone in this unfamiliar, hostile country.

Luckily, the Germans turned out to be just as confused in interpreting and reacting to the situation. They had long realized an Allied invasion of the continent was inevitable. But they didn't know exactly where or when it would come. Hitler and his senior officers believed that Pas de Calais, 130 miles up the coast, would be the main landing point. So entrenched in this theory, they actually scoffed at the first sketchy reports that began coming in about enemy paratroopers landing in Normandy.

In addition, both top commanders charged with defending the French coast, Generalfeldmarschall Gerd von Rundstedt of Oberbefelshaber West and Generalfeldmarschall Erwin Rommel, commander of Army Group B, were at the moment in Germany, far from their commands. Nearly 90 percent of their own senior staff officers were also gone, attending a high echelon *Kriegsspiel,* a war game exercise at Rennes nearly a hundred miles to the south. This particular time had been chosen because everybody felt it would be utterly impossible for the Allies to mount a major invasion during such stormy conditions.

* * *

Anabel Sinclair killed her first man exactly fifteen seconds after Bird opened with his Panzerbuchse. It was a German soldier in his gray *Unterhemd*, undershirt and shorts, lunging out of a field tent twenty yards ahead of her, for a moment silhouetted against a trench berm.

She and Duboudin had been running side by side with the other Resistance fighters, charging through a speckled darkness in frontal assault through the enemy bivouac's wire and mine strips. Their raid was amateurishly carried out, lacking the disciplined fire and movement efficiency of a regular military unit. Yet the men possessed the powerful momentum of pure surprise.

Earlier, they had silently killed the posted guards, two sandbag machine-gun positions, each of the Krauts in camo capes. This particular German outfit was attached to the 716th Division, a static service unit made up of old men and captured Russians and Slavs who had been impressed into the *Wehrmacht* under the threat of death.

Anabel saw her five bullets actually go into the German, tiny flutterings of his undershirt clearly visible in the multicolored light from cluster flares and streams of tracers flooding the sky. Then he was bodily lifted by the impacts and thrown backward, as if he had just run into a taut wire.

All around her, men fought with those vicious gruntings of close combat. Muzzle blasts cracked out. Grenades went off with orange-white bursts and made the earth tremble, the air shift with concussion. A German MP-40 machine pistol abruptly raked the ground directly ahead of her, then lifted, its swarm of bullets crashing through the air close beside her hip. Another grenade exploded to the left, dark silhouettes tumbled through the air.

She was vaguely aware that Duboudin was no longer at her side. She stopped. Her heart pounded wildly in her chest. She swung around, saw bigger shadows loom twenty feet away. She squinted, trying to tell if they were friend or foe. A candle-shaped flame lashed out at her and another spray of bullets rushed past. In reflex, she fired her Sten again, holding the trigger in tight, the weapon climbing in her hands. The shadows disappeared.

She dropped to one knee, realized she was shaking terribly, all the way down into her insides. Everywhere the entire night was being sundered by sounds and sporadic light as distant German flak guns hammered away with staccato poppings and the booms of larger antiaircraft batteries thumped amid the steady, high-pitched raps of machine guns. It reminded her of Luftwaffe night raids she had seen in London. Yet this was horribly different, as if everybody out there were shooting just at *her.*

Gradually the firing within her perimeter began to abate and finally died away. She rose and moved forward. Her legs felt weak. She bumped into something. It was a man's head, the face half gone. A single eye was wide open, staring idiotically upward, as if it were awed by the light in the sky.

"Oh Lord," she croaked, bent, and vomited.

Anabel Christine O'Keefe, tomboy, daughter of Shawn Padrick O'Keefe, who had once built roads in Old Mexico and fought against Pancho Villa. One night in a mud-floored café in Santa Magdalina, Mexico, he had won a partnership in a Montana cattle ranch in a poker game. Within four years, he brokered it into one of the largest meat packers in Chicago.

She was also the daughter of Elizabeth Henry Ashford of Richmond, Virginia, a beautiful debutant descendent of bankers. She met Shawn Padrick at a dance in

Chicago's old Metropole Hotel, where Al Capone, a friend of O'Keefe's, would soon set up his headquarters. Elizabeth fell madly in love with the Irishman's rough-hewn, Wild West ways. Amid the aghast protestations of her parents, she married him in 1919.

When Anabel was ten years old, she could shoot like a cowboy, play bluff poker with the best, and possessed an irrepressible delight for adventure. Sent to the Greenbriar School for Young Women in her mother's native Virginia, she was expelled at thirteen for "unladylike behavior." Then the stock market plunge of '29 hit the country. Her father was one of the few who weathered it fairly unscathed. But then the bloody hunger riots began sweeping through Chicago. Her mother demanded she be sent away to "spare her young eyes the sight of such human bestiality." She was immediately shipped off to her mother's sister, Emma, who lived in Paris with her diplomat husband.

Anabel adored France. Eventually, she graduated from the Sorbonne, although just barely, having majored in art and western European languages. At eighteen, she took up the Bohemian life on the West Bank, wrote ghastly poetry, flirted with narcotics, and took a succession of lovers in intense, wonderfully romantic, though short-lived, episodes.

The group included a strikingly handsome young French naval deserter, a circus acrobat, a flamenco dancer, an artist who mimicked the pointillism of Seurat and Signac, who eventually despaired and drunkenly joined the French Foreign Legion, and finally Vaillant Duboudin, son of a French industrialist who had already won a name for himself on the Grand Prix circuits of the continent.

Then she met Captain Leslie Sinclair of the British Royal Air Force during the British Grand Prix at Donington, England, in 1939. He was dashing yet gentlemanly, loved to fly, and raced motorcycles. He taught her how to sail. Three months later they married and moved into a small flat in Notting Hill, London. Soon after, Leslie was reassigned to a fighter base in Swansea on Bristol Channel flying Spitfires. In the late spring of 1942, he was killed in air combat over Libya.

Anabel mourned deeply for a year in her cottage in Swansea. Then one day she awoke, said, "Enough of this!" and joined the Auxiliary Territorial Service as an antiaircraft gunner. As fluent as she was in French and German, she soon caught the eye of a recruiter for the Special Operations Executive. That summer she joined the SOE.

She passed quickly through special-op training stations at Wanborough Manor and Borman-Beaulieu, learning the techniques and apparatus used by covert agents. From there, she moved on to the grueling Special Training Schools at Arisaig and Glaschoille in the Scottish Highlands where she was taught code systems, radar and radio procedures, demolitions, weaponry, hand-to-hand fighting, and evasion-and-escape tactics.

Her final STS evaluation report stated in part: *Mature for her age in some ways, childish in others. Self-willed, confident, not easily rattled, physically fit, plucky, and persistent with inner strength and courage. Good with weapons. She will make a decent agent if her assignments do not become too boring.*

This was her first mission. She and another SOE agent, Etienne Sufurier, had been flown in in early March during the proper moon period aboard a Lysander Mark III from the 161st Squadron called the Moonrunners, the aircraft equipped with a muffled, nearly silent Bristol Mercury engine. Her false papers identified her as Blanche Marie Lambert, a commercial secretary from Caen. Her operational area included most of Normandy, with its code-named Linen Basket and Greenleaf Maquis circuits. A senior officer within the Greenleaf cell was her old lover, Vaillant Duboudin.

Sufurier was immediately dispatched south into Brittany to work with the Marksman circuit. Both their operational tasks were the same: coordinate SOE operations with the Maquis to assist in sabotage raids, set up air drops, hand off couriers and downed Allied crews along the escape routes to Spain, and send periodic intelligence reports back to London.

Her days in Swansea had been comparatively free of the true face of war. Although the SOE training had been harsh and challenging, in the end it was merely simulation and had failed to fully transmit the true, jolting emotional shock of seeing her own bullets kill a man right in front of her, or of feeling a decapitated human head bleeding on her boot. . . .

Someone roughly grabbed her by the jacket collar and she was wrenched to her feet. Lieutenant Parnell's face peered closely at her. "You okay?" he grunted.

"Yes." She wiped her mouth with the back of her jacket. "I'm okay, yeah."

He shoved her forward, releasing her jacket. "Then get moving. We don't have time for that."

"Wait!" she cried. "What about the wounded? My God, we can't just leave them here."

He stared at her. "Those who can keep up will come with us. Those who can't, stay here. Now *move* it!"

Oberstleutnant Hellmuth Meyer-Detring, counterintelligence chief for Field Marshal von Rundstadt's OB West, stood before a large lighted wall map of France, studying it intently. On the map were clusters of blue pins. All were in Normandy. One group lay within a triangle formed by the towns of Bayeux, Lion-sur-Mer, and Caen. Another triangle pattern ran from the Aure River to the village of Ste. Mere Eglise and the Merderet River.

The colonel was a chunky, red-faced man, his thick hair disheveled. Fifteen minutes earlier, he'd been awakened by his senior duty radio officer. They were in a long concrete room crammed with radios, encryption machines, teletypes, telephone circuit power panels, and numerous sitting operators, several of whom were women. Next to the wall map were tacked at least a hundred photos of enemy agents and Resistance operatives.

This room was part of von Rundstadt's headquarters, a three-story blockhouse a hundred yards long and embedded in a slope beneath a girls' high school in the small town of St-Germain-en-Laye outside Paris. It was now a little after 3:00 A.M., German summer time.

A major dressed in the black uniform and high *Feldmutze* cap of a Panzer officer entered the room. The silver-twist piping on his collar and cap and his Knight's Cross with oak leaves and swords at his throat glistened in the bright overhead lights. He paused a moment, then approached Meyer.

"*Guten Morgen, herr Oberst,*" he said quietly. "Is something up?" As he spoke, a clerk approached the wall map and placed two new blue pins into it.

Meyer-Detring glanced around at him, scowled, then returned to the map. "I'm not sure, Freidrich," he said sharply. "Look at these radio report positions. All over Normandy. But I see no cohesive pattern yet. Do you?"

The major's eyes narrowed as he scanned the pin clusters. His name was Freidrich Land, the physical epitome of a German soldier: powerfully lean with neatly chiseled features, cool blue eyes, and a movie star's mouth and cleft chin. Once he'd been a battalion tank commander with Rommel in North Africa and later part of the *Feldmarshall's* personal staff.

Since he spoke fluent French, he'd been transferred to Meyer's unit as liaison with German agents embedded in the Resistance Movement in western and northern France, particularly in Normandy and Brittany. But personally he hated this cloak-and-dagger business, considering it unseemly for a soldier of the Third Reich. He bore a particular contempt for the Frenchmen who had turned against their own country to work for Germany. In Land's moral code, such a breach of honor and loyalty, even when it was to his benefit, was an unforgivable transgression.

Still, these turncoats *had* supplied good intelligence on the workings of the French Resistance movement. Over the last two months several dozen members, along with British SOE agents, had been arrested following information Land's unit passed on to the Gestapo. Just last night, three British agents had been caught in Brittany using a tip from one of his French operatives.

He shook his head. "Not really, sir. It looks rather random. What do the reports say?"

"Our outposts claim there are enemy paratroopers landing. There have even been some minor skirmishes. But everything is fragmentary so far." He pouched his lips, expelled air. "There *is one* thing, though. That second stanza? It was broadcast by the BBC late last night."

Although Land was a bit inebriated from his late dinner and prolonged sexual romp with his current mistress, a French cabaret singer named Janine Lamiere, that statement got his immediate attention.

Over the last few days, several of his plants within the

Resistance had warned him that two specific messages would soon be coming from London. Each would be coded within a stanza from a poem by Verlain and broadcast over the BBC. Unfortunately, they had not been told precisely what these messages would mean, only that they would signify something highly important.

Despite this seemingly ominous hint that something big might be in the works, the higher echelons of German intelligence paid little attention. Primarily because past reports of similarly "significant" transmissions had proven false or turned out to be decoys. Then on 1 June, the first stanza of Verlain's poem *was* sent out by the BBC. It was repeated three times throughout that day. Now the second verse had just come in.

The major cocked his eye at his chief. "The coincidence here seems significant, doesn't it, sir?"

Meyer-Detring nodded. "I agree. But apparently we're the only ones who think so. I contacted von Templehoff a few minutes ago. Also Colonel Schleiger at Seventh. Both scoffed. They believe these parachutists that have been sighted are merely Allied bomber crews." Colonel Hans von Templehoff was Rommel's operations officer who was acting commander of Group B while the Desert Fox and his chief of staff, General Spiedel, were absent. Colonel Nils Schleiger was the senior intelligence officer of the Seventh Army, which had command control over the Normandy sector.

"But so many sightings?" Land questioned.

"Yes, Schleiger did at least agree that if the sightings continue he would suggest they post an alert." He chortled derisively. "But he won't, of course. Those *die Fotzen* down there don't have the balls to risk their necks with senior officers still in Rennes."

He peered at the map a moment longer, then sighed

and ran his hand through his hair. "Well, until something more significant shows up, I'm going back to bed." He slapped Land on the shoulder. "I suggest you do the same, Freidrich." He left.

Land remained before the wall map, frowning thoughtfully. Finally, he sat down at one of the teletype desks, lit a cigarette, and continued studying the map while a clerk added two more pins to the collection.

Blue Team and the partisans, now numbering thirteen including Duboudin and Anabel Sinclair, double-timed through a moonlit landscape. *Bocage* country it was called, the word meaning *box* from the ancient hedgerows that marked out field boundaries set up during Roman times. They were everywhere, surrounding small fields. Each field always had only two entrances.

The hedgerows themselves were formed of eons of dirt on which beeches and oaks had grown to as much as sixty feet in height, their bases covered in thick brush. The roads that ran between them were narrow and sunken to a depth of six or seven feet. In some places, the rows merged their branches to form dark tunnels through which slivers of moonlight shone. Here and there, the ground opened into apple orchards and a few grain fields and the air was thick with the smell of apple blossoms and summer grass and moist earth.

Observing these dark, leafy barriers, Parnell could visualize what perfect defensive positions they would make. He was quite surprised at how tall and thick the trees were. The preoperation intelligence reports he'd seen had failed to show that, since the aerial recon photos on which they were based had been taken from directly above and didn't indicate depth. He shook his head, picturing the poor bastards who were going to have to capture this countryside. The operation would be a long, slow, bloody process, he suspected. One field at a time.

He was directly behind Sinclair and Duboudin, the rest of the men in column behind them. Fifty yards ahead was Laguna and one of the Maquis acting as guide. His name was Claude, a small wiry fisherman with a whisper like a bellows. Bird was in the middle of the line with Cowboy and Smoker pulling rear guard. Red had ordered everyone into single file to lessen the effect of an ambush. To speed things along, he used Anabel to translate his orders. So far, everybody was still maintaining adequate ground speed, but the first signs of fatigue in the out-of-shape Frenchies were beginning to appear.

It was now twenty minutes after 2:00, Brit time. Red kept checking his watch, constantly aware of the extreme tightness of their schedule. Even after they made contact with the two Maquis posted at the ordnance cache near the village of Sonsui, they would still have to cover nearly six miles to reach the German coastal battery.

Duboudin and Sinclair were to use part of the cache's explosives to blow their rail line target outside Valognes. Then they'd head to the opposite Cotentin coast and link with other Linen Basket and Greenleaf cells near Barneville and Carteret to conduct raids against German communication systems and transport routes.

The Cotentin Peninsula resembled a thick, gloved thumb protruding out into the English Channel. On the western side of the peninsula was the great indentation known as *La Marche*. Across it lay Brittany, which formed the hand portion of the glove. Located at the tip of the Cotentin was the city of Cherbourg, one of the three major, deep-water ports along the Channel coast.

Its occupation was absolutely essential to the establishing of the Allied beachheads. As a result, once the Allied assault forces were ashore, they were to immediately push inland, south toward Caen and west to the *Marche* coastline so as to cut off the entire Cotentin. Once this was achieved, they would then drive due north to take Cherbourg.

Wyatt pulled up beside Parnell, the long barrel of his German Panzerbuchse strapped to his back. "Lieutenant, some of them Frenchies is losin' steam back there," he said.

Red nodded. "Yeah, I hear them." He glanced at his watch again, the luminous dials forming tiny blue lines. "We should reach the cache in about twenty minutes. Just keep 'em moving."

"Right." Bird fell back.

The night had grown quiet again, the German flak guns long silent now with only an occasional burst of small arms fire far off, sounding like hunters in an adjoining valley. At the moment, they were passing under one of the hedgerow overhangs. It was pitch-dark inside and their boots made hollow slaps on the hard-packed dirt.

He watched Duboudin and Sinclair, who were dimly visible ahead, the soft tinkle of their equipment exaggerated under the trees. Both ran with their heads down but the Frenchman was puffing with exertion. Still, both were staying with the rhythmic cadence, stride for stride. He called softly up to them, "How you two holding out?"

Anabel's head instantly snapped around. "Don't worry about us, buster," she snapped.

Parnell chuckled, thinking, *So, the lady's still pissed at me. That's good, pissed is good.* Ever since leaving the German bivouac, the female SOE agent had been glowering at him, giving him curt answers to his questions, openly outraged at his order to leave the wounded Maquis behind.

He didn't blame her. He hadn't liked doing it. In fact, one of the things he firmly believed in as a soldier and an officer was never to leave his wounded or even his dead behind. But that was when it was *possible* to do and still complete his mission.

Here, he'd had no choice. Wounded men would have slowed them down too much, completely destroyed his task schedule, which was and always would be foremost in an operation. Nevertheless, he'd done what he could for them, administering to their wounds and then hiding them far from the scene of the battle. He even left one of the Maquis fighters with them, thereby lessening his force of still another weapon.

But now another problem was coming on swiftly—these Frenchmen lagging behind. Although he had suspected they might break down under the physical strain of such a rapid pace, he'd been optimistic. But now that prickly feeling in his scalp, which always came when things began getting antsy, was there.

As each minute slipped by, he became more and more aware that if they were late reaching that Kraut battery, they might not be able to take it out in time and possibly get caught in the naval bombardment. He also knew that this particular emplacement was inside twelve feet of reinforced concrete and down under sixty feet of earthworks. Could the *Tuscaloosa*'s batteries destroy it if his team didn't? If not, there was going to be a lot of dead and wounded American soldiers down there on Utah Beach.

He pushed that dark scenario from his mind and focused instead on Anabel Sinclair. What in hell was an American woman doing in the British SOE, anyway?

More importantly, how savvy was she? Her training had obviously been good enough to allow her to rattle off weaponry and ordnance nomenclature with ease. But that puking bit back there told him this was probably her first taste of real combat.

He shook his head, sucked saliva through his teeth in disgust. That was all he needed, a greenhorn liaison agent, and a woman to boot. Then he realized he was being a bit unfair. Nobody experienced bloody war the first time without revulsion and horror, that abrupt, shocking, raw introduction to real killing. The important thing was how a person reacted afterward. He decided to give Sinclair a chance, let her prove herself. It wouldn't take long to find out what she was made of.

Seventeen minutes later, Weesay came merging out of shadow to inform him that he and Claude had just made contact with the two Maquis guarding the supply cache.

It was in two British CLE chute containers that had been bomb-bay dropped from a B-26 Marauder the previous night. They were long wood and metal boxes with shock-absorbing pans to protect the contents when they hit the ground. Each was capable of holding three-hundred pounds of gear. They also had tiny flashing red marker lights that the two Maquis men didn't know how to turn off. So they had merely dragged the two containers into a nearby cow-shed and covered them with straw with the lights still blinking beneath.

Inside, wrapped in oilcloth and Cosmoline packing, were bundles of plastique explosives, reels of wire, fuses, extra ammunition, concussion and phosphorous grenades, two updated M9A1 shoulder-fired rocket launchers called bazookas, fifteen 2.36-inch rocket warheads, orange signal flares and pistol along with extra Thompson machine guns and Colt pistols.

Bird and Smoker cracked open the CLEs and began handing out the contents. The shed had a thick layer of manure and straw on the floor that gave to the chilly air and the moss-covered stones a warm fecund odor.

Meanwhile, Parnell, Sinclair, and Duboudin held a conference outside. Anabel was still brusque. She said, "How many added men will we need for the battery?"

Red glanced at her. "We? You're not coming with us."

"The hell I'm not."

"Bullshit."

"Oh, that's so lovely." She faced up to him. "Listen up, Lieutenant. And try not to be too stupid here, okay? How do you intend to communicate your attack orders to these men in your fifth grade French?"

"I'll manage."

"God!" She looked at Duboudin, frustrated, rattled off something in French.

Duboudin nodded and turned to Parnell, speaking very slowly in his own language. "*Je vous en prie, Leutenant.* I think it would be most beneficial for Madame Sinclair to go with you. She is familiar with this country and our safe zones. Thus, you could move faster and hide yourselves more freely. Is that not true?"

Red frowned at him. Damn it, the Frenchie *was* right. He nodded. "Point taken." He turned to Anabel. "Okay, you can come."

"Oh, happy day," Anabel said mockingly.

Parnell ignored her. "How many men can you spare, Lucas?"

"Two. I'll take the youngest and most inexperienced."

"Good." He turned back to Sinclair. "You, go load up on ammo."

She gave him a hard stare before whirling away.

It was nearly three o'clock BDST, everyone doubly loaded with weaponry and ammo. They gathered around the cowshed. Two large white-and-liver-colored cows wandered across the field and stood watching. The night had turned colder. Wispy fog drifted sluggishly along the ground and the moon was lower in the sky but still sharp, casting the pasture beyond the shed into soft blue whiteness while the black walls of the surrounding hedgerows rose like ancient castle parapets.

Anabel and Vaillant discussed the rendezvous point following the battery attack and chose a particular safe house in Valognes in two days. Then she bade him adieu and moved off with Blue Team and nine Maquis men, Duboudin watching as they slipped past, heads down, adjusting their loads on their shoulders.

As one particular man came abreast of him, a stocky Norman named Henri Dupin who was dressed in a thick turtleneck sweater and a beret, his load suddenly slipped from his back and fell to the ground. Dupin cursed and stooped to recover it. Duboudin quickly knelt beside him to help as the others jogged by, Smoker Wineberg, the last man in line, calling out to Henri, "Come on, Frenchie, chop, chop."

Vaillant leaned close, whispering urgently, "Fake illness and fall back. Contact Major Land immediately. Inform him of the battery attack and that I suspect the Allied invasion is coming here. In three hours."

"*Oui*, Valliant," Dupin murmured. He got his load reshouldered and ran off to join the others.

Chapter Three

The countryside was full of rabbits. Smoker Wineberg had never seen so damned many rabbits in any one place, the animals spooked from brush to go dashing off in the moonlight, big, haunchy things running humped over. They always waited until the column had passed before shooting out.

Twenty minutes earlier, there had been an Allied air raid along the coast, most of it farther east. It lit up the sky again with the rolling thunder of explosions that drifted in to them on the sea wind. It had been pretty heavy, even some big bombers invisible up there in the moonlight. Now the country had fallen back into that peculiar silence that always follows horrendous noise.

Smoker was alone on drag, back about thirty yards from the last Maquis. He was loaded down with gear plus the baseplate for Bird's Kraut cannon, the metal weighing a ton. Yet he relished the heated strain on his body, the steady rhythm of his boots striking the ground, his insides working with a smooth, blood-pumping efficiency. An exhilarating tune-up for what lay ahead.

Not like them Frenchies. Jesus, they were a slobby bunch. He could hear their gasps and wheezes coming back to him. He spat and looked around. Funny country this, old country, everything wild-looking and unkept. Not like England, but more lush than Italy. Still, he liked the smell of it, the rich perfume of apple blossoms. It reminded him of another place.

Back when he was on the bum in '37 he'd ridden the rails out West one summer, through the Tennessee Appalachians to Missouri and Kansas and finally Nebraska. With the weather so beautiful and warm, he'd decided to turn northwest, go see the Pacific coast. He crossed Wyoming and Idaho and ended up in a small Columbia Basin town named Moses Lake in Washington State. He got a job bucking hay for a week and then moved on, got roaring drunk in Wenatchee and picked up a woman named Adele at a honky tonk called Junior's. Built like a brick shit house she was, with short, sun-bleached hair and a dark brown tan that offset her blue eyes.

She called him Killer when she found out he boxed and told him she was married to a wheat farmer and had five kids. Every summer she'd get the itch and run off, spend a few weeks hitting the rodeos at Cheyenne and Calgary, getting drunk and sleeping with cowboys until she'd had enough and then she'd return home.

"An' your old man lets you back?" he'd asked, shocked.

"Of course."

"Ever' blessed time?"

"Sure," Adele said, laughing. "Why not? There ain't nobody else in the family can cook worth a shit."

He had spent three days with her in and around Wenatchee and up at Lake Chelan while she killed time until Frontier Days started in Cheyenne, Wyoming. Wenatchee was apple country and the air always seemed filled with the heady fragrance of apple blossoms. At night in bed, he continually marveled at Adele's sexual hunger, her quickly unleashed lasciviousness. He also liked the totality of her tan. It coated every inch of her body, made her look like a Polynesian baby. She explained how she got it: "When I disk the fields, you know? I always ride the tractor bare-ass naked."

He chuckled, remembering her now. A goddamned doozie, that Adele. Mulling it over now, he decided he couldn't blame her old man for taking her back, actually letting her through the door knowing with certainty where she'd been and that she'd sure as hell do it again. No, old Adele was just too good a jelly-roll fuck to let loose of. . . .

A man was lying across the road, part of his body hidden in the fog layer that had formed along the ground. Wineberg stopped, went to a knee, intently scanned the situation. It was one of the Resistance fighters, a thick-chested guy in a worn leather jacket and beret. Smoker advanced and bent down to examine him.

"*Ca va*, Frenchie?" he asked.

"*Je vous en prie*, I am ill," the man croaked, gasping thickly. He clutched his chest. "*Mon poitrine!* It flames!" He coughed violently.

Smoker waited till the coughing subsided and then lifted him to his feet. The Frenchman came up reluctantly, cramped over. "Come on, buddy," Smoker said. "Ya'll's jes' winded. Come on, pal . . . *continue.*" He held him a moment, then let him go. The Maquis fell down again, curled over in the fetal position.

"I can not go more," he wailed.

"Shit."

"*Je m'excuse*, please, I can not go on. " He began to vomit.

Smoker watched disgustedly for a moment, then began taking off the man's gear: two explosive musettes, a spool of blasting wire, and a phosphorous grenade box. Leaving him his weapons and a bandoleer of rounds, Wineberg straightened up.

"*Merci, merci,*" the Frenchman panted. "I will come if I am able. I will come."

"Yeah."

He heard a sound, far off. The sudden whine of an engine. He swung around and looked back up the road, listening. The Maquis said something. "Shut up!" Smoker growled. There it was again.

He sprinted back along the road, running in the triangle of deep shadow the moon cast off the side. Fifty yards out, he paused, squatted, twisting his head back and forth to hear. Sure enough, more engine noise. Then the squeaking jangle of treads. Armor!

He raced back, stopping just long enough to hiss at the Frenchman, "*Allemand, Allemand.*" The Frenchie rolled over and, dragging his weapon, crawled up the roadside, and disappeared into a hedgerow.

Wineberg ran on to warn the others.

The German column came on at a moderate pace, first two motorcyclists and an SD Kfz. 250/9 half-track. A hundred yards back were three dozen *Opel* three-ton trucks filled with troops. They were dressed in field gray and *Einheitsmutze* caps with their helmets slung over their shoulders. The vehicles had tiny blue slit-lights that made the dark column appear as a slithering snake with a hundred tiny sapphire eyes in the moonlight.

As soon as Smoker reported the Germans' approach, Parnell had ordered everyone off the road, into cover in the hedgerows. He ordered that no one fire unless they were discovered. He and Anabel found a spot beneath a thick cluster of vernier fern and prickle brush, the fern smelling like turpentine. The sunken roadway lay directly below them.

The trucks rumbled past, the noise of their engines bouncing off the dirt walls. Their exhausts drifted up into the brush. Each truck had three concentric circles painted on its door and hood that indicated it was part of a *Feldersatz* or field replacement battalion, moving into position at night to avoid being strafed by Allied fighter bombers that now dominated the air space over France.

Anabel leaned close. "Replacements."

Red nodded. "Where are they coming from?" He caught a whisper of perfume, carnations, a tropical scent incongruous here.

"Probably Quettehou. There's a big service depot there. I think—"

"Hold it!" he hissed, touching her hand.

The column had slowed, then finally stopped, the truck engines idling quietly. Some of the drivers got out and stood in the roadway. Several urinated against the wall, talking and laughing softly. A motorcyclist came back, skimming between the vehicles and the road side, the rap of its engine amplified by the narrow walls. He disappeared toward the end of the column. In a few minutes, he was back. Soon after, the trucks started moving again.

Parnell cursed under his breath. They'd already lost over twenty minutes and there was no telling how long this column might be. Anabel once more leaned close. "I overheard some of the drivers. This unit's headed for St-Lô. Taking advantage of between bombing raids. They're going into service reserve with the 91st *Fallshirmjagertruppe.*"

Oh, shit, Red thought, the 91st! That was one of the toughest paratrooper divisions on either side of the war.

Another dozen supply trucks went past, then six gun carriages hauling 20mm flak cannons and two 75mm field howitzers. Two more half-tracks held up the rear along with a small personnel carrier with battalion staff officers aboard. The half-tracks squealed and clanked in the narrow roadway.

Parnell waited, listening to the sounds of the column drawing away. He consulted his watch for the tenth time. It was one minute after 4:00. He tapped Anabel's back, rose, and pushed through the ferns.

Quickly they formed up in the road. Heat from the passing vehicles had dissolved the layer of fog along the ground between the hedgerows. Red and Sinclair took the lead, Bird still on point. He whistled and they started off again, this time Parnell picking up the pace.

In their haste, no one noticed that the ill Maquis named Henri Dupin was missing.

At that moment, thirteen miles to the west, the forward elements of the massive Allied invasion fleet, which had already dropped anchor in seventeen fathoms of water off the five Normandy assault beaches, prepared to debark troops into the swarms of landing barges that had been off-loaded two hours before. The sea was agitated enough to lift the barges and slam their gunwales against the bigger ships' hulls as the heavily loaded first-wave assault teams fought to climb down the boarding nets.

Meanwhile, the bombardment gunships, following their minesweepers' red-and-green-lit Dan buoys that marked the cleared pathways through the German minefields, headed to their designated fire support areas.

Even in the gloomy, cloud-covered darkness, the Allied armada was an awesome thing: seven thousand ships spread from horizon to horizon in columns and ranks twenty miles deep. Fast-attack transports, freighters, tankers, hospital ships, coasters, even small ocean liners. With them came the bombardment and covering Task

Forces, the concentrated firepower of seven battleships, eighteen cruisers, and forty-three destroyers, along with numerous small gunboats and rocket assault ships.

Streaming out of dozens of English loading ports from Scotland to Bristol Bay, the fleet had assembled during the hours of 5 June at a sea rendezvous fifteen miles southeast of the Isle of Wight, code-named Picadilly Circus. Then it turned south-southeast and headed straight for the coast of the Bay of the Seine and the assigned landing beaches. Those of the British and Canadians were to the east, the two to the west the Americans'.

But for Blue Team the only ship that would be time-crucial was the *Tuscaloosa* and her fourteen-inch guns. If they opened while the assault team was inside the enemy emplacement, those big shells could send them all to hell. At that precise moment, she was easing into station in tandem with the British cruiser, HMS *Black Prince,* on the northern flank of Fire Support Area One off Utah Beach.

It was Anabel Sinclair who got the Germans to stop.

They were still double-timing hard on the road to Quettehou, a mile outside the hamlet of Ravenouville. Beyond that, they'd still have to cover two more miles to the Kraut coastal guns.

The country had changed from hedgerows to rolling maritime hills covered in deep flannel grass, pleasantly lush. Still, they kept falling farther and farther behind the clock. Most of the Maquis were now near total collapse. Twice Parnell had been forced to halt because they began pulling leg cramps, their calves seizing up rock hard with excruciating pain.

Now he again whistled everyone to halt. The Frenchmen dropped while he, Bird, and Sinclair squatted.

The tall grass formed a four-foot barrier along the sides, gently bending in the breeze. "This shit just ain't cutting it," he said, breathing deeply but easily. He looked over at Bird. "What do you think, Wyatt?"

The sargeant shook his head, spat, came back. In the moon glow, his face gleamed with perspiration. "Not good, Lieutenant. Even if these boys make it, they ain't gonna be worth a damn in a fight."

"Then we leave them."

"What?" Anabel croaked. She, too, was panting heavily. "You can't attack that battery with so few men."

"It can't be helped," Red shot back. "Wyatt, check out who can continue. Leave the rest. Be certain we take the bazookas and as many grenades as we can haul."

"Yes, sir," Bird said and started to move off.

Laguna came running back along the road, dropped to one knee. "Something's comin', Lieutenant," he said. "Looks like a motorcycle and a car." He chuckled. "The dumb fucks're runnin' without blackout lights."

Parnell looked toward the north. He could see a faint glow about a half mile off. A single headlight appeared, a sharp, bright spot. With it came the distant rap of a motorcycle, which quickly faded off as the vehicle dropped below a low hill. Twin headlights now flashed into view and also quickly vanished.

"Wyatt, you and Weesay set up here. We have to take whoever it is. We need their wheels."

Sinclair touched his arm. "If you start firing here, it could bring patrols out of Ravenouville."

"We'll have to risk it." He rose and headed back along the column of men, the Frenchmen still sprawled in the crushed coral like corpses. Cowboy was standing, chewing on a C-ration candy bar.

Anabel called out to Parnell, "I'll get them stopped, Lieutenant. When they do, use your knives."

Parnell paused. Turned. "How the hell you gonna do it?"

"Just watch. Set up on me."

She immediately began pulling off her bandoleers, then her leather jacket, sweater, and cap. Her short dark hair fluttered in the sea breeze. Next came her trousers. Parnell, Bird, and Laguna silently watched. She took off her shoes and finally slipped off her panties and bra. She lowered herself to the road, completely naked.

The sound of the motorcycle rose again, closer this time. Behind it was the high purr of the automobile. Wordlessly, the three men scattered, Parnell calling softly in French, "*D'accord*, everybody hide." The Frenchmen rolled to their feet and limped into the grass.

He gave a low whistle. Fountain came running up. "Set up on both sides of the road," he ordered. "Just beyond where the woman's lying. When the vehicles stop, take 'em with knives. If they're Frenchies, hold up until I find out who they are. But don't let anybody get a round off."

Fountain nodded, staring at Anabel over his shoulder. "God-*damn*, that little ole spy gal's flat-ass *nekked*."

"Go, go," Parnell growled.

Sinclair was lying fully in the road now, her head up on one elbow watching the men deploy. They ran past her giving open glances.

The German vehicle was a small, open Volkswagen staff car with a driver and two officers in back. Ahead of it, the motorcycle rider abruptly skidded to a stop when his headlight hit Anabel. He shouted back to the Volkswagen. The driver slammed on his brakes, the little car fishtailing.

The cyclist was dressed in a long leather jacket, gauntlets, and goggles. He stared at Sinclair, then turned and called to the car again. The two officers climbed out and walked up to him. They stood studying Anabel suspiciously, murmuring to each other.

They were Luftwaffe officers in dark blue greatcoats with major insignias. At last, they started forward, walking side by side. The headlights shone brightly on the back of their high boots and cast their shadows onto the coral road.

Bird killed the driver in total silence as Smoker jumped the motorcycle rider, both coming at the Germans from out of the grass. The cyclist heard the rustle of the stalks and turned slightly but Wineberg was already on him. Growling, he rammed his knife into the man's throat, cutting in and down into the small bony cup at its base. The rider reeled back and let out a choked howl.

The two officers whirled around. *"Pas blos auf!"* one shouted. They tore their coats open and began clawing for their P-38 pistols. There was a scuffling of boots and Parnell and Cowboy hit them. Red took his man from behind, snapped his right elbow under the chin, his other arm wrapped around the back of the officer's head. Twisting sharply, he broke the man's neck, dropped him to the ground, and turned to assist Fountain.

Cowboy and the other major were entangled. The German was strong and agile. They tumbled into the grass, flailing at each other. Fountain managed to get the officer's head back and stabbed him in the ear. The officer screamed. Coming up, Parnell grabbed the man, lifted him, and rammed his knife straight into his kidney. For a moment, the German froze, then turned as Red released him, falling, his eyes wide open, the whites shining in the moonlight.

* * *

Three minutes later, with Sinclair fully dressed and driving the Volkswagen, they roared off toward the road to Ravenouville. Parnell, Bird, Fountain, Wineberg, and five Maquis fighters with all their gear were squeezed into the little car. Another one clung to the spare tire mounted in front. Weesay and Claude had already roared off on the motorcycle, taking point.

While they were loading, Anabel suddenly realized somebody was missing. She counted heads, saw it was Dupin. She turned to Parnell. "He's one of Lucas's best lieutenants. A damn good fighter. Where the hell could he be?"

Smoker heard her, said, "He musta been the guy pulled up sick. Back before that Kraut column came along."

"Well, we can't do anything about it now," Red snapped. "Let's move."

They soon reached Ravenouville, raced through without slowing, the hamlet completely dark and silent, merely a dozen two-storied stone houses and a small, steepled church. Dogs barked at their engine noise. The moon was low in the western sky now and the air was heavy with the sweet smell of ocean and seaweed and vast, open space.

Parnell, crunched down between the two front seats, arms and legs and gear all around him, could feel Anabel's haunch against his arm: soft-hard buttock flesh beneath her trousers and bandoleer. Again, he detected that faint whisper of perfume.

He turned, studied her profile: short hair, wind-ruffled, eyes squinting with concentration. In the faint back-glow from the headlights, he traced her pert nose, her pouty lips slightly opened. A damned fine looker, he thought. Classy. He pictured her as the Sweetheart of Sigma Chi, homecoming queen.

As if sensing his scrutiny, she turned and smiled down at him. Her smile was triumphant: *I told you I'd get them stopped.* He dipped his head, gave her a thumbs-up. Then, abruptly, the dark specter of the German bunker flashed back into his mind. With it came the absurd reality of this pretty American girl driving them wildly through the French night toward a killing zone. Jesus, it was all wrong, discordantly out of place.

He'd encountered female resistance fighters back in Italy. But they were a far different breed, most of them *born* into a world of violent death, the residue of eons of repression. They fought out of desperation, not choice. What kind of internal hardware did Anabel Sinclair have? What motive to be here? Little Miss Betty Coed come to war. Why? Jilted? A casual choice as epilogue to a summer semester in Europe? He found himself suddenly very angry, and feeling very foolish, too. But he couldn't pinpoint the exact reason for either. *That* pissed him off even more.

He dismissed the whole thing, swung his mind back to the deadly, more important business at hand. He looked out through the windshield, watched the Frenchman out there on the tire hanging on for dear life, his jacket flapping wildly. Mentally, he began going through the procedures of the attack.

Back in England, the team had run through three mock exercises of a surprise attack against a German Type 685 artillery emplacement. Now he methodically went through each step again, forming the natural sequences, figuring unexpected screwups. The trouble was the *biggest* problem was one he couldn't foresee. How would these untrained Resistance fighters perform under fire? They'd done all right against a small bivouac. What they were taking on this time would probably be at least a full company of trained troops who were deeply entrenched.

He felt the old tightening in the belly start. He checked his watch. It said 4:26 A.M. *Shit.*

When Duboudin and his two companions reached the Cherbourg rail line three miles southeast of Valognes, they could hear the distant rumble of a train approaching. Now and then, they actually caught sight of its blue headlamp in the predawn darkness.

He'd deliberately chosen the youngest of his circuit men to accompany him, fishermen brothers from the village of Binic on the Brittany coast. They were new to the Movement. Their father had been murdered in a German labor camp in Russia two years before. Their names were Rene and Georges Gruhier. Both were still excited, flying on the adrenaline from the attack on the German bivouac.

Duboudin slapped Georges's shoulder. "Get up the track about a hundred meters and lay your charges," he said. "When Rene and I finish here, we'll string out the wire and connect up. Hurry!"

Georges raced off, spooking a rabbit that broke from cover and went bounding along the track ahead of him. Duboudin watched him go. Rene was already on his knees, pulling kilo-weight plastique blocks and fuses from his knapsack.

Vaillant gently slipped his double-edged fighting knife from his belt, settled it blade-down into his palm. The rumble of the train was drawing closer. Rene turned, grinning up at him. "Oh, those fucking sauerkraut-eaters. We'll send the *bande de voyous* straight to hell, eh, *patronne?*"

With a backhand move as quick and slick as a snake's tongue, Duboudin slit his throat. With a wild grunt, Rene leaped to his feet, twisting, holding his hands over the wound. He began to gag, a frothy, mushy sound. Blood squirted through his fingers. He tried to speak but was unable. He fell down, thrashed for a moment, then went still. Valliant wiped his blade on the boy's sweater, returned it to his belt.

The sound of the train burst out suddenly as it cleared a hedgerow a kilometer away, starting into a slow curve. Vaillant whistled loudly and shouted, "Georges, come quickly!" The older Gruhier brother immediately came running back along the tracks. Duboudin slid a short-barreled, 8mm Lebel revolver from his jacket and held it against his leg.

As Georges drew closer, he spotted his brother on the ground. "*Mon Dieu*," he cried out. "What happened to Rene?"

He came up, dropped to his knees. He tried to lift his brother upright, felt the blood all over Rene's sweater. He stared at it, then swung around and looked up at Duboudin. The blue headlamp of the train came on, its brightness attenuated into a diffused glow, the bass pound of its engine rolling like crashing surf as it pulled a slight hill. Georges yelled something and lunged for Vaillant.

Duboudin took a half step back and shot him in the forehead. The impact knocked Georges to the side. He shot him again and still again, the bursts of the weapon lost in the larger sound of the approaching train. He quickly dragged both bodies into brush, the ground beginning to shake.

Then the train was there, roaring past, sucking the blue glow of its headlamp away into the darkness. The huge driving wheels slammed against the rails as a thick cloud of soot sparkling with cinders blew up and back over Vaillant. The line of boxcars and flatbeds carrying chained-down German artillery pieces hurtled past, their tiny red running lights bouncing and jittering.

As the last car drew off into the darkness, he dashed across the tracks and disappeared down into an apple orchard, running hard. His destination was Faucogney, a kilometer to the south. There he had a hidden radio set. He *had* to contact Major Land. On the chance Henri Dupin had failed to do so.

Chapter Four

"*Oberstleutnant*," Major Land murmured quietly, giving Colonel Meyer-Detring's shoulder a gentle nudge. The colonel lifted his head from his pillow, stared up at Land, then cleared his throat. "More paratrooper sightings?"

"Yes, sir. Quite a few," Land answered. "Also a heavy air strike at 0330. And a Normandy radar station picked up something out in the Channel. But the images were too distorted for clarification."

Meyer-Detring drew his head back, startled. "Something out in the Channel? What about the other stations?"

"Nothing, sir. Nearly all are temporarily down for repair."

The senior officer swung his thick legs over the side of the bed, sat for a moment rubbing his face. His underwear gave off an odor of oranges from his specially prepared talcum he had shipped from Amsterdam. Finally, he stood and began to dress while the major filled him in on the latest reports.

"Apparently Seventh Army's finally come around," Land said, standing at casual parade-rest. "Schleiger's declared an *Alarmstruffe Zwei*." An A-2 was the highest state of readiness.

The colonel guffawed. "Has there been any word from von Rundstedt?"

"Not yet, sir."

"Rommel?"

"No. Templehoff still considers this a developing situation."

The colonel pulled on his boots, shrugged into his tunic. "What about OKW?" The initials stood for *Oberkommando der Wehrmacht*, the German High Command.

"Colonel Schleiger called Berchtesgaden directly. Jodl dismissed the reports. He and Keitel are both convinced we're all panicking down here. At worst, they believe it might be a feint. They've warned the Pas de Calais units to be on extra alert."

"Have they told the Führer?"

"Jodl refused to wake him."

Meyer-Detring scoffed. "What else would you expect? Those fucking *Nikesel* twins." Generaloberst Alfred Jodl was OKW's chief of operations. He and Hitler's chief of staff, Generalfeldmarschall Wilhelm Keitel, were both known to be the Führer's toadies and disparagingly called *Nikesels* by many senior army officers. The word meant a toy wind-up donkey that constantly nodded its head.

The colonel cursed when he saw the number of sighting-pins on the operations wall map. They had doubled. "What's come in from our buried agents?" he snapped at Land.

"A flood of reports, sir. But no one knows anything specific yet."

A corporal came up to hand Meyer-Detring a teletype message. The colonel scanned it, grunted. "Mannequins now," he said, shaking his head.

"What's that, sir?"

"Several outposts report finding small stuffed dolls dressed like paratroopers out in fields. They even have chutes and equipment packs."

"Obviously decoys."

"Of course." The two men exchanged glances, their eyes questioning: decoys for what?

Another corporal approached Land. "Excuse me, *herr Major*. A triple-X-urgent message just come in for you from one of the Normandy agents. Code-named Nicholas. It's being deciphered now, sir."

Land's eyebrows lifted. "Perhaps we have something at last, *Oberstleutnant*," he said and hurried off to the deciphering room.

The agent code-named Nicholas was Vaillant Duboudin.

Parnell was brusque, trying to keep the explanations to an understandable minimum for the Frenchmen gathered in a tight circle around him in the darkness. They were two hundred yards from the German gun emplacement, in deep grass. Far beyond the cliff the sea lay dark. Low, scudding clouds had moonlight beyond them, the moon itself now just barely above the horizon. The wind was gusty and whipped the tall grass.

He had already dispatched his own team to take out the battery's sentry posts, cut through the outer fence line, check and mark out pathways if there were mine belts inside the bunker compound. Now he was explaining the attack plan to the Maquis fighters, step by step, Anabel translating for clarity.

This was to be a shock attack, he said. Sudden, fast, with coordinated and specific concentrations of firepower. Since they didn't have enough reserve manpower, there would be no base-of-fire set up and, therefore, no fallback line. "We *will* overrun that installation," he said flatly. "Is that clearly understood?"

Anabel translated. Everyone nodded.

The assault would be composed of four fire teams, each

led by a Blue Team trooper. The first objective was the penetration of the bunker itself. For this, they'd use the bazookas and Bird's Panzerbuchse to blow the two entry doors. There would be another team above the bunker that would drop phosphorous grenades down the vents.

Once inside, the teams would link up and spread throughout the emplacement. "Use saturation bursts and your grenades. But be damned sure you know where your bullets are going. Don't go shooting each other."

Again the Maquis nodded with solemnity. They shifted from knee to knee, their weapons nestled in the crooks of their elbows. In their farmer and fishermen garb and work hats they looked like grim peasants waiting to storm the Bastille.

Parnell continued, "There's a main corridor inside the building. Runs the full length of it with individual rooms branching off. We'll secure each room one at a time. Then we hit the gun platforms. They'll undoubtedly be steel-reinforced casings. If so, we'll go in through the on-duty crew's ready room in the center of the platforms."

He waited while Anabel completed the translation, then said, "I know you people haven't been trained in securing a room. Here's how it's done. First you throw in two concussion grenades. The M2A1 types, with the green stamp. As soon as they've detonated, the team leader will order the first man in.

"He takes one step through the door, throws a fan burst, steps to the right. The second man follows immediately with another spray burst and then steps to the left. The last man in is the leader who'll fire a third spray burst and secure the position. Any questions?"

"You went too fast," Anabel said.

He repeated the procedure, waited. She completed the relay, asked for questions. There were none.

Parnell said, "Okay, listen up good. *Ecoute tres bon, oui?* We *must* complete the assault and withdraw within thirty minutes. At precisely 5:40 a naval bombardment will commence on this position unless I signal that we've disabled the guns. *Comprendre?*"

Sinclair had started to translate, then stopped abruptly, turned to stare at him. "So it really *is* on, isn't it? They're actually out there right now?"

"Yes."

"Oh, God!" She quickly told the Frenchmen that the great Allied invasion was already under way and was at that very moment lying off the French coast. Their faces broke into wide grins, the men whispering happily, excitedly: *"Dieu Merci,"* *"C'est merveilleux!"* and *"Viva le Amerique!"* They craned their necks to look out toward the ocean.

He waited a few moments for them to quiet down. "All right, check and lock-and-load your weapons." A sudden thought struck him. "Your new Thompson submachine guns, I assume you people know how to handle them, right?"

"Yes," Sinclair answered. "I trained them myself." There were the sharp *chunks* of breeches snapping shut as the Frenchmen shoved rounds up into the chamber and clicked their safeties on.

"Keep them locked until we reach the bunker," Red added. "I don't want you people shooting each other in the ass while we complete the approach."

Anabel passed that on, then turned to her own weapon. She had given her Sten to Rene, one of the boys with Duboudin. Now she had a new Thompson, too. Parnell looked to his own gear, finishing up by feeling through the canvas of his demo musette to be sure he had his flare gun and three cartridges.

Everyone fell silent. The Frenchmen stared at the

dark ground. One or two made the sign of the cross and kissed their thumbnails. Sinclair leaned on her weapon, nervously ran her tongue over her lips. Around them, the wind lashed the grass and made the stalks hiss.

Red looked out at the ocean. High up a thin gray wash had deepened into solid black over the sea. To the right, along the eastern horizon, a thread of fluorescence was glowing now. As he stared at it, the colors seemed to shift from indigo to a gray blue and finally a merging yellow orange.

He checked the time: 4:36. The salt-saturated air was cold. He took out his toy clicker, rolled it in his hand, felt himself coming up to it again, that tensing of the body, a folding inward of himself into a single functioning, thinking, acting unit. His fingers tingled pleasantly as he watched the grass for his scouts to return.

At thirty-four, Rudolph Bucher was the oldest second lieutenant in his regiment, the 716th *Heereskustenartillerieabseiling,* or coastal artillery regiment. A fanatical believer in Adolph Hitler, he had been in the *Werhmacht* for fourteen years, slowly working his way from *Soldat Schirrmeister,* a supply private, to *Leutnant.* His fellow officers disliked him. He was crude, obstinate, and overzealous, even for their tastes. He also had an unpleasant body odor.

By the spring of 1944, Germany had badly depleted itself of fighting men. Many units were constantly at half strength. The army was forced to seek out any male they could find to fill their ranks. Some were as young as thirteen. For the first time, the military also began using impressed prisoners of war, non-Aryans such as Poles, Russians, and Armenians. They were given the choice: fight for the Führer or get your families slaughtered.

The officer rosters had also been brutally decimated. Old men and previously incompetent officers were now being given commands they ordinarily would never have received. That was how Second Lieutenant Bucher became the battery commander of bunker FKB-124 outside Ravenouville. He gloried in it, his long-awaited chance to prove his loyalty to Fatherland and Führer. He fully intended to die doing it.

He did, however, have good reason to be proud of his Feld Kanone Batterie. In late 1943, Hitler had envisioned a continuous defensive line of deep fortifications, antitank obstacles, and mine belts extending from Norway to the Pyrenees to seal off western Europe against invasion. He named it the Atlantic Wall. Although both Rommel and von Rundstedt scoffed at this wall business, referring to it as a *Wolkenkuckshiem*, which meant *cloud cuckoo land* that could easily be flanked, they nevertheless built the Channel portion of it with great speed and quality using slave labor from France and the Low Countries.

FKB-124 was a modified Type 685 bunker, 150 feet long, sixty feet deep, and constructed of eight-foot-thick walls of reinforced concrete. It had three levels, all beneath the ground. They contained living quarters, an armory, mess facilities, supply rooms, and a powder magazine on the lowest floor. In addition to Bucher, all the noncoms, radio operators, and range-and-track coordinators were German. The gun crews, however, were composed of impressed Russians and Poles, which created a total muster of sixty-two men.

Bucher despised the foreigners under his command. Although some of the Russians had been Soviet Army artillery men, it was impossible to make most of the stupid *schwein* understand his orders.

In addition, he knew how untested he personally was

in the handling of combat artillery and battery defenses. To offset this shortcoming, he had drilled his men constantly. When they failed to meet his time-and-firing standards, he had them lashed bareback with a cat-o'-nine-tails that he'd found in a ruined French naval museum. This particular brutality had already crippled two Russians. The others were terrified of him.

The battery's three 155mm field guns were in individual cylindrical casements in the center of the bunker, each with a concrete dome that slid back to allow the weapon to achieve firing position. The lack of steel had prevented construction of swiveling cupolas on the latest coastal bunkers, so these were mounted on "spider-leg" recoil spring equilibrators and emplaced on hydraulically operated platforms that lifted them from their pits. This allowed enough elevation and traverse to lay down enfilading fire against targets directly offshore of the emplacement's hundred-foot-high bluff as well as on targets as far away as Pointe de Barfleur in the north and Grandcamp-Maisy to the southeast.

The battery's fire control and ranging system utilized a Kommandogerat 40 Direcktor, which provided automatic and continuous targeting data to the guns' own elevating, traversing, and sighting mechanisms and fired each shell electrically. The main components of the Direcktor were located in a firing room beside the noncoms' quarters to the left of the gun pits. Its sighting element, a seven-foot-wide optical instrument mounted on a pedestal, was above it in a small observation bunker with a narrow viewing slit through which the machine collected distance and windage information.

There were only three entrances to the bunker: two stairwells down to the central corridor and a loading ramp with a small crane to off-load installation supplies and ordnance into the magazine. Outside air entered through six vents and a baffled conduit system.

A double electrical fence surrounded the entire installation. Far outside the fence line was a shallow cement channel linked to three external tanks containing a mixture of kerosene and crude oil. If attacked by enemy artillery or air strikes, the channel could be flooded and lit off so as to create a thick screening smoke to obscure the bunker from enemy gunners.

On this particular night, Bucher had been unable to sleep. Restless and brooding, he wandered about the bunker, scowling at everything. Twice he went up to the observation room to look out at the darkness over the ocean.

Then at 0408 hours British time, Seventh Army headquarters' A-2 alert reached him. Within three minutes, he had his battery in full combat status: the entire roster on duty and all outer doors to the installation double-sealed with small arms issued. His firing systems were now in the process of being checked and rechecked.

At first, Bird and Fountain couldn't figure out what the ditch was for. Like a shallow moat, it had a cement coating and was about a hundred yards from the German emplacement's outer fence line. Grass grew thickly along its edges. At this point, it ran on a north–south line from the bluff's edge.

He and Cowboy's task was to first neutralize the sentry post on this side of the bunker, then set up a path through the fence and inner compound to the first entry point. Air recon photos and Resistance intelligence reports indicated there were two guard posts: this one near the bluff, the other at the main freight road into the facility. Wineberg and Laguna had been assigned to deal with that one.

Wyatt decided to follow the moat. It would be easier than slowly probing through the grass for outer mine belts. It might even take them right up to the sentry position. They headed off running nearly upright, hidden by the tall grass. As they neared the cliff's edge, they could hear the wind popping and soughing up the cliff face. From beyond came the soft rustle of surf and the faint calls of seagulls.

A few feet from the edge, the moat made a sharp turn to the right and paralleled it. Soon they came to a branch ditch that led to a half-buried tank about ten feet in diameter. It was under camouflage netting and there was a canvased pump connected to it with a hose that emptied into the moat. German symbols and the words *kerosene-huile* were stenciled on the tank.

Wyatt nodded. "That's what I figured," he said quietly. "The little sumbitch's a smoke screen maker."

"A what?" Cowboy asked.

"A smoke maker. The Krauts flood 'er and light off under artillery attack. Makes a helluva smoke screen to obscure the bunker."

They moved on.

The entire approach to the fence was easier than they'd expected. The grass had deliberately been left wild and uncut so as to give the impression from the air that it was merely deserted coastal savannah. They were able to get within fifteen feet of the sentry post, which was a small semicircle of sandbags backed against the outer fence.

They could make out two guards in camo capes hunkered down behind the bags with their backs to the wind. The post had a single mounted MG-34 machine gun positioned to give it a full field of fire from the cliff edge to the entry road. A leather-cased field telephone hung on a pole.

Bird crawled to the left and took up position ten feet from the sandbags as Cowboy moved a few feet to his right. In the faint light, the sandbags looked like smooth stones, compacted by the rain.

Bird drew his boot knife. He felt his temples thudding softly, experienced the old familiar taste of copper pennies in his saliva. He glanced over at Fountain, coiled his legs, and mentally counted off: one, two, *three!*

Moving in perfect unison, both men charged forward and went over the sandbags. The guards' heads snapped around. Their mouths opened in utter shock and then their eyes, wide, white in the dim light. Before they could react, knife blades were rammed into their mouths with upward strokes that carried the points into the base of their brains. Blood gushed out between their lips.

Wyatt's and Cowboy's momentum took them into and over the two Germans who were spastically thrashing and slamming against the floor of the sentry pit. One tried to get to his hands and knees. Fountain knifed him again, through the folds of the cape into his left back, down between upper ribs. The raw, hot smell of the blood rose and with it the thick fume of excrement. The German had lost control of his bowels.

Bird hurriedly cracked the machine-gun breech, drew out one of the belted 7.92mm rounds, and rammed it into the gun's muzzle to disable it. They turned their attention to the compound fence. Their luck was holding. A low tunnel covered in corrugated tin and sandbags went from the back of the sentry post through both fence lines. Quickly they scrambled through and entered the bunker's inner perimeter. A communications ditch trailed off at an angle to the tunnel. It was for bringing up ammo and personnel during guard mount change. A thin telephone cable ran alongside it.

They followed the ditch through the grass, going slowly at first to check for trip wires. Unbelievably, there weren't any. They reached the northern entry stairwell, paused to listen. Only the moaning of the wind and the soft purr of internal generators.

Wyatt glanced at Cowboy and shook his head. This was one dumb fuck of a battery commander, he thought, leaving his approaches unmined and then failing to lay trip wires in the most obvious pathway to the entry door. Fountain nodded agreement.

They eased down the stairs. It was made into four switchbacks with platforms. The steps had steep risers and were slippery with mud. The walls had dark patches of fungus. At the bottom was a door with a tiny red light above it.

The door was made of riveted steel plating with hidden hinges. Bird felt along its rusted surface, then lightly tapped his thumbnail against it, leaning in to listen to the soft rebound, gauging the steel's thickness. He figured it was two, perhaps three inches in depth. *Good, good.* Their bazookas and the Kraut antitank gun would easily blow holes through this sumbitch.

He signaled Fountain. They darted up the stairs and hurried back along the communications trench.

Parnell kept watching the sky. The dawn light seemed to be coming on too fast. The snapping grass stalks were already beginning to silhouette against the dark gray counterpane high up.

A clicker suddenly chirped out in the grass, twice. He

clicked back, one snap, a pause, another. Bird and Fountain silently emerged. Wyatt hurried over to him while Cowboy squatted near where they had come out, watching their back trail.

"She's a clear run right up to the stairwell, Lieutenant," Bird said. "No sign of mines or trip wires."

"Really?" Parnell said, surprised. "How long does it take to cross through?"

"Maybe five, six minutes."

Another double clicking sounded softly under the wind. Red counterclicked and Smoker and Weesay came in. Wineberg reported. His was the same as Wyatt's. Like Bird and Fountain, they'd used the smoke ditch to get close to the sentries and had quickly and easily dispatched them.

Red ordered the assault fire teams made up. Half the Maquis fighters would go with his group, the other half with Smoker, Cowboy, and Weesay. This was quickly done. He then gathered his own men around him to synchronize their watches: "It's 405 eight and ten . . . now. We hit the bastards at 055 on the button. That'll give us thirty-five minutes before the navy starts throwing shells at us."

He glanced at Wineberg, who would be team leader for the other group. "Smoker, set up your bazookas on the door right off. Even if your vent men aren't in place when it's time to go, blow the son of a bitch anyway."

Wineberg nodded.

Red again scanned the sky. The light was turning to a dull pewter color. He heard birds in the grass now, delicate trills and short whistles. There was a sudden thrashing of wings, everybody jumped as four small, dark objects flashed over them, skimming the tops of the reeds.

He turned to Sinclair. "You stay close to me." She appeared pale, her eyes large. She held her Thompson across her breasts. The bottoms of the shells in her bandoleer shone silvery in the increasing light.

"All right," he said. "Everybody move out."

Bird took point, the grass quickly swallowing him with only the muzzle of his Panzerbuchse visible, cleaving through the tall stalks like a shiny guidon. Red watched as Smoker's group disappeared into cover, then turned to the last of his Frenchmen as they slipped past him.

Anabel knelt close beside him. She looked so small in her jacket and crew cap, her face stiff, determined. Nervously, she kept tapping three fingers of her right hand on the butt of the submachine gun.

Parnell felt an inexplicable tenderness come up into his throat for her, his earlier anger suddenly, completely gone, leaving only this sense of comradeship, the same feel of bonding he had with his own men. There was something more, too. The realization that whatever Sinclair's motives were for being here, whatever gentle place she had come from, she *was* here of her own choice. Kneeling at his side and ready to thrust herself back into that dark violence and death which had already stunned and terrified her. And doing it without a word of protest or hesitation.

Before he even realized it, he had reached out and gently put his hand around the back of her neck. She turned to him. Her mouth trembled into a small smile. He grinned back at her. "Set?" he asked quietly.

She nodded, looking into his eyes.

"Then let's do it," he said. They rose and pushed into the grass.

For the third time Lieutenant Bucher had climbed the stairs to the observation platform to scan the sea, the chilly wind whistling through the ranging slot making the small cement room uncomfortably cold. Yet he still didn't see anything out there, the vast canvas of the ocean not yet free of its lingering darkness.

A noncom operator was seated behind the wide *Kommandogerat* sighting element. From it came the periodic hum as the instrument relayed changing windage data to the firing room as it ran through its high-alert-status pre-firing exercises. The unit, looking like a long telescope resting on its side, smelled of electrical oil and lens cleaner.

The battery's three 155mm guns were still covered. To keep his position hidden for as long as possible, Bucher would not order the cement caps slid back and the field pieces raised until he received specific target coordinates and orders to commence firing from regimental headquarters.

But he could already taste the joy of the coming battle. He knew the enemy was out there somewhere, had felt it all through the night, a sixth sense from the gut. Once he'd received the *Alarmstruffe Zwei*, his unease had evaporated. Now he was keyed up, ready to go. And absolutely certain he would give a splendid account of himself once the action began.

A small gray wall phone buzzed. On its face was an *Achtung* warning against enemy tapping of the lines. The sighting element operator turned to get it. Bucher waved him off and picked up the receiver himself. "Yes?" he snapped.

"*Herr Leutnant,* we've just received a Red-Status message from Oberfehlshaber West headquarters relayed through *Feldnachrichten Kommandantur.*"

Bucher's heart gripped up. *Direct from von Rundstedt's HQ?* "What does it say, *idiot?*" he shouted. "Read it to me!"

"Strong indication your position will be ground-attacked before daylight," the radioman read. "Extreme probability prelude to massive invasion your sector. Must oppose with total force. Do not, repeat, do not allow installation to be overrun."

The lieutenant felt a tingling chill shoot up his back. He turned and looked at the sighting element operator, the young man closely watching his officer's sudden reaction. At that moment, a loud explosion blew through the battery. Both men froze as the floor of the observation room vibrated slightly. They stared at each other as a second explosion came followed almost immediately by a third, the echoes merging to riffle up through the underground building.

Before their sound completely faded, Bucher was racing back down the stairs, bellowing.

Chapter Five

It was all happening again for Sinclair, coming with that same abrupt, horrifying suddenness. Pure silence and then *boom!* and they were into it. Down at the bottom of the stairwell, the antitank gun had blown a six-inch-wide hole right through the bunker door, partially tearing one side off its hinges. The back-blast and concussion swept back up the stairwell, carrying cordite fumes.

Bird was stretched prone on the second landing, angling the gun downward so he could hit the door, his body braced against the wall and railing. The spent shell casing and rotating ring had bounced off the side wall and now lay on the bottom deck, spinning slowly.

Anabel shoved forward, peered around the edge of the upper wall. The Frenchman behind her agitatedly shoved against her, anxious to see Parnell's signal to come down to the attack. She saw Red holding up his hand, indicating for them to wait. The door smoked and the smell of hot metal drifted up.

A muffled explosion came from the other side of the battery, the two bazookas going off as one against the other entry door. Then the Panzerbuchse fired off again with its hissing, slamming rush of sound. This round went through the space between the door and wall, blew the door back, and exploded inside the bunker.

Parnell waved them down. Anabel charged ahead,

went down the steps two at a time, gravity pulling at her. Surges of wild thoughts, images, feelings ripped through her, made her heart ram crazily against her chest wall. Her skull felt prickly, a peculiar taste like gunmetal rose in her mouth.

At the same time, she experienced a strange calmness behind all of it. Somewhere off in another sector of her brain, her subconscious self was thrusting forward with instincts honed by her training to take command of the crazy flood of energy racing through her body.

Halfway down, she saw both Bird and Parnell heave two grenades through the partially blown doorway and duck back. She too dropped to the landing, her Frenchies doing the same. Their hard breathing made sucking sounds against the metal platform.

The grenades went off, yellow-orange flashes. Dirty white smoke and shrapnel flew back through the opening. Metal shards slammed into the stairwell walls. She waited a moment, then pushed herself to her feet and headed down once more.

Parnell and Bird were already gone through the sundered doorway, the Panzerbuchse lying beside it. There was the staccato rap of Thompsons. A man bellowed, the sound fading down into a tight sting of German obscenities. Firing from the other end of the installation, more Thompsons. These were instantly answered by German counterfire, Anabel recognized the tinny crack of Gewehr rifles, the dangerous trilling burr of Fallschirmjagergwehr machine carbines.

She reached the bottom. Shouting for one of the Maquis to bring the Kraut antitank gun, she dashed through the doorway. The inside corridor was misty with smoke and the sharp stink of spent explosives and cordite. Parnell was to her right and ahead, down on

one knee, firing at an angle to the turn in the hall. Bird
was farther in, crouched near the corner in the corridor.

She moved up beside Red, heard him grunt just before he cut loose with another burst, ricocheting his
bullets off the opposite wall and down the corridor.
Spent shells tinkled onto the cement floor.

The fast *thrupping* sizzle of a German MP-40 machine
pistol came from somewhere, sounding hollow. Bullets
cut coronets into the left wall. Cement dust flew. She felt
something slap against the edge of her grenade harness.
A sharp heat that instantly vanished.

Parnell rose and ran forward. He and Wyatt disappeared around the corner. The French Maquis fighters
were abreast of her now, sprinting forward, weapons
ready, their eyes large and wild.

A German soldier suddenly appeared in a side doorway, crouched. He swung his rifle up to his shoulder.
Both Anabel and one of the Frenchies fired at him at
the same moment. The man ducked his head and
started to turn. Their bullets made two perfect stitch
lines across the wall. The back of the German's head
burst open, flinging blood and skull chips ahead of
him like a fan as he dropped.

Sinclair paused long enough to jerk a grenade from
her harness, heard the snap of the tape and click as the
activator arm flipped up. "Grenade left!" she yelled in
French at the top of her voice and flung it over the German's body and through the doorway. The explosion
rumbled inside walls and threw the soldier's body out
into the hallway like a limp doll.

She dodged past it and ran on. Hot spots drifted in
the air from the firing and explosions. The smoky haze
was thick with cement dust. One Frenchman paused to
look around the corner, then vanished. She cautiously

looked around the edge. Four German soldiers were lying in the corridor. One lifted his arm and reached for the wall, his eyes glaring with effort as if it were taking his entire pool of strength to reach it. A Maquis shot him, then stopped long enough to kick the man's head before running on.

Up ahead, Parnell was waving urgently at them, shouting,. "Get up here! Come up!"

She caught a glimpse of the profile of his face in the smoky light, clenched down grimly, his jaw muscles tight, eyes narrowed. Yet there was also a certain stillness there, a quiet control in movement. She felt a rush of warmth for him come swelling into her breasts. *Crazy, crazy.* She ran toward him, her boots slapping on the dusty cement floor.

The phosphorous grenades of Cowboy's fire team blew right back out the air vents, spewing thick white fumes of molten hot oxide dust across the top of the gun casement. The fumes looked faintly luminescent in the dawn light.

"God-*dammit*!" Fountain bellowed. In frustration, he rammed his boot against the vent, looking like a nun bowed in prayer. His two Frenchmen across the roof of the bunker looked at him, their hands spread: *what now?*

He knew what had happened. The vents weren't free flowing, had baffles and filters spaced along the impellor casings. The lighter-charged M3A phosphorous grenades didn't have enough explosive power to blow through the obstructions and saturate the lower rooms with fumes. It was his duty to disable the men in those rooms long enough to allow the penetration teams to isolate the main corridor.

"All right, you sons a' bitches," he murmured, grinning. "I'll jes give you boys some *bigger* shit first." He snapped two M2A1 fragmentation grenades from his harness, held them up for the two Maquis to see. He pointed down the vent. Twisting back, he released the two grenade arms, cooked off the fuse for two seconds, then tossed them down the vent.

The twin explosions blew his vent half off its foundations, shrapnel *whanging* and spiraling out of its mouth. The cement slab under him trembled faintly. Two more explosions went off as the Maquis blew their vents.

Now he held up two phosphorous grenades, turned, and tossed them into the tilted vent. This time only a thin outburst of phosphorus fumes came up. They'd blown right through the obstructions and into the lower rooms. Krauts, he knew, were now down there getting clouds of acid-hot fume particles all over them.

As he lunged into the firing room from the observation platform, Lieutenant Bucher's thoughts were zinging so rapidly through his mind he was unable to form any stable coherency to them. Urgent questions of what his first reactions should be welled. What commands? Snippets of partially remembered lectures on bunker defense and the tactics and countermeasures against enemy assault drifted up, along with a dark underpane of fear and confusion. With that came, tangentially, the bitter remembrance of how he had always been snubbed by his fellow officers. He experienced a renewed rush of determination. This was his moment of testing, what he had waited for. There was no way he would fail.

Forcing his mind to slow down, he examined the situation, its dimensions and depths. Countermeasures immediately popped up into his mind. He paused, glared around the room. His noncoms were already moving, hurling orders, the air thick with the resounding cracklings of firefights out in the corridor and the muffled explosions of grenades from somewhere above. Faint screams erupted from the weapon pits.

"Seal off the guns!" he shouted. Obeying, a corporal rose and raced to the door that led into the gun crew's ready room and lunged through. A senior *Unterfeldwebels* darted past him carrying an MP-40, a lanky fellow with a brush mustache.

Bucher grabbed his tunic, brought him to a stop. "You, take men. Defend the magazine. Don't let the enemy reach the munitions."

"Yes, sir," the sergeant said. He went through the room, chose six men. They rushed back through the firing machines and down the stairwell to the powder room.

At that instant, the upper door to the corridor blew in. A white-hot object sizzled across the room and exploded in the forward bulkhead. Concussion waves rolled through the smoke, heating up the air, fluttering. The men, who had instantly dropped to the floor, now regained their feet.

A grenade tumbled along the ground, blew up with a shockingly loud bang. The concussion sucked Bucher's breath. Another came in. This one stopped directly beneath one of the firing computer units. When it exploded, rolls of data paper were heaved, unraveling, up against the ceiling.

Crouched behind a radio console, Bucher began firing his Luger blindly at the smoke-blurred doorway. "Concentrate your fire on the door!" he kept screaming. A barrage of German guns opened up, the rounds funneling into and through the doorway. A man in farmer's clothing momentarily appeared but was quickly hurled backward by the force of the bullet stream.

A fierce exchange went on for a full half minute, then stopped abruptly. There was a roaring silence. A few seconds passed. As if a switch had been flipped, another vicious firefight erupted down at the east end of the corridor. Within its clattering racket Bucher could clearly hear men shouting, calling out: "Stop! Russkies! Russkies!" Rage flared up into his face. Those cowardly Bolshevik *Ochse* were *surrendering*.

He leaped from behind the console, roaring, "Counterattack them. Now! They must not get in." Several men came slowly to their feet and charged forward toward the doorway, firing as they moved.

As the first men bolted through the door, two were cut down. A third stumbled over one of the bodies and also went down. A fury of gunfire swept over them. Bullets buzzed past and smashed into bulkheads. Another grenade went off like a small thunderclap. Shrapnel spun through the air.

Bucher felt panic grip his insides. Frantically, he searched the smoke- and noise-filled room. He had only four men left, his noncoms. He tried to fire his Luger. It was empty. He wanted to flee. *Nein! Nein!*

"Fall back," he bellowed. "Into the pits."

A sergeant rose, darted to the doorway. It was locked. He pounded on it. Another grenade came tumbling through the air, struck him in the back, and went off. The force jammed him into the door just as it swung open. He crumpled to the floor, a gaping wound in his back, exposing bloody, shattered spinal vertebrae.

Bucher and the remaining men dashed through the doorway, into a narrow corridor, the inner wall of the number-one gun pit curving to the right. Three Russians were kneeling in the corridor, their broad Asian faces waxy-looking in the dim light.

Cursing, Bucher ran past them. They and the noncoms followed, to the doorway of the ready room and through it. Someone slid the heavy steel door shut.

Following the ancient tradition of naval warfare, which stipulates that just before a ship goes into battle her skipper must give his crew a speech, at precisely 0517 hours a boatswain's whistle screeched forth from the loudspeakers of the heavy cruiser, USS *Tuscaloosa*. It was followed by, "Now hear this. Now hear this." A moment later, the deep, steady voice of Captain Norman Gillette came on.

He said, "This is the captain. The time has come to prove ourselves worthy of the trust placed in us by our nation. What we are about to do will be part of a decisive strike against those men who prefer Hitler's slavery to freedom. In this fight, we will hit hard and break clean. There is glory enough for all of us. Good luck and God be with you." The loudspeaker clicked off.

High up in his Primary Fire Control station atop the ship's cage mast, Senior Gunnery Officer Commander Raymond Morrison made a sign of the cross and returned to his duties. At the moment, the cruiser was steaming at four knots inside her assigned Fire Support Area One off Utah Beach.

The core of the armored PFC station was an Mk 38 Mod 2 range-finder/director, a tall metal unit containing telescopic and gyro-synchronized gear to gather range, windage and roll-and-pitch data on designated targets. The information was then transmitted through a self-synchronous or "selsyn" system to the ship's Forward Gunnery Computer Room, which automatically calculated specific-target-sighting instructions for the ship's nine eight-inch/55 guns.

Morrison felt the deck tilt slightly as the *Tuscaloosa* began a slow turn to port. He leaned forward and sighted his binoculars through an armor slit. The sky was a pearly gray out there, the sea still a black, misty expanse etched with whitecaps. A covering destroyer suddenly came into view from his right, its bow cleaving the ocean.

He swung the glasses the other way and saw several transport ships, each trailing an antiaircraft balloon. Around them, faintly discernable, hundreds of tiny Higgins boats carrying the first wave of invasion troops of the 4th Infantry Division bobbed and thrashed through six-foot swells as they patiently awaited the order to form up for their forty-five-minute run to shore and H-hour.

He swung back again and scanned the western horizon. It formed a thin dark line twenty-five thousand yards off the Normandy coast of France. Right there was his first potential target, designated TS-47/8-1, a buried enemy *Stutzpunkgruppe* emplacement containing three 155mm coastal guns. Unless a yellow site-flare was sent up by an elite force that had gone in last night to neutralize the bunker, he'd commence fire on it at exactly 0540 hours.

The *Tuscaloosa* was a veteran of the North African and Sicilian/Italian campaigns where she had performed admirably. But on this combat cruise a glitch was creating worry for Morrison. Because of a Bureau of Ordnance foul-up in England, the ship's magazine had been issued only armor-piercing shells. It had been too late to rectify this.

Armor piercing shells are designed for ship-to-ship duels, steel against steel. Their nose fuses won't detonate unless they strike a dense target. Shore bombardments, however, always use the lighter high-capacity shells to lay in a wider swath of destruction. So, he knew, unless that Normandy coast was made of solid rock, his AP rounds wouldn't go off unless they made a direct hit against the gun bunker.

The deck tilt steepened as the ship came around. It would take her a full ten minutes to complete the turn, then she'd slow to two knots and begin her salvo run. He glanced up at the range clock, keyed the ship's phone, and spoke to his FGCP watch officer. "Stand by to commence firing sequence on turrets one, two, and four," he said. "We are holding at twenty minutes, four-one seconds."

Acknowledgment came right back: "Standing by for CS on one, two, and four, aye. Now holding at twenty and four-one."

The Panzerbuchse's round, the last, blew a perfect hole right through the gun pit corridor, wrenching the door open. Parnell ran forward and tossed a fragmentation grenade through, the twisted metal smoking. As the echoing sound riffled off through the cement bulkheads, he and a Maquis fighter lunged through. Two bodies lay stretched across the narrow passageway.

Bullets exploded back at them. The Frenchmen grunted and fell back onto his buttocks. Red cut loose. The reports were deafening in the enclosed space, cordite smoke drifted. A German soldier staggered forward from a slight bend in the corridor. He tried to fire again. Parnell killed him.

The next door was a bigger problem. It led into the gun crew Ready Room, its steel at least four inches thick. This was now the only way into the three gun pits. He could hear men yelling beyond it. From the cracks seeped a thin veil of white phosphorus fumes.

"Get those bazookas in here," he called down the hall-way. As the order was relayed, he picked up the wounded Frenchman and carried him back to the Firing Room, laid him down beside a dead German. The Maquis's eyes kept fluttering, like a man in dream sleep. He'd been shot in the abdomen. A portion of intestine protruded like a small child's balloon veined with red spiderwebbing.

Weesay and Smoker came in with one of the bazookas and two 3.5-pound projectiles. Just beyond the door, Red saw Sinclair kneeling beside another wounded Frenchie. Two German soldiers stood farther back with their hands in the air, staring at someone out of sight.

The first bazooka rocket slammed into the Ready Room door with a horrendous crack, the back-blast of the weapon sounding like the sudden expulsion of high-pressure air. Shrapnel flew as smoke swirled and then drifted after it. The round had merely dented the steel, leaving a scorched star in the metal.

"Fuck!" Smoker said. He quickly shoved in the second projectile, wired off, and tapped Weesay's shoulder. Once more the weapon's shrill back-blast blew down the corridor, bits of the projectile's head hurling back after again merely indenting the door's steel.

Parnell was squatted a few feet away. Smoker turned, shook his head. Red swung around and yelled, "Wyatt, bring up some plastique. We'll blow the seams." He turned back, still squatted, his eyes narrowed thought-fully. Finally, he waved Wineberg over, asked him, "Did you put phosphorous down in that room?"

"Not that one, sir. We din't have no more M-Threes."

Shit! He thought about that. An idea hit him. "That smoke trench, did you spot the kerosene feeder tank for it?"

"Yeah, Lieutenant. It was near the main gate."

"Go get some. Pour it down on the vent and light off. But make it damned fast."

Smoker ran off. Parnell moved back to Bird, who was quietly hunkered down at the Firing Room door, holding his Thompson across his knee. Behind him was Cowboy and two Maquis. One had a jacket soaked with blood. It dripped slowly onto the floor.

"What's the status?" he asked Bird. The sergeant's face and smock were covered with cement dust save for the skin around his eyes where sweat had cleansed it from his skin. It gave him the look of a raccoon. "The bunker's secure, sir. 'Cept for the gun pits and them Krauts down in the powder room."

"The field pieces come first. If we can't breach in five minutes, we'll lay charges and pull out." He nodded Fountain over. "Cowboy, take one man and seal off the magazine. Don't let the pricks inside out. But tell them they've got a choice, surrender or get blown to hell." He looked at his watch: 0521. "Give 'em five minutes. They don't move by then, pull out and get the hell away from the bunker."

Fountain turned, pointed at the man in the bloody jacket. They dodged across the Firing Room and went down the stairs to the magazine.

"Set up your fire lanes," he said to Wyatt. "They come out shooting, finish them fast."

"Right, Lieutenant."

Red continued on through the door to check on Sinclair.

She was calm and talked quietly. Cement dust made her leather jacket appear to be covered with fine gray snow. He saw that a bullet had partially sliced her grenade harness. She was sitting back on her haunches, looking at the Frenchman. He was dead.

"How many have we lost?" Parnell asked.

"One dead, two wounded." She nodded up the hall. "Out in the entry alcove."

He looked up at the German soldiers standing near the back wall of the corridor. They had broad Slavic faces, their eyes frightened. One had been shot in the arm. He held it tightly against his gray uniform. "These all the prisoners?"

"Yes. They're Russians. They were begging to surrender."

Red nodded. "All right, take one of the Frenchmen and the prisoners. They can carry the two wounded. Get as far as you can from the bunker."

"No," she said. She reached down and closed the dead Frenchman's eyes.

"What?" Parnell glared down at her. In her crew cap and dust-covered face she looked like a young boy, a dirty London waif. "Goddammit, Sinclair. In about nineteen minutes that ship'll open on us."

"There could be more wounded."

"We'll bring them out."

"No." She looked up at him, her waif eyes gone solid.

"That's an order," he hissed.

"I'm not one of your men," she said sharply. She left his eyes, signaled one of the Maquis. He came up. "Take the wounded and the prisoners far from the bunker," she said in French. The man looked at her, then at Parnell. "Go *now*."

The Frenchman turned to the prisoners. "*Allons,*" he shouted at them. "*Va te faire foutre.*" Using his gun muzzle and head jerks, he herded them up the corridor, switching to German: "*Laufschritt marsch.*"

Without another word, Anabel rose, picked up her

weapon, and went down into the Firing Room. Red stood helplessly watching.

The muzzle of Bucher's MP-40 slashed across the Russian gun crewman's forehead, the thick sight ring leaving a deep cut. The man fell back onto the Ready Room floor. The lieutenant glared balefully at him and then around the room. Three of his noncoms stood behind him with raised weapons. A dozen Russians and Poles were across the room.

"Any man who tries to open that door will be shot," he screamed at them. "You Bolshevik trash will fight or you will die right here."

They prowled, scowling like highly agitated tigers behind wire. At the first blast of the bazooka, they had rushed away from the door, yelling out to the attackers in Russian and Polish. The second round pushed them over the edge, the men pleading with Bucher to surrender, telling him in their jibbering languages that it was a massive attack and there was no hope.

Several of the men were part of crews who had been in the gun pits on alert status when suddenly phosphorous grenades blew down through the vents. Many had died of shock and oxide inhalation before the few could get out. Now their uniforms were powdered white and their hands and faces burned, the phosphorus scalding their throats and lungs and eating holes in exposed flesh.

The Ready Room stank of the phosphorus oxide seepage, an odor like the gummy residue off electrical battery terminals. With it was the raw stench of burnt skin. It was a fairly large, windowless cement structure. It contained a bank of four bunks on one side for the standby crew, a table, and four chairs. Spread on the table were grimy playing cards, a small chess set made of a crate wood, and a portable Fu 8 artillery spotter's radio. On one wall was a telephone box with several buttons on its face that linked it to the main sectors of the bunker.

Four doors gave entrance into the room. The one to the Firing Room corridor was solid steel. Now there were two humps in it from the bazooka rounds, the metal scorched and tempered into blue and orange rings. The other three doors led into the gun pits. These were made of steel framing filled with poured concrete. They were two feet thick and swung lightly on counterweights in the wall. In the center of each was a wheel like a vault's lock, which shifted bars inside to seal it off.

Lieutenant Bucher stepped around his noncoms and moved to the corridor door, pressed his ear against it. His beige-colored tropical field tunic with its red collar and shoulder straps was spotted with sweat and blood. It was silent out there. He had a violent headache that seemed to rise up from the back of his head to hold his skull in a vise. His mind roared between stark terror and rage. He noticed one of his noncoms looking at him. Was there an appeal for surrender in the man's gaze?

Never.

He must counterattack, he realized. Of course, his only tactical option now. But the narrow door presented a problem. The attack would have to be carried through with one man at a time, like pigeons exiting a coop. Unacceptable. Wait, he could send the Russians out first, use them as shields for his main thrust. Yes, they were nothing but useless fodder, anyway. He liked that thought. He started to turn, the order coming into his mouth.

A liquid began flushing down out of the overhead

vent, splashing onto the floor and several of the men. Everyone jumped back. It was dark like maple syrup and smelled of kerosene. Smoke screen oil!

Before anyone could react, a blue-yellow flame flashed down through the falling stream of oil. There was a hollow *whoosh* and the entire column of liquid was aflame. It raced across the floor. Dense black smoke began filling the room.

Gunfire erupted, the muzzle blasts horrendous in the enclosed space. Bullets blew chunks out of the walls. A man fell down beside Bucher. His noncoms and the Russians were fighting, tearing at each other in a thickening oily fog. Bellowing, he opened up blindly, sweeping the MP-40 crosswise.

The Russians broke past his men, lunged for the door as the light vanished into a brown blackness. Vaguely he could see shadows moving. He fired at them until his clip was empty. Men coughed and shouted.

A sense of panic seized him. Dropping his weapon, he groped out with his hands, felt a shoulder, a wall. He was aware he whimpered deep in his throat. Felt shame. His breathing had become labored. He could taste the oil in his mouth, his lungs burned. Somewhere in the darkness, the fire hissed sudden flashes of orange flame that glowed in the darkness, then disappeared.

Now his rage returned, the panic dissolving. He was a German officer, he would die as a German officer. That decision told him what to do. He moved along the wall. The heat in the room was becoming unbearable. He touched the edge of the table, felt for the telephone receiver. One side of the table was afire, the smell of burning wood. He knelt, pressed the receiver to his ear. It was hot. He punched the button to the powder room.

There was a buzz, another, then a click and a man said, "*Ya?*"

"Leutenant Bucher," he croaked, then had to pause to gulp in scorching air. "Explode the . . . munitions!"

There was no answer. Another machine pistol roared and a body fell across his back, rolled off. "I am ordering . . . you to set . . . off the magazine. Do you—"

The phone went dead.

There was a sudden movement of air pressure that seemed to break apart the vacuum of the room. A door had just been thrown open. *Nein! Nein!* he screamed in his head. He could feel the solid blackness shifting around him as smoke got sucked through the doorway. With stunning ferocity, the image of death swept into him. Blackness. He began to shake, the thing entwining itself around his chest.

He fought against it, reached up, felt for the spotter's radio. The burning table suddenly fell to one side and the radio slid onto his shoulder. The metal was scorching hot and burned his hands as he grabbed for it. He refused to accept the pain, felt for the face of the unit, switched it on. The plastic mike was beginning to melt. His head swam.

He keyed and began transmitting, screaming out the call sign of his regimental fire-control headquarters, his own name, and his emplacement's coordinate reference. For a moment, he lost consciousness, came back. There was a sudden splurge of static through the radio's speaker and then the remote, clipped voice of a regimental operator requesting his verification code numbers

He blurted them out. Then, speaking in broken, choked phrases, he told the operator exactly what he wanted done.

* * *

They came out of the Ready Room like oil field workers off a burning derrick platform, stumbling and gagging, their hands held up to show they were unarmed. Four soldiers, three obviously Russians, the fourth a German with short blond hair that was partly singed. With them came billowing black smoke that drove everybody back down the corridor and into the Firing Room.

They rounded up the Germans into a bunch. Their faces were bright red from the heat, their eyes slits. Parnell and Bird tried to reenter the corridor. It was useless. The Ready Room was in full flame, roaring like a furnace.

Parnell wiped oil soot from his eyes, looked around, spotted Laguna and then Anabel, over near the upper hall. "Weesay, gimme your charges." Laguna slipped his musette over his shoulder, tossed it to him. "Get these people out and as far from the bunker as you can." He nodded toward Sinclair. "Especially her. Carry the bitch if you have to."

This time Anabel needed no prodding. With Laguna behind them, they disappeared up into the main hall of the emplacement as Parnell and Bird raced the other way, to the southern entryway, demo bags dangling from their arms.

It was daylight outside now, the two men coming up out of the stairwell like dusty gophers from a hole. Parnell glanced back, saw the others crawling through the main gate. He and Bird headed for the pit domes, coming up on them, the cliff edge appearing in view. And there was the Allied invasion armada, stretched as far as their eyes could see in terrifying majesty and panoramic grandeur. It stunned them for a moment, hauled them to a stop, staring.

Rank after rank of ships of every description moving relentlessly toward the shores of Normandy. Minesweepers out front followed by multitudes of landing craft: LCMs, LCIs, LCVs, LCTs. Thousands of tiny water-beetle-like Higgins boats and amphibious tractors and trucks plowing ahead, streaking the sea with matrices of tiny white wakes. Lean destroyers and corvettes cutting bigger wakes among the attack transports and finally, slowly prowling their assigned firing zones, the bigger gunships, the light and heavy cruisers, and way out, the battleships, looking massive and ominously lethal even at such a distance.

The roaring of engines and clanking of machinery drifted in on the wind and with it the smell of bunker fuel and steel hulls. Orange and green flashes appeared twenty miles to the east as the British gunboats, slightly ahead of the Americans, opened on their Gold, Juno, and Sword Beaches. The sound of it rolled like approaching thunder.

Red and Wyatt finally moved again, reached the vents to the gun pits. Black smoke poured from the Ready Room outlet, but the ducts above the gun pits were torn apart and coated with white oxide. Parnell stopped at one, peered down. The lights were still on down there, shifting phosphorus fume like a white sea, lifting and settling gently as if it breathed. He could just make out the breech of a field piece.

He turned and shouted at Bird, who was crouched over the number-three pit duct. "Set up for four minutes." Bird nodded. Parnell tore open one of his demo musettes and began setting up a charge, the whole bundle of kilo-sized plastique blocks, inserting the main fuse and crimping wires.

At that moment, the first German artillery brace came

in, the shells winnowing through the sky like ripping cloth and the dry-seed rattle of fuse heads. Two explosions, one on top of the other, blew grass and earth into the air sixty yards to the left of the bunker.

Jesus Christ, Red thought, shocked, *what the hell was that?* He had heard the rounds coming in, his battle instincts instantly shoving him down flat onto the cement dome, Wyatt doing the same. He looked out at the dirt and smoke lifting into the sky, thinking those goddamned shells had come from *inland* and were German 155s. He twisted around, stared at Wyatt. Both knew what had happened: *the bunker's battery commander had just called in an artillery barrage on his own position.*

Parnell leaped up, looked toward the outer compound. The others were moving through the grass beyond the fence now, cleaving pathways through the tall stalks. As he watched, they suddenly veered west, directly toward the cliff and the impact zone of the two artillery shells. The grass was afire around the strikes. Good boys, he thought, knowing his men were deliberately herding Sinclair and the Frenchies over there since the next flight of shells would land on the *opposite* side of the bunker compound as the Krauts laid in bracketing fire.

He returned to his demolitions, first taking out his flare gun and its three taped cartridges and shoving them into his smock pocket. Seconds later, he had the charge completed. He fixed the timer for three minutes, whistled to Bird, and now held up three fingers. Then he leaned down through the blown air duct and swung the demo musette, generating momentum, and hurled it as far to the left as he could. He knew the gun pit's stack of ready shells would be against that particular wall.

Then he was up and headed for the number-two gun

pit duct just as the second German bracketing brace struck to the south of the bunker.

At their support and bombardment stations off Omaha and Utah Beaches, the cruisers of the four American fleet task forces, Sitka, Alpha, Delta, and Camel, each trailing a reference buoy, began the countdown of their firing sequence.

Last-minute target adjustments were relayed from the PFC stations, computed in EGCP rooms, and then fed into the ship's automatic firing systems. Turrets began slowly swiveling, their guns gracefully lifting to the proper traverse and elevation positions consistent with the entered target coordinates. Inside those turrets, breech blocks swung open to receive the big shells and powder silk bags. Handling room crews, dressed in hooded fireproof smocks, feverishly worked in sweltering heat and the constant slam of rammers and the screeching rattle and rumble of shell hoists and powder cars.

One minute and holding.

Aboard the USS *Tuscaloosa*, Commander Morrison stood with his binoculars fixed on the distant shoreline, now clearly visible in bright gray light. Above him, the seconds ticked off the range clock as sluggishly as floating leaves in a placid stream.

Forty seconds . . . thirty-five . . . thirty . . .

He took a quick scan to the left, then to the right, and back to the target. Training instinct braced his body for the familiar jolting slam of the guns about to come. Behind him, the assistant PFC officer quietly called off the last few seconds before 0540 hours.

At ten seconds, Morrison said evenly into his mike, "All stations stand by."

Three . . . two . . . one . . .

"Commence firing."

There was a crashing flash of green-yellow light. The cruiser heeled to starboard and a rush of acrid smoke blew through the armor slits. For a moment Morrison's ears felt clogged. Then the thunderous, rolling crescendo of the naval bombardment surged into his small space: the ocean-shaking booms of big-gun salvos, the rushing shriek of rocket launchers, the lighter, faster bursts of smaller weaponry.

Beneath it all, barely audible, came the electronic buzz from the Mk 38M2 RF/Director collecting impact data on the target designated TS-47/8-1.

Parnell and Bird had come off those gun pit domes like charging cheetahs on an African plain. They sprinted past the south entry stairwell, turned, and headed for the main gate, terribly aware that any moment the German main barrage would be coming in.

Parnell's mind told him to fire off his flare. *Do it, do it,* it screamed. He held back. No, he had to be absolutely certain his and Wyatt's charges would set off the pit shells. He still believed he had at least two minutes left before the naval guns opened up. So he and Bird, down into the grass now, ran on, side by side, the tall stalks whipping across their faces.

Suddenly it seemed as if the entire ocean was erupting in sound, one horrendous, crashing rumble of gunfire. The gray dawn sky lit up with flashes of white and yellow green and red. He glanced over his shoulder. Thousands of red and white tracer lines formed a crisscrossing matrix just above the surface of the sea. Higher up, hundreds of red fireballs came arching through the air, moving in deadly slow motion and leaving trails of smoke.

He saw something that nearly stopped his heart. *Sweet Mother of Christ Almighty!* There, slightly angled away from the rest of the bombardment fire, were six incoming shells in merging lines a hundred yards across, approaching in that leisurely, humped precision.

He caught sight of Bird's stark face staring at him, and then they were both down in the grass. He heard the shells' deep *shushing* whistles and cowered beneath his arms, his mind stalled in the horrific, numbing realization that he was about to get blown into nothingness.

The *Tuscaloosa's* salvo was slightly low and struck the face of the cliff. A hard jolting concussion wave roared through the ground. A fraction of a second later there were two violent explosions. This time the concussion bounced Parnell into the air. Yet in that small span of time, his mind registered several amazing facts. First, he was still alive. Second, those shells had missed the savannah. Third, the explosions of it had been too small, sounding as if only two of the shells had actually exploded. *What?*

Wyatt appeared in the grass, grinning crookedly, his face deadly pale. "Jesus, we jes' copped a lucky one, Lieutenant. Them boys is firin' AR rounds."

Of course, Parnell thought with a surge of overwhelming joy. Only two shells had hit into solid enough rock to set off their impact fuses.

He and Bird were up again, sprinting full out. Two eyeblinks later, the main German barrage struck the buried bunker, and at least a half dozen 155mm shells crashed in instantaneous sequence across it.

They dove for the ground again as the huge geysers of grass and dirt filled with chunks of cement and metal came exploding outward toward them. Things whirled overhead, other objects slashed through the grass stalks as the concussion bent them as if struck by a violent wind.

There was a moment of ringing silence save for the collisions as debris struck the earth all around them. Unable to wait any longer, Parnell started to shove himself up, his legs, gathering themselves under him. The entire German bunker blew up. This explosion was so violent it literally lifted the ground a whole foot as a huge cloud of black smoke and debris fumed up above the gun emplacement. Bigger shards of cement and contorted steel rods and burst shell casings flew over them, sizzling and hotly buzzing like small comets.

Parnell rolled himself into the tightest ball he could make of his body. Things crashed down around him, some striking his arms, legs; hot metal, stinging. He waited what seemed an endless, desperate length of time. But gradually the rain of debris slowed into isolated thumps and thuds, things smoking in the grass. He could hear the roar of a big fire.

Now! Fumbling with it, he withdrew the flare gun, tore off the cartridge tape. His hands were shaking. He finally got the cartridge in, slammed the gun, raised it, and fired. It had a powerful recoil, like a twelve-gauge shotgun, and a tinny ring as the flare shot upward, trailing sparks. Higher and higher it went, curving slightly as gravity began to pull it into an arc. It finally burst into a bright ball of white-orange and then pure orange light, trailing molten sparks and a thin line of dark smoke as the chute drifted slowly on the sea wind.

"Oh, Christ," Bird suddenly screamed. "Here's another salvo!"

Again there was a shushing whistle of incoming ships' rounds. The shocking terror rushed back into his mind like water being sucked down a drain. Only now his imagined death was not a total sundering. Instead, he mentally saw the dreadful image of an eight-inch round blowing through his insides like a beam of steel.

The shells hit, shaking the ground in three twin impacts that made peculiar, penetrating, cut-off sounds across the savannah. Red remained absolutely still. He could almost hear the ticking of fuses. Two seconds passed. Another two. He lifted his head. *Thank you, God.* None of the shells had hit solid rock.

Before the next two seconds could slip past, he and Bird were up and moving.

They all gathered at the edge of the bluff a half mile from the German bunker to stare and listen in silent awe as the greatest machine of war the world had ever seen bored on in its relentless spectacle toward the shores of France. The entire coastline seemed in flames, columns of black smoke rising high into the lightening sky. Far to their right, the bunker still fumed its own smoke.

There were ten of them left: Parnell and his men, Sinclair and four Maquis, including the wounded one. All were cut and bruised and filthy with blood and sweat and dirt and grass stains. Six German prisoners, all Russian, stood apart, murmuring softly to each other and grinning, knowing they were now, finally, out of it.

After a long moment, Parnell called Bird and Sinclair over to him. They squatted close together. He looked at Anabel. "Okay, now you're calling the shots," he said. "Where to?"

She looked at him, her face distracted. She hesitated, as if gathering her thoughts before speaking. "La Madeleine," she answered finally. "It's about two miles that way." She nodded toward the south. "There's a safe house there. We can rest up and reprovision."

"All right." He recognized her slowness, the normal re- action to initial combat. "I think we should send some of your Frenchies with the wounded man and the prisoners down to the beach. They can link up with the assault troops."

"Yes, of course."

"How many do you want to go?"

"All of them, I suppose. It'll be crowded enough at the house with just the six of us." She rose and went over to the Resistance fighters and talked to them a moment, first checking on the wounded man, who appeared un- conscious. Then the Frenchmen moved off along the bluff, waving back at the Americans. The prisoners car- ried the wounded.

Spread out in an overwatch patrol formation, they started through the grass, double-timing it. Cowboy was point, Bird and Weesay in the rear. Parnell had consid- ered using the German officer's car again, but decided against it. Anything moving fast across a lightening land- scape would draw Allied fire.

He and Sinclair ran close to each other in the center of the formation. He watched her and in the new light saw that his earlier appraisal was definitely correct. She *was* quite pretty, battle grime and all. Now he saw that her eyes were a deep brown. He took a Hershey ration bar from his tunic, undid the wrapper, and offered it to her.

She took it without comment, popped it into her mouth, and began chewing. Her eyes closed. "Oh, God, that tastes good," she whispered.

They went along silently for a while. Finally, he said, "You did okay back there."

Anabel didn't respond to that either, just continued running, eyes ahead.

"But I'll tell you, sweetheart," he added. "I came *that* close to kicking your pretty little ass for ignoring my orders."

Now she turned to him. Her brown eyes twinkled and a tiny smile touched the edges of her mouth. "I know," she said. "That was the only *good* part of back there."

Four minutes later, at precisely 0600 hours, the sky came alive with planes, nine thousand in all, as a second Allied air bombardment began. First came the fighters, U.S. Ninth Air Force Lightnings, Mustangs, and Thunderbolts, along with British Spitfires and Seafires from the RAF Second Tactical Air Force, roaring in low on strafing runs. Higher up were B-26 Marauders, B-25 Mitchells, and British Havoc A-20s. Still higher, their bellies in altitude daylight, roared the big Lancasters of RAF Bomber Command and the Fortresses and Liberators of the U.S. Eighth Air Force.

Amid this horrendous, explosive, thunderous cacophony, Blue Team and Anabel Sinclair doggedly raced for the hamlet of La Madeleine as the morning light of 6 June spread across the landscape.

CHERBOURG

Chapter Six

In the American sector of the invasion of France, it was both a walk-in and a slaughter.

At Utah Beach, the U.S. 4th Infantry Division found almost no German opposition. The biggest reason was the tide. Storm-high, it had driven most of the assault craft over two thousand yards away from their designated landing points. If this had not occurred, positioned and sighted heavy enemy coastal guns would have created havoc in the incoming assault waves. In fact, the beachhead would be quickly established with less than two hundred casualties. By noon, units of the 4th would be past the beach exits and linked with troopers of the 101st and 82nd Airborne.

Omaha Beach was a horrible contrast. Located sixteen miles to the east, it would forever become known as "Bloody Omaha." Everything seemed to go wrong. First, preinvasion intelligence had contained a major error. The assault troopers of the 1st and 29th Divisions of the U.S. V Corps had expected to go up against the relatively weak German 176th Static Division. Instead, they ran into the crack, battle-hardened 352nd Division, which had moved into Normandy in January.

Secondly, the tide again played a decisive role. It swept landing boats far beyond their designated sectors and the water was deep enough to hide Rommel's beach obstacles and offshore sandbars. As the lines of Higgins boats came in, they grounded or plowed into the invisible obstacles and were blown apart by the mines on top of the steel triangles.

The Germans waited until the first wave was four hundred yards from shore and then opened on it with a vicious cross fire of machine guns, small arms, and light field guns. The Americans found themselves in water over their heads, far from shore, and struggling to keep from drowning as the fierce raking fire slammed at them. The troops aboard the boats that did manage to reach shore stepped out into a withering fusillade so intense entire companies were wiped out within the first three minutes.

The first wave quickly stalled, most of its men totally pinned down. Then the second, third, and fourth assault waves came into the killing zone. Soon the entire beachhead became a massive, jammed-up mess of dead and wounded men, destroyed equipment, capsized Higgins boats, scattered gear, and small, isolated groups of troopers desperately seeking cover behind whatever they could find: German obstacles, pieces of explosion debris, even their own dead.

It would be hours before the first, tentative attempts by squads and sometimes individual soldiers to reach the relative safety of a sea wall three hundred yards inland succeeded. Still no concerted effort to push inland would form up until late afternoon. By nightfall, the deepest penetration, made by elements of the 16th Regimental Combat Team of the 1st Division, would be only two thousand yards.

The three British/Canadian landing beaches, assaulted fifty-five minutes after the first American landings, were comparatively moderate in German opposition. Brigade groups of the British XXX and I Corps quickly secured both Gold and Juno and would eventually reach their scheduled inland objectives by early afternoon.

Only at Sword, the most easterly of the invasion

beaches and the one closest to the river Orne, was there a major battle. Also, other elements of the British I Corps in conjunction with the Canadian 3rd Division had been assigned the capture of the city of Caen, ten miles inland; but before they could adequately deploy, they were counterattacked by the German 716th Static Division powerfully reinforced by infantry and armor from Rommel's 21st Panzer Division, his veterans of the North African desert.

The Germans hit hard and nearly drove through the gap between Juno and Sword Beaches, intending to roll up at least half of the Allied invasion force. Two things prevented this: air strikes and pinpoint naval gunfire. The German Luftwaffe turned out to be nearly helpless, allowing the Allies to immediately gain total control of the skies over Normandy. This would remain a decisive factor during the entire Normandy-to-Paris campaign.

Still, across a sixty-mile front, the Allies and Germans continued in bitter fighting throughout and beyond 6 June. But the successes of that particular day would go down in history as the most pivotal in the war against Nazi Germany. Rommel himself said of it, long before it actually came, that it would prove to be "the longest day."

The safe house was a farm, or *masure,* on the outskirts of La Madeleine. It sat inside a two-acre hedgerow box like a small oasis among apple orchards. In it were several buildings of brick and slate or half timbering and thatch: a main house, a barn, a dairy and cheese-processing house, including two underground aging rooms, several animal pens, an apple crusher, a barrel shop, and a duck pond.

The owner was a spry, one-legged sixty-five-year-old Belgian named Henri Jacquemart. He had an elfish face full of wrinkles, a long hooked nose, and tufts of white hair above his ears. Before World War I he had owned a perfume distillery in Le Mans. It was said his nose could identify any of five thousand essences after only one whiff.

He had fought the Germans in World War I and lost his right leg at the knee. He had also lost his sense of smell. Once the war was over, he found he could not tolerate cities. So he became a farmer, grew apples, and made cider and a Roquefort-type cheese called *ciel bleu*. He was a senior leader of the Resistance's activities in the Brittany and the Cotentin Peninsula. His code name was Charlemagne and he spoke decent English.

Earlier that morning, Parnell and the others had come slowly in from the coast. Waves of Allied aircraft kept roaring overhead, coming in from the north on strafing and bombing runs. The distant thunder of battle was constant and great columns of black smoke towered up into the sky. They could see gun duels between Allied warships and German coastal batteries while under the constant racket was the endless tolling of church bells.

They kept encountering groups of fleeing villagers, many on bicycles or with their hastily gathered belongings on small carts and horse-drawn flatbed hay wagons. Some told Anabel that a BBC broadcast had come thirty minutes before the bombardment started, warning people along the coast between Le Harve and Cherbourg to move at least thirty-five kilometers inland.

When they saw Parnell and his men in their jump smocks with U.S. flag patches, they excitedly crowded around them, offering flowers and kissing their hands and tugging at their ears, Norman gestures of great affection. Twice they also saw small groups of Maquis, both with women and all heavily armed and moving fast. Oddly, they didn't see any Germans. Undoubtedly the Krauts were afraid to move during daylight because of the constant Allied air strikes.

Still, Anabel was worried. "You're too damned conspicuous in those uniforms," she told Parnell. "Don't forget some of these people are collaborators and prefer the Germans. You've got to get into civilian clothes."

It turned out to be quite easily done. The villagers were so eager to share their clothing that some of the men even took off their own trousers and wooden shoes right there. Within minutes the entire team was outfitted in red corduroy pants and striped sweaters.

They reached La Madelaine just after 8:00 A.M, a small, fortified market town that dated back to the fourteenth century. It was surrounded by a high stone wall with five watch towers and a small castle in the center. Its houses all had high, triangular roofs of red tile and were tightly clustered around the castle's square. It was deserted.

Jacquemart's farm lay a half mile beyond. He met them on the porch of his main house and led them down into a large cellar. There were pillars and Gothic arches and copper pots and pans hanging from its walls. A stone oven sat at one end. At the other end were wooden barrels of apple cider, which saturated the air with a sharp, varnishlike odor.

They sat at a long packing table and two old women in long black sprigged muslin dresses and white bonnets fed them a breakfast of fried eggs, thick slices of pork heavy with fat, and three-foot-long loaves of putty-colored bread swabbed in butter. They drank cider the color of gold, which was called calvados.

After eating, Jacquemart took Sinclair and Parnell up a back stairway. A large white rain barrel stood at the top of it. He led them across the compound to two trapdoors built into twin mounds of dirt, both mounds densely carpeted with wild jasmine. Steps went down into a room fashioned of thick oak beams like ship's timbers. Racks of ripening cheese in gunny-sack wrapping lined the walls. Between them were mushroom beds on wooden platforms like catafalques. The room was cool and humid and dense with a cheese smell mixed with a musty, fungal odor like old cemeteries.

Henri shifted a panel from one of the mushroom plat-forms and showed them stored British Sten guns and pistols and sealed packets of PE-808 RDX plastique ex-plosive. In the other platform were boxes of bullets and hand grenades and a radio, an SCR-2000 transceiver.

Behind a stone panel on the far wall was a small room made of wood and bracing with sheets of oilcloth tacked between the studs. On a small table was another radio, this one a Hallicrafter JK-180 marine transceiver. A knee-pad Morse code key was connected to it. Three maps were taped to the cloth walls containing small red star markers showing German military unit positions. The roads and rail lines were highlighted with yellow crayon.

Henri nodded at the radio. "It has been busy since three this morning, very heavy traffic. Many are enemy intercepts." All German army units up to regimental level used telephones and teletypes for interunit com-munications, so the Maquis were often able to tap into their lines and pick up uncoded traffic. "They trans-mit heavily in the open. I think they're confused."

"What are our people doing?" Anabel asked.

The old man grinned. His teeth were yellow. "We have hit the Germans very hard since sunup." At one of the wall maps he pointed out where Resistance raids had already been carried out against German targets, from Lisieux to Caen and Falaise and as far west as Coutances and Vire. "So far we've remained relatively unscathed."

He paused. His smile disappeared. "There *is* bad news,

though. Three of your fellow agents were taken by the Gestapo last night."

Sinclair's head snapped around. "Which ones?"

"Etienne, Anatole, and J." These were the code names for two of the main SOE agents in Brittany. Their assigned circuits were named Marksman and Stationer 2. J was the Marksman wireless operator.

"Oh, shit," she said. Both agents had gone through training with Anabel.

"They were surprised at a safe house in Donan."

Distractedly, she paced about, her head down, then came back. "This makes ten arrests in two months in the Marksman and Stationer Two circuits. Their security's obviously been penetrated."

"Yes, of course. Any suspicions? It has to be someone inside those circuits."

"Perhaps so, perhaps not. He could be cunning enough not to strike within his own cell."

"That would mean he's bigoted." The term referred to people within the Resistance who were high enough to have inside data, including the true identities of other circuit leaders, their operational systems, and networks of safe houses.

The Frenchman nodded without comment.

"This is bad," Anabel said. "This person puts the entire movement at risk. You *must* find and eliminate him."

"Now there isn't time to investigate."

"Then you'll have to shut down everything."

"*Non!* We've waited too long for this day to come."

She considered a moment. "Then at least change your code protocols and cipher systems."

"To what purpose? If he's a senior leader he'd know."

"Damn it, you have to do something."

"Madam, if we dismantle the system, we'd be of no use to the Allies. True?"

"True. But our position has become extremely dangerous now. You could be inviting total disaster if you don't go underground now."

Jacquemart shrugged. "Has it not always been thus?"

She glanced at Parnell, returned to Henri. "Where is Lucas now? Have you heard from him?"

"I assume he's at Bricquebec."

"Bricquebec? You mean for the transformer plant raid?"

"*Oui.*"

"That was canceled. There are now more pressing targets."

"Perhaps he disagrees."

"I need to use your radio. Privately."

"*Tres bien.*" The old man turned and headed for the trapdoor.

Anabel looked at Red. "You too, fella. Out."

Parnell and the Frenchman sat on beech stumps, quietly listening to the sound of war that thundered in a rising and fading crescendo beyond the hedgerows. The sky was sunlit but bore a peculiar oily sheen. Thin clouds of dissipating smoke drifted overhead. Although there was a fair wind it didn't penetrate the trees. The farm compound was warm and still with only the occasional scurry of ducks in their pond and the drowsy drone of large black and yellow bumblebees lifting in wobbly arcs among the wild jasmine.

Red examined Jacquemart from the corner of his eye. The man's leg prosthesis was made of leather, dark and moisture stained. It looked medieval.

Henri said, "Where in America you are from, *Lef'tenant?*"

"The state of Colorado."

"Ah, *bon.* Cool-a-*rah*-do. Indians and cowboys, *non?*"

"Yes."

They sank back into silence. Red noted that the man's earlier jauntiness had vanished. Now he looked fragile and weary. He gave off a scent of old things, of stale tobacco and dried juices and compost.

The Frenchman asked, "How long before your troops come to this place?"

"I don't know."

Jacquemart mused for a moment. "It won't be easy. *Non, non.* At least fifty thousand Germans are between here and Cherbourg. They'll fight fiercely to save the port."

As if to emphasize that point, there was the sudden raw crash of bombs to the southeast, probably Allied attack bombers going after transportation lines near Montebourg. In the sky, the explosion flashes flickered off the thin scud of smoke like artificial lightning. There was the rapid, peppery discharges of Kraut AA guns. Over the tops of the highest trees, they could see tracers arching upward, sparkling balls of white harshly bright in the sunlight.

Henri watched them for a long moment, then turned to Parnell. "How long have you been in combat, *Lef'tenant?*"

"Since Morocco."

"Ah, a long time. Did you enjoy it?"

"What?"

"Do not be surprised. *I* did, when I was young. War is such a great adventure. *Ca me glace sang?* Like ice in the bones?"

Parnell thought about that and realized the old man was right. In some insane way, he *did* relish battle, ground combat, its sound and fury, its shock and terror and constant closeness to violent death triggering adrenaline rushes so powerful they created an almost deadly excitement.

If he lived a hundred years, he knew he'd never experience such intensity again. And he'd never be able to explain it to anybody who hadn't shared war close up, didn't have the words to communicate it. For those who *had* seen battle, no explanation would ever be necessary.

Jacquemart was smiling at him, a wistful, melancholy smile. "*Ah, je m'en etais bien doute.*"

"*Oui.*"

Then the old man shook his head. "But you have not seen the trenches yet."

"What trenches?"

"I fought the Germans for two years in the other war. I won myself great glory. But then I saw the trenches and realized it was all so futile. It *always* is. You see?"

"If you believe that, why do you fight now?"

Henri shrugged. "We never have a choice. *C'est pas?*"

The Morse code was finally coming through clean, the pulses of sound so rapid they seemed to form a continuous chain without breaks. Anabel had had difficulty reaching her two first-call SOE contact stations in England, Beta Yellow and Beta Green, the air too thick with traffic chatter and heavy static to get through. In frustration, she finally switched to the emergency station, Alpha Yellow One, located in Norgeby House, Baker Street, London.

Each SOE agent had a totally individualized code used to transmit data to and from the field. It was based on a poem chosen by the particular agent during his training. Combined with it was a deciphering system called a WOK or worked-out key. Whenever a coded message was sent between the contact station and the agent, only he and the station could decode it.

She quickly tapped out her report, informing AY-1 about the successful attack on the German coastal gun emplacement and the capture of the three SOE agents. She explained that a high-ranking Resistance spy seemed to be involved and Charlemagne intended to continue operating. She requested orders.

Before they could come, the Krauts began laying out powerful jamming signals. The Hallicrafter's speaker screeched and growled. She immediately switched to another emergency frequency, broadcast white noise for a full minute to decoy, then switched to a third frequency that was below that of the jam frequency. She reprocessed and again waited for orders. She was told to stand by.

She rose and nervously paced back and forth between the mushroom beds. Her skin felt clammy. The frequency watch light came on. Rushing back to the unit, she hurriedly copied out Alpha Yellow One's order message. She made them repeat it, then signed off and began decoding it.

The pony's name had been Éclair. It meant *lightning*. He stood twelve hands high and could run swiftly with a merry-go-round gait. He was the color of faded sunflowers. Vaillant Duboudin's father, a wealthy Strasbourg industrialist, had imported the Exmoor breed animal from Cornwall, England, when the boy was seven years old.

During most of the year, the Duboudin family lived in the *Grand Ile*, the Old City of Strasbourg. During the summer, the boy and his sickly mother moved to their chateau near Mont St. Odile in southern Alsace where Vaillant and Éclair would ride away the warm hot days tracing the ancient *Mur Paien* or Pagan Wall built by Celts in 1000 B.C. where it climbed up into the thick conifer forests that grew on the slopes of the three-thousand-foot-high *montagne*.

One day Communists killed the pony, shot it from ambush, then stoned the wounded animal to death. Terrified,

Vaillant hid himself among the rocks of the Pagan Wall. A bearded face peered in at him, viciously cursing his father and all like him. He ordered the boy to relay a message: the next time they came, everybody would die.

The incident left Vaillant with two things permanently seared into his mind: a hatred of Communists and a terror of enclosed spaces. Now as he crawled along the rust-encrusted flood pipe that led into the power station outside Bricquebec, his mind raced and sweat poured from his body.

Directly ahead in the lead crawled one of his circuit lieutenants, Roger Mieral. Behind them were fifteen Maquis, all armed and carrying demolition charges. He had linked with them earlier at a safe house near Highway 23. On this particular raid, he had specifically ordered Mieral to take part.

Vaillant had never trusted this man. Now he had become a distinct danger, Duboudin certain his lieutenant suspected him of betrayal. Soon after the Gestapo had begun their successful attacks of Resistance safe houses, Roger began giving him long side studies with sullen eyes. This morning, he had been especially watchful after learning of the capture of the three Brits.

Mieral was a member of the *Parti Communiste Francais*, the French Communist Party, and also a recruiter for the *France au Combat*, a particularly active guerilla group made up of strict Trotskyites. Duboudin knew if Mieral convinced his fellow guerillas that Vaillant was indeed a traitor, they'd kidnap and torture him until he admitted it and revealed the entire network of German agents buried within the Underground. Then they'd hang him.

They reached a junction in the flood pipe. Mieral looked back, hesitating. Vaillant waved him on. This particular raid had been planned weeks before. As soon as the particulars had been okayed by the senior Maquis council, Duboudin had smuggled the entire plan out to Major Land. Then it was canceled but the Germans ordered him to carry it out.

Again Mieral stopped and twisted around. "I don't like this," he hissed. "We're bunched too much. And it's been too easy. This could be a trap."

"Go on, damn it," Vaillant whispered back harshly. "The invasion has confused them, made them careless. Now is the best time to attack." Roger glowered but finally moved forward once more.

Vaillant looked at the dark walls of the drainpipe. They smelled rancid like animal manure souring in the rain. He felt the curving sides pulling in around him, felt his heart thudding. He wiped sweat from his face. His eyes stung and the pain made him suddenly aware that he wanted *out.*

Desperately, he closed his eyes, forced his mind away from the pipe. He drew up pleasant memories, willing the images to appear there in the darkness behind his lids. One memory in particular: himself driving a race car, snug in leather suit, straw bound around his legs to protect against impact. Caught up in the memory, he could almost feel the wind in his face, see the roadside flashing past and a glistening stretch of sea beyond.

He had always loved speed, atop Éclair's back then, and later on the feel of pure power in his race cars, the seat-sinking acceleration as he rocketed away from the starting pit. When he first got the racing bug, his father's wealth had opened great opportunities for him on the European racing circuits. But it was Vaillant's natural talent that took him to the heights.

He competed against the best in the world: the legendary Tazio Nuvolari and lesser greats such as Jean Pierre Etancelm and Papa Trossi, from whom he took the famous Rudge-Whitworth cup in 1937. Also against Emil Taruffi, the American, Tommy Milton, and Denis Murolari, known as the Moroccan.

He usually drove Bugattis, Maseratis, and Mercedeses, big 1500cc cars called *voiturettes,* in races all over Europe, England, and North Africa. From triangular-track courses to the Grand Prix at Le Mans, Monaco, and Milan. He even ran those rough-and-tumble, slipstream races at Greenstone Bridge, England, and the ten-hour endurance runs at Algiers. Twice he'd driven the death-trap track at Switzerland's Bremgarten where he survived a horrendous crash in 1939 with only a broken finger.

His fame allowed him to meet many powerful people. Among them were wealthy Nazis. Once he even dined with Reichsmarschall Hermann Goring, commander in chief of the German Luftwaffe, an avid fan of auto racing. Gradually, he came to deeply believe that Hitler and the Social Democrats were the only ones who could save Europe from Russian Communism. He and other intellectual Frenchmen debated the situation and he eventually decided to help the Nazis.

So far he'd managed to keep his double-agent work completely secret. With the help of the Gestapo, he had even become a Resistance hero. Twice he escaped their custody, once after a wild car chase through Rouen, and again when he killed a German interrogator after being caught during a raid in Caen. Both scenarios had been staged. Now that Mieral had become dangerous, he knew the man had to be eliminated. Today was the day it would be done.

He opened his eyes, saw Roger fooling with a heavy overhead screen directly above him. He was pushing at something with his fingers. Suddenly a cover opened and a flood of light came down into the pipe. He heard machinery, the hum of generators, and saw Mieral gazing upward, his profile brightly illuminated.

There was the hollow blast of a machine pistol and Roger's head exploded apart. Bullets slammed into his body with a thudding sound, the muzzle blasts ringing. Rounds rico-

cheted off flesh. One blew past Vaillant's shoulder. He heard
another impact and the man behind him gave a choked cry.

You fools! Duboudin thought wildly. *Qu'est-ce que tu fous? I'm
here, I'm* here. As he thought this, he was already moving backward, his knees hurting, his claustrophobia sucked away and
lost in a greater fear. "Go back!" he yelled at his men. "Go back!"

The desperate murmurs of frightened men sounded hollow
and filled the flood pipe. He realized he too was panting wild
wordless words in his throat. He scurried along, backing as frantically as a rat in reverse. He heard firing from far back in the
pipe, the rapid, *bruuppping* cracks echoing through the metal
tube. Men screamed, sounding like night creatures in a horror
movie. Another burst of automatic fire came.

Vaillant stopped abruptly as he ran into the Maquis directly behind him, who had stopped. "I'm hit bad," the
man groaned. "Oh, God, what do we do?"

"Go back."

"They're killing us."

He kicked at the man, felt his boot go into facial bone.
The man moaned. Duboudin tried to move backward
again but couldn't against his weight. He began cursing
frantically as he realized he was trapped. The claustrophobia exploded anew into his head. He lunged forward,
crawling wildly. He crossed over Mieral's blood and brain
matter, the stuff smelling raw, a butcher shop stink.

A German soldier peered down at him through the
screened opening. His helmet glistened in the light that
cast his face into shadow. "Come out," he ordered in German.

A terrible memory picture leaped at Vaillant like a panther from cover. *Next time you will all die. Oh, please, no.*

"*Come* out!" The German shouted. "*Mach schnell.*"

"Nicholas," Vaillant gasped back in German. "I am
Nicholas."

The soldier said something, then moved away. There was the soft murmur of voices. Another German soldier looked down. This one was an officer. He pulled open the screen and stepped back, out of sight.

Duboudin could not move. He stared up at the light. Again the officer's face appeared. "Come out of there, damn it," he snapped again. "You are safe."

Cautiously, he lifted himself, put his head through the opening. Three Germans were standing there staring at him. He pulled himself free and slid his feet over the curve of the pipe to the floor. The room was painted a soft green. The Germans continued looking at him until the officer, an Oberleutnant, glanced at one of his men and flicked his thumb toward the pipe opening.

Now the wounded Maquis poked his head out. There was blood all over his face. One of the soldiers grabbed him by the jacket and hauled him out. The man fell halfway to the floor, his back braced against the curve of the pipe, his head lolling forward. The German officer stepped up and shot him through the top of the head, the Maquis jerking sharply and then slumping completely to the floor.

More soldiers came running. They looked at Vaillant with cold stares. For the next five minutes, they fired burst after burst back through the flood pipe, bullets screeching off metal. The muffled sound of other firing came faintly into the room. At last, one of the soldiers crawled down into the pipe and the *Oberleutnant* jerked his head at Duboudin.

They walked along a catwalk above two huge generators. The machines were painted the same soft green and the air smelled like burning electrical circuits. They descended a narrow stairway and went out a steel door. The sun made Vaillant squint as he and the officer walked along a dirt road to a wire fence and through a gate.

Beside the end of the flood pipe through which the raiders

had come earlier, there were eight dead Maquis stretched out on the grass. Some had been shot many times and their clothes were soaked with blood and rust stains from the pipe. The blood was smeared across the grass, coloring its tips.

A dozen soldiers worked at the pipe head. The firing had stopped. As Duboudin watched, they pulled another body out. The *Oberleutnant* walked back and forth, looking down at the dead men. Then he returned to Vaillant. "How many were there besides you?" he asked in German.

"Fourteen."

The officer nodded. He looked back at the bodies, then came back to Vaillant. "You can leave now," he said sharply. He had dark eyes. They, like those of his soldiers, were contemptuous.

"First I must notify Major Land that—"

"I said you leave *now*," the German repeated.

Duboudin looked at him. "Yes . . . yes, of course." He started off, walking swiftly. The German soldiers stopped working to watch him pass. No one said anything.

Sinclair came out of the cheese-aging room, squinting in the sunlight. "London's changing protocol," she told Jacquemart. "They'll raise you at ten hundred to initiate details."

"*Oui.*"

"They suggest you at least evacuate your family."

"I intended to do so. How long will you stay?"

"We'll be leaving in a half hour."

"*Bon.*" The Frenchman's face opened in a bright smile, his old eyes suddenly a-twinkle again. "But first we make a toast. My finest *calvado* for this historic day. *Allon.*"

At that moment, without warning, a pair of American Mustang fighters exploded into view just over the treetops of the compound's western hedgerow, the roaring of their big Rolls-

STORM FRONT   123

Royce Merlin 61 engines like sudden thunderclaps. Out of instinct, everybody hit the ground. The fighters flashed past in the blink of an eye, their prop washes coiling downward bringing the smell of hot metal. As quickly as the roaring had come, it was sucked back into the silence.

They returned to the main house, paused at the stairwell to wash their hands in the rain barrel, a tradition when entering a Norman home. Henri went down. Parnell took hold of Anabel's arm. "What's on tap with us?"

She seemed distracted. "What? Oh, a new mission. We have to check out a church site at Lieu d'Meed. It's about five miles from here. London needs to know if there's an OFCP operating in it. If there is, we take it out." The initials stood for Observation and Fire Control Post.

He studied her face. "Something about this you don't like?"

"Yes. This circuit breach. Now everybody's in danger. There's no way to know who to trust." She nodded toward the house. "Not even *him*."

"The old man?"

"Yeah."

Parnell shrugged. "So we watch everybody and keep on the move."

She nodded, looked up at him. "London's sending in Hunters."

"Who?"

"They're a special SOE black-op crew. They come in, try to isolate the spy, and take him out. We have to lay out a drop site." She gave him a wary look. "These people don't take time to discriminate. Anybody they suspect, they kill." She nodded toward the basement. "Henri's refusal to close off the operation doesn't look good for him. I like that old man. But I've got a bad feeling that one way or the other, he's going to die."

Chapter Seven

Major Freidrich Land dozed, his eyes barely open, the rise and fall of the Opel-AV Blitz staff car jolting his buttocks. It was just after noon. Beside him in the backseat was SS Sturmbannfuhrer Karl Wunsche, resplendent in his black tunic, riding breeches, and cavalry boots. The white metal eagle and death's-head insignia on his high-peaked *Dienstmutze* cap and his silver collar piping and *Sigrunen*, or SS-runes, glistened in the sunlight.

Wunsche had once been an actor. He was quite handsome and had the contemptuous air of a spoiled princeling. Land despised him intensely, a man of poses. He could easily picture the bastard standing erect above a ditch filled with people begging for their lives and then, with the flick of his hand, ordering them shot. *Schaum,* scum!

They were now halfway between the cities of Évreux and Lisieux, bound for Caen. Two hours earlier, a furious Colonel Meyer-Detring had ordered Land into Normandy. "This fucking Resistance rabble is exploding all over the goddamn place," he had roared, his face scarlet. "You get over there and put a stop to it. You hear me, Freidrich? Get those goddamned secret agents of yours earning their fucking Judas money."

He sent him with Wunsche and two platoons of Gestapo who were now strung out behind them in four

Opel-AV three-ton trucks with a motorcycle leading the small column.

Land opened his eyes fully and gazed out at the rolling grass hills dotted with stands of beech and mahogany trees. To the north and west smoke columns rose into the sky like dark wraiths and there was the continuous grumble of artillery audible over the car's Horch V-8 engine. Soon, he knew, they would be entering the *bocage* country.

They had already begun encountering villagers moving toward the east, responding to those BBC broadcasts ordering them to do so, the French peasants staring sullenly at the Germans as they sped past. But so far, they'd seen only minor movements of their own forces, and those mainly mounted infantry units and some columns on foot. It was obvious why. Ever since they got beyond Évreux, the sky had become thick with enemy aircraft. Twice they had to stop and scatter for cover as American Marauders came over on low-level bombing runs. Fortunately, the planes were after other targets.

Still, Land couldn't understand why at least *some* of Rommel's Army Group B and Dietrich's 1st SS Panzer Corps units weren't moving. He knew the Desert Fox's battle philosophy well. Unlike von Rundstadt, who believed in a flexible front that allowed for counterattack, Rommel steadfastly held that the only way to stop an invasion was to destroy it at the shoreline. To do that, he must have concentrations of fast-moving armor.

What he didn't know but strongly suspected was that Hitler had personally canceled von Rundstadt's request to move his Panzers. In truth, the Führer would not okay the request until later that afternoon, when it was nearly too late.

He rolled his neck and asked, "Where are we?"

"You have been asleep?" Wunsche shot back sarcastically.

"No, not quite."

"Then you should know."

Land looked at him, a sardonic smile playing on his lips. "Tell me, Karl, are you truly an asshole?" he said. "Or do you just masquerade as one?"

Wunsche's neck instantly went tense and grew red. His mouth stiffened with tight rage. Since both were of equal rank, there was nothing much he could say to that comment. Chuckling, Land turned away, noting with pleasure that up ahead the sergeant riding shotgun had also stiffened, his cheek aquiver as he tried desperately to suppress a grin.

Two minutes later, the column was strafed by three British Spitfires, the aircraft sweeping in so low their sound had been hidden until they were there, coming in in echelon. Rounds exploded in dual lines along the road ahead of the staff car, rushed back and over it, the slam and jolt of their impacts sounding like someone striking garbage cans with a rapidly swung club.

Land felt bullets crash into the seat beside him. Wunsche gave a stifled cry. The staff car careened off the road and went over, pitching Land free and rumbling on. He had rammed his shoulder into hard dirt, a jab of sharp pain going through his neck, and his arm went numb. His head rang with tiny, shrill spikelets of sound.

Up in the sky, the Spitfires had already executed tight, climbing wingovers and were headed back for another run. The lead truck was already burning. Land shoved to his feet, his head whirling for a moment, and began waving his good arm frantically. "Off the road!" he bellowed. "Get off the road! Fire at their prop hubs."

He pulled his pistol, awkwardly having to do it with his other hand, and started firing. The first aircraft came in high, its bullets slashing past overhead. Instantly, the second was there. He saw the muzzle bursts from its eight .303-caliber machine guns, the bullets hurtling out trailing thin ribbons of smoke. They tore up the road, threw huge clods of dust.

The third Spitfire had a hub 20mm cannon. Its first two rounds struck one of the trucks. As the aircraft roared past, its prop wash stinking of hot cordite, the truck exploded in a huge ball of orange flame and smoke. Metal parts skidded through the air. Land had followed the aircraft with his pistol, the weapon already empty. He watched as the three planes reformed and disappeared toward the northeast.

Wunsche was dead. The bullets had torn his left arm off, split his skull. He lay beside the staff car in a grotesque, twisted posture. His arm lay a few feet away, the silver Gothic-lettered *SS-Inspektion* on his sleeve cuff still as shiny as a new coin.

Twelve soldiers were dead, fourteen wounded. Major Land radioed for medical assistance and transport, then walked up the road to the wounded motorcyclist. The man sat staring at his leg, which had been torn open from knee to thigh, the wound as bloodless as an illustration in an anatomy textbook.

Land bound the rider's wound with his scarf, then whistled up Wunsche's aide, a young, pale-faced *Oberleutnant*. He instructed him to load the unwounded soldiers onto the two usable trucks, leave a squad with the wounded and dead, and continue on to Caen.

He examined the motorcycle. It was a 200cc military model Bordfunk Fusilier. Pulling it upright, he settled into the seat and cranked down the kick starter. It roared into life. He flexed his arm and fingers for a moment, letting the feeling come back, then gunned back to the road and sped off toward Caen.

* * *

Major Land's suspicions had been on the mark. As the Allies tenaciously pushed inland off the Normany beachhead, Hitler had continually hesitated to throw his Panzer divisions into the Normandy battle. He still believed this attack was only a feint and that the real invasion would soon hit Pas de Calais.

On Utah Beach, forward patrols of the U.S. 4th Division had reached Pouppeville and Ste. Marie-du-Mont by early afternoon. Soon after, they would link with the 3rd Battalion of the 301st Airborne Regiment and enter St. Mere Eglise. Other units would push through the flood zones and be six miles inland by evening.

Omaha Beach was still bloody ground. But gradually, under the leadership of such men as Brigadier General Norman Cota, who, with pistol in hand, walked coolly back and forth in the face of the enemy fire issuing orders, and of individual noncoms and ordinary soldiers who also defied death, the troops began to move up the beach.

Still, it wouldn't be until 1300 that radio messages reached General Bradley, commander of the U.S. First Army, that the bluff four hundred yards from the water had finally been reached. By evening, elements of the 1st and 29th Divisions would break out of Easy and Dog sectors of the beach and drive inland as far as St. Laurent and Vierville-sur-Mer, two thousand yards from the ocean. This narrow beachhead would cost the Americans 4,200 casualties.

Meanwhile, the assault troops of the British XXX Corps had met moderate resistance at Gold Beach because the Germans hadn't completed their defenses in this section of the coastline. And also because those partially constructed defenses had been hit with intense

Allied covering fire, including the heavy ripples of five-inch rocket fire from LCRs lying directly offshore.

Quickly DD tanks were landed and units of the Royal Hampshires and the 1st Dorsets moved inland. Before 1600, over 25,000 troops were solidly ashore along a front that was four miles deep and six miles wide. Forward units were already swinging to their right to link with the Americans off Omaha.

At Juno Beach, three brigades of the Canadian 3rd Division had landed. For many, this was a return to France since many had fought and died in the ill-fated Dieppe Raid in August 1942. The "Canucks" would achieve the deepest penetration of the day. As late afternoon approached, they'd occupy a beachhead of twenty-five square miles, completely isolating dozens of German units.

Accompanied by shrill bagpipes playing "Blue Bonnets Over the Border," the British 3rd Division came ashore at Sword Beach, the easternmost sector of the invasion that lay between the village of St. Aubin-sur-Mer and the mouth of the river Orne. They were supported by an impressive naval bombardment group made up of the battleships HMS *Warspite* and *Ramillies*, five cruisers, and thirteen destroyers.

Their primary objective was the major communications and transport center of Caen, nine miles to the south. But before they established a secure beachhead, Hitler finally agreed to hit them with his 21st Panzer Division backed by the 12th Waffen-SS-Panzer Division and the Hitler Jugend, which was made up of crack veterans of the Waffen-SS-Panzer Leibstandarte.

Mounting a major counterattack, this German armor engaged in tank exchanges with elements of the British Eighth and Twenty-seventh Armored Brigades and nearly pushed them back to the coast near Lion-sur-Mer, thus opening a gap between the 3rd Division and the Canadians. Again naval covering fire helped stop the German counterattack. Nevertheless, by the end of the day, the Brits would be totally stalled three miles from Caen.

Lying in a field slightly west of road D-42 between Valognes and the small town of Montebourg, Parnell slowly glassed the small church atop the Lieu d'Meed that sat out there in the sunlit *bocage* like a phallus.

He studied it minutely. The base was about two hundred yards wide and gradually tapered to a nearly needle-shaped summit 160 feet high. It was situated at the end of a narrow, half-mile-long spine of land half its height. Its rocks and soil were pinkish white and the entire shaft was dotted with brush clumps and small, tumbled stands of juniper.

As a mining engineer, Red immediately recognized it as an oceanic upthrust pillar, probably twenty or thirty thousand years old. Eons of wind and rain had worn away its connection to the main spine, leaving it isolated. Steps cut into the stone wound all the way to the small, gray-white church perched at the top.

It formed a perfect watchtower, he could see, giving any defending force an unobstructed view of the flat ground for hundreds of miles around it. Undoubtedly, he figured, it had been doing just that across all the centuries of warfare hereabouts. The reason why it hadn't already been blown to hell was also obvious to him.

He started to lower the glasses. Two German soldiers came out of the church and stood looking toward the coast, one using a pair of binoculars. After a few minutes, they went back inside.

Oh, yeah, Parnell thought.

He turned to Anabel, who was lying beside him, Bird

on his other side. "It's a spotter's position, all right," he said. "I just saw two Krauts." He stared at her. "Wouldn't that church be yellow lined?" Certain structures, either for historical or religious reasons, were often placed off-limits to artillery barrage or bombing by both the Allies and the Germans. Such sites were always marked in yellow on battle maps.

Sinclair nodded. "Yes, of course."

He snorted. "Never easy, is it?"

"That's a very holy place, Parnell. A pilgrimage site, actually. If I remember my French history, it was in that very church that the Viking chieftain Rollo got baptized. Tenth century, I think. That single act saved Christian Normandy."

"That's all interesting as hell. But does London really expect us to assault that thing in broad daylight?"

"Yes."

"Well, that's plain bullshit." He turned to Bird. "Thoughts, Wyatt?"

Bird turned his head, spat, came back. "I figure we'd make it about halfway up before we got our asses nailed, Lieutenant."

Red sucked spittle through his teeth. "If it was dark we'd have a chance."

"But we can't wait for night," Anabel interrupted. "We have to do it now. Remember, we've got to be at least five miles from here by sundown to mark out the drop zone for those Hunters."

Parnell stared hard at her. "Sweetheart, a whole goddamned battalion couldn't take that position in broad daylight without artillery."

She shrugged. "So how will we do it?"

Again he thought a moment. "Can you call in barrage fire or a close-support air strike?"

"No, of course not. Even if I could, they'd check the coordinates, find out what the target was, and countermand the request."

He nodded. "Okay, then we do it ourselves. You got any heavy guns cached around here some place? Anything twenty millimeters or bigger?"

"My God, you can't blow up that church."

"The hell I can't. Look, if you think I'm sending my men up there without cover fire and in broad daylight to save a pile of stones from the tenth century, you and London're nuts. Now, do you have any light artillery pieces nearby or not?"

Anabel started to protest again, then sighed. She knew he was right. "Yeah, there're two captured Raketepanzer-buchse 54s in Crique d'Chiota. That's a hamlet near Valognes." These were German versions of the American bazooka but carried much more power and fired an 88mm rocket.

"How many rounds?"

"Two canisters with four rockets in each."

"How long to get there an' back?"

"Couple hours."

Parnell cased his glasses. "Then let's go get 'em."

Moving back across country this time was much harder than before. Although most of the fleeing villagers were now gone and the little, sunken country roads totally deserted, they kept spotting small German units far off, racing from cover to cover, dodging Allied air strikes.

They passed through tiny hamlets of little more than three or four stone houses. Here and there were dead Germans and burned-out vehicles, a few civilian corpses, too. The bodies were black and distorted. Fires burned in some of the hedgerow fields and cows and goats wandered about, spooking easily.

They came upon a lone Frenchman dressed in a black suit and a derby hat. He carried an old, beat-up Belgium FN Saive automatic rifle and was herding eight wounded German soldiers down a country lane. Their field caps bore the light blue cords of an administrative unit and their uniforms were coated with explosive powder. Several were mere boys, the others old men.

Proudly the Frenchman informed Anabel that he was the mayor of the hamlet of St. Bounier and had captured these Nazi pigs running terrified in the woods after aircraft had destroyed their convoy. She asked him where he was taking them. He said he didn't know exactly but that he would march them for a week if necessary until he found the *Americaines*. He also warned her of German snipers.

They first saw the smoke when they were still a mile from it, slanting thinly in the wind over the distant tree line. It had an oily pall to it. As they drew closer, Anabel's face got tighter and tighter.

They passed along a narrow, sunken road that ran between towering walnut and cottonwood trees. The road was as lumpy as pickles, the side stones coated with moss. As they crossed a small stream, it turned sharply and climbed and they could see the hamlet of Crique d'Chiot.

All its buildings were gutted, some still burning. The bodies of its residents were strewn along the road, men, women, and several children. They were so newly dead that save for the bloody clothing, they looked merely asleep in the road. One was a priest. The exiting rounds had ripped great holes in his black cassock. It indicated he had been facing the guns that killed him. There were also several dead Percheron horses, one still harnessed to a wagon, and three large, gray cows. Everything had been machine-gunned and then the houses set afire. The air stank of wood smoke and that cloying, unmistakable fetidness of death.

They walked among the corpses and the ruins, stepping gently. The stillness, like the quiet after all battles, seemed inhuman. Sinclair's face had turned pallid. She paused above the priest, then made the sign of the cross, knelt to touch his hair, and moved on. When Parnell and his men looked at each other, their own eyes were frozen, opaque, and they didn't hold each other's stare.

The arms cache was hidden below what had been the church. Its old beams and flooring had gone up quickly, the walls acting like a flue. It left the dark odor of scorched stone. They pulled up the floor slabs behind where the altar had been. The cache contained two long wooden boxes. Their tops had been seared but the weapons inside were untouched.

The two Raketepanzerbuchse were folded and had firing shields. Their rocket canisters were made of metal and had red German writing on them. Besides the rocket guns, there were four French MAS 38 machine pistols, small and odd-shaped, along with five cases of 7.65-caliber cartridges and three tarnished British Webley-Fosbery .455-caliber revolvers.

Ten minutes later, carrying both Raketepanzerbuchse and the rocket canisters, they left the hamlet and headed back toward Lieu d'Meed, the sky beginning to cloud over and the smell of rain coming in on the wind.

The rain had brought out the phlox blossoms, lemon drops in the foot-tall grass, and released the spicy sweetness of wild lupine and sweet pea. Fountain was already soaking wet, crawling with the extended five-foot-long Raketepanzerbuchse. Its firing shield kept poking him in the side, but he couldn't discard it.

Unlike American bazookas, these weapons required a protective suit for the person firing it against the muzzle flash. Fortunately, the shield on this one took the place of the suit. A few yards behind him, dragging one of the forty-eight-pound rocket canisters, was Laguna.

The rock pillar of Mont d'Meer rose up a hundred yards away, silhouetted against the gray overcast. Typical of Normandy's unpredictable weather, this rain front had moved rapidly off the ocean. Although it was only 5:30, it was cold and dark enough for lights to be burning in some of the scattered farmsteads where there were peasants who had refused to evacuate. The rain had turned the pinkish white soil of Mont d'Meer a slaty umber.

Cowboy kept checking his position, keeping the tiled roof of the church on top in his view. They were crawling across a small field enclosed by hedgerows. Several cows had come to the gate of the adjoining field and were watching their progress with that stolid, fixed curiosity of such animals.

Weesay paused to look over at them. Then he said under his breath, "Hey, *vacas estupidas,* chu better move yo' asses."

Fountain glanced back at him. "What?"

"I was tellin' them cows over there to move off. When we cut loose, them Krauts're gonna send mortars in here, baby."

Fountain said, "What, *chico,* you talkin' to cows now?"

"Sure."

Cowboy snickered. "When they answer you, what do they use, Spic or Frenchie?"

Weesay shook his head. "*Meng*, you one ignorant fuckin' shit-kicker."

Parnell had split the team near a swampy area a quarter mile from the mount, the place smelling of sour mud and the surface of the water all dimpled. A flock of gray ducks drifted bobbing among the reeds. He and Sinclair had taken the other rocket launcher with Bird and Smoker on security, one man flanked on the outside of each fire team.

The attack plan called for Red to fire the first two rockets at the German spotter post, then sprint to a parallel position fifty yards away in case any German units in the area opened up and homed to the rockets' trails. As they moved, Cowboy and Weesay would cover with two rounds and then make the same change of position with Parnell doing the covering.

They reached the hedgerow and went up into it. It was formed of a six-foot-high dirt mound covered in brush and trees, beech, walnut, and oak. The foliage was dense, the tree trunks thick as barrels, and the air smelling of wet soil and mossy tree bark. The rain made a delicate pattering in the higher leaves.

They quickly set up, Fountain half kneeling beside an oak tree with his firing shield resting on the trunk. He took a bead through the shield's slit window, swinging the fore and aft sights slowly from left to right until the church roof sat squarely in the center of the crosshairs.

Weesay loaded the launcher, sliding one of the rockets into the rear and listening for the click as it seated itself into the lock slot. The projectile was two feet long with a circular tail fin and carried a seven-pound hollow charge. He tapped Cowboy on the shoulder and slid down and to the right of the tree. Fountain jacked back the cocking lever and resettled himself, again aligning to the church.

They waited.

Four minutes later, the hissing, whooshing rush of Parnell's first round cracked through the rain. It hurtled through the air, angled sharply upward, looking like a sizzling fireball trailing a thin string of smoke. It struck just below the church and erupted into a flashing fume of amber mud. Several seconds passed. Then the second rocket went out. This one struck the front wall of the church and blew chunks of stone and red tile into the air, obscuring it.

Cowboy waited for the debris to settle, the smoke drifting off in the wind. Hazily the contours of the church reappeared. He breathed in, let a bit of air out, held, and squeezed off, sending an electrical spark to the propellant charge. From the rear of the launcher shot out a ten-foot-long, candle-shaped flash of heat and light that blew brush and leaves back into the field.

Cowboy felt the heat on his back and the muzzle flash threw a tiny square of heat through the shield slit. His eyes snapped shut for a tiny moment, then he reopened them and watched the rocket go spiraling upward and explode into the base of the church's steeple. Before the debris settled, he felt Weesay shoving in the next round and cursing as his hand touched the hot barrel.

Parnell was following Anabel, both of them skirting the backside of the hedgerow, Sinclair carrying the launcher across her chest like a rifle at port arms, Red lugging the heavier canister and both Thompsons and bandoleers.

Damn, he thought, and was again impressed at how physically fit this woman was, sprinting through the tall

grass with that hot, twenty-pound weapon. He heard
Cowboy's first round go out and strike target, the explosion sounding hard and solid, a direct hit. He
pictured the Kraut spotter team in there, most of them
probably already dead.

So far, there had been no enemy response. Cowboy's
second rocket went out and also hit with a dense, vicious
blast, another bull's eye. They reached the corner of the
hedgerow, went through it, and down into the next field.
Sinclair turned and looked back. He waved her on. Hugging the next hedgerow, they went another forty yards
and then disappeared among the brush and trees.

His last two rockets both hit what was left of the
church of Mont d'Meer. The entire roof and steeple had
been blown away. The remnants burned fiercely, sending up a dark, dirty brown smoke. Then as Cowboy's two
rockets struck, they sent up fiery chunks of stone that
sparkled and flashed against the sky.

The first German mortar round struck the field just behind their first position. It heaved up a sudden "tree" of
grass and dirt. "Mortar!" he bellowed and hit the ground,
catching a quick glance of Anabel twenty feet away going
down into the grass, too. In quick succession, three more
rounds came in, the clicks of their fuses clearly audible.

He was up and moving two seconds after the last blast.
He saw Sinclair lying, looking up at him. He reached
down, grabbed her by the arm, and lifted, pushing her forward at the same time. "Go, go!" he shouted. "The next
ones'll walk right here."

They were shelling Cowboy and Weesay's first position,
too. As he ran, part of Parnell's mind registered the explosions. Experience told him they were from a 50mm
Leichter Granatenwerfer 36. Somewhere to the south, firing at its seven-hundred-yard maximum range. Possibly

from a position on the mount's spine. Good, he thought, that gave them a head start to the northwest.

The shelling stopped. In the silence that followed, they heard ducks quacking out in the marsh, a single dog howling. Red called to Anabel, pointed, and they started directly across the field to the opposite hedgerow.

He heard the *pop* of a bullet going past nearby, the round creating a vacuum into which the air rushed with its riflelike crack. "Sniper!" he shouted and again hit the ground just as the rifle's muzzle report caught up with the round. He saw Sinclair stumble and go into the grass on her side.

Jesus, she's hit, he thought. Then realized he hadn't heard flesh impact.

He lay with his head just below the top of the grass, scanning. His combat instincts had already estimated the sniper's distance from them by using the time between the bullet and muzzle sound. He figured the son of a bitch was at least two hundred yards off, probably right there in that hedgerow.

Another *pop* came. He closed his eyes, straining to hear the muzzle report so as to gauge its true direction. There it was, due south. He rose and emptied one Thompson at the hedgerow, the weapon turned on its side so its upward pull would sweep the rounds in a level line. At the same time, he heard Wyatt, farther back and on his right, open on the position. Leaves and dirt clods in the hedgerow blew into the air as he dropped back to the ground.

Silence.

Twenty seconds slipped past. He began to crawl to where he'd seen Anabel go down. A deluge of rain swept over him. The droplets were heavy and smacked solidly into his back. He saw her boot, reached out, and touched it. She turned and looked at him, her face streaming water, her eyes round and calmly brown.

"You hurt?" he asked.

"No. Did you get him?"

"I don't know. We'll find out soon enough." He lifted, checked the distant hedgerow, swung back toward Bird's position, then ducked down again. "Ready?"

"Yes."

"Go!"

They rose and headed for the hedgerow near Wyatt, running full out. They heard Bird immediately lay in covering fire, his bullets streaking past them twenty yards to the left. Then they were into the hedgerow, the rain still pounding down through the leaves as Wyatt came along the backside of the tree line, jogging, hunched over.

Fifteen minutes later, they linked with Fountain and Laguna and headed northwest toward the drop zone for the Hunters.

They came in at 2115 hours, the long summer dusk still glowing faintly beyond the clouds. The assigned drop zone was two miles outside Volognes, at the edge of *bocage* and the coastal savannah.

Since Sinclair had no R-E homing system or an S-phone to guide in the Lysander jump plane, they marked out the DZ with flashlights. The aircraft came in low from the northeast, made one pass, climbed slightly, and then three parachutes appeared, the men jumping at just barely four hundred feet.

The leader's name was Captain Dodds-Parker, a tall, lean, sharp-faced man with a David Niven mustache. He didn't introduce his companions. They were all special agents from the Security Project Unit of SOE's

MI-R Section, all veterans of covert operations in Norway, Greece, and Italy. Once, Anabel told Parnell, these same men had made a spectacular escape from the Gestapo by stealing a six-hundred-ton coastal steamer and sailing it alone back to Aberdeen, Scotland.

The three were dressed as French farmers, their weapons in musettes. They quickly buried their chutes and then huddled with Sinclair while Parnell stood aside, listening. She began by going over the penetration of the Brittany circuits.

Dodds-Parker stopped her: "No need to rehash, old girl," he said. "Do you have any suspects?" He had a clipped, Oxford twist to his words.

"No one stands out."

"Very well." The captain rose, the others doing the same. The meeting seemed to be over.

Sinclair said, "Wait a minute. We haven't established contact procedures."

"No need to, old girl," Dodds-Parker said.

"How will we know if you're successful?"

"If we surface within the next fortnight, it shall mean mission accomplished. If we don't, we will have been canceled." Matter of fact: *canceled, killed.* He smiled at her. "Well, cheerio."

The three men rapidly moved off and were soon swallowed by the deepening darkness.

Chapter Eight

Although 6 June was a benchmark in World War II and the beginning of the end for Nazi Germany, other significant events throughout the world had also occurred but were overshadowed by the massive invasion of Europe.

On 4 June, the rearguard of the German Fourteenth Army, made up of crack troops of the IV Parachute Corps, had crossed the river Tiber in Italy, abandoning Rome to the forward elements of the American Fifth Army. This marked the completion of the race to Rome and the end of the southern Italian Campaign. On the previous day British and Indian battle groups had finally driven the Japanese 31st Division out of Kohima, Burma, securing India once and for all in what some would later claim was the most savage fighting of the entire war.

On 8 June, the Russians launched a massive offensive, code-named Operation Bagration, in order to siphon German divisions from the western front. On the same day in the Pacific Theater of Operations, U.S. Task Force 58 began a heavy bombardment against the Mariana Islands in preparation for the next day's major landings on Tinian by units of the U.S. 2nd and 4th Marine Divisions.

In Normandy, once the Allied beachhead had been firmly established, German resistance firmed up. Although the flood of troops and supplies pouring ashore quickly gave the Allies numerical and firepower superiority, along with total control of the air, the German Army was still a powerful and skillful fighting force.

Under Rommel's direction and pinpoint artillery shelling, they were able to hold the Allies within their beachhead using a strategy of static defense and a slowly yielding front. In this way, the Desert Fox hoped to position his forces for a massive armored counterattack. But on 11 June, Hitler intervened. He forbade his generals to give up a single inch of ground. They were to hold in place or die.

He did, however, release two crack SS Panzer Divisions, the 1st from reserve in Belgium, and the 2nd from Army Group B in Toulouse in southern France. A profound tragedy involving this division occurred as it headed for Normandy. On 10 June, after constant Resistance raids against the transiting German units, the Nazis savagely retaliated. They chose the small town of Oradour-sur-Glane as an object lesson. They locked every villager in barns and the church and set fire to the whole village. Anyone able to escape the flames was machine-gunned. The death toll was 642 people, men, women, and children.

Although British/Canadian forces had linked with the Americans to form a consolidated front from Touffreville east of the river Orne to Bayeux, the Brits quickly became stalemated in their push for Caen.

Meanwhile, in the American sector, the initial plan had been to push northward, toward Cherbourg. Despite the successful use of artificial harbors called Mulberries off the Normandy beachhead, Cherbourg remained the only sheltered, deep-water facility capable of handling the tremendous amounts of supplies needed to keep the Allied offensive going. Its capture was absolutely essential.

Unfortunately, the *bocage* was perfect country for static defense. The Allied senior commanders then decided to

turn their main thrust westward, directly across the Cotentin Peninsula to the sea. Once done, Cherbourg would
be cut off. Now the fighting became a slogging, bitter
slugfest, infantryman's combat, one hedgerow, one field,
one house at a time. As the bloody days ground past, the
American momentum slowed until the beachhead could
no longer be developed and the forward thrust stalled to
a dead halt. The situation verged on crisis.

Then, on 14 June, General "Lighting Joe" Collins's VII
U.S. Armored Corps began an intense attack across the
Cotentin. Led by the 9th Infantry and 82nd Airborne Divisions, he drove to the west coast, reaching Barneville
on the seventeenth. Cherbourg was now totally isolated
and the Americans immediately resumed their push
northward.

These first days following D day were for Blue Team
and the Normandy circuits of the French Resistance a
melange of rapid movements and quick raids. Their general operational area formed a triangle with points at
Volognes in the north, Carentan inland from Utah
Beach, and Coutances, which lay west of St- Lô.

In conjunction with Duboudin and fifteen Maquis,
Sinclair, along with Parnell and his men, struck a
transformer/high-power installation at St. Sauveur.
Next, they hit a railway repair facility outside the junction town of Periers. Then, splitting from Duboudin
and with a new contingent of Maquis fighters, they
turned northeast to raid a gasoline tank farm at St.
Jean-de-Daye. Afterward, they rushed back across the
Cotentin to destroy a bridge on Highway D 903, the
road between Carentan and the western coastal town
of Carteret.

In the rare moments of rest, the team taught the Frenchies the fundamentals of special-op soldiering, such as setting up firebases for an attack and using proper raid-and-evade tactics; how to operate at night, to fix positions and maneuver, to use sounds and smells rather than sight to gauge enemy locations and strengths; and how to control the tempo of an attack.

The clamor of war continuously surrounded them as they crossed back and forth through shifting fronts: the distant rumble of artillery, the sudden racket of firefights, or the ground-shaking thunder of bombing runs. Sometimes, they encountered German troops on the move and hid in the brush while they passed, hearing that distinctive crack of hobnailed boots and smelling the Kraut odor of sweaty leather and tobacco.

In between the sudden, adrenaline-saturated raids, they crept through dark, silent hamlets, traversed *bocage* fields and sunken roads so recently the sites of battle that the bodies of Americans and Germans were still strewn about, the foliage ripped and showing fresh yellow wood and the edge of shell holes still coated with explosion powder before the wind could blow it away. Some of the bodies had no arms or legs or heads, and many were being eaten by escaped farm pigs. They always killed the animals.

The land was scarred and torn, filled with the burned-out wrecks of trucks and tanks and even the hulks of downed aircraft looking lonely in fields. Once they came across an amazing sight. In a shallow forest of beech trees lay the carcasses of the horses and men of an entire company of Cossak mounted cavalry who were fighting for the Nazis. The horses were all jet-black and the men wore black boots and trousers and cream-colored jackets with bullet loops. They were armed with sabers and sidearms and their Persian lamb

hats, red capes, and silver belt buckles were embla-
zoned with swastikas.

18 June 1944
1823 hours

Anabel was cleaning everybody's clock at poker: Laguna, Fountain, Wineberg, and a Resistance officer
named Georges Soustelle, all seated at a rough, round
table. Low ball, stud, blind, and straddle, she knew all
the variations. They had found the playing cards in a
closet, grimy with pornographic photos on their backs.

She and the team with nine Maquis were in the tiny village of Larregier. It had once been a castle. It sat on a low
hill that overlooked the Douve River and was surrounded
by a wall and a moat now thick with moss islands and water
lilies. As the evening twilight darkened, frogs began filling
the night with sound.

The hamlet was completely abandoned, even the bigger animals gone, only chickens pecking in the streets.
In the center of the village was a tall grain silo that had
been the castle keep. The houses and tiny shops were all
flat-roofed and built directly onto the ground. The main
castle building had been turned into apartments. The
village had a dark, medieval feel to it, a place filled with
the ghosts of churls and wandering minstrels.

They had chosen the butcher's shop to set up momentary camp since it was adjacent to the main gate. The
other Resistance fighters took the blacksmith's house. Together, they quickly secured the area. While doing so, the
men had found several caches of wine and calvados, the
powerful apple cognac peculiar to Normandy. Now everyone was a little tight.

After posting guards on the hamlet's walls, everyone settled down to eat and clean weapons while Anabel and Soustelle prepared dinner, a stew made with long pork sausages and vegetables and fresh apples they'd discovered in a ground box outside the shop. In one of the houses, Sinclair found a big copper *saucie* pan and bags of flour that she used to whip up a batch of biscuits called Johnny Browns, which, she said, her father had taught her how to make from when he was a trapper in Wyoming.

She said, "I call."

Everybody laid down their cards, checking things out. Laguna grinned broadly, his perfect, white teeth gleaming in his dirt-stained face. "I got chu this time, honey. T'ree niners."

Anabel's eyebrows bounced as she gave him a dimpled smile and spread her cards out. "Look 'em over and cry in your beer, gents," she said. "Four big daddies."

"God-*damn*," Weesay said.

Soustelle scowled at her. "*Qu'est-ce que tu fous, dame?*" he growled.

"Just showing you people how it's done, *mon cher*," she said.

The Frenchie was a small man, puny even, with a narrow, ratlike face. Yet during the raids they had made together, he had repeatedly proven himself to be a vicious fighter. All the Americans liked him. Still, scowling, he snatched up the bottle of calvados and took a long pull.

Cowboy said, "Where ya'll learn how to play poker like that, sweet thang?"

"My daddy taught me," Anabel answered, gathering in the hardtack crackers they were using for chips.

"Oh, well, shit," Weesay said. "Her *daddy* taught her. Daniel Boone of Wyoming."

"What was he, a goddamned Mississippi gambler, too?" Fountain said.

"Yeah, among other things." She picked up the cards, began shuffling. "Okay, boys, what'll it be this time? Spit in the ocean? Cincinnati?"

"I no longer wish to play, Madame," Soustelle said stiffly. He pushed away from the table and, carrying the bottle of calvados, silently walked outside.

"I'm out, too," Smoker said. "Twenty-five crackers, that's my limit." He also took a bottle, slung his Thompson, and followed Soustelle out.

"What?" Anabel cried, looking at Weesay and Cowboy. "You guys quitting too?"

Laguna gave her a narrow-eyed look. He lifted his hand, fingertips pressed together, and poked them at her, like a snake's tongue. "I jes' put the Chihuahua's curse on you, *nina*."

"The what?"

"The Chihuahua curse," he said. "A terrible thing. Chu don' wanna know how terrible."

She laughed. "God, what weenies."

Laguna and Fountain went upstairs. Anabel sat nibbling on one of her crackers. The room was dark, its walls and beams coated black from the butcher's fat kettles. It smelled like boiling leather and the deeper, thicker odor of spoiled meat.

She felt wonderfully alive, despite the constant stress and physical exertion they had all been under for nearly two weeks, eating on the run, grabbing sleep when they could. And going cold-fleshed at the killing and the horrible things she had seen, such things she could never have conceived of in her other world.

Yet despite all that, her spirit seemed genuinely elated with some inexplicable energy, here in *this* dingy, smelly place among bearded, smelly, red-eyed men whom she had come to respect and bear such affection for, so deep, that if she thought on it, it would have made her heart ache and brought tears to her eyes.

She focused on the sounds of war that came faintly from beyond this house, beyond this hamlet's thick walls, so constant now they had become a perpetual backdrop to which she had to deliberately listen in order to realize they were there at all. Yet here, now, she felt comfortable, cozy, and utterly safe. She took a drink of calvados, almost as thick and yellow as sunflower honey. It burned nicely going down, warming her belly.

Across the room, Parnell was still listening to their radio, a new SCR-1500 that had been in one of the airdrops. Whenever they stopped, she would monitor BBC broadcasts, watching for her code letters and messages indicating London wanted her to make contact with SOE headquarters for orders and updates.

Thus far, no word of the Hunters' mission had come back to her. There had been shadowy hints of someone tracking the Maquis circuits, particularly in Brittany. Everyone assumed it was the Gestapo. The Germans had made four more lightning-quick raids on safe houses, three in Brittany and one in Normandy, arresting twenty-one Maquis. Now everyone was running on high alert, the circuit and cell leaders shifting their operational areas without notice, making last-minute changes to attack plans, and always staying constantly on the move.

She poured Red a glass of cognac and took it over to him, placed it on the floor where he sat cross-legged, the earphones pressed to his ears. He glanced at her, nodded silently, and then took a long pull of the drink.

"There's a Kraut tank battalion somewhere nearby," he said.

"Where?"

"Can't tell exactly. They're running Panzer code. But it's

strong as hell." He listened for a moment longer, then took off the earphones and rested them across the radio. He turned around to look at the card table. "Cleaned 'em out, did you?"

"Of course."

He grunted. "You're a hot little mama, ain't you?"

She tilted her head, studying him. "You don't like me, do you?"

"That's a helluva leading question."

"*Do* you?"

"Does it matter?"

"No, not really."

"Then why ask it?"

She took a drink from his glass, her eyes never leaving his face. "Is it because I haven't folded like you figured I would?"

"What makes you think I figured you'd fold?"

"It was written all over your face the first time I met you."

"You see it now?"

"No."

"Then that's a stupid assumption."

She leaned back, felt sudden anger come hot up into her face. "My *God*, you can be an unbearable pain in the ass, Parnell."

He gave her a moment of hard eyes, then lifted his forefinger and pointed it at her like a pistol. "Right back atcha, sweetheart," he snapped. Without another word, he stood up, slung his Thompson over his shoulder, and went outside.

Fifty miles to the south, Henri Dupin woke with a start and lay listening. Nothing but distant artillery.

He stretched, flexing his muscles. His legs were stiff. He had been on the move all day, bicycling from Avranches to St. Pois, southeast of Vire, the country full of small canals. He had been continually stopped by nervous German sentries.

Still, he didn't mind it. He enjoyed his new job. Duboudin had made him a courier, running messages between the Normandy circuits and those in Avranches and Fougères. It made it easier for him to pass on Vaillant's coded notes to the Germans without raising suspicion.

Still, Henri figured a man deserved a bit of relaxation, a chance to tickle the doe's vagina, *non*? To this end he had stopped to see one of his old mistresses, a Madame Elie Borrel. She was the wife of a Maquis in the Oakleaf circuit of Brittany. Dupin had been sleeping with her off and on since 1939 when she was a barmaid in St-Malo. Now she lived with her sister aboard a canal boat, a gross woman, *un grand cheval*, like a horse, who favored sailors but who could be deliciously inventive in bed.

Yet, oddly, not this afternoon. Instead, she had seemed passive, almost remote. He wondered if she might have another lover. He looked about, perhaps unconsciously searching for a man's possessions, a sign. The cabin of the boat was done in a faded red, thick overhead cross-members, a ladder to the deck. The air reeked of wet wood and canal water, the musky essences of vaginal secretions. He closed his eyes. What did it matter if she had another? he thought. How absurd of him to be jealous.

He let his mind drift lazily, but almost instantly it fixed on the image of Vaillant Duboudin. Henri felt his stomach tighten. His friend and the leader of the Nazi conspirators inside the Normandy Maquis was getting way too careless, as far as Henri was concerned. Too overconfident, stupidly taking too many risks. That could lead in only one direction: exposure.

Especially now. Over the last week, two of their fellow operatives had been killed. Not in battle, *murdered*. But by whom? Certainly not the Gestapo. He had thought about it and come up with a fairly good idea. It *had* to be the *maquereaux*, the bloodiest of those Communists in the FTP. Now that the Allies were actually here on French soil, they were starting their elimination of rivals so as to control the midlands once the Germans were driven out.

He heard a noise, a rustle. He opened his eyes. A man was kneeling beside the bed. He had a lean, white face with a thin mustache. He smiled pleasantly at Henri and gently placed a revolver against his head. It had a long silencer fitted to the barrel. In perfectly accented French, he asked, "You are Henri Dupin?"

"*Mon Dieu!*" A splay of pure, icy terror rose though Henri's chest. "Who are you?" From the corner of his eye, he saw Elie standing at the top of the ladder, wearing only her dirty black sweater, her thick legs dimpled, the dark triangle of her pubic hair as large as a highwayman's mask. Her arms were crossed coldly over her breasts.

The man waited a moment, then turned to look at her. She nodded silently. The man came back. "Cheery bye, old boy," he said in English.

Henri heard the snap of the pistol's hammer and then the crack of the exploding round. The muzzle blast, blowing sideways through the silencer's vents, seared his eyes. Inside his head a burst of white-hot light exploded and his senses instantly crashed into chaos. Sounds roared up, smells became solid, colored lights flashed and faded and flashed again. Yet he felt absolutely no pain. And then he was dead.

* * *

The rain had stopped and Parnell could see breaks in the night's overcast, stars showing faintly. Soon air strikes would be coming in again, he knew. Far away, a walking barrage was going on, the artillery men conducting RBF, or Reconnaissance By Fire, salvos to locate and flush enemy positions. The sporadic rumble sounded as if someone were dynamiting in a distant quarry.

He was seated on the top of the wall that surrounded Larregier, standing his turn on watch. It was nearly eleven o'clock. From the moat came the raucous croaking of frogs, a sharp overture of individual calls. He leaned his back against ancient stone and listened to it, the noise so of-the-night.

Abruptly, it stopped, every single frog going silent at the same precise moment. Instantly alert, Red quickly scanned the ground beyond the wall, even though he was certain it was nothing, simply a peculiarity of all frogs. He had always wondered about that oddity, how a group of frogs could all stop at once, as if a boss-frog had telegraphed a signal collectively into their tiny reptilian brains.

He waited for them to start again. Several minutes passed. Then isolated croakings began, here and there, until there was once more the full swelling chorus. He listened. It drew up the memory of another similar moment in time.

A night back at the University of Colorado beside Varsity Lake, all silvery in moonlight and only faintly etched with the reflections from the lights of Old Main Hall, the frogs going full bore like a glittering in the night. Him and Sally Ann Tanner lying in the pine tree shadows, urgently fumbling with each other's clothing, her saliva tasting of salt and lemon and the feel of her breasts and nipples exuding a goose-pimply heat. Then there was the smooth curve of belly under his fingers and Sally's lush, warm wetness into which he plunged as she whispered breathless urgings in his ear.

Then the frogs stopped.

She instantly went stiff, gasped, "Oh, God."

"What?"

"Someone's coming."

"No one's coming."

"The frogs. They stopped making *noise.*"

"The hell with the frogs!" He was so close, could feel himself bunching down there, ecstasy trembling on the edge. She struggled to get out from under him. He was embarrassedly aware that he whimpered, staring stupidly into the shadows.

Oh, Jesus! . . .

He laughed now, remembering. Sudden banshee cries erupted in the night as a rocket battery opened up to the north, the ripples going off so rapidly they made a continuous sound. He listened for the impacts. They came like stitchings in the earth. Then the night dropped back into semisilence again.

Sally Ann's image lingered. Yet slowly it changed into someone else: Anabel Sinclair. Red felt a quick, tight desire rush through his stomach. Before he could stop it, his mind pictured her naked, her face staring up at him with hot, arousal-slitted eyes, her mouth parted, her breath . . .

A man's voice called softly, "Tough-ski."

Parnell roused himself, felt stone, the chilly Normandy air. "Shit-ski," he countersigned.

Wyatt came up onto the wall, squatted, bracing himself with his Thompson. "A message from Quarterback's comin' through, Lieutenant," he said.

Parnell grunted, pushed himself to his feet, and went back down to the butcher's shop.

It was from Colonel James Dunmore, operational commander and creator of the Mohawkers. Although he had desperately wanted to go into France with General Omar Bradley, now commanding the U.S. First Army in the invasion, he'd been personally tagged by General Patton to oversee his intelligence analysis for a major operation in England.

Since January of 1944, the Allies had created a huge dummy force called the First U.S. Army Group, or FUSAG. General Patton was given command of this monumental deception plan. It was designed to make the Germans believe the invasion of Europe was coming at Pas de Calais so they would keep their powerful Fifteenth Army stationed there.

Headquartered in Dover, FUSAG was an entire fake Army Group composed of phony encampments throughout England, hundreds of make-believe tanks and landing craft placed where Nazi overflights could photograph them, huge artificial storage areas and even embarkation ports.

Despite his heavy workload, however, Dunmore continued periodic contact with Parnell and Blue Team. To do this, he worked through a newly formed Special Forces Headquarters unit, which was a collaborative between the SOE and the American OSS. This unit was now overseeing all clandestine operations in France.

Before leaving England, he and Parnell had worked out a method of transmitting messages using a code based on certain words and phrases from the games of

football, baseball, and basketball, pure American sports
that would be little understood by Nazi interceptors.

Dunmore's code name was Quarterback, Parnell's
Tight End. To further secure the messages and link
them to the correct one of three maps, each transmission was preceded by an identifying reference. The
football code and map was Notre Dame, baseball's was
Cooperstown, and the basketball reference was YMCA.

Anabel was seated at the radio table when Parnell
came down. Seeing him, she keyed transfer and gave
him the chair. He quickly tapped in his code name and
ID number sequence in Morse code and cleared for reception. It came rapidly, only once. Red immediately
recognized Dunmore's peculiar rhythm on the key.
When it was completed, he tapped acknowledgment and
ended the transmission.

Deciphered, the message read: *barneville on coast
taken . . . cotentin/cherbourg cut off . . . hold station and
monitor twenty-four hours . . . possible mission . . .*

19 June 1944

Major Land pulled his Mercedes Benz Type-170 light
staff car off the dirt road and parked beside a thick oak
tree. He switched off the engine and got out. The mid-
morning was beautiful, the sky clear and blue. Long
grassy hills dotted with stands of Douglas pine and fir
sloped way to the west and the Orne River glistened in
sunlight far below.

He had noticed this particular oak several times in the
past when he traveled the Suisse Normandie District between Caen and Thury-Harcourt. It had a distinctive
wound that had grown into folds of wood that reminded

him of a vagina. He sat down beside it now and lit a cigarette.

The bucolic serenity was a pleasant relief from the chaos and ruin of Caen. Allied bombers had repeatedly attacked the city since the start of the invasion, destroying over half of it. But here the war seemed far away, only the columns of dirty smoke rising here and there to mark its existence.

For the past ten minutes, he'd watched a lone bicyclist coming up from the river, bundles of kindling wood tied to his handlebars and rear bracket. He approached, came abreast of the German officer, a tall man in a shabby peasant jacket and cone-shaped hat. He was sweating heavily from the climb. He didn't look at the major as he passed.

Land let him go by, then called out in French, "You, come here."

The rider stopped, dismounted, and pushed his bicycle up the slope to the tree. "You're late," he said. The rider was Vaillant Duboudin.

Land looked him over quietly, his blue eyes holding a faint, amused smile. Finally he said, "A fitting disguise that, Nicholas."

Duboudin took his hat off, swept perspiration from his forehead, put it back on again. "This isn't wise, Major," he said. "I don't like meeting in the open."

"But it's so . . . pleasant here. Don't you agree?"

"Let's get on with it. What's the purpose of this meeting? Why couldn't you have relayed it by radio or courier?"

The smile went from Land's eyes. "I'm no longer certain of whom to trust. Your circuits have become compromised and are unstable."

"Nonsense," Duboudin scoffed. "It's only the Communists. They're attempting to maneuver for control now. But I watch them very closely."

"Is that so?"

"Of course."

"And it's they who are killing your agents?"

"Yes."

"Including Wrestler?" *Wrestler* was Henri Dupin's code name.

Vaillant was jolted. "*He's* dead?"

"Yes. The body was found this morning in a canal." Land paused, watched Duboudin stare at the ground. "We don't believe it's the Communists."

Vaillant raised his head. "Then who?"

"An assassin team from British Intelligence."

Vaillant considered that a moment, then shook his head. "No, that can't be. I've seen no signs of infiltration."

"Then you're a damn fool," Land snapped. "They've been sent here to clear your circuits, man. And sooner or later, they'll get to you."

"I don't believe it."

Land tilted his head, studied the Frenchman. "Whether you believe it or not, you're becoming a risk, Nicholas . . . perhaps even expendable." He and the Frenchman locked eyes. Finally he said, "How much pain do you think you could stand?"

"As much as I have to."

"Good answer. I hope you never have to test it."

Doboudin was the first to look away. Two tiny wrens suddenly burst through the oak branches and went skimming down the hill. Duboudin watched them, turned back. "Is there anything else?"

"Yes. The Americans have reached the coast. That means they'll turn north against Cherbourg. From now on, you will confine your operations to the Cotentin and send us data of their moves and intentions. You understand?"

"Yes," Vaillant said. He closed his eyes, inhaled, opened

them. Lifting the bicycle, he swung it around, mounted, and rode away without another word.

Colonel Dunmore's mission-message came through at 0110 hours, 20 June. It read:

> *te-1818b des Notre Dame: zlog:2208*
> *3 quarter and 4 gameday . . . buttonhook right, blue*
> *lead . . . grid 191501 . . .*
> *slot right, x-stop . . . handoff to middies, slot right . . .*
> *25 song leader minus 2 . . . gateman mascot*
> *second-string pregame . . . grid 197322 . . .*
> *groundskeeper soccer players . . . chalktalk 24 . . .*
> *qb-1818a*

Deciphered, it stated that Parnell would receive an air-drop at 10:00 P.M. that night at Notre Dame map grid position 191501, which lay on the eastern bank of the Douve River. He was then to execute a deep penetration of the port of Cherbourg so as to act as a forward observer for a naval bombardment scheduled for 25 June. His contact would be an agent code-named Mascot.

Meanwhile, the remainder of Blue Team would execute a demo raid against a German radar station at Notre Dame grid 197322. These instructions were to be kept totally secret, even from other SOE agents. Until then, Parnell was to maintain a constant radio watch for further orders.

Chapter Nine

23 June
2310 hours

Parnell was impressed at the easy, expert way Pierre Touissant handled the thirty-foot whaleboat, a double-stemmed, open-decked, lug-rigged sailer with a main and foremast. The tail of the big storm still carried gusts of twenty-five-knot winds that swept in off the Channel, so the Frenchman had furled his foresail and reefed the main. Its boom was now angled straight to starboard as he kept them running free before the wind.

Touissant was seventy-six years old, his body as taut and wiry as steel cable. He had been a fisherman all his life, spoke sparingly, and constantly chewed tar, which kept his teeth a brilliant white. He was now taking them directly into Cherbourg Harbor.

The ocean was cast in fog. Black-faced waves loomed in, their tops feathered with spindrift. Sitting far forward, Red could hear the hiss of the bow as it cut water and the wild surging of the wind and sometimes in the lulls the pound of surf off the lee shore a mile to starboard.

The storm had been one of the worst in twenty years. It had come up in the afternoon of the nineteenth and pounded the Normandy coast for thirty-six hours. Although Parnell didn't know it, it nearly destroyed

Mulberry A and Mulberry B, artificial harbors that had been floated across the Channel from England and set up off the assault beaches to handle the massive flow of men and material for the push inland. Both were now piles of twisted steel and cement blocks. Over seven hundred ships and small craft had also been shoved aground.

He moved aft, squatted beside Anabel. She was sitting just aft the main mast, scrunched down in a thick black sou'wester. Two waterproof gear bags attached to inflated inner tubes lay on the duckboards at her feet. "How you doing?" he shouted over the wind.

Her face looked pale and drawn in the dim light. "Sick."

"What?"

"I said I want to puke my guts up."

He grinned, slapped her on the back, and returned to the bow. Unlike her, he was thoroughly enjoying the rough trip. There was something about storms that had always drawn him, particularly those at sea. Their wild power and vastness transmitted a pure, joyous energy down into him.

Before entering college, he'd worked six months in the oil fields in the Gulf of Mexico, first as a jug-hustler on an exploratory shooting crew, and then as a tong man on Standard Oil's number 174 rig in the Coopers Field twenty-five miles off Galveston. Three times, big tropical storms had slammed into the rig from the Caribbean. Off shift each time, he'd ridden the blocks up to the derrick man's walkaround and happily huddled there, listening to the shrieking wind, which made the safety cables sing and the derrick groan and pop. . . .

It was now nearly midnight. They had started two hours before from a tiny cove at the base of the sheer, five-hundred-foot-high chalk cliffs of the Cap de la Hague, the northernmost tip of the Cotentin Peninsula. A few drift-wood shanties were nestled at the edge of the cove with a small jetty and net racks and rowing dinghies pulled up on the small beach.

Touissant whistled and Sinclair crawled back to him. They spoke for a moment, then she came forward. She leaned into Parnell's shoulder. "He says we're entering the outer *digue*, the harbor's breakwater system," she shouted. "From here on in, keep absolutely silent."

Red felt her trembling with cold. He put his arm around her. She felt solid and firm beneath the heavy jacket.

"Once we're into the main harbor, he'll take us into the Bassin du Commerce," she continued, her voice quivering. "We'll go under a bridge, the Rue du Val de Saire. Beyond it, watch for a red light on the eastern bank." He nodded. She returned to her seat.

Thirty minutes passed. Although Red couldn't see anything beyond a few feet, he could sense the presence of land, of man-made things on both sides of them. Buoy horns moaned like wounded elephants. Inside the main breakwater, the wind grew calmer, smoothing the surface, which allowed the whaleboat to go lightly.

Another twenty minutes slipped past. Now he heard the surge and fade of machinery, caught the thick smell of wharf tar and diesel fuel and steel. Since Cherbourg was under blackout, the only lights he could faintly make out were blue, casting blurry sapphire halos like Christmas lights seen through gauze.

Without the shifting power of open ocean wind, the fog thickened. It was as damp and cold as mountain rain. They passed another, smaller breakwater and entered the main harbor, passing what were obviously wharves and big ship mooring docks. Here the noise was louder: the shushing rush of grain conveyors and the rumble of cantilever cranes working their boom trolleys as they off-loaded cargo from German freighters that had run the Channel out of Spain and Portugal.

They now entered another body of water, the feel of it narrower. It was the Commercial Basin. Ten minutes into it, a dark object suddenly eased by directly overhead, the Val de Saire Bridge, which separated Cherbourg from Old Town on the east. Below the span was the powerful stench of bird guano and rusted steel. A heavy vehicle rumbled across the bridge, its noise gently fading off.

A hundred yards beyond the bridge, Parnell's heart went cold. Above the wharf sounds, he had detected the faint grumble of diesel engines, the gentle hissing whisper of water being cleaved. He glanced around to look at Touissant. He could just barely make him out at the tiller. The main sail, nearly limp now, luffed gently, making a soft, canvas sound.

He swung back. The engine sound grew louder. It was close, somewhere off the port bow. He leaned over the stem post and squinted into the fog, his whole body tense. It was difficult to pinpoint the direction of the engine noise.

He felt the air shift suddenly, displaced by the approach of something moving. Staring hard, he thought he saw a shadow. Nothing. The hiss of the bow wave was quite loud now, just out there. The shifting fog thinned slightly. For a fleeting moment, he saw a long black hull passing, bow cutter teeth, deck gun, then the double-high sail skimming past about forty yards away. He could hear the soft hum of blowers as a cloud of warm diesel exhaust rolled over the whaleboat. It was a German submarine standing down the Channel at about seven knots.

It disappeared. The whaleboat hit the sub's stern wave and rocked violently for a moment, tossing the masts sharply enough to make them squeak softly with strain. Once through the turbulence, Touissant swung toward the east bank and they ran parallel to it for another ten minutes.

The red light snapped into view, a tiny star in the fog: *blink, blink,* pause, *blink, blink.* Toussant countersigned with his own light and swung the tiller hard over again. The whaleboat heeled around in a 180 and lay to, the main sail luffing gently. He hurried forward. "Quick," he whispered harshly. "Go over."

Red grabbed the gear bags and inner tubes, eased them over the side. Holding them against the hull so they wouldn't drift, he waited until Anabel had slipped over the gunwale and into the water. Then he shook the Frenchman's calloused hand and went in himself.

The water was shockingly cold. Ahead about twenty yards the red light flashed again. Pulling the tubes, he and Sinclair kicked toward it. They reached a stone step. A hooded figure appeared, helped them up onto a stone ramp. No words were spoken. The figure turned and headed up the ramp.

They crossed a grassy embankment and went down along a drainage pipe. It smelled of chemicals. Every fifty feet it had a cement brace block, the surfaces slimy with moss. They reached a coral road, went along it for about a hundred yards, then turned into a narrow, cobblestoned alley. Half-timbered houses rose on both sides with flower boxes in their lower windows.

They reached more water, the area smelling oily. Canal boats and water shanties were moored along the near bank. They followed their guide across a wide-plank catwalk and stepped onto one of the floating shanties. It dipped slightly with their weight. The hooded figure unlocked the door and stood aside. They went in.

Inside, the air felt compressed, saturated with the scent of soap and wildflowers and the more prevailing stench of wood rot. A light came on. It showed a neat sitting room with a settee and two side chairs, all three covered in a flowery pattern, a Welsh dresser that contained several black-and-white photographs in silver frames, two of a young couple in clothing of the twenties, others of them in ski togs or swimming trunks. The room had a single large window with flowered curtains and dainty valences and a blackout shield made of tar paper.

Their guide turned, pulled back the hood. It was a woman with short brown hair and merry blue eyes, mid-forties, slightly worn around the edges yet still quite pretty. "I'm Mascot," she said, smiling graciously. "Welcome to shit-hole Cherbourg."

As General Collins turned his VII Corps north for the drive to Cherbourg, the rest of the Allied line remained in static positions outside St-Lô and Caen, both key to a complete breakout from the Normandy beachhead. Still, the Krauts were paying a heavy price for containing the British and Americans. Both the German Seventh Army and Rommel's Panzer Group West had already been reduced to mere battle groups by constant artillery barrages, air strikes, and naval shelling. Many infantry battalions were actually down to less than 150 men.

On 20 June, Hitler, still believing the main Allied thrust would come at Pas de Calais, had ordered von Rundstadt and Rommel to mount a six-division counterattack through the gap between British and American forces at Bayeux. He agreed to send four Panzer divisions to carry it through, two from Fifteenth Army, one from southern France, and one from the Eastern Front. But these immediately came under constant air attack, which knocked them to half strength by the time they reached *bocage* country.

Viewing this fatal disaster in the making and the Führer's maniacal refusal to see what was actually happening right before his eyes brought most senior commanders in the German army to finally realize that the war was hopeless and that Hitler, probably on the brink of insanity, would ultimately destroy Germany completely. His fight-to-the-death order to the troops hopelessly caught in the seal-off of the Cotentin Peninsula strengthened that belief.

The push into the northern Contentin, with Collins's VII Corps now bolstered by three fresh infantry divisions, two squadrons of motorized cavalry, and two tank battalions, had great initial success. Some forward units covered as much as ten miles a day. But the Germans were deliberately allowing them such speed, falling back to a powerful defensive perimeter outside Cherbourg, a belt of field works that extended four to six miles around the city. The port itself contained forty thousand troops under the command of Generalleutnant Karl von Schlieben. In addition, there were twenty big gun casements along the coast, firing 88mm, 150mm, and some 280mm field howitzers.

Because of the storm damage to the Mulberry harbors, the Allies now *had* to take Cherbourg as soon as possible. But on 21 June, advance patrols of VII Corps's 4th and 9th Divisions ran head-on into the Cherbourg perimeter and the drive north was stalled.

Frantic, the Allied Chiefs of Staff realized they had to assist Collins. Thus far, Cherbourg had been spared intensive bombing attacks so as to keep the vital harbor facilities from damage. Earlier, there had even been a plan to send naval gunships in to shell it; but that, too, had been sidelined since concentrated time-on-target fire presented too big a risk to the harbor.

Now the naval bombardment plan was put back on the table, with a proviso. Destruction to the harbor could be held to a minimum if a forward observation officer were inside the city, calling in the fire missions onto specific targets and then immediately assessing the damage.

A small commando landing party was considered first, then canceled. If they were spotted, the Germans might be tipped to what was coming. Besides, why not use personnel already on the ground, possibly even Resistance members? The matter was sent to the Special Forces Headquarters in Bryanston Square, London. There, Colonel Dunmore convinced the senior officers of OSS and SOE to dispatch Lieutenant Parnell. He was already in country and was an experienced shore fire-control officer. It was also decided to send agent Sinclair with him since she was familiar with the city of Cherbourg.

By early evening of the twenty-third, the gunships for the Bombardment Force began marshaling across the Channel at Portland, England. It would be under the command of Rear Admiral Morton Deyo and would consist of two Fire Groups.

The first would include the American battleship *Nevada* and the cruisers *Tuscaloosa* and *Quincy*, the British light cruisers *Glasgow* and *Enterprise*, along with six destroyers. The second group would consist of the battleships USS *Texas* and *Arkansas*, with five destroyers for escort.

Clearing a transit lane straight to Cherbourg would be the ships of U.S. Mine Squadron 7 and the British 9th Minesweeping Flotilla. At dawn, P-38 fighters and TBM-3S anti submarine aircraft out of fields in southern England would rendezvous with the armada to supply air/sea cover.

The Bombardment Force was scheduled to leave port at midnight of 24 June.

Parnell and Sinclair, seated in Mascot's tiny, neat kitchen drinking strong, cognac-spiced coffee and downing jelly croissants, listened while the Resistance agent showed them her disposition map of German forces in Cherbourg. It was astoundingly thorough with red circles indicating concentrations of troops, transportation yards, arsenals, supply dumps, forts, even the locations of large gun emplacements. In the harbor area, she had designated normal mooring berths of German warships, including the two submarine nests, one in the Commerce Basin, the other on the far side of the harbor, along with warehouse, cargo, and fuel storage sites.

Anabel said, "My God, woman, how were you able to learn all this? They know they're going to be hit sooner or later. I'd think the Germans'd be nervous as hell, suspicious of everybody even coming near a military installation."

The French woman nodded. "Oh, yes, the strutting pricks *are* frightened," she said. "They make shit in their trousers. But, you see, I work in the shipyards, a welder. I'm extremely proficient. Sometimes the Nazi bastards send me to do repair jobs on military equipment." She winked. "I have observant eyes, *non*?"

Mascot's real name was Madame Giselle Chaffin. As a younger woman, she had run brothels in St-Germain-en-Laye and St-Denis outside Paris. Her husband, Christian, had been a jockey and racing *revendeur*, a tout. When the Germans occupied France, Christian was arrested because he was a known Communist. They shipped him off to a labor camp in Poland and she never saw him again. She herself was sent to Cherbourg to work on the docks.

"Has London given any specifics about this operation?" Red asked.

"Only that we are to be attacked. And that you will observe for ships."

"No time schedule?"

"*Non.* Perhaps they will come tomorrow, perhaps later. We'll know when the shells come, eh?" She flashed her bright smile. "Whatever, we will have to move quickly. When dark comes tomorrow, I'll guide you to an observation point on Montagne du Roule." This was a steep, forested mountain just east of the city. From it, they would have a panoramic view of the entire port. "Till then, you rest up here."

"Does the Gestapo ever make sweeps around here?" Anabel said.

"Sometimes. If they do, you will know. The boat dogs bark excitedly. Like they are smelling game, you see?" She chuckled, stood. "Come, I show you where to hide your equipment and yourselves in case that happens."

Wyatt Bird shifted the cigar to the other side of his mouth and studied the high rim of the sea cliff, a black line up there with faint stars beyond. The cigar was no longer lit, but it seeped a sweet taste into his saliva, like brandy. Father Emmanuel Benjeloun had given each member of the team one from a polished mahogany box in the rectory of his tiny church in St-Pierre Eglise. They were precious, he told them, smuggled in from Spain. But, of course, this was a very special occasion.

The Catholic priest was a dark-skinned Moroccan who spoke precise English, very tall and thin with beautiful teeth and a gentle voice and delicate way of using his hands. He was their contact guide for the raid on the Kraut radar station. Anabel Sinclair had vouched for him, considered him one of the few in the Cotentin circuit she could truly trust.

Their target was not a fixed radar station. Instead, it was two mobile picket vehicles that periodically moved to various sites along the remote coastal cliffs between St-Pierre Eglise and Cherbourg. For months Father Emmanuel had monitored their movements, each crew driving a half-track and pulling a generator/antenna trailer.

German radars were far inferior to those of the Allies. These particular units, Wurzburg 1000s, used only 2.4-meter wavelengths, which was not even a quarter of what the British CH and American SCR-270 sets utilized. As a result, these could only probe arcs of about forty miles out to sea.

During his observations, Benjeloun had noted that the radar crews always returned to the same sites, following a strict rotation schedule: same day, same hour, and always just before dawn. They would scan for about twelve hours and then move on to another designated position.

Utilizing this information, Bird had set up Fountain and Laguna just after midnight in ambush position at the spot where Father Emmanuel said one of the vehicles would show up this morning. Then he, Smoker, and the priest moved three miles down the coast to where the second truck would park.

Each ambush team was armed with a bazooka with three rocket rounds and fresh explosives that had been air-dropped near the Douve River. The drop's A-5 gear containers had also included an SCR-511-CN marine transceiver, which Parnell would use to call in the naval fire missions. In addition, there was fresh ammunition, and coded material issuing mission instructions, ship call procedures, and frequencies to be used.

There were also forged ID documents for Parnell: a passport and seaman's papers in the name of Zahi Hawass, an Egyptian sailor crewing aboard a freebooting Portuguese tramp steamer. The SOE had even supplied him with oil-stained seaman's clothes, a woolen watch cap to cover his red-blond hair, a lambskin P-coat, and Arabian leather seaman's deck shoes.

During his OSS training in Cairo before the Italian campaign, Red had picked up enough Arabic to fool the Germans, throwing a jumble of meaningless words at them if he were stopped and questioned. After all, what were the chances a Kraut field soldier would know Egyptian-Arabic?

Wyatt checked his watch. It was 3:13. They were now hunkered down in a small crescent cove at the foot of the cliff where the German radar unit was scheduled to appear. The cliff was sheer limestone, serrated into ridges by the wind. It was sea-cold with a layer of fog lying on the ocean surface and combers periodically crashing along the outer curves of the cove.

He asked Father Emmanuel. "What kind of cover we got up there, Padre?"

"Grass, mostly," the priest said. "Quite tall. Perhaps a bit of moor scrub and some thickets of sea juniper. It will give adequate hiding."

"Is there a way up there, or do we gotta scale it?"

"Yes, there is a path."

Wyatt turned, spat, came back. "Okay, Padre, let's get 'er done."

Once at the top, they set up their ambush position in a particularly dense clump of sea juniper. The branches were prickly, the leaves smelling like peppermint. Forty yards away was a flattened, grassless area where the truck usually parked. It was littered with rusty German ration cans and parts of several empty wire boxes that the soldiers had dismantled to use as firewood. Tracks led back through the savannah grass, which was about three feet high here and permanently bent by the wind.

Bird lay down in the sand, shifting his body to make a comfortable indentation. Smoker took up position to his right while the priest moved farther back on the same side and lay down in another juniper thicket. Wyatt rested his cheek on the folded-out bazooka tube, the metal cold against his flesh and smelling of Cosmoline and rocket residue.

Wineberg, breaking out the bazooka rounds from their oilcloth sheaths and laying them side by side in the sand, said, "You figure they'll show, Wyatt?"

"Hell yeah. Krauts always shit in the same hole at the same time."

Smoker studied the bare parking site. He snickered. "Jesus, if we can't clip 'em good from this close, we better fuckin' go back to Basic."

Bird was also studying the position, picturing the radar vehicle, figuring where he'd put his rounds: first one in the fuel tank, second in the cab, third into the trailer. Then he got to wondering, What kind of armor did these radar rigs carry? He'd never seen one before. What if they had combat armor?

He knew bazooka rounds were rarely effective against the plating of German Panther and Tiger tanks when struck head-on. Instead, the shooter had to put them in the tracks or underbelly to bring it to a stop. He decided to change his firing plan. First he'd nail the vehicle's metal treads, bring it to a complete halt, then put the next rocket through its windshield or viewing slits. The trailer could wait. *Okay*, yeah, he decided, *that's how it'll be.*

He waited. Inside, he felt completely calm, comfortable, with the sea juniper taking the whip out of the wind. High in the sky, the stars were faint, jiggling slightly as he looked directly at them, as if he were seeing them through a sheet of cloudy water. He didn't think about the men he was about to kill, they were simply the enemy.

He heard the clatter of the half-track's treads first, cracking and fading and coming back. Instantly, he was out of his doze. He glanced at his watch: 4:08. He whistled softly. "They're here."

"Right," Smoker called back.

The half-track came on slowly, its blue slit headlights like devils' eyes in the grass. It pulled up into the bare spot, made a 180, and stopped. Lifting the bazooka into firing position, Wyatt recognized the vehicle, a refitted Bussing-NAG three-ton prime mover. He'd seen them in the *bocage*, transporting disabled tanks on big flatbeds, a service unit, lightly armored with only 5mm steel. Built over the half-track section was a van box for the radar gear and crew's sleeping space.

The vehicle's engine died, left only the gentle hum from the generator trailer. Bird nestled his shoulder snugly against the weapon's padded rear bracket, eased his finger to the trigger housing. Traversing his sight from the front of the half-track back across the steel-plated viewing slits, he quickly changed his firing plan again. The bazooka moved slightly as Smoker inserted the round and clicked off. He felt him tap his shoulder. He fired.

His first rocket went right through the left viewing slit, the weapon's back-blast blowing juniper branches toward the cliff edge. The round exploded inside the vehicle, a vivid red showing for a second through the hole and other slit, the thunder of the explosion muffled. Then there was a strange hissing, like air rushing out of a punctured tire.

Smoker tapped his shoulder again. This second round smashed into the front corner of the van box. There was another red flash, muffled explosion. Then the entire vehicle blew up with a sucking rush. The ground trembled. Things flew through the air, making smoky arcs.

One of the objects was a German soldier, his body twirling, covered with flames. He landed a stone's throw from their position, coming down on both feet, screaming, his legs already moving, running blindly as he tore at his clothing. They caught a glimpse of his face, contorted like a soul in Dante's Hell, caught a whiff of burning flesh that was instantly whipped away by the wind.

Father Emmanuel leaped up, tried to grab the man. The soldier ran past him. A second later, he disappeared over the cliff, the light of his flames etching the rim for a second and then vanishing. He screamed all the way down, the wind riffling the sound.

Wyatt felt his lips draw back against his teeth, felt his face go stiff. The bazooka shifted. He felt Smoker's tap. Quietly, calmly, he fired, putting the last rocket dead-center into the generator trailer, which blew it to pieces.

At 5:13, Major Land was awakened by a runner from Seventh Army headquarters with a deciphered message from Duboudin. He was billeted with another intelligence officer in one of the rooms of the bomb-shattered Hotel des Quatrans in central Caen.

He read the message in his undershorts. It said: *codex 855//IN des major land v Nicholas: rumor british intelli-*

gence operative and american special forces officer now in Cherbourg . . . purpose uncertain. xxxxxx

Land ordered the runner to notify Colonel Franze Weinbach that he would be in immediately. Wienbach was now command officer for Generaloberst Dollman's Seventh Army intelligence section.

He quickly completed his toilet, washing his face in a bucket of fresh water, dressed, and headed across the two blocks to the Chateau de Caen, the enormous fortress begun by William the Conqueror in 1060, which now served as Dollman's headquarters.

The city lay in shambles from constant Allied air attacks. Tall piles of rubble and deep shell holes filled the streets. Most of the buildings were damaged, some completely gone. There had been huge fires in several sections and now the cold dawn air was rank with the stench of burnt stone and explosive powder and death rot. A few citizens, some children, poked among the ruins.

Weinbach was highly agitated, chain-smoking as he darted about the intelligence section, a large room with vaulted ceilings and ornate pillars. It was filled with radio operators and clacking teletypes that gathered updated reports from field units of the I and LXVII Panzer Corps, which were now handling the defense of Caen. Tactical field maps were taped all over the ancient stone walls.

The colonel was a short, powerfully built man, pectorals showing clearly through his shirt. He had a round face, closely clipped black hair, and a week's growth of stubble that made him look like a waterfront thug. He saw Land and boomed across the room, "You have seen your agent's message?"

"Yes, sir," Land answered, moving quickly to the colonel's side.

"Come with me," Weinbach snapped. "There is something I want you to see." He hurried to a map of the Cotentin, pointed at it. "Our only two northern mobile radar units have suddenly disappeared. Somewhere between St-Pierre Eglise and the Point."

"Disappeared?"

"We've received no reports from them since 0200." He turned his head, glared at the major. "Put your agent's message with that fact and what do you see?"

Land studied the map for a long moment, then said, "A possible sea attack against Cherbourg."

"Precisely. Very probably a commando raid in force."

"Then, sir, I'd advise you notify von Schlieben immediately so he can shift troops to the harbor entrance and dispatch patrol boats."

"Already done."

A sergeant approached. "Excuse me, *Oberst*, a report from—"

The colonel cut him off harshly. "Yes, yes, in a moment." He turned back to Land. "I have a specific task for you, Major. You're a tank man so you'll know. I want combat-status reports on the Second and the Lehr." The 2nd Panzer and the Panzer Lehr were the two armored divisions west of Caen. "By evening."

"Yes, sir," Land said. He braced, spun, and hurried away.

Parnell opened his eyes to near darkness, just a single line of light from under the doorway. Instinctively, he reached for his weapon, this time only a Colt .45 resting beside his hip. He lay, listening.

He was stretched out on a mattress and wool blanket that smelled of old woman and cigar smoke, on the floor off Madame Chaffin's bedroom. He and Anabel had slept there, Sinclair on the bed. He remembered the look of the room in lamplight: small, done in shades of red with a vanity on curlicue legs, a brass bed, on one side a curtained bathroom containing a toilet with a wooden box above it and a long pull chain and a claw-footed porcelain tub, a douche bag hanging from its spigot and the area smelling of vinegar douche. The place had a flouncy, nineteenth-century feel, cancan girls and Toulouse-Lautrec posters.

They had both bathed before retiring, glad to get the coating of salt off their bodies. The three-in-the-morning silence had been broken only by the always-present distant rumble of artillery. He had slept fully clothed, Anabel in panties and a sweater. They didn't say much to each other before she turned off the bedside lamp. Red noticed that there were ashtrays with cigar butts and half-empty bottles of gin on the side table. Apparently Madame Chaffin enjoyed entertaining.

There was a light tap on the door and Anabel eased it open. "You up?"

"Yeah."

She came in carrying two mugs of coffee. He sat up, took one of the mugs. Anabel moved to the window and slid back the blackout curtains, filling the room with sunlight. Outside lay waters of an estuary of the Commerce Basin, dazzling in morning sunlight. Directly across from them was a dockside where fishing boats were moored.

She sat on the edge of the bed, one leg curled up under her. "How'd you sleep?"

"Okay." It wasn't exactly true. Like all combat veterans, Red was never quite able to come down completely, let himself go into deep sleep. Instead, he would drop into a watchful slumbering, coming back to consciousness periodically before drifting away again. "You?" he said.

"Not so hot."

"Where's Mascot?"

"At work, I guess." She laughed lightly. "I can't picture her welding. Then, again, I can. She's a spiky lady."

"Mm." The coffee was heavy and very powerful. It warmed the inside of his mouth, drew off the gummy taste of sleep. They sat quietly. The sounds of machinery seeped into the room, a woman called to someone.

He looked up to see Anabel watching him. Their eyes held. She said, "Do you ever get really frightened, Parnell?"

"All the time."

"Does it ever go away?"

"No. You just learn to live with it."

She inhaled, brushed a hand through her short dark hair. She looked very pretty sitting there, now taking a sip of coffee and holding the mug with both hands, so youthful, like a teenage girl at a slumber party. He saw the smooth curve of one leg against the bottom of the sweater and felt a tight sexual urge riffle through him. He looked away.

"You know, you still haven't answered my question," Anabel said.

"What question's that?"

"Why you dislike me."

"Not *that* again."

"You know what I think?" she said. "I think it's because you want me and won't admit it."

He turned back to her. She was smiling slightly, but it seemed much more than playful coquettishness. "That's what you think, huh?"

"I see the way you look at me."

"I suspect a lot of men look at you."

She didn't answer immediately. Instead, she simply

looked back into his eyes. Finally, she said, "But those can't have me."

The tightness he'd felt a moment before blossomed fully, a warmth that spread all through his groin, up into his belly. He sat there, feeling suddenly, uncomfortably juvenile.

"Is it because you're just too scared to let yourself feel human again?" Anabel said.

He chuckled, embarrassed. "You don't have to feel anything but horny for a roll in the hay."

She closed her eyes, her mouth curved up in dimpled frustration. "You truly *are* an ass."

The moment hung in the air like static electricity. Red felt his scalp tingle, felt desire well like a wind. Before he even realized it, he was on his knees, moving to the edge of the bed. When Anabel opened her eyes again, their faces were inches apart. He saw her irises widen for a moment, then a dark smokiness come into them, and he kissed her, gently, then harder, feeling her tongue probe his lips and taking it, drawing it into his mouth.

In urgent haste they undressed and lay naked on Madame Chaffin's brass bed, exploring each other quickly, Parnell feeling his body growing in power and possessiveness. They made love as hungrily as sweethearts who had not seen each other for a long time. When he entered her, she was heatedly moist and sighed and clung to him as they lunged together, Anabel whispering and moaning and then arching up tightly, her face contorted. A few moments later, he too reached orgasm and buried his face in her hair.

No words were spoken. They simply continued fondling and caressing each other, Parnell touching all of her with fingers and tongue. They made love again, this time with Sinclair above him, charging on and on and on until they were both spent, panting. Slowly they came down and Anabel inhaled deeply and whispered, "My *God*, that was good."

Heated silence.

Finally, she slipped from the bed and went to the bathroom, pulling the curtain, the rings making a little metallic rustling. He caught the strong odor of vinegar, heard water dribbling into the bottom of the tub. After a while, she came out, pulled on her sweater, not looking at him, and went to the window. She stood gazing out at the sunlit basin.

"Is something wrong?" he asked.

She shook her head. "You're the first one I've been with since my husband." Her voice was so soft he hardly caught the words. He didn't know how to answer that. He slid his legs over the bed and began pulling on his trousers.

"May I have a cigarette?" she asked.

He glanced up, surprised. "I didn't think you smoked."

"I'm starting again."

He took out his pack of ration Luckies, handed her one, and lit it with his Zippo. She turned back to the window, one arm across her breasts, the other resting on the back of her hand.

He paused, studying her, noting her nicely shaped legs, the sweet, round curvature of her buttocks below the sweater, the skin of them showing slightly red where he had clenched her as he plunged. From somewhere down the bank he heard a dog bark, then another.

She said, "I feel like I've just made a big mistake."

"Oh?" He sounded defensive.

"No, it's not what you think." She stopped, was thoughtful for a moment. "When my husband was killed, I had a terrible sense of guilt. You know? There I was alive in my safe, petty little world and he was dead. That's why I joined the

SOE, so I could kill Germans. I hated the bastards so much. That's what got me through some rough spots in training, kept me going. It's the same thing that allows me to handle what I see over here. A motive to explain it all."

She turned and looked at him. "Now I've undone it." She came and sat beside him, frowning, trying to explain. "Hell, I don't know how to put it . . . I accused you of no longer being able to feel human, didn't I? God, what rubbish. You were right, Parnell. Over here when you feel too much, you die. On the *inside* if nowhere else. There's no place in war for emotions, *any* emotions."

"No. You're just learning what we all had to learn. It'll take time. And this"—he nodded at the bed—"this was only—"

She cut him off sharply. "Don't say it, Parnell. Please, just don't say it."

He stopped.

"I think I'm falling in love with you." She said it simply, matter-of-fact. Then she gave him a crooked, sad, helpless smile. "God help me, I already have."

That jolted him. *Wait a minute,* he thought, shaken, *hold it right there.* He stared at her and realized the sudden rush of exhilaration he was feeling was also mixed shock. *She loved him!* But goddammit, it was *nuts!* Love here, now, in this insane place?

He didn't have time to think any more about it. He heard the front door of the shanty suddenly slam open and he was scrambling for his weapon, clothing, Anabel doing the same.

A moment later, Giselle Chaffin lunged through the bedroom door. "Gestapo!" she hissed. "They're coming!"

Chapter Ten

The space was barely a foot and a half high, three feet wide. It ran the length of the shanty, down under the floor of Giselle's kitchen, the place hot and airless, foul-smelling with rat feces and moisture-soaked wood and flaking caulking. Pipes from the sink ran through the flooring, their metal rusted and the rubber seals hardened and cracked. Earlier, they had stowed their equipment bags and automatic weapons down here. Now Parnell and Sinclair were crunched together, making no sound, even breathing softly, listening.

Four minutes after they entered the hiding hole, Gestapo agents pounded on the front door and then burst in, the waterborne shanty rocking slightly from their sudden weight. Boots pounded directly over their heads, moved about. They could hear the Germans talking to Chaffin, her talking back in a mixed patois of Kraut and French. They followed the footsteps throughout the house, fading at the other end, heard things crash to the floor. Then they were back in the kitchen, directly overhead again, stomping on the boards.

Parnell brought his hand up along his body holding the Colt .45. He rested it beside his chin as a heavy drop of sweat ran off his forehead and into his right eye, stinging. There hadn't been time to extract and assemble his Thompson, just enough to slam a round into the pistol as they scrambled down into the hiding hole, Giselle's face peering down through the narrow trapdoor, then closing it, sinking them into a pitch-darkness.

He lay there aware of the thick pounding of his heart. Anabel's body, still only in sweater and panties, pressed tightly against him, so close he could smell her hair, French soap, the faint muskiness of their lovemaking. He wore only his trousers and one sock. The rest of their clothing was stuffed between them and the bulkhead. He felt her heart racing, too, the thudding of it coming through the flesh of her throat.

The minutes seemed eternal. Red could swear he actually felt the seconds moving through the darkness, dragging past as sluggishly as caissons in deep mud. *She loves me.* The thought leaped out at him. No, he refused to look at it. Couldn't help it, came back to it, then veered away again. He flexed his finger along the side of the pistol's trigger guard, felt the distracting smoothness of the metal.

At last another Gestapo man came to the door and shouted something. The others left, the shanty rocking again. They waited. Madame Chaffin didn't open the trapdoor immediately. They listened to her lighter steps moving about. Finally, there was a click, the squeak of hinges, and light came down into the blackness.

Huddled in the kitchen, cautiously peering out the window, Parnell said to Giselle, "Jesus, we were lucky you showed up when you did."

"I told you to listen for the dogs, idiot," she said angrily. She still had her work coveralls on, stained with welding powder and grease, goggles around her neck. "And you better also thank Him they weren't SS Einsatz kommandos. We'd all be dead right now."

"How'd you know they were coming here?" Anabel asked.

"I heard a rumor that intense sweeps were in effect. Since early this morning."

"You can just walk off your job like that?"

The Frenchwoman chuckled. "My German supervisor thinks I sleep with *Wehrmacht* officers. I told him a captain friend of mine was in great need of a good fuck before he returned to the fighting."

"And he believed it?"

"He's too afraid not to. Besides laying the officers, I also lay a sweet welder's bead." The laughter snapped out of her eyes. "I don't like how sudden these sweeps came. No warnings. That means they were looking for something very specific. Like maybe two Allied agents newly arrived?"

Red and Anabel exchanged shocked looks. "That's not possible," she said. "Only Parnell, his team, and I knew about our mission."

"And the priest?" Parnell said.

"Father Benjeloun? No, I won't believe that. His parents were *killed* by the Germans in Libya, for God's sake. He'd *never* help the Nazis."

"It got out somehow."

"Maybe somebody just put the pieces together."

Giselle interrupted. "It doesn't matter now. What does matter is that it's going to be more difficult to move." She was thoughtful for a moment. "*Attendez,* you both be ready when I get back. We'll leave as soon as darkness comes. I don't think the Germans will return. But damn it, *fais gaffe,* listen for the dogs this time."

She left.

* * *

Charles Milassin had a grossness about him that was like an odor. His code name was Lalba. A railroad worker stationed at Coutances at the base of the Cotentin, he was always filthy with grease and Babbitt powder on his hands and clothing. Once a staunch Socialist and member of the *Confederation Generale du Travail*, the French Confederation of Labor Unions, he was now a bitter enemy of the Communists who had taken over the CGT. As a circuit courier, he was one of Duboudin's selected agents working for the Germans.

He was to meet Vaillant this forenoon in the tiny hamlet of Caillou dur Seulles four miles west of Coutances. It sat beside a stream, barely a dozen houses of stone and thatch. All had been badly damaged by Allied strafing runs targeting German columns moving through the pastureland that surrounded the town. Now it was deserted.

Duboudin waited inside the kitchen of the last house in line, the one nearest the stream. Most of it had been destroyed by the 20mm cannons and .50-caliber machine guns of American P-51s. The kitchen was strewn with stone rubble, pieces of furniture, and crushed cooking utensils. A large woodstove stood at the opposite wall beside which Vaillant had rested his bicycle. Rats rustled behind the stove.

Angered by Milassin's tardiness, he paced, pausing now and then to study the approach road through a blast hole in the kitchen wall. Across the stream stretched pastureland, the grass deep and richly green.

A German burial detail had dug a line of graves about fifty yards from the stream, the area looking like a scar in the grass. There were twenty-two mounds of raw earth, each with a small white wooden cross at the head. A hawk drifted past, casting its shadow on the graves, searching out mice hunting insects in the newly turned earth.

At last, he saw a pug-nosed, flatbed truck approaching. It was Milassin, railroad tool boxes and acetylene equipment strapped down on the back of the vehicle. The courier skidded to a stop on the stream's stone bridge and surveyed the hamlet. Duboudin waved him in.

"Must you *always* be late?" Duboudin snapped harshly at him as he crawled through the rubble of the front door.

"What difference?" Milissan said sarcastically. "The war moves slowly, does it not?" He had a bulbous face filled with fever scars on his cheeks, which he puffed up for a moment and then spat out a stream of dark tobacco juice.

"You have the money?" Vaillant demanded.

"Of course."

"How much this time?"

"Fifty thousand."

These were occupational francs counterfeited by the Gestapo. Periodically they were supplied to their buried agents to pass on to members of the Resistance. Each bill contained a tiny code visible under ultraviolet light that gave the Nazis a way of tracing it back to the Underground.

"All right, let's get on with it."

The sound of a speeding vehicle came drifting through the shell hole. Cautiously both men peered out at the approach road, finally spotted a German Volkswagen officer's car. It flew over the bridge and pulled up beside Milassin's truck. Three German soldiers dressed in black Panzer uniforms got out. One was an *Oberleutnant*, the other two *Oberschutze*, ordinary tank men armed with MP-40s.

Without hesitation, they approached the house and stepped through the doorway. The officer was tall, lean, with a thin mustache. He pointed his Luger at the two

Frenchmen and snapped in German, "Who are you? What are you doing here?"

Duboudin smiled pleasantly. "*Guten morgen, Herr Leutnant,*" he said. "We are merely two friends about the Führer's work."

"Is that so? And what would that be?"

"We are counterintelligence agents working with General von Rundstadt's intelligence section. My code name is Nicholas. If you will contact a Major Land in Caen, he will verify what I say."

The lieutenant turned his eyes to Milassin. "And you would be Lalba, then?"

"Yes," Milassin said. Then he turned and frowned at Vaillant.

Duboudin's heart jumped. *How does he know that? He shouldn't know that!* He watched the German lieutenant smile suddenly and say in English, "Damn bloody stupid of you chaps." He shot Milassin in the forehead.

Then things happened so fast Vaillant was never quite sure afterward what the sequence had been. Milassin falling backward as a solid chunk of blood blew out the back of his head, then something rolling from under the stove. *Mon Dieu!* A German Eihandgranate 39, round as an ostrich egg, the sizzle of its igniter like the hiss of a snake. The grenade tumbled and turned and everyone threw themselves backward. It went off with a blinding flash, the sound so close it was almost muffled, the quarter pound of TNT hurling shrapnel.

Stunned, he lay on the stone trying to connect things in his head, half-thoughts flying. *Who? How?* He felt himself trying to rise. God, so difficult. He put a hand flat against stone, pushed. The ringing in his ears rose to a stinging pitch. He looked over his shoulder.

The three Germans, no, they were *not* but *Englishmen!*

One was crawling toward the wall. He blindly rammed his bloody head into it, numbly turned, and started back. The other two were obviously dead, twisted in those heavy, carelessly thrown positions of death.

A French boy of about fourteen abruptly squirmed out from behind the stove. He had dirty brown hair and a soot-smeared face. His right arm hung limply with a filthy bandage around the elbow. He started across the kitchen, not looking at anything.

Vaillant fell onto his back again. He clawed for his sidearm, brought out a Walther .38. His head hummed. He lifted, pointed the weapon, and shot the Englishman in the shoulder, again in the top of his head. He slumped. Duboudin turned slowly, looked at the boy. *He knows I'm a counteragent now.*

He killed him.

Red and Anabel had waited out the long day and drawn-out twilight, alert and watchful, listening for the dogs and cautiously peering through windows. They did not make love again, nor even speak of it.

Parnell continually watched Anabel on the sly. She'd catch him at it and hold his eyes for a moment, then turn away. He still couldn't formulate what to say to her. Yet he had the profound feeling that suddenly things had changed and would never quite be the same again. As in everything, it was a winning and a losing, all at the same time.

Early in the afternoon they heard Allied bombers crossing overhead, headed in to hit the German defensive line six miles to the east, the deep droning of Lancasters and B-17s in triple Vs up very high. The German AA guns opened up immediately, the racket of their explosions scattered and random, like carnival fireworks.

The sky was filled with sudden puffs of black smoke and, as they watched, first one and then another American aircraft was hit, sudden bursts of light in their fuselages and flakes of debris flying out. Both planes turned aside as if veering and then rolled into slow-motion wingovers that went into agonizingly ponderous spiraling as they fell to earth. Only four crewmen's chutes popped into view like tiny blossoms drifting in the wind.

It wasn't until after 9:00 that the twilight finally left the sky completely. An hour later, Chaffin came for them. They crossed the secondary basin in a rowboat called a *canot*, flat as a slab, Parnell working the oars, the women in the stern. They could hear vehicles and half-tracks moving somewhere near the basin, but only tiny colored lights were visible.

They reached the opposite shore, Old Town Cherbourg, near a partially sunken barge. People were living on its above-water stern section. They silently watched the three of them pass. Centuries before, this entire area had been a marshland. Now it was a thick warren of decrepit houses and empty nineteenth-century industrial buildings that stretched away from the maritime section of New Cherbourg.

Chaffin led them through dark alleys strewn with refuse, narrow as coffins, quickly across thoroughfares. Despite the German-imposed curfew, shadowy figures loitered in wall recesses and prostitutes openly strolled in their aimless promenades. They whistled at Parnell as they passed. Dim red lights hung over stairs leading down to cellar saloons and bordellos.

They came to a series of ramshackle tenements. Giselle told them to wait. She went up to the first door and lightly knocked. A man peered out, said something, then closed the door. In a moment, he reappeared wearing only undershorts, T-shirt, and boots. He unlocked a large door, swung it up, then silently went back into his apartment.

A small black Fiat taxicab shaped like a loaf of bread was parked inside, the rest of the space filled with paint cans and tarps and painter's tools. Chaffin waved them in. They climbed into the cab, Red and Anabel in the back. It had torn seats and stank of vomit. Giselle backed the cab into the street, went back to close the garage door, then drove slowly up the avenue, the masked headlights casting tiny rectangles of blue light on the cobblestones.

It was a German checkpoint, red lights and sawhorses across the road, a personnel carrier and two motorcycle policemen parked on the Rue Rossel, east of the Commercial Basin.

Chaffin said, "*Oh, merde!*" and eased the taxicab to a stop. She leaned her arm over the seat. "We got Pigs! Get out your papers, hurry." To Parnell, "And you, get your Arabic ready, *mon ami.*"

Parnell looked out through the windshield, his mind jumping. He instantly thought about their gear bags and radio, up in the rear wheel wells. If the Krauts gave the vehicle a thorough examination, they'd find them sure as hell. It would be all over.

"Maybe we can back up," Anabel said to Giselle.

"*Non.* They've undoubtedly seen us."

Red caught a thought, mentally examined it. It *might* work. Damn well better. He turned to Sinclair. "Strip off your clothes."

"What?"

"Get naked, fast." He tapped Chaffin's arm. "I'm getting a piece of ass off a whore. You understand?"

Chaffin grinned. "*Ah, bien oui,* I see, I see."

Anabel hurriedly disrobed, giving him a stare. "Whore, huh?" she murmured. She got her sweater off, her bra, slipped out of her shoes and trousers, Giselle already moving the taxicab forward. Then the panties were gone onto the floor and Parnell pulled down his pants and shorts and made to mount her, one of her legs up and hooked around the small of his back, the other resting on the floor. He started to kiss her, stopped, remembering that you never kissed a whore.

Two German soldiers approached the vehicle, MP-40s and magazine pouches across their chests, their helmets etched in blue from the taxicab's slit headlights. He shone a flashlight on Chaffin. "What are you doing here?" he barked.

"Completing my final fare, *mein Herr*," she answered in German. "Then I go home."

From the backseat, Parnell popped his head up, rambled off some Arabic jibberish, his voice making it sound as if he was angrily asking, "What is this?"

The Kraut skidded his flash's beam into the backseat, the light showing Red scowling, Anabel sitting up, insolently brushing back her hair. One arm lay halfheartedly across one breast. The other breast looked nakedly smooth and creamy in the harsh light.

The German laughed, said something to his companion, who peered over his shoulder and laughed, too. Both wore the battle tunics and green-on-black insignia of infantrymen. The first man said to Chaffin. "Your papers, *Tussi*." She handed him her ID card and the cab's registration. He studied both closely, looked up. "This is not your vehicle."

"*Nein*, it belongs to my brother. He is ill tonight."

"What is his birthdate?" he shot back.

"January the sixth."

The Kraut handed Giselle's papers back, pinioned Parnell in the light again. "You two, papers. *Auf die Schnelle!*" Red and Anabel had already withdrawn their papers. They handed them over. The soldier also studied them meticulously, holding the flashlight close to the cards, lifting it to their faces to compare the photos. After a moment, he held the beam on Parnell's face. "What is your name?"

"He doesn't speak German," Giselle quickly interjected.

"Then ask him in French."

"He doesn't speak that, either. I think he's Egyptian."

"I want your name, *Schweinehund,*" the soldier shouted, pointing at the ID card, then at Red. "Your fucking name, you know, *name?*"

Red went "Ah," like he had just gotten it, nodding. "Zahi Hawass."

"*Agypterin?*"

Red pointed at his papers, rattled off more Arabic. The soldier swore impatiently and shifted the cards in his hand, going to Anabel's. He read it, his head tilted, snorted, and put his light on her. "You are a seamstress?"

"Yes," Sinclair answered him in German.

"But you fuck for money."

"Of course." Sounding very cool.

"How much do you charge?" He played his light over her face, then her breasts, and finally lowered its spot to her crotch, letting it linger there.

"Five hundred, francs occupation," Anabel said.

The light darted back to her face. "*Scheisse!* You are so good?"

"But of course."

"Maybe I try you myself."

"Any time, *Liebling.*"

"Maybe now."

She shrugged nonchalantly. "When I finish with this fish-smelling sailor, you pay me and we have much fun."

He chuckled, shook his head. "Not this time, *Hure.* Now you pay *me.*" He disdainfully flipped their cards back at them, rested the back of his hand on the windowsill, and made come-on movements with his fingers. "Hand it over . . . everybody, *Verdammte Scheise.*"

They gave him all they had, Parnell acting stupid until Anabel cursed and took his money from his pants. Then he angrily started throwing Arabic phrases again, shouting, "*Tsenna, tsenna, wash kain shi tubis lmatar!*" Translated it said, "Wait, wait, is there a bus to the airport?"

The German pocketed the wad of bills and whistled toward the parked vehicles. One of the motorcycle riders dismounted and moved a sawhorse to make an opening in the barrier. The one with the money jacked his thumb in the air and said to Giselle, "All right, *verzich dich!*" She geared up, moving slowly through the sawhorses, and disappeared back into the night.

Parnell watched Anabel as she quickly redressed. Finally, he asked jokingly, "What would you have done if he'd called your bluff?"

She pulled on her sweater, gave him a hard look over the shoulder. "Whatever a whore would do," she snapped.

The Rue Rossel was the main avenue out of Cherbourg and led into the foothills of the Montagne du Roule. Within a few minutes, they could smell the rich odor of rape fields and cattle on the night air. A mile beyond the Kraut checkpoint, the road began a gradual climb.

Chaffin abruptly swung the taxicab off the avenue and onto a rutty dirt road and quickly parked in a stand of scrub oak. "German column coming," she said tightly. A few minutes later a line of German military vehicles approached and rumbled past, a stream of blue lights, half-tracks, and armored cars and Opel three-tonners filled with soldiers, the vehicles dust-covered and battle-scarred. It took twenty minutes for the column to pass.

By 1:00 in the morning, they left the Rue Rossel for good and went up another narrow dirt road. It passed through a small meadow and then climbed swiftly up into stands of beech and cottonwood. A half hour later, she stopped and told them to get out. They were among pine trees, pitch-dark, the ocean-smelling breeze brisk and wet-cold.

Quickly retrieving their gear bags, Parnell and Sinclair followed as Giselle double-timed it up a narrow footpath using a small red flashlight that made everything look eerie. The path wound among rock faces, dipped into ravines and up along ridges, always climbing. In some places it was so steep they had to haul themselves up by grabbing roots and rock holes.

At last they reached an overlook, a small rock promontory that protruded from a limestone sheer that was pockmarked with small caves. Up here, the wind was gusty and made their sweat feel like ice. Two thousand feet below them, Cherbourg lay in darkness. Beyond it, the black sea stretched out, a darker darkness that went out to a horizon line over which the flood of stars shone, sharp flecks of light holding motionless.

There was no long good-bye. Chaffin simply wished them good luck, they thanked her, shook hands, and then she was gone, back down the slope. Parnell chose one of the caves. It went in about fifteen feet, narrow at the back. There was a thick layer of powdery stone on the floor, and discarded wine bottles lying about.

They hauled their gear bags in, both of them suddenly, oddly awkward with each other, alone again. While Anabel assembled and charged their weapons, Red unbagged the transceiver and hooked up his Morse code key.

The instructions that had come in with the airdrop stipulated that as soon as they achieved their Cherbourg observation point, they would transmit a signal three times in Morse code. Then quickly switch to a second frequency so as to hear the acknowledgment. Finally, a third frequency would be used, this constantly guarded until they were raised by the Bombardment Force's monitor ship for further prestrike instructions. For this particular operation, the ship assigned was the American destroyer USS *Plunkett,* code-named Easter Basket.

At precisely 0203 hours, Parnell tapped out his arrival signal: *blue boy . . . paint dry . . . shellack.* Again and then again. He swung the dial, fixed on the second assigned frequency. Only static and white sound riffled through the speaker. Then a rapid string of dots came that indicated his message had been received by the monitor ship. The dots were simply the letter *e* in Morse code repeated rapidly. Each tiny pulse snapped like an ice crystal in the air.

Red fixed in the third frequency. Again there was only the furry nothingness of white sound. Fifteen seconds later Easter Basket came on again, this time with a full coded message: *shellack already applied . . . prepare for viewing on Easter.*

It told Parnell that the Bombardment Force was already on its way and would arrive at sunrise.

Since nightfall of the previous day, Collins's VII Corps had been staging all along the German defensive outside Cherbourg for the final offensive push to capture the crucial port city. In his vanguard, he had placed his most seasoned troops: the 9th Division on the left flank, the 79th in the center, and the 4th Division on the right.

Over the last three days, Collins's advance had continually met extremely stiff resistance with mounting casualties. Although the northern third of the Cotentin Peninsula was not *bocage* country, it was still highly defensive ground with low, rocky mountains, shallow but steep gorges interspersed with stretches of open savannah. All of it gave the Germans excellent enfilading fire positions against the front of the U.S. assaulting force. Still, by the twenty-fourth, Collins's forward units had achieved a semicircle about two miles from Cherbourg.

Now as dawn began to fuse up from the east, a massive Allied artillery barrage opened up. For forty-one minutes, 105mm and 75mm field howitzers along with rocket launchers hurled Time-on-Target fire against specific German strongpoints surrounding the port city. Then, at precisely 0602 hours, infantry units, supported by armor, moved to the attack along the entire German defensive line.

An hour after midnight, Admiral Deyo had received a last-minute adjustment to his Bombardment Forces' mission task protocol from First Army headquarters ashore in Normandy.

Originally, the admiral's MTP had called for a three-hour shelling of Cherbourg and the heavy coastal batteries to the west and north of the port. It was scheduled to commence at 0700 hours. Then General Bradley, at General Collins's insistence, changed it. He ordered that the gunship fire would last only ninety minutes, the targets would be specified by the army through its liaison officer, Colonel John Campbell, aboard the USS *Tuscaloosa*, and the barrage would not start until late in the morning.

Infuriated, Deyo immediately called Bradley. After a passionate pleading, he managed to garner permission to engage in direct fire against at least three of the coastal batteries at his discretion and he could send in counter-fire against any others that opened up against his ships.

Still, he was forced to alter his schedule, shift his approach lanes, and reposition his two Groups. By blinker he immediately notified his ship commanders of the change in orders. Soon after, the Bombardment Force began executing big 360s out in the Channel so as to elapse the difference between the old and new commence-fire times. The armada moved through a calm sea with only an eight-knot northwesterly breeze, their battle ensigns still furled.

However, the minesweeper squadrons had already made landfall some fifteen miles north of Cherbourg in Fire Support Area One. Before turning into their holding patterns, boatswain's pipes squealed through loudspeakers aboard the MSB ships, followed by, "Now here this. Stand by to recover trailing gear." A few moments later came, "Commence recovery. Train in and secure."

The bombardment of Cherbourg had just gone into full hold.

At 0414, the watch light on Parnell's radio indicated a message was coming through. Decoded, it said the bombardment had been postponed until late morning.

They had spread Madame Chaffin's map onto the floor of the cave. Laid over it was a clear plastic target-positioning sheet marked off in black inch squares. Each square represented a fifty-yard impact zone and carried a five-digit ID number.

This bombardment's procedure was slightly different from the one Parnell had used when he called in naval fire missions at Salerno. Since these salvos were going into Cherbourg itself, their impact zones had to be far more precise, the RPEs, or range probable errors, narrowed down so as to minimize colateral damage. That had been the main reason for an on-ground observer in the first place, to pinpoint specific targets within a smaller impact zone rather than using mere coordinates.

Now when Red called in fire missions, he would simply give the target's description and its square ID number. The monitoring ship would then assign the target's position and gun need to the proper ship whose fire-control system would then automatically translate the position into range, windage, and elevation data. After the first salvo, Parnell could then call in adjustments as he had done in Italy.

After decoding the message, Red had restlessly wandered back outside while Anabel curled up beside the radio and tried to grab some sleep. The cave dust smelled faintly sour and reminded her of the stables at the Cherry Point Horse Barn back in Chicago where her father had taught her to ride when she was a little girl.

Her mind tried to fix on that faraway time. It faded. She hurriedly drew up other memories, other places, other faces. They, too, faded. Hell, it was useless, she couldn't hold off thinking about Parnell. So okay, she decided defiantly, let's *think* about the son of a bitch. And immediately realized anew, as she had back in Giselle's bedroom, that she had made one damn fool mistake, telling him she loved him. Good *God*, what a schoolgirlish thing to do.

Well, she asked herself for the fiftieth time, *did* she love him? And answered herself, Yes, damn it. Why? Did something about him remind her of her father? His strength, his manly good looks? She sighed, dejected. Such questions were always stupid and useless. She had certainly been around long enough to know that nobody *ever* understood why they fell in love.

In her whole life she'd only said those particular words to four men: her father, fifteen-year-old Mathew Rawlings Kendrick, who had taken her fourteen-year-old virginity one snowy day in a Chicago loft, her dead husband, Leslie, and now Lieutenant John Parnell.

Well, damn!

Outside, the wind had died down, the air turning ever more predawn cold. For a moment, she listened to the intermittent rumble of guns sounding like bowling balls rolling in a near-deserted, four-o'clock in-the-morning alley. Quickly Parnell's face returned, in a rush, and again she saw the look of shock on his face he'd worn in Madame Chaffin's and felt again that stab of surprise, of rejection, and then the countering anger. *Stupid, stupid.*

She didn't hear him, or sense his presence, until his hand touched her cheek, soft as a whisper. Her eyes snapped open, she turned her head. His shadow was right there. She caught the man-smell of him, dimly saw his eyes holding the faint reflection from the radio's watch light.

He leaned forward and kissed her, gently, then simply brushed his lips back and forth across hers. She reached up to caress his face. They pulled apart, looked into each other's eyes, seeing and not seeing, feeling, and then knowing.

He said, "Baby, I—"

She stopped his words with her fingertips. They would have been superfluous. He kissed her again, stretched out beside her. They held each other, not speaking, hands exploring until neither could bear the desire any longer and they pulled off clothing and he made love to her, slowly and deeply this time, both murmuring, their voices rising breathlessly as each rose into another place, shuddering. Afterward, they lay together and watched the light at the mouth of the cave grow ever brighter.

Then the barrage guns started.

Forward headquarters of 2nd Battalion, 105th Infantry of the 79th Division, was set up in what had once been an open-air café in the southwestern suburb of Cherbourg. It was called the Istanbul. The opening American barrage had nearly destroyed it, hurling most of its front facade out into the Rue de Tanneries. From two blocks to the north came the clatter of small arms, the cracking blow of rifle-grenades, and the occasional jolting backlash of a tank round as the battalion's forward assault units engaged the Germans in street-to-street firefights. It was 0647 hours.

Sergeant Wyatt Bird wove his way through parked vehicles, paused to peer through the café's rear door, then stepped through and briskly approached a lieutenant seated at the bar, studying several patrol maps spread out in front of him. The space was littered with broken bottles and furniture. Some of the tables were still set with cloths and eating utensils, everything covered with explosion dust. Four battalion staff officers were huddled around one of them, which had been brushed clean.

"Sir," Wyatt barked, snapping to attention. "May I have a word, Lieutenant?"

The officer turned his head, frowning, irritated. He had a narrow face, stubble-darkened. "What is it?" he snapped.

"I'd like to request a temporary assignment for me and my men, sir?"

The lieutenant leaned slightly to the side so as to see Wyatt's Mohawk shoulder patch. He jacked his chin at it. "What the hell outfit is that?"

"A special recon unit, sir."

"How many men?"

"Four, sir."

"That's it? Only four?"

"Yes, sir. We've been on a special op out at Cap de la Hague."

The captain's eyebrows lifted. "Behind enemy lines?"

"Yes, sir."

The captain grunted. "Were you successful?"

"Yes, sir."

Following their attack on the radar truck, Wyatt, Smoker, and Father Emmanuel had moved east, following the cliff line to link with Cowboy and Laguna. Soon after, the priest left to return to his village. The team continued on along the coast until they reached the outskirts of Querqueville where they began spotting German patrols and truck columns. Veering south, they crossed Highway S-29, then turned east again, searching for the Allied lines outside Cherbourg.

Just after dawn, they spotted a column of four American Sherman M4 tanks racing along a meadow road. They were painted a brown-and-cream camouflage, their long-barrel .50-caliber machine guns cranked up. Tree branches were affixed to the turrets and aprons.

Bird and the others stood out in the road with their Thompsons held over their heads. The commander in the lead tank held up his arm and it skidded to a stop about fifty yards from them, the others doing the same, slightly flared off the road, protecting the platoon leader's flanks against ambush. Slowly their ball-mounted hull machine guns swiveled until they were trained directly at Blue Team. Nobody moved.

Suddenly, a roaring burst echoed in the air and two P-47 Thunderbolts appeared from below a low, coastal hill. They went flashing close overhead, chunky and silver, their big Pratt & Whitney R-2800 radials leaving prop-wash trails in the savannah grass. They carried napalm canisters and drop tanks and were gone in the blink of an eye, hugging the contour of the land.

As the sound of their passing riffled off, the lead tank commander climbed out of the turret. He was a sergeant in tanker's coveralls and helmet and carried a Thompson with the butt resting in the crook of his right arm. With his other arm, he pointed at the ground in front of Wyatt and the others and shouted, "*Waffe, der boden. Schnell,* you sons a' bitches, *schnell.*"

They laid their weapons down, straightened. "Hey, cousin," Bird hollered back, "we're Americans, for chrissakes."

The sergeant studied them a moment, turned his head, spat, came back. "Americans, huh? What outfit?"

"Mohawkers."

"Mohawkers? What the hell outfit's that?"

"Special recon, detatched."

The sergeant sucked air through his teeth. He had heavy stubble and a crushed pack of Chesterfield cigarettes rubber-banded to his helmet. He nodded toward Bird. "You, advance up here." Bird walked slowly to the tank. By the time he got there, the sergeant had moved to the edge of the tank's apron. "Let's see your dog tags, buddy," he said.

Wyatt hooked his thumb under his neck chain, pulled it free of his shirt, and held out the tags. The tanker leaned out to peer at them, then grunted. "Okay, I guess you boys're all right." He grinned. "Sorry, Mac. We been gettin' rumors Kraut deserters are sneaking through our lines wearing GI uniforms."

Wyatt turned, waved the others in.

"Where you headed?" the tank commander asked.

"To any CP on the line."

"Climb aboard. You just became *mo*-bile," the sergeant said.

A voice called across the café, "Bird? By God, is that you?"

The lieutenant glanced up. Wyatt remained at attention. He felt a hand clap his left shoulder, a man saying, "At ease, at ease, Sergeant." Bird unbraced, turned to look into the broad smile of Major Patrick O'Donnel.

They shook. "How are you, sir?" Bird said, grinning back.

"You know this man?" the lieutenant asked.

"Hope to shit in your eye, I do," the major answered. He was short, slenderly built, and resembled a slightly aged Frank Sinatra. "Best damned platoon sergeant in the Twenty-fifth back at Schofield." He returned to Wyatt. "Last I heard you were still instructing at the AI school at Bliss."

Wyatt quickly explained.

"Special forces, huh?" O'Donnel said. "Well, that's about where I'd expect you to be, fella. Did you know old Lightning Joe's corps commander now?" Before being assigned to the European Theater as commander of VII Corps, General Collins had commanded the 25th Tropical Lightning Division stationed at Schofield Barracks, Honolulu, Bird's old outfit. That was how Collins had gotten his nickname. Soon after Pearl Harbor, he and his division were part of the bloody invasions of Guadalcanal and New Georgia in the Pacific.

"Yes, sir, I heard."

"So," O'Donnel said, "what do you need?"

"Our team leader's in Cherbourg with a buried British agent, sir. Acting FO for a naval barrage. We'd like to go in with one of your lead companies, see if we can locate him."

The major nodded. "Yeah, we were scheduled to get some Dixie Cup fire. But the sons a' bitches're late." He glanced at the lieutenant. "Is Company E still our point unit?"

"Yes."

"Arrange a runner for Sergeant Bird and his men, Frank." He turned back to Wyatt. "CO over there's a Lieutenant Dick Andrews. Tell him I sent you. Well, good luck."

"Thank you, sir," Bird said.

The final battle for Cherbourg proved to be a hell of a fight. From their mountain perch, Parnell and Sinclair watched the entire thing unfold down there below them, Sinclair's face flushed, staring, *Lord*, actually seeing a full-scale *battle* for the first time. No set-piece fighting here, instead a cauldron of fire and explosion, intensifying in one direction, then diminishing to allow another area to erupt.

Using binoculars, they were able to actually see individual squad-sized units of infantry probing the city's outskirts, house-to-house firefights with tanks giving cover, hauling up now and then to blast a building fifty yards away, blowing hell out of it. The rattle and boom of the fighting drifted up on the clear, warming morning air.

Earlier, as soon as the American assault barrage stopped, German field guns inside Cherbourg had opened up. Most seemed to be located around the main harbor and also from two small forts built onto the inner breakwater. Even some of the moored cargo ships began firing their stern pit guns from the dock. This brought instantaneous American counterfire. Unfortunately, it was blind fire, unspotted, and most of the rounds went uselessly into the harbor.

Twenty minutes after the beginning of the assault, they saw two U-boats exit the main submarine pen, swing about, and stand up the Commercial Basin, moving fast, one cutting the other's stern wave. Artillery rounds splashed harmlessly around them. They quickly reached the main harbor and went to flank speed, raced through the twin breakwaters, and made for open ocean. Soon their black hulls glided smoothly beneath the surface, both at the same time, the hulls remaining visible for a minute, twin shadows, and then they were gone.

Red cursed and went on cursing at the missed opportunity of nailing two prime targets, these U-boats going out to lay into the incoming Bombardment Force. The ships were barely visible out there on the rim of the horizon, at least two battleships, their hulls down. So many other prime targets, too.

He and Sinclair were stretched on their bellies, swinging their glasses from gun-flash to gun-flash, marking the positions on Chaffin's map overlay. Then Allied aircraft came screaming in from the sea, P-38s first, Admiral Deyo committing some of his air cover but holding back the Avengers. They flashed low over the breakwaters, their shadows skimming, trailing segmented streams of white smoke as their .50-caliber guns slammed rounds into the docks and train yards. But they didn't remain long because of fuel restrictions and soon headed back out to sea, leaving a few burning targets but nothing substantial.

Agonizingly the hours passed. The sun grew hot, heated the land, which drew in an offshore breeze. It pushed the pall of smoke and dust back against the surrounding hills. Nine o'clock came and passed. Then at 0932, the first German coastal battery opened on the Bombardment Force. This one was located ten miles west of Cherbourg at Gurchy, launching 150mm fire. Two minesweepers were immediately straddled and covering destroyers moved in with smoke and counterbattery fire. But their shells were apparently too small to silence the Kraut guns. The cruiser USS *Tuscaloosa* picked up the mission, hurling eight-inch gun salvos, which did the job.

Parnell whooped. "All *right*! Now let's start kicking some ass."

He was premature. Ten o'clock arrived, then eleven, and finally noon. Still no further fire from the ships. At 1122, the radio watch light began blinking, an incoming message. The speaker crackled, "Blue Boy, this is Easter Basket . . . stand by."

Jesus, at last! Parnell thought. He keyed, "Easter Basket, go ahead." Nothing else came back.

Thirty more minutes passed sluggishly. By now they could see two of the battleships with their cover destroyers moving farther west, Group 1 shifting into its new Fire Support Area. Then, at 1159, a powerful gun blast came from somewhere northeast of the city. It was so strong they had actually heard it over the general battle noise.

Anabel tapped Red's arm. "That's Battery Hamburg at Fermanville," she said. "Big eleven-inchers. Besides a whole cluster of smaller batteries. I wondered why they hadn't come online before now."

One of the battleships, the USS *Arkansas*, quickly got bracketed, huge geysers climbing up out of the sea close-in. As her cover destroyers laid smoke, she opened with counterbattery fire, her shells coming in in double banks, leaving streaks across the sky. But all fell short of the shore-line. The other battleship, USS *Texas*, surged forward and cut loose with fourteen-inch salvos. Red and Anabel watched fascinated. They didn't know it, but this was the first major gun duel of World War II between naval ships of the line and similarly powerful shore batteries.

The radio light blinked again. "Blue Boy, this is Easter Basket. Stand by for shoot relay, over."

Parnell pressed his mike button. "Easter Basket, standing by." He leaned over, studied the map overlay, quickly decided what his first target would be: the arsenal and its train yard.

"Blue Boy, go ahead."

Click. "Easter Basket. Request fire mission. Grid set three-four-four-niner-one. Main arsenal and train yard. HC only. Commence fire immediately." Since Armor-Piercing shells were useless against casemented guns, Parnell had asked for High-Capacity shells, which had instantaneous fuses and more general sundering power.

"Blue Boy, we have it."

Parnell put his head down, knowing what was happening out there: Easter Basket evaluating his FM's ordnance requirement, then passing it off to the necessary gunship capable of carrying it out.

He squinted against the glare off the ocean. Seventy-one seconds later, he saw double copper-colored flashes far out, halos of smoke blowing across the sea as four shell trails appeared like comets rising in that peculiar slow-motion way. At the same time, the radio crackled and a new operator came on, this one a fire-control radioman aboard the USS *Tuscaloosa.* "Salvo, Blue Boy," he said.

Red watched the salvo spread arcing, floating in, watched the individual shells hurtle the last few hundred yards rapidly as if they had suddenly been regripped by gravity. The ship's radioman said, "Splash, Blue Boy." And then the jolting impact as the shells struck a dock a hundred yards north of the arsenal. The explosions heaved dark geysers of smoke and debris into the air.

He keyed. "Blue Boy, two hundred right, one hundred down."

Another wait, more orange flashes and halos, another brace of shells coming in. These struck the arsenal on the northwestern side of its complex. Violent explosions. A small locomotive went spiraling into the air, boxcars, twisted track. Fire flashed through a main building.

"Dead on," Parnell shouted. "No change. Rapid fire for one minute." He swung to Anabel, shouted, "Mark the time." She nodded. He leaned over the map, scanning, again deciding target priority. He chose a battery of 88mm guns.

Anabel told him their position was Fort des Flamand, which sat on the eastern side of the harbor entrance. Earlier it had been slamming rapid-fire rounds at Collins's troopers attacking through the foothills. Counterartillery shelling had silenced it for a while. Now it was firing again.

Anabel called, "Mark sixty seconds."

He keyed. "Target neutralized. Good shooting. Blue Boy shifting fire to new target, over."

The *Tuscaloosa* fire control came right back: "Blue Boy, passing you off."

Almost immediately the monitor ship came on: "Blue Boy, Easter Basket. Go ahead."

"Request fire mission. Grid set three-four-three-one-six. Eighty-eight battery. Commence fire immediately."

"Blue Boy, hold for reassignment."

This time they had to wait two and a half minutes. Now a full-out naval battle was in progress, the battleships, including the USS *Nevada*, which had come up to assist the other two and was now exchanging with Battery Hamburg. The cruisers also shifted as they engaged other German shore batteries with direct fire, the ships out there about fifteen miles. Much closer in, the destroyers dashed all over hell, laying smoke to protect the minesweepers who were trying desperately to dodge the German shelling. The smoke was a dense gray white and thinned slowly in the mild wind, drifting sluggishly toward the shoreline.

Abruptly the new assigned gunship's fire-control operator came on: "Salvo, Blue Boy."

Now a tremendous explosion came as one of the powder magazines in the arsenal blew apart, erupting into a boiling cloud of black and gray smoke, the entire mass rising to eight hundred feet with tremendous speed, showing internal bursts of red as hot gasses continued igniting.

Distracted by the suddenness and size of the detonation, both Red and Anabel failed to watch the shell streaks of the incoming salvo until the ship's radioman notified them, "Splash, Blue Boy," just as the spread of four six-inch shells descended in a slight offset and struck Fort des Flamand dead center. Their explosions threw stone debris a hundred yards in all directions, scattering it across the water.

* * *

For the next eighty-three minutes, Parnell continued calling in fire missions, his mind filled with that dark, awed excitement that always hit him when he was able to control such massive firepower so efficiently. Lying beside him with her binoculars, Sinclair, her own face flushed and wide-eyed, continued calling out the target designations, cautiously avoiding reflections off her lenses since the sun had now passed the noon zenith. After each call, they had to wait longer and longer for a ship assignment since the Bombardment Force was still in full engagement with the German shore batteries.

Using fourteen-inch salvos from the *Nevada*, he demolished the main submarine pen, hurriedly shifted target, and took out the patrol boat base and smaller sub slips across the harbor. Next, he knocked out the two batteries that guarded the entrance through the outer breakwaters, Fort de l'Est and Fort du Centre.

Then the German jamming began, his radio erupting with a loud squealing that went up and back down low before rising again. Swearing, he twisted around and spun his frequency dial, brought up his second assigned transmit frequency, keyed, repeating over and over, "Easter Basket, Blue Boy. Receiving jamming on primary. Switch to secondary. Come back, over."

Four long minutes later, the Naval Gunfire Liaison Ship's operator came on: "Blue Boy, I have you. Proceed, over."

His next target was a nest of 75mm howitzers just west of the bridge that crossed the Commercial Basin. Then a five-truck column of trucks loaded with soldiers that was moving near the western edge of the harbor. Five minutes later, a double spread of five-inch fire came in. The gunship's Splash call was suddenly cut off as his radio again went off into a wild screeching.

Shit, they're triangulating us!

He turned, glanced at Anabel, and felt a sudden, jolting surge of fear go through his heart for her, the thought that she might be killed. He considered immediately breaking off transmitting and moving out. *No, not yet.* Once more he adjusted his frequency, went to the one he'd used for his initial contact with the Bombardment Force.

This time, the Easter Basket operator came right back, anticipating that Parnell would immediately go to this third frequency. "Blue Boy, I have you," he called. "Advise you vacate location. Enemy homing to your signal."

A burst of automatic fire slashed overhead, slammed into the sandstone face behind them. Parnell dropped his face to the ground. *Shit, they've found us!* He shot his eyes to Anabel. She was staring at him, her face gone stiff. Another spray of bullets cut overhead, sundering the air with loud percussions.

He heard the peculiar, hollow *thrup* of a mortar and his heart went to ice. He heaved himself to the left, landed on Sinclair, covering her, shouting, "Mortar!" He lay still, waiting out those long, tremulous moments while the missile arched in silently, his mind racing, replaying the sound of its firing tube, picturing it, trying to identify it: *Leichter Granatenwerfer 36 . . . platoon support weapon . . . 5cm, 2.2-pound shell . . .* What the hell was its range? Right, right: *four-hundred yards . . .*

Jesus, at least forty men and very close.

The double click of its fuse sounded just below them and then the impact explosion shook the rock promontory, bits of stone whirling up and past. Parnell waited, letting the flying debris settle. Then he shouted for Anabel to bring the map. He grabbed her by the sweater with one hand and the radio with the other and, half crawling, scrambled back to the cave, lunging in just as another sweep of bullets crashed against the cliff face above them.

He came up, his face inches from hers. "Find the grid reference for our position," he growled. She nodded mutely and smoothed out the map on the floor. Red keyed his mike. "Easter Basket, Blue Boy. Urgent. Request high-priority fire mission. Grid reference . . ." He turned. "Come on, come on."

Anabel was bent over the map and grid overlay, furiously running her fingers over the lined foothills of Montagne du Roule, searching out their present position.

"Easter Basket," Red said into the mike. "Stand by. . . . God dammit, *find* it."

"Here . . . yes, right here. Three-three-one-niner-three."

He quickly repeated it into the mike, adding, "Position under attack. Overrun imminent. Fire short, high-capacity. Smoke, if possible. Commence firing immediately."

The Easter Basket operator came back, "Negative, Blue Boy. No longer on FM status."

What the hell? Red keyed again. "Listen, you son of a bitch," he blurted. "I repeat, urgent, urgent."

"Blue Boy, hold for clearance. I repeat, hold—" The rest of it disappeared into a rising scream of static. The Germans had just jammed his last frequency.

Click, click.

The second mortar round exploded forty feet up the side of the cliff face. The floor of the cave heaved, dust showered down. They could hear the reverberations of it riffling way into deeper stone, sounding like collapsing bubbles in water.

Sweet Jesus! Parnell looked into Anabel's stark face. "We gotta get the hell outta here," he shouted. "They've bracketed us."

* * *

Three minutes earlier, Admiral Deyo, aboard his flagship, *Tuscaloosa*, readjusted his binoculars to sweep the shoreline with one final, slow scan. Much of it was now obscured in smoke and battle dust. Hundreds of small white birds, looking like bright confetti, flashed and twisted against the blackness of the smoke. The admiral had seen this strange phenomenon before during other naval bombardments.

Standing with him on the ship's port wing was the *Tuscaloosa*'s XO, Commander Erik Cole, along with a radio talker in his oversize helmet. A communications lieutenant approached. "Excuse me, Admiral," he said. "The deadline is coming up on one-twenty seconds, sir."

Deyo cursed and then cursed again, frustrated that Bradley's order had cut his barrage time in half. Those goddamned German coastal batteries were still plenty alive and now he'd have to cease fire and withdraw. It was bullshit.

He lowered his binoculars, glaring, then snapped to the lieutenant, "All right, signal the force to break off action and achieve steaming stations."

"Yes, sir."

Disgustedly, the admiral lifted his glasses again. He watched as blinker signals transmitted his order. One by one, the ships of the force stopped firing and began to wheel back toward open ocean. He felt the deck of the cruiser roll slightly as the captain put her into a shallow turn to starboard.

"Goddamned army," he growled.

"I second that, sir," Cole said.

Four minutes later, the communications officer again approached. "Admiral, a blinker message from *Plunkett*.

They've picked up an urgent fire call from their shore observer. He's under attack and about to be overrun. He's requested a shoot on his own position."

Deyo glanced at his watch: 1:34 P.M. Four minutes past Bradley's deadline. He squinted out at the shoreline for a moment, then turned to Cole. "Those are buried agents," he said. "If the Gestapo gets them, they're dead. And it won't be easy."

Cole nodded silently.

The admiral put his head down, scratched distractedly at his chin. Finally, he lifted his eyes, turned to the communications lieutenant. "Order *Plunkett* to assign the fire request. And inform the captain of whatever ship he chooses that this is being done on my specific order."

"Yes, sir." The young officer hurried away.

Deyo gave Cole another narrow-eyed look. "God help the poor sons a' bitches," he said.

Covering each other, Parnell and Sinclair managed to work their way off the promontory, down into heavy brush and scattered stands of pine trees. The brush was filled with tiny mosquitoes buzzing in the shadows. The German fire was sporadic now, occasional bursts, bullets whipping through the trees.

The brushy slope began to climb. They came to a narrow ravine, perhaps fifteen feet deep. There were exposed roots on the sides and the water-rounded stones on the bottom were covered with strings of moss. They dropped down into it and continued moving up, Anabel ahead, Red constantly watching their rear, pausing occasionally to listen. Once he heard a German voice calling far downslope, another answering close to his right.

His mind raced through dark thoughts. Anabel was an

agent, a *spy*. If they caught her, they'd put the torture to her and then hang her. He felt his insides heave at the image. An even darker reality came, a choice he might have to make. If there was no chance for escape, would he have to kill her to save her from what lay ahead?

No, Jesus, no!

They didn't hear the first salvo coming in. It was just there, a double spread of five-inch shells. Chaos exploded all around them. The ground violently lifted up with a horrendous sound and the air was suddenly sucked back, pulling at their skin, then rushing forward again, creating a wind as the concussion waves swept over them, ballooning their clothes. Rock debris flew, branches and chunks of tree trunk whirled outward.

He held Anabel tightly against his chest, her head buried against his shoulder. Another spread came in, these detonations carrying a flatter sound, higher up the slope. The stink of cordite was thick in the air. Now came a great comber of yellowish smoke rolling downslope, engulfing the trees, filling crevices like flowing water. It inundated the ravine like a hot fog. Their eyes burned, the air filled with the sharp, chemical stench of titanium tetrachloride, smelling like powerful bleach. Then sounds became muffled.

A third spread of shells came in, impacted downslope somewhere near the promontory. The ground shook as the sound roared overhead, sweeping on through the trees with an odd, pulsing oscillation deep in it.

Then silence, thick and heavy as the smoke. Red waited. He felt light-headed, oddly detached, the effect of close-in explosions that had thrown his body senses into momentary overload. He forced himself to focus, listening. All he could hear was the high ringing in his own ears.

A minute passed. Another.

Move, his mind ordered him. *Now!* He pulled himself to his feet, reached for Anabel. Her nose was bleeding from the concussions, her eyes a bit dreamy. They started up the ravine, stumbling. Sinclair fell down. He hauled her up, went on. The smoke began to lift. He could see ten feet ahead . . . fifteen. The smoke coiled around objects like liquid taffy.

A German soldier was sitting against a tree, staring at him. Parnell froze save for the reflexive move that brought the muzzle of his Thompson up, his finger tightening on the trigger. The soldier didn't move, he just sat there, his head tilted slightly as if he were listening to someone calling his name. His infantry gray-green uniform was spotless and in the yellow mist looked blue. He had no legs below his crotch.

They moved past him and kept going up, higher and higher, the air clearer now, the trees thickening into true forest. Sparrows darted through the sun-dappled dimness. They reached a ridge, went over it and down into more forest. They repeatedly saw distant German patrols, glimpses of motion among the trees. Neither of them spoke. They just let their bodies carry them farther and farther away from Cherbourg and ever closer to the sound of fighting.

At 1903 hours, with the sun casting long shadows, they made contact with a probing patrol from the 4th Division, the battle-dirty troopers covering them, waving them in as they came down the slope, their weapons over their heads.

ROMMEL

Chapter Eleven

After intense street fighting that had eventually driven the Germans into positions with their backs against the Cherbourg Harbor, Generalleutnant Schlieben finally surrendered the city on 30 June 1944.

Except for a small contingent of holdouts on the Cape de la Hague, the entire Cotentin Peninsula was now securely in Allied hands. Unfortunately, Kraut demo teams had spent the last hours before giving up destroying the port's facilities. It was so badly damaged it would take six weeks to get it back into operating condition.

Meanwhile, the battle for Normandy went on and was now stalled along a 127-mile front running from Caen in the east across the base of the peninsula to Coutances near the western coast of the Cotentin.

General Bradley, always methodical, committed corps after corps along this front in an effort to break out of the Cotentin. Each offensive met tenacious resistance, despite the fact that the Germans were exhausted and heavily depleted of men and material. During the first three weeks of July, American units suffered over 24,000 casualties.

Back in England, Eisenhower grew more and more impatient at the impasse. With Montgomery's Brits and Canadians still unsuccessful in taking Caen, and the month-long delay in taking Cherbourg, the strategic situation was deteriorating badly. Something had to be done, and done quickly and decisively.

Months earlier, plans for a second landing in France had been completed. Code-named Dragoon, it was to invade at Provence on the Mediterranean coast. But Churchill had continually put off giving his okay to the operation. Now, with the pressure to draw off German forces from the Normandy campaign, he finally agreed to let it go ahead. It was scheduled to jump off on 14 August, and would eventually go down in history as the most perfectly executed amphibious landing of the entire Second World War.

But for now Eisenhower was too anxious to wait for the effects of Dragoon to develop. He flew to France to meet with Bradley and Montgomery. A decision was reached to mount an immediate offensive in the *bocage* to crack through the German perimeter and thrust deep into central France. Part of the plan included the activation of a new Third Army under the command of General Patton.

On the German side, every passing day deepened the desperation of the frontline units. Constantly hammered by air strikes and pinpoint artillery barrages, their casualty lists steadily increased as their supplies and replacements dwindled to nearly nothing. Yet they fought on, knowing that once the Allies broke through their lines, they'd have a clear path straight across France and into the heart of Germany.

In late June, Hitler had relieved von Rundstadt from his command of OB West for suggesting peace talks with the Allies. His replacement was Generalfeldmarschall Gunter von Kluge, a Führer toady. He immediately sent back glowing reports that the French situation was well in hand, and that if he was allowed to mount a major counteroffensive, he would hurl the Allies back into the Channel.

General Rommel vehemently disagreed. He was by now completely disgusted and frustrated at the blind idiocy issuing from Berlin. On 16 July, he sent what amounted to an ultimatum to the Führer via von Kluge. In it, he bluntly pointed out that unless fresh supplies, troops, and armor were immediately sent to the western front, the battle for France was already lost.

In his original draft of the message he had placed a telling sentence. It read: *It is necessary to draw the political conclusions from this situation.* Jolted by this obvious reference to the making of peace ovatures, his staff pleaded with him to delete the statement. If not the entire sentence, they begged, at least the word *political.* Rommel finally conceded. But his views were now clear and this single sentence would soon set into motion a daring operation.

On the very next day, a British Typhoon fighter-bomber strafed Rommel's staff car, badly wounding him. Two days after that, a plot by a group of senior German officers would nearly kill the Führer with a bomb placed in his headquarters' bunker in East Prussia.

17 July
2314 hours

The Westland Lysander Mark III suddenly appeared out of the rainy darkness, flashing into momentary view over the line of placed torches, its underbelly black and the big Bristol-Mercury XXX engine throttled off. Farther down the field, the pilot flared and a moment later eased the big rubber wheels onto the grassy ground, rolled out, then spun and came lumbering back to where Anabel Sinclair stood soaking wet and shivering in the wind.

The cargo door swung open and two incoming SOE agents quickly, wordlessly leaped out. As soon as they were cleared, Anabel tossed her big musette up into the passenger compartment and climbed up after it. She quickly buckled herself into the port seat, one of four. The compartment smelled strongly of canvas dope and parachute silk and harness.

The engine revved, its specially built mufflers giving it a peculiar burring sound like a trilling tongue. They swung around to face into the wind. Then, bouncing over ruts, the heavy-bodied Lysander, affectionately called a Lizzie, struggled along the ground for a few moments, then began picking up speed, the tail coming up as the elevators developed lift. After a short run, it once more lifted back into the wet night sky.

The field was in a remote section of low foothills outside Rambouillet, four miles southwest of Versailles and ten miles from Paris. Anabel had come to Paris with Vaillant Duboudin to sit in on a meeting of high-level Resistance officials who were attempting to stop vicious in-fighting among the Normandy and Brittany Maquis circuits.

Sensing an Allied victory drawing ever closer, the disparate factions of the Resistance in these sectors began forming their power bases for when the fighting was over. The most active was the Communist *Tireurs et Partisans*, or FTP. They were actually attacking other Maquis units, and had even betrayed some of their leaders to the Gestapo.

The officials attending the Paris meeting would be from the four most powerful factions within the Resistance: the FTP, De Gaulle's *Comite National Francais*, the *Carte Organisation*, and members of the far-right *Liberation Nationale*.

Sinclair had been included as a monitoring liaison from the SOE.

They convened on the night of 14 July in ultrasecrecy in the loft of an abandoned warehouse on the West Bank near the Pasteur Institute. The long, low room was filled with bats, litter, and human excrement from squatters, alcoholic artists, prostitutes, and petty criminals who inhabited this quarter of the city. The meeting was conducted in very dim light and many of the participants wore masks. It turned into an acrimonious mess with little being accomplished, and ended after only one night when gunfire erupted.

Anabel now found herself having to expend nearly thirty hours before the Lysander came for her. She decided to wander around the city, see some of the things she had known so intimately in the past.

Paris had changed. Germans were now everywhere. Even, good God, goose-stepping down the Champs Elysées. There were no taxis or double-decker buses anymore, the only traffic German military vehicles and the clumsy wood-burning *gazogenes* with their huge boiler tanks on the roof. There were also little two-wheeled vehicles like rickshaws with old men who had once raced in the Tour de France pedaling them. All the street signs were now in German, and when the Parisians passed her on the boulevards, they *clopped,* everybody wearing wooden clogs because of the scarcity of leather.

Still, some of the smart restaurants like Maxim's were open, and night clubs such as the Moulin Rouge put on shows with Edith Piaf and the famous dancer Zizi Jeanmaire for audiences of German officers and their collaborator girlfriends. But she did find one thing exactly the same: the shop of her favorite couturier,

Edward Molyneux, at number 5 on the Place de la Concorde.

Giddy as a teenager looking for her prom dress, she rushed in and ended up purchasing two sweaters, a gold jersey, and a beautiful red crepe evening gown. Modeling it, she gazed at herself in the mirror and pictured the look on Parnell's face when she showed it to him in soft candlelight. In another shop down on the rue Royale, she bought a beautiful pair of ruby earrings to go with the dress.

The bill was 37,000 francs, roughly 215 pounds sterling. She knew precisely what the SOE financial officer would say when she ran these sales chits on her mission expense account. Well, she thought gaily, screw him.

The day following the surrender of Cherbourg, Sinclair and Parnell parted ways. SOE headquarters had ordered her to link up with Duboudin in Lessay on the west coast of the peninsula and compose a comprehensive report on the status of Maquis cells in Normandy and Brittany.

They would then cross into German-held territory beyond Coutances to make contact with Resistance units operating near Vire and Flers in the east. Afterward, they'd attend the Paris meeting and Anabel would return to England for a thorough debriefing on the entire French situation.

As for Parnell and his team, they were given twenty-four hours of rest, refitted and then sent south to link with the U.S. First Division now stretched out in static positions between St-Lô and Marigny. They were to conduct intelligence patrols deep behind enemy lines south of the St-Lô/Coutances highway.

It had been very difficult for Anabel to say good-bye to Parnell, standing together in the privacy-less noise and clamor of a division on the move, the rest of his men, combat filthy in their smelly, gas-impregnated jump gear, hunkered down a few yards away, quietly watching the columns of fresh replacement troops streaming past in spotless new battle dress who gave their lieutenant and Sinclair salacious whoops and hubba-hubba-mamas.

Ignoring it all, the two looked at each other for a long time without saying anything. Words would have been insufficient. Finally, they kissed, long and hard, and then Parnell said, "Goddammit, woman, you take care of yourself, you hear?"

"I will. You too, mister."

"So I'll be seeing you," he said.

That damned near broke her down. But she managed to hold back tears. A friendly regimental A and P officer had offered her a jeep and driver. She swiftly climbed in and was driven away, looking back only once.

In the days that followed, she immersed herself in her new duties. Sometimes she wept, sometimes she cursed. Once she even got very drunk on calvados and woke with a hangover that sent knife points into her skull. But mostly she moved forward with the hope, no, the *belief*, that one day she and Lieutenant John Parnell would see each other again. For now, it was all she had. . . .

The sudden light was like an explosion in its intensity, flooding through the windows of the Lysander. Anabel had been on the edge of a doze, gently feeling the swivel-and-buck of the aircraft moving through the night. Now all this light was there and then abruptly gone, off somewhere yet still casting shadows inside the plane. Instantly, she knew, *oh, shit*, they'd just been spotted by German ack-ack batteries.

A metal partition stood between the cargo compartment and the pilot's cabin. She heard a tiny buzz. It came from a set of earphones hooked to a mike bracket that hung from the back of the seat ahead of her. She slipped it over her head and double-clicked the mike.

The pilot's voice came on calmly. "Seems we've drifted a bit too close to a Jerry airfield, miss," he said. "You'd best hold tight now."

The aircraft suddenly dropped, as if it were dead weight, going down at a sharp angle, the sound of its engine rising, then fading off sharply as the plane built up dangerous airspeed. Anabel felt her stomach shift around inside her body, a happy memory feeling, doing aerobatics with her father. The Lysander came out of its dive, the engine roaring up again as they went into a steep climb. A moment later, it whipped over in a snap roll, quickly another, then fell off once more.

She peered through the window. Darkness and searchlight shafts tumbled crazily around and around outside. Then flak bursts appeared, sudden smoky flashes, their muffled pops caught inside the surge and fade of the Lizzie's big engine as the pilot put the plane into repeated, convoluted turns and spins and hard pull-ups, trying to evade the enemy fire. Now and then, bits of shrapnel struck the fuselage and came flying through the inside of the plane, smoking.

For ten minutes, they tumbled and swooped through the sky like a windblown leaf. Finally, they managed to work their way beyond the searchlights and flak. The pilot leveled off and came onto the intercom. "You all right back there, miss?"

She keyed. "I'm fine."

"Sorry for the cock-up," he said. "Bloody careless of me."

They continued northwest, steadily climbing until they were in clouds. The air grew cold and damp, but luckily their cover held all the way across the Channel. Two hours later, they touched down beside the headquarters of 161 Squadron at RAF Tempsford in Bedfordshire.

18 July
0534 hours

The 75mm tank round slammed at them like a sizzling comet. It crashed into the ground fifty yards to their right, hurling mud and grass and shrapnel. Everybody hit the ground, slithering, crawling furiously for the nearest bomb crater. There were dozens of them all over the hedgerow field.

Parnell and Cowboy went into the same one, hugged the side. The earth was mushy and stank of cordite. There was a foot of rainwater in the bottom. Both men squinted, listening, trying to figure the tank's position from the sound of its incoming shell and the faint, metallic clatter of its hull as it bounced back in counter-recoil.

Two more rounds hurtled in, exploding high. Shell fragments zinged into the inside walls of the crater. The Kraut gunner was fast, but they quickly realized he couldn't depress enough to put his shells directly *into* the bomb craters.

They waited, expecting the vehicle to move at any moment, find a better firing angle. They knew it would likely come right through the nearest hedgerow and stop on its downside so the gunner could have a clear trajectory to them.

The firing ceased. Cowboy glanced over at Parnell. "I make him about a hunnert yards up and to the right, Lieutenant," he said quietly.

Parnell nodded. They waited in the impacted silence. High above them, the sky was a pewter color that cast the entire landscape into swatches of gray and black like an old movie. Thin fog lay just above the ground, thickening in the shadows.

Cowboy frowned. "Why ain't that sumbitch movin' on us?"

"Maybe it's emplaced," Red suggested. He moved up to the edge of the crater, cautiously peered over, made a sweeping scan, and slid back. "I couldn't spot him. But I think he's in an apple orchard on the right side. If he is, he's laying those rounds in through the south gate."

Cowboy started to say something. There was the soft, deadly rustle and double click of a mortar round. Both men quickly buried their faces in the mushy dirt. It exploded thirty yards behind them, showering them with mud and grass.

Aw, fuck! Parnell thought angrily, *the bastard's got a covering mortar crew with him*. From its firing sound and explosion, he suspected a light, 50mm Granatenwerfer 36. Two more mortar rounds came in abruptly, off to their left, the gunner searching out their defilade positions.

Parnell tried to recapture the fleeting image of the surrounding ground: the gates, the breaks in the trees, firing distances. Looking at the mental picture, he realized they were now in serious trouble. Even if the tank didn't reposition, that mortar crew could sure as hell high-angle them, drop rounds right down into every bomb crater in the field.

Before the tank opened on them, they'd been moving between hedgerows, angling through a small field with wild daisies in the grass, spread out in normal patrol overwatch formation, two men always moving at a time, then halting to cover the others coming up. The tank round came in when they were about thirty yards from the opposite side of the field.

Click, click.

This mortar round struck twenty-five feet directly ahead, between them and the hedgerow. The next one came down near it. Parnell waited the length of a three-count, then whistled sharply, twice, and yelled, "Make for the hedgerow, straight ahead."

The next round was from the tank's 75, the deeper, slashing rush of the shell coming straight in. It passed directly over them, four feet above the crater, and slammed into the ground with a shuddering impact forty yards away.

"Now!" Red bellowed.

He and Cowboy came up out of their hole like cheetahs attacking from ambush, going full-out as soon as their boots hit flat ground, dodging, dipping. The other three were off to their left.

The tank put another 75 round into the hedgerow dead ahead, blew tree trunk and leaves sky high. Its hull-mounted machine gun joined in, throwing a long, traversing burst that went high.

Quickly, they got beyond the angle of the hedgerow gate, out of the tank's direct line of sight. But its MG kept firing blindly, spraying through the trees. A moment later, they went lunging up into the hedgerow's thicket of brush, through the oak and hazel trees, and down into the comparative safety on the other side.

Parnell rolled over, checked Cowboy, then swung around. He spotted Wyatt first, then Smoker and Laguna a few feet beyond Bird. Red held up his right arm and chopped it through the air, indicating they attempt to circle to the left, come up on the tank's right flank. Wyatt nodded. They started off, running hunched over.

Red pushed to his feet. "Let's go, Cowboy," he called

quietly. "We've gotta take out that goddamned mortar crew."

Ever since midnight, Blue Team had been on the move, trying to get back to the American lines before dawn. They'd been out for two days, reconnoitering a concentration of German tanks and antitank vehicles ten miles southeast of Periers. They'd lie up in cover through the day and then move right down among the tank formations at night.

It was apparent that the Kraut armor had obviously taken a heavy beating from Allied air strikes. Nearly all the armored vehicles, mostly Panthers and Mark IVs, were damaged and being worked on, their crews and motor pool mechanics having to scavenge parts from other, more seriously damaged vehicles. Many of the soldiers also appeared drunk, a very dire sign.

To Parnell, these German units looked to be in a state of rapid disintegration and also in a perpetual state of Condition Red, which was badly demoralizing them. Their supply depots were almost totally depleted with a mere trickle of incoming replacement troops, equipment, food, and medical supplies. Once the team had actually watched as German surgeons operated in bombed-out farmhouses using flashlights and apparently without anesthesia.

The land all around was also in terrible shape, like a moonscape. The ground had been punctured by thousands of bomb craters and shell holes. There were burned-out villages and churches and monasteries. Whole networks of hedgerows had been completely flattened or thinned out until they formed only lines of skeletal trees. Many roads were no longer usable. Shattered equipment and destroyed vehicles and field guns were littered everywhere.

The most gruesome part of it was in those areas where the Germans had been caught moving in the open. Dead bodies and parts of bodies along with dead horses still harnessed to their artillery and supply wagons, their bellies blown open by internal decay gas, were scattered all over. Apparently the German mortuary crews were unable or unwilling to collect and bury the dead.

As they moved through this devastation, Parnell and his men went with the neck bands of their T-shirts pulled up to cover their noses. It did little good against the stench that had spread like a dark pestilent cloud for miles around. In fact, it would later be said that Allied fighter pilots making low strafing runs would actually vomit at the thick stench that seeped into their cockpits.

The German mortar crew came straight toward them, three soldiers in Waffen green and brown camo battle gear and helmet covers, SS eagles on their sleeves. One man carried the Granatenwerfer mortar, its silvery barrel and baseplate a single unit. His companions lugged metal canisters of the 2.2-pound HE rounds, running bent over through an apple orchard in which the trees were all leafless, some upended or blown apart, showing yellow wood.

Parnell and Fountain had reached the north corner of the field. Going to their bellies, they crawled around the exposed gate opening, worked back, and then went over into the inside of the opposite hedgerow. It was eerily quiet now, windless, no bird sound, no rumble of distant artillery. It was so still they could almost detect the silent drop of the dawn light like snowflakes.

A man's voice shouted from the other side of the trees. Red and Cowboy dropped, listening for the direction. Then, stealthily, they moved up into the hedgerow brush. Inside, the earth was wet and smelled of fungus, a cold odor like the floor of an icehouse. Mosquitoes droned about their faces.

Parnell held up his palm for Cowboy to hold position, then worked his way through the brush, slithering close to the ground. He crossed between two oak trees. There were bullet holes in the trunks and a gold-colored sap had oozed out. It had hardened into what looked like dusty glass. He pulled aside a leafy branch and looked out.

The German soldiers had paused thirty yards from the tree line, down on one knee to check the hedgerow. He cut his eyes left, right, but couldn't spot the tank. Twisting his head, he silently signaled Cowboy: *three . . . move to the right . . . key on me.*

Fountain vanished into the brush.

Now the Krauts rose and came on, their bread-can canteens tinkling softly. The one carrying the mortar had a Walther P-38 in a black holster, the others shoulder-slung MP-40s. They all had black clip pouches and potato-masher grenades stuck into their webbing belts.

When the lead mortarman reached the hedgerow, he didn't pause but shoved right through the brush and started up the incline, holding the weapon over his head so it wouldn't catch in the tangles.

Parnell's burst caught him in the top of the shoulders. A bullet slammed off the mortar's baseplate and two others made two perfectly round black holes in his helmet. He stumbled and fell flat on his stomach, groaning.

Cowboy's burst took the other two in one sweep, knocking them both backward, their legs disjointedly under them. There was a long moment of silence, their gun smoke drifting gently. In the quiet, Parnell's German groaned again, a gurgling sound. Then another, sharper sound came, the tiny sizzle of a friction igniter.

Parnell had already started to lift himself off the

ground. *Oh, shit!* his mind cried out. One of Fountain's rounds had apparently sundered the porcelain head of a German grenade and set off its igniter. In pure reflex, he hurled himself back and down just as the thing went off with a hard cracking burst. Shrapnel slashed through the trees. Bloody intestines and body parts showered down around him, dripped from the brush.

Now Parnell was up, hollering, "Recover the canisters." He shoved through the tangled weeds to reach the lead mortarman. The man's eyes fluttered. Blood ran out of his helmet and the back of his smock was soaked with it.

Parnell heard Fountain crash through the brush and start out on solid ground. He grabbed up the mortar, saw where his bullet had creased a streak across its barrel. It shone like a sliver of mercury. He tossed the weapon toward the top of the hedgerow, then swung his Thompson around, located Cowboy, and threw a quick burst over his head, covering him just as Fountain scooped up two canisters, whirled, and headed back.

With a heart-jolt, Parnell heard another tiny sound, like a buzzing insect, as the swiveling motor inside the tank's turret traversed its 75mm around. He threw himself down on the side of the hedgerow, hollering at Cowboy, "Tank round! Tank round!"

Fifteen feet away, Fountain tossed him one of the canisters. It smacked him right in the belly. They both hurtled back into the brush and crawled, scrambling up the spongy incline. They crested the top, Red grabbing the mortar as he tumbled down the other side.

The hollow, rushing boom of the taper-barreled 75 came and then the hot *whooshing* of its shell crashing at high velocity through the air. It exploded with a shuddering sound on the other side of the hedgerow. The concussion blew through the trees, hurling shrapnel and torn branches and trunk. Its force jammed painfully down into Parnell's ears.

It made him feel woozy, wobbly legged, and he couldn't hear anything except a loud, intricate buzzing. A few feet away, Fountain was on his knees, twisting his head back and forth. Otherwise, he appeared unhurt. Fortunately, they had both been so close to the explosion they were under its arc of out-throw and saved from the shrapnel.

Red staggered to his feet. Carrying the Granatenwerfer and round canister, he headed off along the hedgerow in the direction of the tank. Fountain followed, his face ashen. From the other end of the field, Wyatt and the others opened up with their Thompsons, going for the tank's viewing slits, trying to knock off the gunner or at least distract him. But their rounds smacked uselessly against the armor plating. A couple ricocheted off, screaming, as the gunner continued laying in rapid rounds, saturating the area where he'd seen the two Americans enter the trees, walking his fire toward the north, then back south again.

They set up the mortar near the south gate. Leaving Cowboy to do it, Red crawled to the top of the hedgerow and lay on his belly to look out. He finally spotted the tank. It hadn't been emplaced but was undoubtedly disabled, probably waiting for a PM to haul it back to a repair depot. His head hurt and the buzzing had diminished only slightly. Beyond it seemed a soundless vacuum.

He held up his arm so Fountain could tell how to adjust the mortar's traverse position, then used hand signals for the range, assuming Cowboy had also been made deaf. Their first round was far right and short. He signaled the adjustments. The second one blew an apple tree ten feet to the right of the tank all to hell. Their third one was dead on. It exploded right on top

of the turret and pitched it upside down, like an over-
turned cup. Smoke began to gush from the ragged
cavity. A tanker climbed out, skidded over the side on
his buttocks, and ran off. Another appeared, then a
third, dragging a wounded man.

Wyatt, Laguna, and Weinberg had come up, dodging through the trees. They engaged the fleeing
Germans. A short firefight followed in which all the
tankers were killed.

At 0743 hours, Blue Team crossed back into their
own lines. Parnell's and Fountain's hearing had returned by then. Red reported to the regimental G-2,
then went to bed.

"John?" a man's voice called.

Parnell was deep in a dream, lying on a rock under
the icy rush of a Colorado waterfall. He could actually
smell moss, feel the watery thunder in his head. He
shifted slightly, thought he felt the gentle tapping of a
woodpecker on his arm.

"Parnell."

He came up into consciousness in a burst of adrenaline. His eyes snapped open, his hand already on the
stock of his weapon, which was leaning against his bunk.
He remained motionless, scanning.

"Whoa, fella," the man's voice said, laughing. "It's just
me, Colonel Dunmore."

Parnell sat upright, rubbed his face. "Damn, sir, I'm
sorry."

"Relax, relax. Sorry I had to wake you."

They were in a low ceiling dugout, the walls tamped
dirt, the overhead made of beech limbs and ammunition
boxes. It was about the size of an average bedroom and

had two bunks, a desk formed from a board and two jerry cans, and a Coleman lantern. Battle gear hung from the walls, beside pinups of movie actresses and black-and-white Italian porno photos pinned to the dirt with .30-caliber cartridges.

The place stank of body odor and lantern smoke and the faintly gamy stench of whale oil, which the men used to prevent automatic weapons from overheating. The dugout belonged to a platoon lieutenant in Second Battalion, 1ˢᵗ Division, named Stan Terry.

Since being attached to the division, Blue Team had been billeted with B Company. Terry was a skinny balding San Franciscan who talked continuously, always seemed to have a fresh bottle of liquor on hand, and bragged on how many mademoiselles he was going to lay when he got to Paris.

Dunmore said, "So how you doing?"

"All right, sir."

"The men?"

"Worn out, but okay."

"Hell, why not? You people've been on the line for forty-two straight days."

"Seems like forty-two weeks."

Dunmore chuckled mirthlessly. "I suspect so. Incidentally, congratulations on the Cherbourg mission. SFHQ considers it a real coup. Get a bit hairy, did it?"

"A bit."

"By the way, I met Agent Flapper in London." The colonel was dressed in starched field fatigues, his college-dean face clean shaven and healthy looking. Behind his glasses, his eyes twinkled as he rose to sit on Lieutenant Terry's bunk. "A very fine and lovely young woman, that Sinclair."

"Yes, sir, she is." He felt a little lift come to his heart hearing her name spoken.

"Well, I've got a bit of good news for you," Dunmore said. "The team's headed for England. For at least an entire week."

"That's great, sir." Parnell looked quietly at him, blinked slowly. "Rest or training?" he asked, quieter.

"Both." The colonel offered Red a cigarette, took one himself, lit them. "Truth is, we've been stalled here in defensive positions too damned long. Ike and the CCS want movement. Now. So he's ordered a major offensive, scheduled for the twenty-fifth. If the goddamned weather holds up, of course."

He was interrupted by a sudden roaring as a flight of fighters passed close overhead, heading for low-level bombing and strafing runs deeper inland. Dunmore waited until the sound faded back into the ever-present grumble of distant field guns, the murmur of motors and voices calling, summer bivouac sounds periodically disturbed by the rattle of small arms from somewhere near Highway 27.

"This time Patton'll be in it, commanding Third Army." He took a drag, blew the smoke up toward the ammunition boxes. "I'm back with him permanently. Chief analyst of his G-2 section."

"Congratulations, sir."

Dunmore nodded. "It's damned good to be back." He chuckled. "So, you know Old George. The moment his lead units hit the ground, they'll be moving. Fast. That's where you come in."

He went on to explain. One of the most powerful battle systems that had come to full fruition during the Normandy campaign had been the concept of CATs or Coordinated Attack Teams, which concentrated infantry, armor, artillery, and air cover into a single offensive unit. Since the Allies controlled the skies over France, quick-response air strikes by fighters and attack bombers had proven highly effective. The Krauts were as terrified of these as they were of pinpoint artillery barrages.

"But there's one big bottleneck in the system," Dunmore said. "The time it takes to field and relay initial fire mission requests, as well as the handling of adjustment fire. It's all just too goddamned time-consuming. Under this present system, once Third Army gets rolling, it'll overrun its own forward observers. Particularly the tactical air controllers.

"So, we've worked out a solution. Every tank platoon leader will be taught to call for fire missions himself. No more going through that damned FO priority assignment bullshit. We'll be cutting out two steps. He'll be in direct contact with both his artillery and the AT pilots themselves. That gives him the ability to call his own fire and adjustments.

"But that means all the tank commanders will have to learn spotting procedure. There isn't enough time to run everybody through formal training, so some will have to learn on the run. I've assigned you and your men along with Yellow Team to do the instructing out in the field."

Parnell thought about that for a moment, frowned. "But some of my own team's never called in fire."

"Doesn't matter. They know the basics and they'll have at least four days of further orientation at Chelton Cross Air Base near London. The main thing is, you're all experienced recon men." He stood. "So you'll be flying back with me. I've already arranged a driver for you." He checked his watch. It was 1:45 in the afternoon. "He'll be by at 1800 to take you and your gear to the fighter strip outside Periers."

"Yes, sir." Parnell started to stand up.

"As you were, John. Look, you got a few hours yet. Grab some more sleep." The colonel paused to scrutinize Parnell's eyes for a long moment. Was there a question in them? Then he grinned, said, "See you this evening." He clapped Red on the shoulder, turned, and went back up the dirt steps.

Parnell lay back, closed his eyes. He felt as if he had not slept at all. *I met Agent Flapper in London.* He thought about Anabel, smelled, tasted her in his mind. *Well, at least she's back there now,* he thought thankfully, *not still in this shit hole.*

He tried to return to sleep, got halfway down there, but was not able to recapture that dream of a Colorado waterfall.

Chapter Twelve

The Gestapo officer wore a black overcoat even though the day was hot, Nazi Secret Police written all over him. He had a small, Slavic face, wrinkled forehead. His neck protruded at an angle from his coat, pushing his face forward. It gave him the appearance of an animal suddenly halted at the sight of game.

He and Duboudin sat on a marble bench in the Jardin du Luxembourg, a fifty-acre park filled with formal terraces and chestnut groves in central Paris. The bench stood beside the Fontaine des Medicis, a long, ornate fish pond with water the color of *café latte* and the odor of dying gardenias. Several small French boys were sailing their toy boats in it, the sails pure white and filled with patches, all heeling in a gentle breeze.

Nearby, an artist had set up his easel and painted the bronze statue of Marie de Medici; people strolled; tiny black sparrows flitted through the horse chestnut trees. To the east stood the Florentine splendor of the Luxembourg Palace, built by Henry IV for his consort, Marie des Medicis, its chimneys and bright copper roofs glistening in the sun.

The Gestapo officer said, "So, what do you have for me?"

Vaillant turned, shocked. During such clandestine contacts made in public, neither participant *ever* spoke.

Communication was always conducted by furtively exchanging notes or ciphers, perhaps folded inside left-behind newspapers or tucked into a purposefully dropped cigarette package, which was then politely handed back.

He said, holding his lips as tightly together as he could and still get the words out: "Why are you speaking openly?"

"Never mind it."

"Where is Major Land?"

"Elsewhere."

"You are to be my contact now?"

"Yes. Code name Gauner." It meant *rogue.*

Vaillant shook his head. "I don't like this." He stared straight ahead, afraid to seem too apprehensive to the passersby.

"It is of no importance what you like or don't like," the Gestapo man snapped. "Give me what you have."

Duboudin had lingered in Paris after the Resistance meeting, staying with a friend he had known during his racing days, a fellow driver named Raoul Thivenet who had lost both legs in an accident in Italy. Now he moved about on a wheeled cart and lived with his spinster daughter in a small walk-up near the Bastille. Vaillant suspected the man fornicated with her, probably with her consent.

For two days he had tried to contact Major Land without success. An officer at OB West's intelligence bureau finally told him to wait for a half hour each day at three alternate contact sites in the city, the first at one o'clock, the second at two, the third at three. He would eventually be met by Land. The Jardin was the last of the three.

He watched the boys with their boats, the children in shorts and summer caps. How thin their legs seemed, he thought. He felt a pang of sorrow. Food had always been scarce in the major cities of France since the German takeover. But now many people could barely keep their families fed. How odd that starvation always showed first in the children's legs.

"Hurry it up," the Gestapo officer growled. "I haven't got all day."

Two German air officers came strolling by with a young, redheaded woman. The men wore spotless, deep blue uniforms, probably staffers from the main Luftwaffe headquarters for Paris, which was housed in the palace.

Duboudin waited till they passed and said, "There was a meeting of Resistance officers here two nights ago."

The Nazi's head snapped around. "*Scheisse!* Why weren't we notified of this well ahead of time?"

"I tried to. I even sent a man to tell Land."

"Who was there? What happened?"

"Nothing, actually. Everybody got into a big argument."

"Who was there?"

"I couldn't tell. Anybody of importance wore a mask."

"*Scheisskerl!*"

Duboudin felt blood rush up the column of his neck, into his face. This Gestapo pig had just called him a *shit-head*.

"All right, what else?" the Gestapo officer said.

"I have four names. All members of the FTP from Brittany."

"These are leaders?"

"Not all, only one."

"Well, well, hand it over."

Vaillant leaned forward and, as if accidentally, dropped his briefcase onto the ground. Both he and the Nazi bent to retrieve it. As the German grabbed the handle, Vaillant slid a folded sheet of paper into his hand. He retook the case and sat up.

The Nazi calmly and arrogantly settled back, unfolded the paper, scanned it, and shoved it into his coat pocket.

"Good God, man," Duboudin hissed. "Are you an imbecile?"

Once more the man's face whirled to stare at him. "What did you say?"

Duboudin put his head back, closed his eyes, tried desperately to gather himself. Abruptly, he lunged to his feet and started to walk away.

"Stop right there!" the Gestapo officer barked. Vaillant froze. The German glared up at him. "If you ever speak to me that way again, Frenchman," he said ominously, "you won't live long enough to regret it."

"Yes, of course," Duboudin said, flustered. "Yes, I apologize."

There was a long silence before the other man spoke again. "In the future, you will bring us better information. And you will be much more *prompt* with it. Understood?"

"Yes."

The man laughed, a snigger. "Otherwise, we might be forced to terminate your services, mm?"

Duboudin nodded, wordlessly turned, and walked away. Distractedly he heard the small boys laughing as two of their boats crashed together, saw the street artist step back to examine his painting. He went right on past them, suddenly feeling very cold.

Chelton Cross Airbase, England
21 July 1944

Smoker Wineberg thought, *This is the goddamned life, man!* Perched up there in the commander's seat of an M4A1 Sherman tank from B Company, 8th Tank Battalion, 4th Armored Division, of Patton's newly formed Third

Army, hotdogging along at thirty miles an hour over hill and meadow, torsion bars smoothing out the lunge and pitch like a big D-8 bulldozer gone ape-shit.

Hot fucking damn!

Only *this* old tractor carried heavy armament: a 75mm M3 main gun, twin hull-mounted .30-caliber machine guns, and a turret-mounted .50-caliber MG just for his use. Even though in a one-on-one with a Kraut Panther or Tiger it had to scoot and duck, it was still a flat-out ass-kicking machine that, at least for the next two days, he would be in command of.

Since arriving back in England, he, Lieutenant Parnell, and the rest of Blue Team had been running rotating live-fire exercises in the six-square-mile base firing range, working out the kinks of Patton's new Coordinated Arms Tactical Attack of *spearhead* doctrine, adapted specifically for artillery- and air-supported armor along with mechanized infantry used in rapid-penetration warfare.

For today's exercise, Smoker was acting commander of the lead tank of Second Platoon. Laguna was with First Platoon, Fountain with Third, in reserve. Parnell and Bird were coordinating the mission calls: Wyatt with a forward spotter team, and Parnell up in a Piper L4 Grasshopper observation plane monitoring the exercise.

He and Weesay were now in the middle of a flanking approach to an enemy-marked road that ran parallel to a low bluff designated G7-1 on their tactical maps. Laguna's platoon was a thousand yards to his right, both of them moving in a wedge formation with their lead tanks on point and two flankers on each side and back. During this particular exercise, they'd be focusing on a rapid-response tactical air strike instead of calling up an artillery barrage.

Most of Third Army's armor and infantry, including their supporting units, had already departed from their original headquarters at Breamore near Salisbury and from training depots in northern Scotland for demarcation ports in southern England. But Companies B and E of the 8th had been sent to Chelton Cross for a week to run Blue Team and two other regular artillery spotter squads through their CATA exercises. The other Mohawker crew, Yellow Team, was operating with A and C Companies back at Breamore. Two days earlier, General Patton and his staff had crossed the Channel and were now in field headquarters at Nehou, France, south of Cherbourg.

Each tank had a five-man crew: a commander, gunner, driver, second driver, and loader. In Smoker's M4A1 the regular commander, a sergeant from Tennessee named Joe Stringer, was now acting gunner for this exercise.

Smoker lifted his binoculars and swept them across the ground far ahead. Green rolling fields interspersed with stands of oak and yew trees, everything bathed in brilliant, late morning sunshine. He wore a commander's skull-fitted radio helmet with his goggles hiked up onto his forehead.

A mike bracket with a selector switch curved around to his mouth. He could speak on intercom to his own crew, talk to the rest of the platoon or to the battalion's operations center, and finally to the fighter pilots themselves, the ones who would respond to his mission call. The main radio console, a specially adapted SCR-385 mobile transmitter/receiver capable of high-frequency ground and air communications, sat to his right under the turret bustle.

He spotted a line of mock vehicles strung out on the bluff road. Steadying the glasses, he continued a slower scan to the left, then moved back to the right. Twenty-two trucks, canvas-and-stick duece-and-a-half troop carriers.

He keyed the intercom, shouting, "Driver . . . stop."

The M4A1 lunged to a skidding halt, then pitched back

to rock on its torsion bars. He keyed again: "Gunner . . . truck column." He let the binoculars hang loosely around his neck and began traversing the turret, coming around quickly, lining up the vane sight on his turret telescope to form a rough aim of the gun.

The gunner came back: "I have target ID."

For a moment, Wineberg lifted his eyes from the scope, squinting, estimating range. He had always had an uncanny knack for reading ground, estimating distances, a feel for where he was in space. He keyed. "Loader . . . Willy Peter." This slang term referred to a WP smoke-marker shell.

He returned to the scope. "Traverse left . . . Steady-on . . . One thousand."

"Ready."

"Fire three!"

The 75mm cut loose with a sharp *crack* that was muffled by his helmet, the tank jacking back hard and then counterrecoiling, rocking slightly as its automatic gyro-stabilizer held the main gun on target. From the twin vent outlets on either side and behind him shot streams of cordite fumes back and away.

Two seconds later he saw a geyser of white smoke lift into the air near the center of the column of fake trucks. Two seconds after that the second round went out, then the third. Before this impact, he was on intercom: "Driver . . . coordinates."

A slight pause, then the driver called back, "Double Q-dash-zero-two-three-four-one."

Smoker twisted, whirled the radio console's frequency dial to the preset one for the Battalion's OC, keyed the mike. "Daddy Bear, this is Red Two. Request fire mission, truck convoy. Smoke. MR is G-seven dash-one. Coordinates double Q-dash-zero-two-three-four-one, over"

The OC came right back: "Red Two, stand by."

He waited, glassing the hits. The smoke from the Willy Peters had lifted into the air and was now drifting gently toward the northeast, thinning out. Thirty seconds went by.

Battalion OC came back: "Red Two. Two flight is inbound, ETA two and a half. Contact Snow Leader on one-five-niner-point-two. Transferring. Will monitor, over."

"I copy that, Daddy Bear." He quickly adjusted to 159.2 on the frequency dial, keyed. "Snow Leader, this is Red Two. Do you copy? Over."

A crackle of static, then, "Red Two, go ahead."

"Snow Leader, truck convoy," Smoker called. "MR G-seven dash-one. Smoke marked. Two clicks southwest tree line, three clicks north of canal. Possible double-A one mile southeast." He had thrown that last one in just to see how the flyboys would set up their strike approach with ack-ack guns off their right flank.

"Roger that, Red Two."

He listened to Snow Leader talking to his wingman. Then there they were, two P-51 Mustangs of the XIX Tactical Air Command coming in at tree level from the north, silver fuselages flashing in the sun, each carrying two napalm wing tanks, flying a tight leader-wingman formation.

As he watched, they climbed slightly and then rocketed toward the line of mock duece-and-a-halfs, their engines sounding high and powerful in the distance. Snow Leader released first, his twin napalm tanks tumbling in slow motion. They struck near the middle of the column, laying out a long sheet of roiling orange-red fire that billowed up into black smoke. The wingman released and another strata of fire and smoke burst upward as the Mustangs kicked hard over to the right and dropped back to tree level, headed due west.

Grinning broadly, Smoker keyed. "Snow Leader, fan-fucking- tastic," he yelled, then caught himself, *whoa!* "Great drop. Thanks."

"Roger that, Red Two. Good hunting. Over and out."

He returned to the Battalion OC: "Daddy Bear, Red Two. Column destroyed. Advancing. Over and out."

Twenty minutes later, Parnell called from the *Grasshopper,* congratulated him on a solid target demolition, then ordered him to let Sergeant Stringer take the next phase of the exercise. Smoker spent the rest of the day and early evening as second driver, down in the sweatbox, a job he didn't think was worth a shit.

Nigel Flynn neared the end of a story he was relating to Anabel Sinclair, about a classmate at Eton named Rodney Evanscott. The story had something to do with a pigeon and a headmaster. "So guess what happens," Nigel said, his freckled face all grin. "Old Killebrew in his silkie vest and pants sits right *down* in this awful mess."

"You're kidding." Anabel laughed.

"No, on my honor. Oh, I say, can't you just picture it?" He shook his head and gazed off, relishing the memory. "Lord, that old Charlie was positively *livid.*"

Flynn was a low-echelon staffer with SFHQ. He and Sinclair had trained together. He had ginger-colored hair and innocent hazel eyes and Anabel adored him. They were in the Cheshire Cheese Tavern on Fleet Street in London, the place done in black paneling and dark-coated windows and polished brass. They were seated at a black table just beneath the huge portrait of Dr. Samuel Johnson, sharing crustless cucumber sandwiches and crumpets with clotted cream, Nigel drinking tea, Anabel white wine.

Since her return, she had been working with SFHQ's

Etat Major des Francaises de l'Interieur department at Bryanston Square, analyzing agent reports on the French circuits. The situation in country had worsened among the various Resistance groups and their alphabet-soup acronym offshoots. Not only in the Normandy and Brittany area, but also in those cells in the south and middle of the country.

Along with trying to get a handle on the increasing internal fighting, British Intelligence was still desperate to isolate leak sources and double agents within the various Maquis sectors. So far, they had developed some suspects, one a man planted with the *Abwehr*, code-named Heinrich, and two highly placed SOE agents in the Toulouse sector, Roger Bardet and Jean Kieffer. Still, two of the Hunter teams they'd sent out had simply disappeared, without any word. Now they were strongly considering withdrawal of all support to some of the more chaotic circuits.

Anabel had been scheduled to return to France sometime in mid-August, to the Le Mans circuit, code-named Cartwheel. Three months earlier, its SOE head there, Emile Garry, and his wireless operator, the beautiful Indian-American Princess Imayat Khan, had been taken by the Gestapo and executed at Buchenwald.

Then, on 21 July, she had been abruptly transferred to a newly created department within SOE's F Section. Its offices were in Somerset House, at the foot of Fleet Street where the river Thames swung past Blackfriars Bridge and the Victoria Embankment. Although she still had no idea precisely what was in store for her, she sensed it was something big.

Nigel started another story, then spotted Brigadier Stanton-Ferryman, overall head of F Section, enter the pub. He immediately stopped talking. The brigadier spoke to an elderly waiter, then approached their table.

Nigel leaped to his feet. "Sir," he said stiffly.

The section chief smiled. "At ease," he said. "Mind if I join you?"

"Please do, sir," Anabel said.

Stanton-Ferryman settled himself. He was quite tall, slender, dressed in a precise dark blue suit, brilliant white shirt, and a moderate blue tie. He always walked slightly bent at the waist as if trying to hide his excessive height, wore his dark brown hair with a stark left part, and perpetually exuded the rich scent of nutmeg from his pipe tobacco.

Flustered, Flynn glanced at his watch. "Please excuse me, sir," he blurted. "I seem to have forgotten the time. I really must be getting back to the office."

"Ah, indeed?"

"Yes, sir. Thank you, sir."

"Bye, Nige," Anabel called lightly as he hurried away.

The waiter approached with the brigadier's tea, the service a set of eighteenth-century John Emes silverware. He delicately poured the tea, reached for the sugar tongs. "That'll be fine," Stanton-Ferryman said. The waiter moved away.

The brigadier took two lumps and a shot of cream from the jug, sipped, and sat back. "Well, now, have you settled into Somerset House nicely?" he asked pleasantly.

"Oh, yes, sir."

"Good." He took another sip, gently set the cup back down. "I say, how long has it been since you've seen your parents? They live in Chicago?"

"Yes, sir, Chicago. It's been quite a while."

"What would you say to a bit of holiday? A fortnight,

perhaps? You could dash right over and surprise them. I'm certain a flight could easily be arranged."

A tiny frown furrowed between Anabel's eyes. *What's this?* "That would be wonderful, sir . . . But things are awfully busy right now."

"Nonsense. Never too busy to see the home folks, mm? You've done splendid work for us, Sinclair. You deserve some time off."

"Well, thank you, Brigadier."

He took another sip. "Yes, let's do that. You notify Jacobs of when you want to leave. He'll make all the arrangements." Mathew Jacobs was her immediate superior in the F Section. Stanton-Ferryman studied her a moment, then said, "Puzzled?"

"Yes, sir, somewhat."

"Understandable. I imagine you're also wondering why you were transferred in the first place. Well, let's just say that we're planning something quite extraordinary. Some might even say slightly mad. But I've always believed boldness justifies itself in its dividends."

Anabel nodded. "So it's to be dangerous."

"Indeed."

"I see."

"Well, so that's settled, then." He took a final sip and stood. "Oh, by the by, Jacobs has a message for you. From that American special forces chap you were with in Cherbourg?"

Anabel sat forward, felt her heart leap. "Lieutenant Parnell?"

"Yes, I believe so. Seems his unit is temporarily back here for training somewhere in Berks County. In any case, Jacobs will know."

God, she thought joyously, *Oh, God.*

She noticed the brigadier's eyes watching her closely.

After a moment, he said, "You'll forgive my prying, but might I ask if there's a larger picture here?"

"Sir?" She was caught off guard but quickly recovered. "Oh, no, nothing like that, Brigadier."

"Good. You know, emotional connections in our . . . *peculiar* sort of business often create delicate and dangerous complications."

"No need to worry about that, sir."

"Good." He nodded. "Well, I'm off for Bryanston, then." He flashed her a smile, diplomatic and sleek. "Enjoy your holiday."

"Thank you, sir." She watched him leave, pausing to pay for his tea. So totally aristocratic. Like a Rolls Royce, he did not walk, he *proceeded*. She had a crazy, tangent thought: did the brigadier ever get a hard-on? Did he writhe in uncontrolled lust? She giggled, shook her head, completely unable to imagine such an absurd picture.

She downed her wine and stood up, her heart singing. She was going to see Parnell!

She picked him up at the main guard gate of the Chelton Cross Air Base. It was near the town of Henley-on-Thames west of London. He was talking to the sentry, Parnell in his officer's pinks, which gave Annabel a warm, glowing shock, seeing again how tall and wonderfully handsome he really was, now all clean and polished.

She had borrowed a friend's black 1939 SS-100 Jaguar, a two-seater roadster. As he came up, smiling, she called, "Hi," and he said, "Hi," and tossed his musette behind the seats, walked around the car, looking through the windscreen at her, the smile still in his brown eyes, and then he cranked his tall frame into the little car's passenger seat.

It was late afternoon, the air cool with a thin overcast. She wore a light raincoat over her evening gown and, for the driving, her sensible SOE shoes. He kissed her. It was as it had been after their first lovemaking, a bit awkward. She geared up and they darted away.

"Where are we going?" he asked over the rush of the wind.

"Delham," she called back.

"Where's that?"

"In Essex County, northeast about fifty miles. We'll have dinner there and then go on to Clacton-on-Sea. I've let a small cottage for a couple of days. From an SOE liaison major of Engineers I met in training. You'll love it."

He nodded, turned, and looked out at the countryside.

She'd had a difficult time reaching him by telephone at the base, kept running into security roadblocks. Frustrated, she finally asked another agent to see if he could break through the security grid using the SFHQ links. He did manage to at least leave a message for Parnell at the base headquarters with Anabel's number at Somerset House.

Red called at 8:30 that night. He sounded tired and didn't say much while she trembled inside. He told her he and the team had been given a double class-B pass, forty-eight hours starting at noon the following day.

She hadn't been able to get out of London until afternoon. It was now three o'clock. Watching him out of the corner of her eye, Anabel felt herself trembling again. Yet at the same time she was a bit hurt and, frankly, miffed. He seemed so distant, preoccupied. What the hell was wrong?

It took them three hours to reach Dedham, bypassing London and going through St. Albans and then on to Colchester before turning toward the sea. The restaurant she'd chosen sat beside the Stour River on a rise of land called Gun Hill, its downslope terraced with flower beds. It was named the Vale, set in a lovely seventeenth-century, half-timbered building with dark oak ceiling beams that were so low and intimate Parnell would have to duck when he moved about inside.

In the parking lot, Anabel slipped on her heels and took off her coat, laid it across the seat. Parnell stood staring at her for a long, silent moment. Then, without a word, he swept her up in his arms and they held each other tightly. She could smell the scent of his soap, feel the muscled roundness of his shoulders and back, and felt her own body, her secret, delicate places, warm with longing.

She did all the ordering, which turned out to be a sumptuous meal. First they had starters of the world-famous Colchester oysters, then cock-a-leekie soup and leg of lamb and breast of pheasant with braised cabbage, accompanied by three different wines, all good but quite strong. Their awkwardness quickly vanished. They became light, laughing, teasing, and feeding each other. Afterward she let him drive, both of them a little drunk, her leaning against his shoulder pointing out where to go.

The cottage was a storybook house of stone, cob, and plaster, with a thatched roof, the eaves round as the top of a muffin, and lopsided mullioned-and-leaded windows with diamond-cut panes. Once inside, they left the lights off and, giggling like children, explored in the dark until they found the bedroom and lay together on the musty-smelling coverlet, undressing each other.

Three times they made excruciatingly passionate love. Later, naked except for blankets around their shoulders, they went outside and stood looking down a long slope toward the sea. The air was filled with the headiness of roses and hawthorn. The sky, clear now, gleamed with stars and they could see the faint edge of the quarter moon beginning its rise.

Then the bombers came over. Several flights moving east, way up, lightless, only their shadows crossing against the stars. It shattered the moment. Red and Anabel went back into the house and lay in bed, murmuring, touching, until Anabel mounted him, thrusting and thrusting desperately, her body silhouetted against the dim, diamond-sundered moonbeams coming through the window.

As her climax drew thunderously close, she suddenly grabbed his head between her hands, pulled his face up to her own, and breathlessly cried out, "Do you love me? Damn it, do you *love* me?" And he whispered back hoarsely, "Yes, oh, God, *yes!*"

Afterward, she wept.

The next day they walked into the village, Clacton-on-Sea, all of it on a hill with a steep stone-paved main street like a staircase up from the sea. The shops and houses all had walls covered with creepers. They ate wartime iced lollies at Jeffery's Ice Cream Parlour and then bought Cornish pasties and blackberry fool along with several bottles of blond ale and a round straw basket to carry it all in.

They hiked out across the moor meadows. The land was all rolling hills filled with low stone walls and heaths and fens and marshland lakes called "broads" that glistened in the sun like pools of mercury. The thick greenness of the fields here and there was interrupted by great colored carpets of wildflowers: golden trefoil and crimson ladyfingers.

Picknicking beside a narrow stream with water clear

as air, Red tried to catch trout that hovered near the rocky bottom with his hands but couldn't. After eating, they went swimming naked in a deep rock pool, the water icy cold. They tossed four of the ale bottles into the pool to cool and drank them on the mossy bank, shivering. Afterward, lying in the sun beside a gnarled yew tree that Anabel told him was called a cow's tail pine, they made love.

That afternoon, they stopped in at an alehouse called the Dirty Duck in the tiny hamlet of Clovestowe where they ate a plowman's lunch and played darts. Anabel won three straight times and Red nicknamed her Babe Ruth Sinclair, but then said he'd actually let her win and she called him a liar.

Arm in arm, they walked back home through the evening's blue, salt-scented air. In the cottage's main room, pleasantly done in muted greens and pinks softened even more by the coppery light of an oil lamp, Parnell made a fire and got out a bottle of Canadian Club whiskey he'd scored at the airbase.

They huddled on a couch with a Jacobean needlepoint coverlet, talking, telling each other things from their pasts, tales that were funny and wild and foolish and sad. Yet, neither spoke of their present missions, nor did they venture forward into the future, beyond *this* moment, *this* time and place. It was as if, by subtle agreement, they had decided that if they avoided speaking of it, they could deny its reality.

Eventually, the fire died and they fell asleep. Sometime in the night, Parnell woke to the sound of aircraft again. The fire was out and the room chilly. He carried Anabel into the bedroom, tucked her in, then went out and had a cigarette, studying the sky. The moon had risen, looking like a white drumhead with a spotlight showing only on its rim.

When he returned to the bed, Anabel was awake. She clung to him. They didn't say anything, or make love, but just lay holding each other.

Anabel was up at dawn. She sat in the dark kitchen and smoked a cigarette, then dressed and walked into the village. At a small greengrocer's she bought some eggs and sausage, Shelton cheese, a bit of flour, salt, and coffee.

She scrambled the eggs and sausage on an old, cast-iron wood stove with a leaf motif and made pan biscuits using a recipe she'd learned as a little girl during a summer vacation with her parents in the Grand Tetons in Wyoming. Parnell watched her, drinking his coffee spiced with whiskey.

Suddenly, midway through the meal, Anabel asked, very softly, "What if one of us doesn't come back?"

Parnell glanced up, then gently laid down his fork. "We'll both come back, Anabel," he said.

She held his eyes. "But you can't be sure. God, nothing is sure in that . . . *insanity* over there."

"I know we will, I *feel* it." He smiled. "Never doubt a soldier's instincts."

She turned away, looked out the kitchen window. On the hill road, a young girl herded a line of white geese. The garden flowers made pure dabs of bright color in the sunlight, which glittered and sparkled off the diamonds in the window.

At last, she came back, forced a smile. "Yes," she said. "Both of us."

Parnell began to eat again. The food had lost its taste. He had lied to her, of course. And knew that she knew he had. Still, they had to continue the game, didn't they?

Dance the dance? To do otherwise would have been unbearable.

When they left, they placed a pair of twopenny coins on the cottage's doorsill. According to custom, she said, it meant they would one day return. The drive back to Chelton Cross seemed endless and yet too swift. They didn't speak much. She drove with her hand on his leg, his on hers. It was eight minutes after noon when they arrived at the main gate.

They kissed good-bye. Parnell looked into her eyes and ran the backs of his fingers along her cheek. "Soon," he said.

"Yes, soon," she answered..

He walked away. She didn't watch him go. Instead, she immediately geared up, spun a U, and raced back up the road.

Chapter Thirteen

The offensive to break out of the Cotentin, code-named Operation Cobra, was scheduled for 24 July, its goal to drive through to Avranches at the western foot of the peninsula and open the way for deeper thrusts into Brittany and eastward to Le Mans, Alençon, and Argentan. In the north, strong German divisions still held off Montgomery outside Caen.

Early that morning, 2,500 American bombers and fighter aircraft took off from five fields in England and headed for Normandy. Their primary target was a narrow section of the frontline midway between St-Lô and Periers. But a rapidly moving cloud front had swept ashore earlier in the night. It completely obscured their target zone. Soon, SHAEF issued orders that the bombardment was to be canceled and rescheduled for the following day.

Tragically, over five-hundred pilots of the strike force never received that call-off order. They carried out the raid and, because of the murky cloud cover, dropped many of their bombs onto the American assault units that were poised to move into the attack the moment the bombardment ended. Several hundred were killed or wounded.

Next morning, the air force made another try. This time, the sky was clear, perfectly blue. Over five thousand tons of bombs were dropped. So many, in fact, that the dense dust from their explosions drifted across the U.S. lines. Another six-hundred American soldiers were hit.

Nevertheless, this bombardment decimated the Germans, the brunt of which was Generalleutnant Fritz Bayerlein's elite Panzer Lehr Division, which suffered 70 percent killed, wounded, or driven mad. Still, SS Generaloberst Paul Hausser, who had taken over Rommel's armor, was a confident, resourceful officer. He still believed he could stem the American thrust and thereby keep the Allies locked in the Cotentin until Hitler sent him reinforcements.

Cobra's main thrust was carried out by Lightning Joe Collins's VII Corps and Major General Troy Middleton's VIII Corps. Actually, Middleton was to have been Patton's vanguard in Normandy once he got activated. But at the last moment, Bradley had shifted him along with several other units to his First Army.

Both corps quickly smashed through the German defenses and began racing southward: Middleton through Periers, and Collins toward Marigny on his left flank. That night the Germans struck back with a strong armored counteroffensive mounted by Hausser's 2nd SS Das Reich Panzer Division and the 17th SS Gotz von Berlichingen Panzer Grenadier Division.

It was a useless attempt. Coordinating with air strikes and artillery, the American armor mauled both of Hausser's elite divisions, destroying the 2nd Panzer as a functioning unit. Collins and Middleton bored right ahead. By 28 July, they reached the outskirts of Coutances and Roncey. That evening the 4th Armored Division occupied Coutances after a savage flanking attack. The way to Avranches and the approaches to Brittany now lay wide open.

* * *

Parnell spotted a large dust cloud, six miles to the east. Something big on the move. Three hundred feet directly below the tiny L-4 spotter plane, the country was open farmland, no longer *bocage,* now mostly triangular fields and pastures and scattered orchards with a few farmsteads and small, burned-out hamlets. Here and there the earth had been torn apart, blackened and filled with bomb craters and wrecked German vehicles still seeping smoke.

The spotter plane pilot was Lieutenant Pete Cassaneres from Detroit. Blue-eyed with jet-black, curly hair and a gunfighter's mustache that made him look like Jesse James. He was one of the best liaison flyers in the ETO and could make his little Piper *Grasshopper* do things it had never been designed to do.

He'd flown in North Africa and Italy and had been shot down three times. He was also the only pilot in Europe to score an air-to-air kill against a Kraut Fieseler Storch by exchanging pistol fire. Like Red, he was now attached to the 35th Tank Battalion of the 4th Armored Division. At the moment, they were flying three miles south of Coutances near the German stronghold of Roncey.

Back in his tandem seat, Red keyed the intercom. "Dust at three o'clock, Pete. Six miles out."

"Yeah, I see it. What do you think, armor or convoy?"

"That much dust, I figure either armor or mobile artillery."

Cassaneres snapped a tight turn. It was nearly one o'clock in the afternoon. The sun was hot and bright and made the countryside that stretched off to the horizon look pastoral-sleepy and summer-pleasant.

As the plane leveled up, Parnell glassed the dust cloud. From inside the drab green interior of the aircraft, its Continental A-65-8 engine sounded like a motorbike while the canvas-and-tubing frame and wings bounced and waggled as they drifted slowly over heat updrafts.

Earlier, Blue Team had been ordered to remain with the 4th Division until Patton was ready to begin his drive into Brittany and to the east. Bird and the others were now cadres in the division's Combat Command B's three tank battalions, while Parnell and Cassaneres performed aerial forward observation, Pete handling all artillery missions and Red the tactical interdiction air strikes.

They began a slow climb. He could clearly see the source of the dust cloud now, a column of Mark IV tanks, at least nine, and several Nashorn 8.8 Pak 43 self-propelled antitank guns. Farther back, moving in single file on both sides of the road, was at least three companies of dismounted infantry.

"Bingo, baby!" Pete called happily. Red heard him switch to the battalion OC's frequency and begin a request for an artillery fire mission.

He watched the column, close enough now to see individual Kraut soldiers looking up at them as they came in slowly. Earlier in the war, spotter planes had been easy targets for ground fire. But after such intense bombardments and artillery barrages, the Germans were terrified whenever one appeared, knowing that if they fired on it and exposed their exact positions, it would be only a matter of minutes before Allied artillery or fighters would hit them.

Still, Red was puzzled. What was this force doing out here? He knew German units *never* moved in broad daylight. As they drew closer, he began to see the reason for it. First off, the armored vehicles were moving too fast, their commanders anxious to gain distance. Secondly, the infantry troops looked worn out, disorganized, their march discipline ragged. At the very sight of the L-4, many had broken from the column and were trying to hide out in the grass.

The poor sons a' bitches were in full retreat, he realized. No, actually in a *rout*. The ceaseless poundings they'd taken over the last three weeks had obviously disrupted their unit integrity and morale. He felt a moment of pity but quickly squelched it so as to focus on the best way to handle this prime target. He decided to wait till Cassaneres's artillery barrage was over, then see whether or not he should bring in fighters for strafing runs to take out the survivors.

A spray of bullets suddenly slammed into the little plane, hitting like a wind gust, the rounds sizzling by after making hard pops as they blew through the doped canvas. One tore a hole in the back brace of Pete's seat. Red heard a tire explode. There was a sharp cracking sound and the engine stopped abruptly. A thin layer of oil droplets began layering the outside of the Plexiglas.

"Aw, *shit!*" Cassaneres yelled.

Another spray of bullets came. Seat cushion stuffing flew and one of the port struts blew apart, creating a large rip in the wing. Parnell felt a bullet cut across the top of his thigh, stinging like fire.

He keyed. "Pete, are you all right?"

"I been . . . fuckin' . . . *belly* shot!"

The plane tilted hard over, then snapped back and over in the opposite direction. Beyond the Plexiglas, the horizon fell away, reappeared, rushing past. He could smell burning oil. A slash of smoke flashed by.

Up front, Cassaneres kept flopping over, then straightening up again. The plane suddenly pulled up sharply. For a moment, it hung near a stall, everything shaking. Pete released all controls and the weight of the engine pulled the nose down again. They floundered and began rapidly losing altitude.

Parnell saw the ground four hundred feet away, grass and stones. The plane finally leveled out. A line of trees loomed directly ahead. The aircraft was still sinking but in a partially controlled glide. Red braced himself. The tops of the trees came at them in slow motion, everything silent now save for the soft slurring sound of air crossing over the wings.

They just barely cleared the trees. Branches snapped across the wheels and undercarriage, twisted the plane sharply to the right. The ground came up as they slid in sideways. Cassaneres managed to kick the tail around at the last moment and they skimmed, the tall grass blades flashing by just feet away.

They struck hard, slightly nose high, the main wheels and tail stud hitting at the same moment. The L-4 bounced wildly as its speed dissipated. Suddenly they hit a ditch and ground-looped, the nose plowing into dirt.

Parnell punched his seat release and kicked out the Plexiglas. He dropped to the ground, twisted around, and pulled the door open. Pete stared at him from upside down. His flying jacket was drenched in blood, looking like black wax on the leather. His eyes were glazed and looked peculiar inverted. He tried to grin but only managed to croak, "Ain't this the shits?"

Red got him unhooked and down onto the ground. At that moment, he heard the unmistakable rippling sound of incoming artillery, the first salvo of Pete's mission call. It passed overhead and slammed into the ground about two hundred yards away, shaking the earth violently. The roar of the explosions and the concussion waves raced out across the grass, bending them as if they'd been struck by a powerful wind. Black smoke fumed up into the sky and whirling things flashed high up in the sunlight.

In the pause between salvos, Red retrieved the medical bag and his Thompson from the cockpit. He got Cassaneres's jacket off and his shirt ripped away. He'd been shot in the stomach below the belly button, two bullets, one going straight in, the other ripping him open like a samurai's knife in hara-kiri. Blood pumped out in spurts. The edges of the wound showed fatty tissue, yellowed like spoiled mayonnaise.

He gave Cassneres a shot of morphine, then bound the wounds as tightly as he could with a sterile bandage. It immediately filled with blood. He put another on. He could feel the squishiness of the intestines as he shoved them back into Pete's body. Another double salvo came whistling, rippling in. He lay over Cassneres, hearing the shells hit, hearing and feeling the roaring, rumbling sweep of the concussions rocketing out through the ground.

Silence, full of ringing sounds and hummings. Did he hear men's voices? He shook his head. It ached horribly. *There, again.* He lifted slightly, looked toward where the barrage shells had hit. His heart went to ice and then exploded with a surge of adrenaline. Running across the field directly toward him were twenty German soldiers.

Oh, Christ Almighty!

He lost all conscious thought, all rationality gone in a flash. Now he moved on a soldier's pure instinct, his blood up there sparking with adrenaline. *Kill them!* He opened with his Thompson, sweeping from right to left. Four soldiers went down instantly. Another fell back, rose, fell back again. The others bored on, screaming.

The Thompson's receiver locked back, the clip empty. He popped it out, tore off his spare that was taped to the stock, rammed it in, and released the receiver. Once more, he fired, fanning, too far to the left this time. Only two soldiers went down.

The second clip emptied. He hurled the weapon away and fumbled for his Colt .45 pistol. The Germans were forty yards from him. He aimed, then stopped. They had their arms in the air and had no weapons. Their faces were gaunt, their eyes wild. *What? What?* They were shouting, *"Komerad! Gefallen, Komerad!"* Jesus, they were *surrendering* to him!

Another salvo of American 105s came in, farther to the right, the gunners, without adjustment calls from Casaneres, now laying in time-on-target fire at will. The Germans dropped to the ground.

Something suddenly flashed by less than thirty feet over Parnell's head. Another L-4. Like Casaneres's, its nose was painted a bright red and the prop tips formed a crimson ring in the sunlight as it pulled up into a climbing turn. A stretcher rack was fitted to the left wing strut.

The Germans didn't appear to notice it. They had plunged to the ground when the salvo came. Now they leaped up and started running again. Some were sobbing. All but three ran blindly past the crashed plane, their terror gone beyond control.

Parnell lowered his weapon. He glanced at the three who remained but couldn't look at them. Instead, he watched the Piper go past, turn around, and come back, lowering, its engine idling. It landed, bounced, touched again, and held, coming abreast of him.

He lifted Cassaneres. Pete sighed. It ended in a gurgle. He appeared unconscious. Parnell ran to the aircraft. The three Germans, still on their knees, watched him with empty, stupefied looks. The pilot had an M1A1 carbine on them, the barrel sticking out the side window. He wore a

4th Fighter Group baseball cap and had a cigar in his mouth.

"Don't shoot," Red shouted as he came up carrying Pete. "They're shell-shocked."

"Okay, fella," the pilot called calmly. "But make it goddamn fast."

Parnell slid Cassaneres onto the stretcher and strapped him in. The wound had saturated the fresh bandage with blood. Pete's face was gray white. Red ran around the tail and started to climb into the plane.

One of the Krauts suddenly appeared, running in close by the spinning prop. He lunged for Parnell, got a hold on one leg. His face was contorted and he babbled incoherently and refused to let go. The Piper's Continental engine wound up and the plane started to move forward slowly, then faster. The German continued clinging to Parnell's trousers although he was being dragged backward. He tried to climb up Red's pant leg. Parnell kicked at his hands but couldn't dislodge him.

"Godammit, get him off," the pilot yelled. "We won't be able to lift off."

Parnell reached down, tried to pry the man's fingers away, couldn't. The plane was struggling to rise into the air, the throttle full to the wall, the prop hurling wash back. Again it started to lift, lopsidedly, then dropped back, lifted, dropped.

Red felt something hit his shoulder. He turned. The pilot shoved his sidearm at him. "For chrissakes, shoot the son of a bitch," he hollered.

Parnell took the gun. The German was frantically trying to climb over the strut now. He whimpered and sweat whipped away from his face. Red looked into his eyes. He would never forget them. He shot him in the forehead.

The soldier tumbled away and the L-4, freed of its

overload, instantly took off, banking sharply as it responded to the imbalanced weight of the stretcher on the other strut. The pilot leveled and they turned westward, holding to less than a hundred feet as another barrage salvo came in, the shells making streaks in the sunlight.

Pete Cassaneres was dead by the time they landed at a fighter strip outside Coutances.

On 29 July, Bradley unleashed Patton and his Third Army. Over the next two weeks, Old Blood and Guts would attack in four directions, rolling over German defenses as if they weren't even there.

Combining with the XIX Tactical Air Command, which quickly became known as Patton's Air Force, he proved out his air–ground team doctrine magnificently. Able to call up air strikes any time, anywhere, his armor commanders moved so fast some actually ran right off their own tactical battle maps.

Middleton's VIII Corps, now back with Third Army, drove hard into Brittany, while XII Corps quickly moved through Avranches and turned eastward toward Fougères, Laval, and Le Mans. The XX Corps turned southeast and headed for Nantes and Angers on the river Loire, and Major General Wade Haislip's XV Corps struck northeast toward the key cities of Alençon and Argentan. Meanwhile, in the north, Monty's troops finally took Caen and were now headed for Falaise to the southeast.

Back in the strategy rooms of SHAEF, the Combined Chiefs of Staff studied their maps and saw that the rapidly developing situation in France was about to present them with a tremendous opportunity. If the British and Canadians were able to quickly move through Falaise and link with the Americans coming from Argentan, their combined force could trap over 300,000 Germans in what would later be called the Falaise Pocket.

The moment Patton had taken the field, Dunmore transferred Blue Team to the XV Corps' 5th Armored Division, specifically to the 34th Tank Battalion of Combat Command B, as it moved east toward Alençon.

Since their tank commander students had learned the procedures for call fire so rapidly, their cadre duties were over and they had been freed to return to their primary duty of probing enemy defenses on deep recon patrols. To facilitate this, they were assigned to F Company, the 34th 's reconnaissance squadron.

They continually ranged far ahead of the CC B's leading tanks. But since they were moving so swiftly, Parnell and his men had to use jeeps to stay out ahead of them. On the fourth of August, just outside the key rail junction of la Ferte Mace, they came on a twenty-two-car train hauling German field howitzers. Red immediately called in an air strike, destroying the locomotive and every single gun car.

The next day they flushed out an entire company of Krauts from the German 708th Infantry Regiment, which had been withdrawn from the area two days before. These men were lost, exhausted, and without food or ammunition. They readily surrendered to Parnell. He sent Weesay, Cowboy, and Smoker in one jeep to escort them back to battalion headquarters while he and Wyatt continued ahead in the other vehicle.

At dawn on 9 August, at a road junction a mile from the town of Carrouges, they caught up to the tail end of the

German 5th Artillery Battalion in full retreat. There were fourteen horse-drawn artillery pieces and the accompanying gun crews.

A Panther tank suddenly appeared on a hill five hundred yards away. It spotted their two jeeps and immediately opened on them with its long-barrel 75mm turret gun. The tank's gunner was very fast and accurate. Before Blue Team could withdraw into a nearby cherry orchard, he bracketed them, lighting up one of the jeeps.

Parnell immediately radioed for air support. Two of Tactical Air Command's newly arrived A-26 Invader attack bombers with two Mustang fighters were vectored to the target. The A-26s came in first, diving out of a lightening sky to hit the artillery column from both ends with their two-hundred-pound bombs and 37- and 75mm nose cannons. After two runs, they broke off to let the Mustangs strafe the survivors.

Afterward, Parnell and his men went down into the killing field. As battle-hardened as they were, the sight sickened them. Wounded men crawled about crying out, some with limbs completely blown off. Corpses and unidentifiable parts of human bodies along with dead and wounded horses, down in their bright harnesses, lay strewn about. The animals screamed, the sound high-pitched and throat-constricting in the morning stillness. Explosion dust and smoke formed a yellow haze in the new sun and the air stank of blood and freshly sundered flesh and cordite.

They administered to the wounded soldiers, only twelve who looked as if they might survive their wounds. Then they walked among the carnage and shot the horses. The German Panther watched from its hill but did not fire on them again.

Finally, Parnell signaled it, using Morse code with his

dit-dot mirror: *come for wounded.* The tank didn't move
for a long time. At last, it came down slowly, its steel
treads clanking. It pulled up near where they had laid
out the wounded men. The crew climbed out, their coveralls battle-filthy, their faces gaunt. No one spoke. The
Americans helped them load the wounded inside the vehicle and on its hull apron. Blood dripped down onto
the treads and bogie wheels.

When it was finished, the tank commander, a *Feld-
webel,* or staff sergeant, snapped to attention before
Parnell. He was thick-chested and bull-necked with dark
eyes. Red touched the tips of his fingers to his forehead
in a casual salute. The German held for a moment, then
climbed back into his tank. It spun slowly and moved
back up the hill.

The following day, Patton ordered XV Corps to begin a
concerted attack against the battered remnants of the German LXXXI Corps defending Alençon. As the 34th moved
into attack positions, enemy resistance was minor, only a
few small skirmishes. But then General von Kluge shoved
his Fifth Panzer Army, commanded by Heinrich Eber-
bach, along with every aircraft he could muster from the
badly depleted Luftwaffe, into the defense of Alençon.

Wyatt Bird much preferred night patrols. The dark was
a friend, engendering in him a profound patience and
total alertness to his surroundings. He could hear and in-
terpret every sound, every smell, the tiniest distortion of
his immediate environment. He'd learned such things as
a boy in the hardscrabble country of central Louisiana.
Then it had been hunting, now it was survival.

He lay behind a low rock, scanning the ground directly
ahead of him. Off to his left was Wineberg. Parnell had

sent them far forward of the battalion's jumping-off position a mile back to probe for minefields in the approaches
to Alençon. The night was cool, filled with moonlight and
large clouds that moved across the sky like arctic icebergs.
Whenever they crossed over the moon, he and Smoker
were able to advance from point to point.

Down a gentle slope fifty yards away was a small stream,
glistening like a strip of cellophane in the blue-white light.
Farther on was a footbridge and what appeared to be two
drainage ditches that emptied into the stream. From his
terrain patrol maps, Wyatt knew that beyond it the ground
rose slightly and then flattened out until it reached a line
of trees far to the right. A half mile in the other direction
was Alençon.

Suddenly, he heard the tinny *pa-thong* of a flare gun and
he clamped his eyes shut and froze in position. German
sentries often randomly shot up flares along their defensive lines trying to catch enemy recon patrols testing their
front. The sound of the gun had been very close, a sentry
post somewhere just beyond the footbridge.

Even through his eyelids the flare light appeared brilliant. Its pop-and-crackle grew steadily louder. *Jesus, it's
coming right down on us,* he thought. Still brighter and
brighter it got. Wyatt held his face close to the ground,
caught the smell of wet soil and mildew and weapon
packing. His skin crawled, waiting, knowing that at any
moment they could be seen.

Abruptly the light went out and he heard the last fading
sizzle of it from somewhere close behind their position.
He opened his eyes. Now the air smelled of flare smoke.
Good, good. They'd lucked out. The Kraut sentry post was
beyond the footbridge, which had shielded them from
being spotted.

He waited a full fifteen minutes before moving. A distant barrage started, stopped. Crickets orchestrated in the brush. A frog in the stream croaked, calling with the same four tones over and over again. In the silence, it sounded as if it were saying Cin-cinn-*a*-ti.

At last he hand signaled Smoker and began crawling down the slope toward the stream. He quickly reached it. The bank was three feet high and covered with reeds. He slipped into the water, squatted. A moment later, Wineberg pushed through the reeds and silently slid down beside him.

They moved along the streambed, pushing their shoes slowly, soundlessly through the water until they reached the drainage ditches. They crawled up into the second one. It was filled with refuse: tin cans, ration cartons, pieces of grenade boxes. There was a strong, sickly-sour smell. Obviously, a German soldier had recently crapped down into the ditch. In the moonlight, blowflies, their backs shiny, droned over the dark pile of excrement.

They inched past, moved on, stopping every few minutes to listen. Soon they were at least a hundred yards beyond the outer rim of gun posts. The moon, almost directly overhead, shone down brightly into the ditch. Using its illumination, Bird constantly scanned directly in front of him, searching for the tiny reflection from a trip wire. So far, there had been none.

Thirty minutes later, he spotted one, a hair-thick gleaming line stretched a foot off the bottom of the ditch. There was another one four feet beyond. He stopped, then stealthily rose and peered over the rim of the ditch. At that moment, a cloud moved across the moon. He waited for it to pass. Again the surrounding ground was flooded with light.

He immediately saw that it was mined. Where each mine was placed, the cover dirt had been compressed by rain, forming a small circular indentation that created a moon shadow. He was able to make out three distinct belts, each one staggered to the next and all laid out in eighty-foot, overlapping arrowhead patterns.

Here and there were the longer, square indentations where wooden high-explosive boxes with pressure fuses had been placed. A double-apron fence ran along the minefield's baseline to his right and mine stakes were set along the corners of the arrowheads. They were made from tree stumps with the sides shaved and the letter M painted on them.

For the next hour, both men studied the field, section by section, imprinting the entire picture on their minds: a ruined farmhouse there, a tree line over there, a double tank ditch curving to the right and then running parallel to the inner baseline of the field.

It was nearly three o'clock when Wyatt finally signaled Smoker and they turned back along the ditch. Fifty feet from the small stream, they heard Germans. Both of them dropped to their bellies, down there among the empty cans and human shit. Two German soldiers came to the edge of the ditch and stood there talking. By now the moon had moved and was casting a shadow across it. One Kraut was directly above Bird. He began to urinate. The stream hit Wyatt on the shoulder and the back of his neck, warm and sticky.

Fuck!

One soldier, sounding angry, said, "*Ah, dass dieser Koter. Der Torfkopf!*" The edge of his helmet gleamed dully in the moonlight.

The other said, "*Na, komm schon. Lass Franz in ruhe, Gerhard.*"

"*Geh weg!*"

"*Ah, Scheiss drauf!*" The second soldier walked off.

The flow of urine stopped. Bird heard the rustle of cloth, the German mumbling angrily to himself. Then Wyatt's heart jumped as he caught sight of his wristwatch. In the moon shadow, its phosphorescent dials were glowing brightly.

The Kraut soldier abruptly murmured, *"Was ist . . . ?"* He bent down to peer into the ditch.

In one snake-quick movement, Bird grabbed his helmet strap, shoving his knuckles into the man's throat to keep him from shouting, and hauled him downward. The soldier flailed, off-balance, as Wyatt pulled his boot knife and rammed it deep into the German's lower stomach. The blade went in to the hilt, no bone to block it. Putting his shoulder behind it, he slashed across. As the soldier dropped heavily, he shoved him onto the opposite side of the ditch, the man landing on his back as Bird came to his knees.

The German made a soft moan and gripped his stomach. Coils of shiny tissue pushed through his fingers, his intestines erupting through the wound, smoking in the cold. He lifted his head. In the moonlight, his eyes shone like large, blue-white pearls. His lips trembled and he made another soft, muttered moan. Twisting his knife, Bird swung the blade backhanded and sliced across the soldier's throat. Blood burst forth, a black fountain. The German slumped.

They wired two grenades to the dead man's helmet and belt. If someone lifted his head, they'd trigger them. Then they retraced their way back up the stream to their entry point. They were nearly to the distant tree line when the grenades went off. A few seconds later, two flares arched into the sky, flooding the landscape. A machine gun started firing, then another farther down, the Germans recognizing the blast signature of the American M3 grenades. Their tracers crossed each other's field of fire. After a while, the firing stopped.

At 0235, Bird and Winberg crossed back through their battalion's perimeter.

19 August 1944
0143 hours BDST

"Surprise, surprise," Anabel Sinclair shouted over the roar of the bomber's engines. Grinning, her pretty features distorted by the light from two flashlights, she laid out her cards onto the aircraft's corrugated aluminum deck. "Full house, gents. Read 'em and weep."

Her two opponents were Howard Hopkins, the SOE dispatcher assigned to oversee the forthcoming airdrop, and a fellow agent, Paul Guiet, code-named Nestor. She and Guiet were to jump near the Lorraine District city of Brumath, north of Strasbourg on the French-German border. Once down, Anabel would link up with the Crisp circuit of the Maquis, while Paul would travel with the Bistrot circuit.

They were aboard a British Armstrong-Whitney MkV medium bomber from 161 Squadron, the Moonrunners, sitting inside a stack of steel crates containing supplies and weapons, playing draw poker by flashlight. It was icy cold in the aircraft, both agents dressed in heavily padded jumpsuits, gloves, and football-like helmets that made Anabel look like a young boy. Hopkins wore a fur-collared jacket and a woolen crew cap.

"Bloody hell!" he cried now and disgustedly threw down his hand. "That bloody well flushes me, woman." He pulled himself to his feet and climbed out of their cubbyhole to go forward to the flight deck.

As Anabel gathered in her winnings, Guiet asked, "Are

you always so lucky?" He was a dapper little Frenchman with a gigolo's cool smoothness.

"At poker, always." She had taken them for nearly twenty-two pounds during the three-hour flight from RAF Tempsford, in Bedfordshire, the Moonrunners' home base. "Want to go again? Two-handed play?"

"*Mon Dieu, non,*" Guiet cried. "I know when to cease." Then he smiled. "I will console myself that it is a sign we will both encounter good luck down there."

"I'll second that, pal."

Guiet sighed, folded his arms, and rested his head back against one of the crates. He closed his eyes. Sinclair watched him and her cheeriness instantly vanished. She had learned a long time ago how to hide her inner feelings. People needn't know what was inside. Now she inhaled deeply and let the air slip out slowly through her lips.

Beyond the stack of gear crates was the rectangular drop hole in the aircraft's deck through which she and Guiet would jump. Afterward, as the bomber made a second pass, the chute packs on the crates would be hooked to a static line, then slid on roller slots and pushed out. Now the wind, full of engine roar and the smell of hot oil, rushed up through the hole sounding like heavy rain.

She flicked off the flashlights and in the abrupt darkness her mind shifted, the anxious thoughts that had been hovering way back there like storm clouds coming forward. She felt her stomach tighten. It was partly from fear and partly from a sense of excited anticipation. Operation Oasis was finally beginning.

After saying good-bye to Parnell, that day seeming so terribly long ago, Anabel had decided to cut her holiday short and return immediately to F Section. It would have been senseless to brood away the remaining days in a blue funk. No, she needed busywork, to keep the edge of sadness away.

No one at Somerset House seemed surprised to see her back so soon. Some gave her sly, knowing smiles. Apparently word of her Yank lieutenant had seeped out. Surprisingly, even Brigadier Stanton-Ferryman appeared pleased to see her back already. He asked after neither her soldier "friend" nor her parents.

Three days later, Anabel was informed she was to accompany the brigadier to what was known as a Warning Order conference. This was the first phase in the inception of a new operational mission. All he would say was, "I think you'll find this most interesting."

They were driven in his chauffeured Bentley to the New Public Offices in central London. Far beneath this building was a huge bombproof bunker made up of a sixteen-room suite, all grouped around a main map room. The facility was called the Cabinet War Rooms. In it Prime Minister Churchill and his Chiefs of Staff met to conduct the war. Also within it was a small cubbyhole containing a SIGSALY scrambler telephone connected by transatlantic cable to the White House so Churchill could speak directly with President Roosevelt at any time.

They were ushered into one of the conference rooms by a female naval ensign. The space was done all in white with a long mahogany table and leather chairs. A large map of Europe covered one wall. Before each chair was a gold-edged notepad, two sterling silver pens, and a carafe of water and a glass. SOE's liaison chief for the Foreign Office, Sir Maurice Peterson, was already there.

Over the next ten minutes the assistants to the Chiefs of Staff of the three military branches appeared: Admiral Gerald Aston, General Sir William Capstick, and

Second Assistant Air Chief Alan Laine. The last to show up was General Bruce Stanfield, who was Churchill's appointment to chair the Committee for Imperial Defense.

Anabel sat like a little girl in church, overwhelmed by all the brass. *Jesus, what the hell am I doing here?* She didn't have a clue as to why she was being included in this galaxy of military big shots. So, she said nothing, occasionally sipped water, and smiled pleasantly when she was introduced.

General Stanfield opened the meeting. He was a short, brisk man with a ramrod-straight back and dark eyes that seemed to have sufficient intensity to bore holes through cement. He quickly got to the business at hand, the plans for the new operation code-named Oasis. In clipped tones, he summarized its beginnings, its mission purpose, and the parameters of its execution. He spoke without notes and only occasionally pointed to something on the wall map.

As the intricacies of Operation Oasis unfolded, Sinclair was stunned. The thing was *brilliant.* Of course it would be risky, and might not even work in the end. But it was a wonderfully bold stroke. One that could conceivably end the war in Europe. And, holy crap, *she* was going to be a part of it!

For a long time, British Intelligence had known of Feldmarschall Erwin Rommel's realization that the war was lost, and that if left unchecked, Hitler would bring complete destruction to Germany. Although he hadn't taken a direct hand in the failed assassination of the Führer, he knew of it. Moreover, with his being the most respected military man in Germany, "the People's General," the conspirators had intended for him to replace Hitler and then negotiate an immediate peace with the Allies.

At the moment, Rommel was convalescing at his

home in Wiener Newstadt, a small mountain town south
of Vienna, Austria. But intelligence reports had begun
streaming in about Hitler's purging of the German High
Command in revenge for the 20 July plot. It was only a
matter of time before he got to Rommel.

So the primary mission of Operation Oasis was to
bring about a meeting between the *Feldmarschall* and
General Stanfield, who would act as Churchill's personal
envoy in an effort to persuade Rommel to defect to England, declare himself the *ex propio* leader of Germany,
and once and for all bring down the Nazi regime.

Anabel's part of it was to coordinate the links between
SOE and those Resistance cells in northeastern France,
southern Germany, and central Austria which would help
her get Stanfield to and from Rommel's home. Its challenge and obvious danger titillated her, made her giddy
with expectation.

Before the meeting broke up, the general went around
the table, calling for comments and suggestions. When he
got to her, he asked only one question: "Agent Sinclair, are
you up to the task of delivering me to Rommel?"

She came right back. "Yes, sir, I am."

"Good," Stanfield said.

On the ride back to Somerset House, she could hardly
contain her excitement, so many thoughts and ideas racing through her head. Beside her in the vacuumed
silence of the Bentley sat Stanton-Ferryman, poised in
his splendidly fitted dark suit and gloves and exuding
the delicate scent of lime.

Finally he said, "You did quite well back there, Sinclair.
I must say, I was particularly impressed by your immediate response to the general's question. Jolly good, that."

"Thank you, sir." She watched pedestrians hurrying

along the sidewalks. It was cloudy and chilly outside. She turned back. "Might I ask a question?"

"Of course."

"Why was I chosen for Oasis? I mean, I'm a relatively junior agent. Why me?"

"Actually, there were several reasons. Admittedly you're *not* the most experienced agent on our roster. Nevertheless, you're a good one. You speak German like a native. And you're exceedingly familiar with the particular parts of Germany and Austria through which you'll pass." He paused for a moment. "In addition, Stanfield asked for you."

What? How the hell could that be? "Why? How could he even know of me?"

"Perhaps it might be more accurate for me to say he wanted someone *like* you."

"I don't understand."

The brigadier chuckled. "Come along, Sinclair, don't be naive. You're an American, of course. An expatriate but still an American. As you now know, this is to be strictly a British operation. Our Allies won't know of it until it is a fait accompli. Thus the inclusion of an American on the team would, well, let's just say, dull the edge of potential criticism."

Aw, yes, she thought, the eternal bureaucratic BS, that endless one-upsmanship: *Nah, nee nah, I've got a better plan than you.* God! "What if things go completely cock-up?"

"I trust they won't."

Irritated just enough to push it a little further, she said, "What if we're captured and the Krauts broadcast word of it?"

Stanton-Ferryman's eyes narrowed slightly. "In that case, there would be red faces and mutual outrage all round."

The car pulled smoothly to the curb in front of Somerset House. As the driver hurriedly got out and turned to open her door, the brigadier said, a bit stiffer than before, "Tomorrow we'll begin strategy sessions on your phase of the mission. Till then, I suggest you bone up on anything and everything that could possibly have an impact on your task. I'll of course expect some solid input from you."

"Yes, sir."

A faint, cold smile touched his mouth. "I trust my little disclosure hasn't dampened your enthusiasm?"

She gave him back her widest, prettiest grin. "Not one damned bit, Brigadier."

The driver opened her door, she climbed out, and a moment later the Bentley skimmed away.

Hopkins tapped on the top of a crate. "Best get harnessed up, people," he called. "We'll be over drop zone in ten minutes."

Here we go!

He helped the two agents into their chute harnesses, the damned things tight as hell between Anabel's legs, across her breasts. She could feel the adrenaline coming fast now, the beginning of something utterly new. Actually, she enjoyed jumping, its wild sensation of free-falling and then floating.

She lowered herself heavily to the edge of the jump hole and hung her legs over the edge. She would be first out. The wind tugged and sucked at her legs. She felt Guiet getting down directly behind her, his legs straddling her buttocks, his chest pressing against her chute pack.

"One minute and counting," Hopkins shouted.

As he leaned closer, Anabel handed him her poker winnings. "Give this to the flight crew," she shouted. "Tell

them to buy a few rounds on me." She winked at Guiet.
Hopkins took the money, shoved it into his jacket pocket.

They'd be going out at eight hundred feet, single chute,
no backup. She braced one hand against the edge of the
jump hole, and with the other she gripped the chute's pull
ring. She looked down. There was only blackness outside,
yet it seemed tinted a faint blue from the moon, already
far across the sky. She heard, felt the bomber's engines
changing pitch, dropping in sound, the pilots slowing the
aircraft as they approached the jump zone.

Hopkins again leaned down close, bellowed, "*Merde.*"
It was the traditional last word always spoken to an SOE
agent when he departed on a mission. No one knew how
the practice had started. In French, it meant *shit.*

She leaned forward. A moment later, his hand slapped
her hard on the shoulder. She heard "Go!" and was already pushing off, dropping heavily. There was the
sudden, jolting blast as the prop wash hit her, threw her
into a wild tumble, over and around and over again. The
western horizon formed a pale, fuzzy blur as she caught
sight of the Armstrong-Whitney's wide stablilizer and double rudders as it flashed away, a big dark object against the
stars.

Then there were the drop zone lights, four white spots
forming a box way down there in the darkness. They
quickly rolled out of her line of vision as she made one
more, slower spin, reappearing as she came around, now
slightly off to the right.

She pulled the ripchord. There was a pop, the noisy,
clothy stream-out of the main chute and the sudden,
groin-grabbing shock as the canopy opened. Her momentum carried her into a pendulum swing, the zone
lights jacking back and forth yet drawing rapidly closer.
The air was cold and filled with the thick, turpentine odor

of trees, the only sounds now the snap and whip of her risers and the distant drone of the bomber as it made a long, reaching turn to swing back over them for the cargo drop.

Anabel hit hard, down onto packed dirt, her boots striking first. Drawing in her legs, she rolled, the risers coiling around her shoulders and then the canopy, all silky and dumping air, settled down around her legs. She had rolled onto deep grass, wet and crispy with frost. She popped the quick release of her harness and came to one knee.

Two men were running toward her, their flashlights bouncing. Anabel pulled her sidearm, a Webley & Scott 7.65mm blowback model pistol, jacked a round into the chamber, and flicked off the safety.

The men stopped twenty yards from her. One shouted his code name, "Hamlet." Anabel relaxed. *Friendly.* She called back "Roxanne," which was her newly assigned code name for Operation Oasis.

The men started forward again just as the bomber came roaring over. One ran past her, headed for where Guiet had landed. The other came up, grinning. She could see his white teeth in the back glow of his flash. They embraced.

In French, he said, "*Bon Diem, mon petit.* It is so wonderful to see you again."

"*Oui, et tu, mon ami,*" she said happily.

He released her, stepped back. They could hear the cargo crates coming down, their dark chutes big moving shadows. Other flashlights, farther down the field, were converging onto the spot where they would hit. "Come, we must hurry," he said. "Patrols sometimes pass through here before dawn."

Together they began collecting and rolling up her chute, which would be buried somewhere among the trees. The man's code name, Hamlet, was also newly issued, specifically for Oasis. In truth, he wasn't an official SOE agent at all. Instead he was a senior officer with the French Resistance. His original code name had been Lucas.

He was Vaillant Duboudin.

Chapter Fourteen

Throughout the remainder of July and into August, the Allied drive into western France continued unabated. There were occasional fierce battles, stubborn resistance from pockets of elite Kraut units. But overall the German Army was in headlong retreat. In the process it lost twenty-five of its thirty-eight Normandy divisions.

Patton's Third Army had moved with exceptional speed. Aided by decodes of intercepted German Enigma messages and the constant air cover from XIX Tactical Air Command, his armored units swept across Brittany to Dinan and Rennes, struck southeast to Le Mans and Orleans, then rolled due east through Chartres and Dreux by early August.

The only major disappointment had been the failure to close the Falaise Pocket. Because of a lack of coordination between British and American units and a fanatical defense of a corridor out of the Pocket, two-thirds of the remaining Germans had been able to slip through and escape toward the Seine.

But now Bradley grew anxious that Patton was moving *too* fast, exposing his flanks. On 14 August he ordered Old Blood and Guts to stop advancing and hold along the Orléans-Chartres-Dreux line.

Patton was livid. "To hell with my flanks!" he roared. His aim had been to continue all the way to the Seine, cross it, and then turn northwest, trapping Paris and the entire German Seventh Army between him and the British and U.S. First Army driving from the west.

It wasn't until the nineteenth that Bradley was finally convinced to let him loose again.

By 23 August, his spearhead units had taken Melun, Sens, and Troyes. Including the five days lost due to Bradley's hold-order, Third Army's eastern thrust from its first major battle outside Mortain had carried it over 250 miles into the heart of north-central France in only nineteen days.

This lightning maneuver completely unhinged the enemy's plan for the defense of Paris. On 25 August, the city's German commander, Lieutenant General Dietrich von Choltitz, ignoring Hitler's specific orders to destroy it, surrendered Paris. As a concession to the French, Eisenhower ordered that Major General Jacques Philippe Leclerc, commander of the French 2nd Armored Division, would be the one to lead the victorious Allies into the City of Lights that same day.

8 September 1944

Anabel couldn't get over how unpriestlike Jean Couteau looked, with his shoulder-length dark hair swept back in the Byzantine style, his black turtleneck sweater and trousers. Actually he was an *ex*-priest, from the Sacred Trinity Priorate in Reims. Tall and athletic looking, he appeared much younger than his thirty-six years.

As a militant member of the Communist FTA and chief of the Crisp Maquis circuit, he was able to use his considerable skills as a painter for a cover identity. Actually, he had already won some renown as a Fauvist, much in the style of Gauguin and Matisse. He lived and worked in Huguenau outside Strasbourg with his mistress, Valerie Pompidou, an occasional bar girl and prostitute. In addition, he had been a champion skier as a younger man and possessed an infallible ability to secretly transport things across borders.

They were in his studio, a small, cluttered affair on Rue de Ralliement, a block from the city's famous *Tres Pointe* statue of the Madonna and Child cast from twenty-three captured Russian field pieces from the Crimean War. The walls of the studio were covered with half-completed paintings and rough sketches. All were of nudes. The room was heavy with the smell of paint pots, old wood, and the vague scent of unwashed nakedness.

Couteau continued working as they talked, viciously slashing his brushes across the canvas. Anabel and Valerie were his models. Both were naked, Sinclair partially reclining in a posing chair, one hand to her breast, with Pompidou's blond head resting in her lap. The pose strongly suggested lesbian lovers.

Sinclair liked Jean's work. His nudes were faintly distorted, voluptuous, and big-nippled, yet they were done in bold strokes of primary color. The backgrounds were varied, one a lavish red-draped boudoir, another a farming scene. The one she particularly liked was of a coquettishly smiling prostitute counting out her fee, the painting done totally in bright reds and yellows.

Now she said. "With the London go-ahead on Rechberg, will you be able to give us a definite time estimate?" Dr. Eric Rechberg was a physician from Vienna, an old friend of Rommel's. He was known to be highly sympathetic to the movement toward a negotiated peace. London hoped to use him as a go-between.

"A week," Couteau snapped. "Perhaps two." He always spoke in little word bursts.

"CS's getting awful antsy about this guy. So am I."

"Antsy? What is antsy?"

"Anxious, unnerved. Intelligence reports say Rommel's arrest could come at any time."

"*Absurde.* Hitler would never arrest that man."

For Operation Oasis, Sinclair had been given a new identity and code name. Her cover was that of a shop girl named Maxine Milanier who had been recently jilted in Nancy by a German officer. Her code name was Roxanne. Pompidou had gotten her a job as a waitress at a place called Café Poupee. She posed for Couteau so her frequent visits to his studio wouldn't appear suspicious and also on the chance that German secret police might unexpectedly pay a visit.

Valerie piped up irritably, "Hurry up, Jean. I'm getting hungry. And my ass is cold."

"Just a few more moments, *mon chou.*"

Pouting, she twisted around, took a cigarette from a nearby table, lit up, and returned her face to Anabel's lap. Her expelled smoke felt warm against Sinclair's crotch.

"Can we really trust Rechberg?" she asked.

"Of course," Couteau said.

"What if he isn't as sympathetic as we think? After all, he *is* a German. If he turns us in, everything goes down the crapper."

"He won't. When we approach him, he'll know *we* know. Then he *must* cooperate. Or we expose him. Besides, there is no one else." He stepped back, tilted his head this way, that, studying the canvas.

Anabel sighed. "Well, I gotta tell you, this joker's the one weak link in our chain."

"All chains have weak links."

"*Oh, foutaises,*" Valerie cried. "I'm hungry, damn it."

Couteau tossed down his palette and brushes with a flourish. "*La voila!*" he cried happily. "*Rapproche-toi,* see what you think."

"It's beautiful," Valerie said moodily. She got up and went into the kitchen, didn't even bother to look at his painting.

Anabel studied it. "*C'est merveilleux,*" she said finally. It was true, it really *was* quite beautiful, filled with brilliant washes of yellow and orange, the sky framing the two women a deep glowing blue. Jean had captured a feel of fleshy, sensuous passion in the turn of Anabel's lowered head, in the fragile touching of her own breast, in the rich curve of Valerie's buttock. Oddly, it made her feel suddenly, terribly *naked*. She shot him a quick, embarrassed glance, then reached for her bathrobe and slipped it on.

"Ah," Couteau cried happily. "You see, *mon cheri*, you *respond* to it. Good, good. So will the pig major." This particular canvas, he'd told her earlier, had been commissioned by a major in the Strasbourg Gestapo. This was the third painting the German had bought from him. "You know where he places them? On the ceiling over his bed. So he can enjoy classic masturbations as he looks at them."

"How lovely," Anabel said. She turned and walked into the kitchen. Valerie was already eating a lunch of cheese and grapes and wine, still naked.

Strasbourg, France
12 September 1944

Fish made little swirls in the perfectly flat, lead-colored canal water. For a moment, Major Freidrich Land paused beside the weathered handrail of the watchtower

quay, looking down at the bank twenty feet below. Then
he flicked his cigarette away and continued on down the
stone steps. The sky was overcast, the feel of early fall
rain in the air.

The quay was shaped like the bow of a boat. Several
canals came together here. A lone fisherman sat beside
the water with a long pole poked into the dirt between
his shoes. He didn't turn to look at the German's approach. He was dressed in a shabby black coat and a
wide-brimmed hat, his face bearded.

Land stopped directly behind him. "You look ridicu-
lous, Duboudin," he said, chuckling. "Like a silly French
hand-puppet."

Vaillant Duboudin grunted.

Land gazed about curiously. This was his first time in
Strasbourg. This particular spot was near the Ponts Cou-
verts, the ancient defense works of the old city. To the
right and left were other watchtowers built on quays.
Half-timbered houses and tall, fortresslike buildings
lined the canals, while deeper in the city the spiked
Gothic spire of Strasbourg Cathedral rose like a tall
lance point, dominating the skyline.

"So," he finally said. "You wished to see me, here I am."

"What I have to tell you is very big," Duboudin said.
Over the last week, he had been desperately trying to locate the German major. The information he held burned
a hole in his mind. But he absolutely refused to hand it
over to that arrogant dog of a Gestapo officer from Paris,
Gauner. He finally managed to get word to Land through
his previous superior in OB West's intelligence section.

It had been a stroke of luck when the British notified
Valliant that he was to be part of an important mission,
Operation Oasis. He'd been chosen, they said, because
of his intimate knowledge of the Resistance circuits in

northeastern France, his home district, and also because he and Sinclair had worked so well together on their previous mission.

When he was told the particulars of the Oasis plan, it shook him. If Rommel actually defected, he could bring Hitler down completely. Then what? God, he'd given up so much to support these Germans, believing them to be the only power capable of preventing an all-out Communist takeover of Europe. But now the vaunted Third Reich was on the run. And in the vacuums they were leaving behind, the Commies and their FTP chieftains were already generating an ever-stronger power base in France.

"Ah?" Land said. "So, tell me."

"First I want to know what the hell is happening," Duboudin growled. "You Germans are *losing*. Some say the war is already over. I see signs of it every day. What good will you Nazis be to me if that happens? What good will *Hitler* be?"

"I'd watch myself, Duboudin," the major said softly.

"*Merde!*" Vaillant angrily reeled in his line, viciously cast it out again. It made little ripples on the mirrored surface, like wrinkles in gray silk. "Give me some hope that there will be a turnaround soon. Can you at least do that? I've sacrificed my honor for you people. I feel my conscience—" He stopped abruptly.

Land glanced around. Two young women in fur-lined coats were standing at the railing. Both were quite pretty. The handsome German major dipped his head, smiled at them. One smiled back shyly. They turned and walked away, giggling.

"Well," Duboudin demanded as soon as the women were gone. "*Can* you reassure me?"

Land didn't answer. Turning away, he walked along the bank, his hands behind his back, staring down into the water. No, he couldn't reassure this sniveling Frenchman. Because he didn't know the answer himself.

Over the last five weeks, he'd witnessed things that had shocked and humiliated him. The great *Wehrmacht,* his own beloved Panzers, getting bested, literally *running* from the field of battle. As the Normandy crisis had steadily worsened, High Command had decided he could be more useful in one of General von Kluge's newly formed *Vorwarts Beobachtung Gruppe,* Forward Observation Teams. As such, he'd been free to travel throughout the battle front.

He was near Mortain when von Kluge, on Hitler's direct orders, threw four of his best panzer divisions against the Allied Mortain-Avranches line in early August, only to get them slaughtered. Later, he watched as American armored units plunged across western France like a giant steamroller, taking town after town: Fliers, Domfront, Mayenne, Le Mans, Alençon.

Finally, he was there during the horrors of the Falaise Pocket, where thousands of German troops tried desperately to escape through the narrow corridor that ran between Falaise and Argentan. He saw good German soldiers fleeing in blind panic, leaving their weapons and big guns on the field; saw entire companies surrender; beheld *Wehrmacht* officers abandoning their own men, some so terrified they attacked and killed fellow Germans in order to steal their vehicles.

It appalled him. Finally, disgusted beyond bearing, he reacted. Taking command of a platoon of three Mark V Panzers, remnants of the 9th Panzer Division, he charged through the routed columns, passed safely beyond the Falaise corridor, then swung around and held off advancing Allied units so more men could get through. He used the tactics he'd learned with Rommel in North Africa: hit savagely and withdraw.

Four other tank crews soon joined him. Over the next forty-eight hours, they engaged the enemy in nine close-in firefights, destroying four American Sherman tanks, two half-tracks, three mobile 75mm guns, some infantry, and a small convoy of trucks hauling gasoline.

But it was futile. The combined Allied air and ground strikes were simply too powerful to counter with what the Germans had left. For the Americans, it was like shooting fish in a barrel. By 21 August, the battle for the Falaise Pocket was over. Land and his one remaining tank withdrew to l'Aigle and then to Dreux where he turned it over to a battalion captain of the 1st Panzer Grenadier Division.

Stealing a motorcycle, he headed for Paris and reported to the headquarters of OB West. His old intelligence boss, Oberstleutnant Meyer-Detring, was still there, thinner and more agitated. By now, General von Kluge had been replaced by another Hitler appointee, Feldmarschall Walter Model. Meyer-Detring quickly ordered Land to eastern France, to gather what information he could from Resistance double agents about the Allied strategy of moving on the German frontier.

"They're going after Rommel," Duboudin said up the bank.

Land swung around. "What?" He hurried back to him. "What is this about Rommel?"

"They're smuggling in a personal envoy from Churchill to convince the field marshal to defect to England. They want him to set up his own government in exile."

"Is Rommel aware of this plot?"

"Damn it, don't stand so close to me," Vaillant snapped. "It does not—"

The major grabbed the back of his coat, lifted his face

around. "Does the *Feldmarschall* know of this plot?" he hissed.

"No. He's being approached by an old family friend." Duboudin pulled free, glared up at him.

"Who?"

"A doctor named Eric Rechberg from Vienna."

"When?"

"We're waiting on word from him now."

Land pivoted, walked a few steps, his mind rapidly clicking through shocked thoughts. His beloved Rommel *defect?* Unimaginable. Still . . .

Unlike the ordinary line soldier, Land, as an intelligence agent, had learned about the earlier attempt on Hitler's life, and also about the subsequent purge of high-ranking *Wehrmacht* officers. Once even the Desert Fox's name had been mentioned. If Hitler *did* eventually intend to arrest him, then the *Feldmarschall* might conceivably accept the British offer. No, he couldn't conceive that. Rommel was not that kind of man. Honor and loyalty, even in the face of death, meant something to him.

So what should he, Land, do? Let Rommel defect if he so chose and perhaps save his life? Or, take away his opportunity to flee and let him die by Hitler's hands if that was to be his fate? For a moment, he was ensnarled in the dilemma. Where did his ultimate loyalty lie? With a beloved commander or with his country? He did the only thing a Major Land could do. He chose his country.

"I want all the specifics of this operation," he snapped. "Names, routes, photos if you can get them."

"But how do I reach you quickly to set up another meeting?"

"No meeting. That would take too long to arrange. We'll use a dead drop." Land took a small pad and pencil from his tunic pocket. He scribbled something, tore off the page, and handed it to Vaillant. "Remember, I want *everything*. Call this number and let me know the drop site. Code the message with the word *Trojan*. You understand?"

"Yes," Duboudin said.

Wiener Newstadt, Austria
19 Semptember 1944

Rommel turned in his chair. Seeing Dr. Rechfeld, he smiled, nodding. "Ah, Kanin. It's good to see you again." Kanin was a nickname he'd given his friend when they were schoolboys together. The word was short for *kaninchen*, which meant rabbit and referred to Rechfeld's swiftness in footraces. "Come, sit, sit."

The day was beautiful, cloudless, with the clear crispness of mountain autumn in the air. Rommel lived with his wife, Lucie Maria, whom he called Lu, and their young son, Manfred, in a large Alpine chalet made of redbricking, thick support beams, and sharply slanted roofs. It was nestled among mountain pines and had a neatly groomed garden to the side.

The general had been reading there, dressed in riding breeches and a dark desk sweater. He still had a small bandage around his head. Although always lean and militarily spare, he now looked pale and drawn in the bright sunlight.

Rechfeld sat on a wrought-iron lawn chair and Lu brought them glasses of sweet schnapps. She had short brown hair, always worn in bangs, and dark eyes that, to the doctor, now seemed cauterized with a look of deep sadness. It was a look he now often saw in many others.

The two men talked casually of past things, of mountaineering and skiing trips and their mutual fascination for flying small aircraft. At first, Rechfeld deliberately avoided mentioning the war. But finally he attempted to ease into it.

"Are you eating well, Erwin?" he asked.

"Of course."

"Still black bread and canned meat, eh?" It was a familiar gibe of the doctor's. One of the reasons the ordinary German soldier so loved Rommel was that he had always shared their dangers and discomforts in the field, even eating only what they ate.

The field marshal chuckled. "Old habits are hard to break."

"Indeed." Rechberg rose, walked about, then stopped to gaze distractedly at a cluster of late roses.

Rommel watched him, then said quietly, "You have something to say, Kanin. Out with it, then."

Rechfeld came back, sat on the edge of his chair. "I fear for your safety."

Rommel nodded but made no comment to that.

"Worse, I fear for our country," Rechfeld went on earnestly. "We've been friends a long time, Erwin. I've never hidden my true feelings from you."

Again Rommel nodded, his eyes still and watchful.

"Hitler and his mongrel entourage are destroying Germany. There, I've said it." He held the general's steady gaze. "Everything we ever honored has been twisted, *diseased*. To what purpose? This war is lost, you know it and I know it. Why do we continue? Only to feed the sick delusions of a madman?"

"Be careful, Kanin," Rommel said gently.

"No, I no longer want to be careful. One day they'll come for me. I accept that. But what is worse, one day they'll come for *you*."

"I know that."

"Then you must do something. For yourself, for Germany. Dear God, you're our last *hope*." Overwhelmed by his passion, he again thrust himself to his feet and quartered the garden. Once more he paused beside the roses. Staring at them, he said, "I've been approached by the Allies."

Rommel said nothing.

The doctor came back, stood beside the table. "Agents from the British have contacted me. They want me to arrange a meeting between you and a personal envoy from Churchill." He stopped, intently watching Rommel's face for a reaction.

Outwardly, there was none. The general simply looked silently up at him with those piercing, dark eyes. After a long moment, he said, "Sit down, Kanin. Calm yourself."

Rechfeld sat, waited.

"What do they intend to say to me?" Rommel asked.

"They want you to escape to England."

"To defect."

"Yes."

"Do they believe I would do that?"

"They hope. *I* hope."

Rommel shook his head. "You really think I could be that disloyal?"

"Disloyal to what? To this . . . this *insanity*? *That* is itself insanity. You have a greater, truer loyalty, Erwin. To our Fatherland."

"What of my family?"

"They'll go with you."

Now it was Rommel who rose and walked slowly about the garden, gazing up at the sky, his hands pressing into his back. An old picture, the Desert Fox working out his next maneuver, drawing on that brilliance under fire in which he threw away the textbooks and relied only on his soldier's instincts, what his men had called his *Fingerspitzengefuhl*, that sense for the battefield.

Rechfeld waited. Sparrows chirped in the shrubbery. A mountain hawk drifted across the sky, drawing a delicate shadow of itself on the cobblestones. Rommel returned to the table.

"I'll see them," he said simply.

All through the long afternoon of the twentieth, Anabel nervously waited in her room for a message from London, giving her the final green light to initiate the main phase of Operation Oasis.

Late last night Couteau had come to tell her he'd received word that Rechfeld had been successful in getting Rommel's consent for a meeting. She immediately radioed her watch operator at Somerset House with the news and was told to listen for further orders via a coded message on the BBC, which would be broadcast within the next twenty-four hours.

That meant she'd have to keep a constant radio watch on her compact B2 agent's transceiver, which she kept hidden under the floor near her bed. To do this, she instructed Jean to send Valerie to tell her boss at Café Poupee that she was ill.

Sinclair lived in a rented room owned by a Mme. Tulle, a seventy-year-old woman who also operated a small lace-making shop on the ground floor of the building. It was located in the Dockland district outside Haguenau, between a *garage de bicyclettes* and a *confiserie*, a candy store.

Mme. Tulle, fragile as her own lace, was gossipy and firmly believed that Anabel was a *fille de joie grasse matinee*, a part-time hooker. After all, this young lady *was* a bar girl. She continually probed Sinclair with questions about the profession, lurid questions asked with a bright-eyed fascination.

At precisely 6:17 that evening, the BBC message came through. In stentorian tones, the announcer said: "Now for an item of interest for those living in Brenden Hills, Somerset. The Reverend Jonathon Greenfield will give a slide presentation this evening after Vespers in the Rectory of St. Bernard of the Wood. His subject will be the flora of the Bourjeimat Oasis of Mauritania, West Africa.

"Reverend Greenfield and his wife, Roxanne, conducted extensive botanical studies there in 1936 while on mission for the Anglican Conservatory of Tempsford. All wishing to attend must contact the Rectory Office before nine o'clock BDST. Parking facilities will be as usual."

By extracting certain coded words, identification phrases, and inserting German time for the British double summer time, she quickly deciphered the message. London was issuing a full clearance to proceed with the operation. Further, General Stanfield would arrive in France at eleven o'clock that night, using the same drop zone she and Guiet had used outside Brumath.

Stanfield was late. The sky had a thick overcast and the delivery plane, a B-24 Liberator bomber from Carpetbagger Squadron out of Harrington, Northhamptonshire, overshot the field flares and had to turn back for a second run.

Waiting on the ground were Anabel, Couteau, and Duboudin. They had driven out in the same large black Citroen Couteau used for the earlier pickup. There was to be no cargo drop this time, the general jumping from the aircraft's bomb bay.

Everybody got anxious when the plane missed the first

pass, its sound fading away as the pilots tried to reorient themselves. Then it came again, lower this time, its exhausts showing orange as it roared past. And there was Stanfield's parachute suddenly appearing in the darkness.

He was already folding his silk when they came up, Anabel calling out her code name as challenge. Stanfield responded with his own code name, Pericles. She said, "Good jump, sir." She started to introduce the others, but he cut her off sharply.

"Time enough for that later," he snapped. "Let's just get on with business, shall we?" They extinguished the field flares, buried the general's chute, and had soon disappeared back into the night.

At 0425 hours the next morning, a telephone call came into the signal section of the German Second Army's intelligence section located in the Chateau des Rohan in Strasbourg. It was code-tagged Trojan. The senior watch officer immediately called Major Land, rousing him from sleep.

Fifteen minutes later, he arrived at the section and was handed a transcription of the message. It was from Duboudin. Claiming the impossibility of using a drop site, he had given his entire message to the watch officer. It said that the British envoy had arrived and would be attempting to cross the German frontier near the small village of Rastatt this very night. It went on to specify the make, color, and license number of the automobile the party would be using, who would be aboard, how they were armed, and precisely what road they would be taking.

Land called the watch officer. "Get Gestapo headquarters on the line," he ordered.

"Yes, sir," the man said and hurried away.
21 September 1944
2310 hours

The Germans had set up their barrier of logs perfectly, thirty yards beyond a curve in a dirt road two miles outside Rastatt. On one side of the road was a slight bluff with a stone barn built close to the edge. On the other side vineyards stretched away into the darkness, the air dense with the dusty bouquet of the fruit.

The Citroen came around the corner going well, Couteau at the wheel. Beside him was Duboudin with Stanfield and Anabel in the back. They were all dressed like peasants: field caps and faded jackets and bandannas.

Stanfield's kit bag with his dress uniform he'd use with Rommel and a leather briefcase sat on the floor of the car along with weapons under a blanket: two Sten Mk II submachine guns and a clip belt with spare rounds. Jean and Vaillant were both armed with French MAS 38 machine pistols, odd-looking guns that fired 7.65mm long rounds. In addition, everyone had a sidearm.

As they cleared the turn, Couteau suddenly hit the brakes, the car skidding for a few yards. "Something's in the road," he said tightly, peering ahead, the dim blue blackout headlights throwing only a faint sheen onto the road.

Anabel leaned forward to look out the windshield, too. Beyond the dim glow, she could make out a solid dark shape across the roadway. Then she spotted sparks like fireflies and her heart went frigid. They were uniform insignias faintly reflecting the headlights.

Beside her, Stanfield said almost peevishly, "Bloody damn, it's a roadblock."

A bright spot flicked on, pinning them in its beam, the burst of light pouring through the windshield like a white explosion. Another spot appeared, this beam sweeping first to the right, then also homing to the car.

Couteau uttered an obscenity and jammed the car into reverse. It leaped backward, Jean hauling the wheel over, attempting to spin a 180. The right rear wheel went over a bump and down into a small ditch. Still cursing, he shifted again and gunned the motor. The wheel spun. They were stuck fast.

A German shouted something. There was a pause and then an MP-40 machine pistol opened up. The bullets slammed into the car's roof sounding like someone striking it rapidly with a chain. One of the side windows blew in, scattering shards of glass into the backseat.

Everybody hit the floor. Stanfield clawed for a Sten, pulled it free of the blanket, and jacked the cocking handle back, chambering a round. Anabel found the other and did the same. The German gun stopped firing. There was a slight pause and then it started up again. This time the bullets ripped into the engine compartment. The engine immediately stopped and a twin hissing came from the radiator. Once more the MP-40 quit firing.

The German voice shouted again, in French: "You are ordered to surrender immediately. It is useless to resist. Throw your weapons out and step from your vehicle with your hands in the air."

"We're surrounded," Duboudin said. His voice was shaky. "It's of no use to struggle."

Stanfield ignored him, shouted, "Did anybody see how many there are out there?"

"*Non*, it was too quick," Jean called back from the floor of the front seat. "*Merde!* I can't believe this. This road is *never* guarded."

"It's no use," Duboudin said again. "They *have* us."

"Oh, bollocks!" the general growled. "I bloody well intend to fight the bastards."

Anabel shifted her knees and felt fear in her like a freed beast. Her heart pounded crazily and terrible images rocketed through her mind. *We're spies. They torture spies!* Her hand gripped the trigger guard of the Sten so tightly she could feel the nail of her finger gouging into her palm. She focused on the tiny pain, forcing herself to calm down. *Breathe deep, breathe deep.* She became aware of the solid metal heft of the weapon. It drew up reassurance and with it a surge of anger.

Goddammit, we will *fight the sons of bitches.*

The front passenger door suddenly opened and Duboudin dropped from the seat onto the ground. Jean shouted, "No, don't run, you fool!" In the silence, they heard Vaillant crashing off through the vines. Nothing happened for several seconds, then the Germans let loose another fusillade.

The doors on the other side of the car flew open. Both Couteau and Stanfield dove out. Still huddled on the floor, Anabel waited till the German weapons went silent again, then lifted up enough to get the barrel of her Sten out the window. She fired a burst. The weapon jerked lightly against her hand and its spent rounds slapped like flung marbles into the overhead.

Jean and the general also opened up. They managed to knock out one of the spotlights. A Kraut screamed in pain. The other spot momentarily slid to the side, then was pulled back to the vehicle. Another firestorm of bullets shattered windows and tore up the automobile's body. Sinclair felt a slug actually whip through her jacket collar, saw the others blowing seat ticking into the air.

It went on for several more seconds but finally stopped. Instantly, she slid backward on the floor and out of the car. She saw Couteau kneeling at the front, Stanfield at the rear. She crab-walked to the general.

He suddenly rose to a crouch and opened fire, spraying from right to left. His first rounds got the other spotlight, which plunged everything back into darkness except for the dim back glow of the headlights.

They waited tensely for another fusillade. It didn't come. Then in the humming silence, they heard another sound, the rhythmic cadence of boots hitting the road from beyond the bend. Stanfield grunted. "Seems the buggers're surrounding us. Bad show, this."

Jean scooted over. "Quickly," he whispered. There was the musk of fear on his breath. "We must get out *now*."

"Agreed," Stanfield said. "It's now or never. I think it best we scatter. Better chance for evasion."

Couteau shoved a fresh clip into his MAS 38, the click loud. "I'll take the bluff, you head through the vineyards. A river is a mile to the south. If you can reach it, your chances will be good."

Anabel asked, "Where do we meet?" The pound of the boots was closer. A German barked an order.

Jean considered a moment. "Drusenheim. A shoemaker there, his name is Claude Paccaud." He nodded, a quick dip of the head. "*Bonne chance, mes amis.*" He turned and darted away, hunched over, then went springing up the small bluff, his shoes breaking off pebbles that tumbled down noisily. The Germans immediately fired, the hot streaks of their bullets faintly visible in the darkness.

Stanfield tapped Anabel's shoulder. "You go first," he ordered. "I'll fire cover."

"Sir, I think —"

"Damn it, woman, off with you." He lifted and opened up.

She went, running low, the grape rows breast high, tooth-edged leaves slapping against her arms. Behind her, Stanfield was still throwing short bursts. The Germans switched their aim back to the car, the bullets hitting the body with hollow, metallic collisions.

She paused to look back. Flashlights probed the darkness from near the roadblock and from back around the curve of the road. The beams darted out over the grape rows and up along the walls of the barn. She could hear Germans moving into the vineyard, calling to each other.

She threw a burst toward the flashlights, hoping to cover Stanfield's run from the car. Instinctively dropping to the ground, she immediately realized how stupid she'd been, her muzzle flashes exposing her position. Bullets instantly came snapping, zinging over her head, tracers drawing white-hot lines and vanishing, the images lingering on her retinas. She scurried deeper into the vineyard, running and clawing along the moist ground.

She got beyond the firing zone, straightened, and broke into a dead sprint, squinting ahead, repeating in her head over and over: *God, don't let me hit an intersection or one of the post-and-wire lines.* Instead, she collided headlong into a stack of big metal harvesting tubs. A burst of pain exploded in her chest as she crashed through the tubs and hit the ground.

She couldn't breathe. It was as if all the air around her had suddenly been sucked away. Desperately she fought to fill her lungs, couldn't. Her eyes fluttered, her head rang. Slowly, air began to enter again. Gasping violently, she tried to get up. Her legs buckled and she fell back down.

A flashlight beam appeared up the grape row. She watched it approach, her eyes blinking, her hands searching for the Sten. *Damn it! Damn it!* The beam caught her.

A voice shouted, "*Hier etwas es. Hier! Genau da draussen?*"

The thud of boots. She could almost feel them make the ground tremble. *Oh, God!* The light was close to her face now. She heard the soft tinkle of equipment. She closed her eyes. A hand roughly grabbed her sweater and hauled her to her feet.

Chapter Fifteen

0143 hours
22 September 1944

Neue Bremm Prison had once been a hunting lodge of Frederick the Great, king of Prussia. It sat on a hill in a thick forest four miles from Saarbrücken, Germany, a dank and ugly structure, more medieval than eighteenth century.

Anabel Sinclair sat on a straw mattress in total darkness, staring straight ahead. She was in a long narrow cell with stone walls covered with moisture and fungus colonies that smelled like vomit. Around her right wrist was a metal bracelet attached by a thick chain to a similar bracelet around her ankle. The chain was so short she couldn't fully straighten up. It was very cold in the cell.

On the right and left other cells lined away. She could hear the faint snores and phlegm-thick coughs of other prisoners, all women. A wide corridor connected the cells. In its fore walls were harness pegs and tie-down rings still embedded, indicating it had obviously once been a horse stable.

Her whole body hurt. She could still taste blood in her mouth and the right side of her face was swollen and throbbing. Her chest ached. She sat very still and tried to focus on nothing. It was impossible. Images kept leaping into her mind, carrying with them other sharp, fear-wrenched thoughts. But she kept at it. After a while, her steady gaze began to make the darkness shift as if it were slowly turning solid. Subtle lights shimmered and coiled against her retinas. She watched them. They seemed terribly dangerous.

Oh, God, oh, God.

She forced herself to refocus on nothing again. At the SOE Special Evasion-and-Escape school in Glaschoille, she'd been put through mock imprisonments, long interrogations, threats of torture. The key, they had told her, was to always control your mind. Don't ever let *them* have it. Cast it far away, create a mental world that you could feel and smell and touch. That gave you the ability to abolish time, fear, even pain.

The shimmerings came again. She blinked rapidly and suddenly felt an upwelling of horrible sorrow, deeper than she'd ever felt in her life. She dipped her head, wept softly. It was merely a momentary catharsis. She stopped. The seconds, the minutes did not seem to move in the darkness. Had hours passed? Their demarcations had become blurred.

She returned to her staring. But this time she drew up specific images: landscapes, seascapes, trees, clouds. She tried to imagine their colors, feel the warmth of sunlight pouring out of an endless sky like a liquid. But gradually, inexorably, her mind was drawn back to the now. Finally, exhausted, she let it come.

They had beaten her as they dragged her back to the road, screamed in her face. Gestapo men and SS soldiers were all over, some still out in the vineyards, their flashlights darting. She caught a quick glimpse of General Stanfield. He appeared to be wounded in one leg. She saw neither Jean nor Vaillant.

They transported them in separate Opel personnel carriers in a convoy of a dozen other vehicles filled with SS troopers. A Gestapo captain sat beside her like a stone statue. His uniform smelled of mildew, as if it had been left somewhere damp.

It took three hours to reach Neue Bremm, much of the way between tall forest walls and the sweet turpentine scent of pines filling the night air. During the ride, she played and replayed the ambush scenario in her head. Obviously, they'd been betrayed. These Krauts had known exactly when and where they would be. But who had it been? Couteau? Valerie? Someone within his circuit? Still, there were only a handful of people who actually knew all the parameters of Operation Oasis. It could have been *anybody*, even someone in the government back in London.

Picturing it all again, she kept coming back to the sequence of actions during the ambush. Something had been *wrong* back there, out of place. She tried to draw it out, but it remained just beyond the fringes of her consciousness. She kept trying, going minutely through every step, every word, looking for clues.

And suddenly there it was. *Duboudin's* actions. Of course. He'd wanted to surrender, hadn't he? Why? It wasn't like him. Vaillant was no coward. Yet he *had* tried to persuade them that it would be useless to fight. When they refused, he ran away.

She felt a cold, dark thing shift in her heart. Now she mentally saw something else. When he left their vehicle, the Germans had held their fire for several seconds although he had been clearly visible to them in the glare of the spotlights. They could easily have killed him but they didn't even try.

Oh, God, it was *him.*

She heard the hard crack of boots out in the corridor. She froze, felt her insides grip up. They came on, stopped at her cell door. Locks clanged. The door swung open. A flashlight flared in her face, hurting her eyes. Two men came into the cell. One grabbed her chain and hauled her to her feet, sending stabs of pain through her ankle and wrist.

He swung her around and roughly shoved her through the door.

Now it begins, she thought in terror.

Claude Paccaud met Couteau at his kitchen window with a revolver in his hand. He was an immensely fat man, massively calm. He said, "I assume something has happened."

"We were ambushed by the Gestapo," Jean blurted, panting, as Paccaud let him in. He was soaking wet. "Has there been a sweep here tonight?"

"*Non.*"

"Be very careful. There will probably be one before dawn."

His escape from the Gestapo and SS soldiers had been very close. He'd hidden in the rafters of the barn near the roadblock. The Germans, thinking he had fled off through the vineyards, did not search it thoroughly. It was fortunate they didn't have dogs, not needing them, thinking they would take the Resistance party easily without a full-scale hunt.

Through a crack in an eaves slat, he watched them bring Sinclair and then Stanfield back to the road. The general was wounded in the leg. He saw them beat the woman but no one touched the general. Two officers talked to him, both majors, one SS, the other dressed in the black *Einheitsfeldmutze* uniform of a panzer division. They held their flashlights respectfully out of his face. Then he and the woman were driven away in an armed convoy, leaving two platoons of soldiers behind to continue combing the vineyards.

Paccaud shook his head. "This is not good." He had obviously been asleep. He had on a sleeping cap like a long stocking. A woman in a robe came to the kitchen, saw who was there, and went away. In a moment, she returned with a blanket, then left again without uttering a word.

Jean had managed to elude the soldiers and make his way to the river. He floated halfway to Drusenheim, the water low and swift and already filled with winter cold. He ran the remainder of the way to Paccaud's house, always staying at the edge of trees, his good ski legs and wind allowing him to maintain a steady, sprinting rhythm.

"Someone betrayed us," he snarled.

Paccaud shrugged fleshy shoulders. "Perhaps it was merely ill luck."

"*Non, non.*" Jean wrapped himself in the blanket. Perspiration dipped from the tip of his chin. "They knew, the German dogs *knew.*"

"But who could it be?"

"I have a suspicion. Only a few of us knew the precise schedule. It had to be one of *us.*" His eyes narrowed. "Hamlet."

"Ah? Duboudin?"

"Yes. He turned coward and ran away. But the Germans *didn't* fire at him."

Claude grunted ponderously. After a moment, he poured some wine and handed it to Couteau. Jean drank it down in one gulp.

Couteau said, "Raise Paris, tell Napoleon what's happened." Napoleon was the code name for Rene L'Hote, FTP chief for northern France. "He can notify London. Then warn the circuit chiefs a big Gestapo sweep will be coming. They'd best go to ground for a while. And post an *etoile* against that fucking *traitre* Duboudin." *Etoile,* the word for starfish, was also the code symbol the Maquis used when identifying a suspected turned-agent or enemy assassin.

Claude's radio was in the basement, the place thick with a sour odor from vats of vegetable tannin solution made from oak, valonia, and hemlock bark in which he soaked his animal skins, deer and goat, to make shoes and gloves. In the opposite wall were two large drying ovens. The radio was an old Swiss-made Zietz 200 FX, bulky as a stove. He had it secreted under one of the vats.

While Paccaud transmitted, Couteau paced and peered through the small basement window, cursing. After a few minutes, Claude slipped off the headphones long enough to tell him something. "Bad news, Jean. The Gestapo has torn up your studio. And they've taken Natalie."

Couteau stared at him, then walked to a box and sat down with his hands in his lap, staring at the floor.

At 3:23 A.M. British time, Stanton-Ferryman was awakened by the watch officer of Somerset House and told of General Stanfield's capture. Since the beginning of Operation Oasis, the F-Section chief had been sleeping in his office. He immediately began making phone calls.

Thirty-one minutes later, he and his Deputy for Intelligence, David Keswick, arrived at the War Rooms. General Capstick, Admiral Aston, and Sir Robert Dalton, Minister of Security for the Foreign Office, were already there, in meeting with the prime minister.

Winston Churchill was a notorious nighthawk who rarely retired before dawn. Then he would sleep until noon. Often he'd hold conferences in his bedroom while still in his pajamas, puffing on his morning cigar and sipping brandy. Now he sat on the edge of his bed, legs dangling, bulldog face ascowl, while Stanton-Ferryman filled in the data.

When he finished, Churchill growled, "We're certain Stanfield was taken?"

"Yes, sir. One of the accompanying agents who escaped said he clearly saw them in custody."

The prime minister scanned faces, his eyes dangerous. "What happened out there?" he finally said.

Everybody exchanged glances. Finally, Admiral Aston said, "Obviously there was a penetration of our Oasis network. The Gestapo *knew* precisely when and where they would be crossing the German border."

"Where was the leak? Here or there?"

"It had to have been someone within the Resistance circuits who was privy to Oasis," Stanton-Ferryman said immediately. "It was no one in my system. Of that I'm absolutely certain."

Churchill puffed, nodded. "Well, then, we'll just have to go and retrieve them, won't we?"

General Capstick spoke up. "That was also my immediate reaction, sir. As was everyone else's in this room. Unfortunately, we don't know precisely where they're being held."

Churchill took another healthy pull on his cigar. The room was already heady with the vanilla scent of it. Through the walls seeped the faint sound of machines. "Judging from where they were taken, can't we extrapolate where they most likely would be?"

"We've already done that, sir," Standon-Ferryman said.

"There are three Gestapo prisoner-holding points in the general area. One in Strasbourg, another at Karlsruhe, and the third is Neue Bremm Prison near Saarbrücken."

"How quickly can we find out which it is?"

"A bit sticky that, I'm afraid, sir," General Capstick said. "With someone as important as General Stanfield, it's likely he could be sent directly to Berlin. As for the agent, she'll probably be held temporarily at any of the three prisons and then transferred to Ravensbruck sometime later. Most female political prisoners are sent there."

"I repeat, Sir William," Churchill said caustically, "how quickly can we pinpoint where they are at this moment?"

"I'm sorry, Prime Minister," Capstick pressed on. "But the only real source of such intelligence must come from the Resistance itself. At this point, we have no way of knowing whom we can trust."

"Goddammit, I don't want extenuations," Churchill rumbled, his lower lip protruding pugnaciously. "We *must* resolve this immediately. Within the next twenty-four to thirty-six hours. Beyond that, it becomes postulate. Now give me some *options*."

Again there was a quick exchange of glances. The Foreign Office security chief, Dalton, spoke up. "I believe we have only three, sir. A rescue, a release through diplomatic channels, or a prisoner exchange."

The prime minister shook his head immediately. "Not diplomatic channels. Too sluggish. And without the specifics of where they're being kept, a rescue attempt at this time would be unrealistic." He thought a moment. "Whom do we now have that Berlin might consider a fair trade?"

"There's Strubreiter," Dalton said. Generaloberst Franz Strubreiter had been chief of staff for Feldmarschall Albert Kesselring, commander of German forces in northern Italy. He was captured by an American patrol near Florence on 7 September 1944. "He's certainly Kesselring's chum and a known favorite of Goering's."

"Is he here or still in Italy?"

"He's here, sir. In Dunsbury."

Churchill looked around. "Anyone have anything better to offer?" No one spoke up. For a long moment, the prime minister considered, then gave a sharp nod. "Very well, it's Strubreiter. We'll use the Swiss ambassador as liaison to Berlin. A very good man, that. Hopefully, he can convince those maniacs an exchange would be beneficial to them. However, be absolutely certain he fully understands the necessity for utmost speed."

"Yes, sir," Dalton said, made to turn away.

"Excuse me, Prime Minister," Stanton-Ferryman said quickly. "My agent will, of course, be part of the exchange?"

"Yes, the agent," Chruchill said. "We bloody well can't leave her to those dogs. All right, then, we'll need another prisoner for the negotiations. Whom can we afford to lose?"

"How about Starr, sir?" Dalton said. John Starr was the cover persona for an SS Sturmbannfuhrer named Otto Luttich who had been planted in England by the German SD. Six months earlier, he'd been taken in Cambridge.

Churchill's eyes narrowed. "Wouldn't that be dangerous? After all, he knows a great deal about us."

"Actually, sir, we don't think he does. Everything we've been able to uncover seems to indicate the bulk of his information was gleaned from deliberately planted untruths. Whenever we've interrogated him, we've always subtly reinforced the belief that what he has is still factual and valuable to Berlin. Even if he were to pass it on, it would be totally useless."

"Good, we'll go with him." Churchill now gave everyone a final scan, speaking as he did so. "I need not emphasize the importance of this operation, gentlemen. Although I have complete confidence that Stanfield and our agent will maintain their silence, regardless of Gestapo brutality, we know the Germans will use this incident for propaganda purposes. They'll paint us as a covey of bumbling nincompoops. Worse, they'll attempt to create a sense of duplicity and disunity between us and our American Allies.

"I therefore intend to contact President Roosevelt immediately and explain the entire Oasis Operation to him." He snorted mirthlessly. "I suspect he'll not be pleased that his people were kept out of the loop from the start. Can't say I blame him. In any case, gentlemen, I will expect you to bloody well get *cracking* on this. Understood?"

Everyone nodded. Churchill slid his feet to the floor, the signal that the meeting was over.

"Prime Minister," Stanton-Ferryman quickly put in. "There's one other item. It relates directly to your very point of disunity with the Americans. Might I suggest that if Berlin accepts our proposal, we send an American unit along to accompany Strubreiter and Starr to the exchange site? A sort of symbolic gesture that would give the Yanks a feeling of inclusion."

Churchill puffed, nodded. "Yes, I think that *would* be sensible. A bit obvious and certainly after the fact. Still, it could prove effective. Do you have any specific American unit in mind?"

"Yes, sir, I do," the brigadier answered. "It's a small, elite U.S. Army unit called Blue Team. Made up of only five men, I believe. But they've worked with the OSS in Italy, and were extremely effective for us in the Cotentin. Particularly during the bombardment of Cherbourg. Actually, our own agent Roxanne, the one with Stanfield, operated directly with them throughout most of the Peninsula campaign."

"Fair enough," Churchill said. "Get them."

"Yes, sir," Stanton-Ferryman said and hurried away.

Anabel woke to freezing cold and fever. She was on her mattress but could not remember being returned to it. Her teeth clacked loudly and her entire body was wracked with spasms of violent trembling. She felt her breath hesitant, as if it were partially blocked somewhere along the line of her throat. She lifted her head. Her hair and clothing were stiff from the cold. When she moved, the clothing crackled.

Noises came from out in the main corridor, cell doors slamming, a heavy shuffling of shoes. Now and then a sliver of light would seep under the door. The other prisoners were being herded out to their day's work. Nobody spoke. It was like a troop of zombies passing beyond her door. The shuffling faded as a klaxon sounded far away. She closed her eyes and was aware only of the cold.

It had been bad. She was interrogated in a room at the end of the prison corridor. Its walls had previously been painted white but were now faded to a dirty yellow. Horse harness chains still hung from pegs. There were two metal chairs in the center of the room. Against one wall was a tall surgeon's cabinet with glass doors. Beside it was a metal bathtub, two-thirds filled with water. Little drifts of straw were banked in the corners. The room might have once been a veterinarian's operating stall.

The interrogator was an SS Hauptsturmfuhrer in a gray uniform with black and silver collars. He was middle-aged, with a tight mouth, large ears, and rimless glasses. He resembled an aging schoolteacher. With the standard Gestapo technique called *Anschauzen,* everything he said was shouted loudly in a voice that was a bit nasal.

For a full hour, he asked her the same question: "*Stuck* LL835, was Feldmarschall Rommel involved in this plot?" German prisoners were always referred to as *Stuck* along with their ID number, the word coming from a particularly foul-smelling soap. Either sitting directly in front of her with his face close or pacing about, the SS officer repeated the question over and over, his words without stress, said monotonously as if by rote. Periodically, he'd strike her across the face with his open hand. He did that perfunctorily too, as if he were adhering to a prescribed procedure straight out of a manual: *ask here, slap here.*

At first, she gave him only her cover name and background. He ignored it, went on with the question. She finally went completely silent. It didn't alter the man's attitude or voice.

Then, abruptly, he ordered two burly *Alufseherinin,* soldier guards, to unlock her from her chair. They did so, carried her to the bathtub, and held her head under the water.

It was freezing cold. The shock of it went right into her brain like a blow to the skull. Frantically, she struggled, terror overwhelming her. Holding her mouth shut, she tried desperately to keep the water out, her eyes rolling, the sides of the white tub blurry. Her chest began to ache as if it were being held to a fire. Her head thundered. She couldn't hold any longer. Water rushed into her mouth, flooded down into her throat.

They pulled her out, gagging and gasping for air. The SS officer repeated his question. Three times. Then they shoved her back into the water. They did this fifteen times. The last three times she lost consciousness. The terror had vanished. Now it was only endurance. Even the prayers she had been saying in her head were now only disconnected murmurings.

0918 hours
22 September 1944

Blue Team had just returned from probing German defenses east of the Moselle River southeast of Nancy when Parnell received a radio message ordering him to immediately report back to the 4th Armored Division's headquarters at Nuevos Maisons on the outskirts of Nancy.

For the past two weeks, they had been attached to Combat Command A of Brigadier General Manton S. Eddy's XII Corps after the XV Corps went into reserve as part of a reshuffling of Patton's units. Ever since the occupation of Paris, the Allied push eastward had continued well. Unfortunately, bickering and bad decision-making on the highest level of command had begun to slow it to a walk once the Moselle River was reached.

The first major mistake was Montgomery's. Earlier that month, he'd finally convinced Eisenhower that a roundhouse strike into Holland could easily open the way to the German Ruhr Valley and create a bridgehead in the heart of Germany. On 17 September, Operation Market-Garden was launched, spearheaded by a massive airborne assault by the U.S. 101st and 82nd Divisions along with the British 1st Division and the 1st Polish Airborne Brigade. Their goals were the bridges and canals of the Maas-Waal-Rhine sector of Holland. It was a stunning failure that cost the Allies thousands of men killed or captured.

The second fatal blunder occurred because of General Patton's stubborn insistence on capturing rather than bypassing the strongly fortified city of Metz on the Mozelle. The attempt stalled his forward momentum. Once that happened, the remnants of the still-powerful German Seventh Army were able to slip safely back beyond the Rhine.

Colonel Dunmore was waiting for Parnell in the division's intelligence tent. He looked tired, the eyes behind his glasses not sparking energy as usual. He shook Red's hand and the two of them walked along a nearby stream while he filled in the details of their new mission.

"We're still waiting for the go-ahead on this thing, John," he began. "But I want the team ready to move out if and when it comes. In full battle dress. They stressed that point."

Parnell chuckled. "What, are we gonna be in a parade?"

"No. You're to act as an exchange escort."

"A what?" A pair of swallows suddenly came skimming along the stream, just off the surface. Nearing the men, they flared, squealing, and shot straight up into the sky.

"The Brits're trying to set up a prisoner exchange," Dunmore said. "You take their people out and bring ours back."

"Who is it?"

"A big-shot Limey general, guy named Stanfield. Also his SOE agent."

SOE? Parnell thought, abruptly tense. No, it couldn't be.

"Apparently they tried to set up a meet with Rommel, get him to defect," the colonel went on. "Went at it all on their own, didn't tell us squat. Somebody talked and the general and his agent got picked up by the Gestapo.

Now the sons a' bitches want the appearance of Allied unity. That's why they requested an American escort for the exchange."

"Who's the agent?"

"You know her, Anabel Sinclair."

He heard her name and his heart went solid. *Oh, sweet Mother of God, they've got her!* A searing rush of horrible images hurtled through his mind, made his bowels grip up. He forced his mind to slow. *Whoa, she's coming back, coming back . . .* if *there's an exchange.*

Dunmore watched him narrowly. Finally he said, "There's something else here, isn't there?"

"What?"

"From the look on your face, I suspect this has suddenly become personal. Will you be able to handle this one?"

"You're goddamned right," Parnell said sharply.

"Okay, fine, John," Dunmore said. "Go draw clean gear and report back to me."

Red turned and sprinted away without acknowledging the command.

The clearance came from London four hours later. The exchange site had been chosen, a small churchyard in the junction town of Chateau Salins, fourteen miles northeast of Nancy. The two German prisoners were to be flown to a fighter strip at nearby Toul. Then they and their escort would board a train flying white truce flags for the forty-five-minute run to Chateau Salins.

Three times they came for Anabel. The same *Haupsturmfuhrer* with the same question. Each time they put her in the bathtub sooner. The SS officer referred to it as the *Kuhler*. Mixed with the water now was her own urine, which she had released as she lapsed into unconsciousness.

The third time they brought her to the old veterinarian's room they shaved off all her hair before the interrogation began. They used scissors and a straight razor and cut her scalp. The blood ran down into her eyes. Her entire face was swollen now from the periodic slapping. The fever spasms shook her repeatedly. She could feel it in her head, in her breasts, as if all the heat left in her had converged there.

Between the questionings she lay in the fetal position on her mattress. She tried to project her mind away but could not get past the reality of this horrible place, become free of the realization that it would all go on and on until they broke her. Already she wanted desperately to tell them things they wanted to hear. Then they would stop. But she refused her own pleadings.

Still, she was close. She had already weakened once, helplessly cried out, pleading with them. It hadn't mattered. The SS officer went right on as if he had not heard her. Later in her cell, she whispered to someone in the darkness, explaining her momentary failure. It seemed very important she do that. *You see? You see?* Sometimes it was Parnell she spoke to, sometimes her father, Shawn Padrick. They did not answer.

She no longer wept. The terror and near drownings had dissolved her capacity to do so. She thought about death. It seemed a welcome release. If she had a weapon or a sharpened utensil she might have killed herself. But, no, even now that seemed abhorrent. There was always the cold and the fever—they infested her body like foreign entities come to ravish her.

After the fourth interrogation, they did not use the *Kuhler*. Instead, each of three guards raped her, one after the other, and then all again. She lay on the hard stones of the veterinarian's room and closed her eyes and tried again to close off her mind. This time she did.

The locomotive was an old French de Glehn 241A-class engine, black with faded red trimmings, everything soot-layered. It pulled only its tender and a single passenger car. The car was from the Orient Express, blue-and-cream with a tarnished silver-domed roof. It had originally been a smoking carriage with mahogany benches lining each side, the white overhead patinaed from years of cigar and pipe smoke.

Generaloberst Strubeiter sat stiffly in his greenish brown tropical field tunic and red-striped breeches. They'd been freshly washed, yet the appointments, the red and gold shoulder boards, the knight's cross with swords, the gold-bullion breast eagle were all unpolished.

He was of medium height with a full face, closely cropped blond hair under a black field cap, a drawn-back mouth that gave him a perpetual look of impatience, as if he had just witnessed an underling in a blunder. He remained silent.

The SD agent, Luttich, alias John Starr, was the exact opposite. A slender, mongoose-faced man, he sat ensconced in a heavy raincoat, chain-smoking and playing with a handheld, pegged chessboard. Occasionally he'd lift his eyes, black as agates, and stare with open insolence at the Americans.

Parnell had placed two of his men at each end of the car, all of them armed with Thompsons and spare clip pouches on their battle harnesses. He himself sat across

from the *Generaloberst,* watching the German officer
closely. Strubeiter never connected with his eyes, always
keeping his own gaze steadily on a point slightly above
Red's helmet.

The windows of the car had blackout drapes. Periodically Parnell slipped the edge aside and peered out. An
overcast had moved across the sky. He could see troops
and armored vehicles beyond the sides of the tracks, first
American and then German, the soldiers watching
silently as the exchange train passed them.

It was nearly 5:30 when they reached the church on
the edge of Chateau Salins. Several German vehicles
were parked among the headstones. Ancient yew trees
partially ringed the cemetery, the grass unclipped. The
church itself was as small as a country schoolhouse, its
stone walls dark with moss.

The train eased to a stop. Parnell looked around the
drapes, then moved to the forward end of the car. He
said to Bird, "Keep them in here till I give you the
signal to bring 'em out."

"Right, Lieutenant."

He went out and down the car steps. The twilight air
was cold. The only sound was the regular hiss and blow
of the locomotive's pressure valves releasing steam. At
least twenty SS troopers stood in a semicircle facing him.

In the center was General Stanfield. He was dressed in
his formal uniform, still creased from his kitbag. Under
his right trouser leg was the bulge of a bandage. Standing a few feet in front of the others was a Gestapo officer
in a long, black leather coat and fedora.

Parnell strode forward, stopped in front of the German but actually faced toward General Stanfield. He
came to attention and saluted the British officer, held
the gesture until Stanfield saluted back. He then turned

to the Gestapo officer, a husky man wearing odd, gold-tinted glasses. The man lifted his right hand in a casual Nazi salute. Parnell did not return it.

"I have your people," Red said brusquely. His eyes scanned the Germans. He felt a coldness in his chest. Anabel wasn't there.

"And I yours, Lieutenant," the Gestapo officer said in perfect English. They stared at each other.

"What will the procedure be?" Parnell asked.

"We simply exchange our prisoners simultaneously."

"Where's the British agent?"

"She will be along. Now, shall we conclude this?"

Parnell returned to the smoking car. With two men on either side of the Germans, he escorted them back to the Gestapo officer. The Germans exchanged salutes. The Gestapo officer turned, jerked his head. Two SS soldiers brought Stanfield forward. Without any words being spoken, the exchange was made.

The Gestapo man smiled faintly, nodded. "So, it is concluded, then." He started to turn away.

Before Parnell could say anything, General Stanfield barked, "Stand fast there, you. Where is my fellow prisoner?"

Again the Gestapo man gave a faint smile. "I'm afraid, sir, our previous agreement has been somewhat altered." Instantly, Strubeiter's head snapped around and he scowled at the man.

Parnell felt blood rush into his head. He stepped forward menacingly. "Listen, you son of a bitch, get her out here *now*." From the corner of his eye he saw his men instantly lift their weapons. The SS troopers did the same.

"Stand easy there, Lieutenant," Stanfield said quietly. He turned to Strubeiter. "This is an outrageous breach of the exchange agreement, *Generaloberst,*" he said angrily in German. "How can you permit this?"

Strubeiter had momentarily turned his attention to him. Now he swung back to the Gestapo officer. "What the hell is this idiocy?" he growled, also in German.

"I'm sorry, *mein Herr,*" the man answered. "I am merely following orders."

"So? I hereby countermand those orders."

"That cannot be done, sir. They come directly from Berlin."

Strubeiter drew back, shocked.

Stanfield said, "In that case, there will be no exchange at all." He immediately stepped forward, headed for the SS troopers. The Gestapo man intercepted him, placed the palm of his right hand on the general's chest. Stanfield slapped it away. "How dare you put your filthy hands on me!" he shouted.

"Forgive me, sir," the Gestapo officer said hurriedly. "But I'm afraid you have no choice in this matter. You and your men are free to go. If you attempt to disrupt the exchange, you will be shot."

Stanfield glowered, his face aflame. "Then do your worst, you chummy bastard, and get bloody stuffed!"

Strubeiter quickly intervened. "Please, one moment, General," he said to Stanfield, then returned to the Gestapo agent. "What is your name and rank, idiot?" he demanded.

"Rittmeister Georg Wohlfarth, *Generaloberst.*"

"And you refuse to carry out my direct order?"

"*I* have no choice, either, sir. But, please, I must warn you, if you also interfere with these proceedings, you will be placed under immediate arrest."

Strubeiter trembled with rage. He reached out and roughly shoved Wohlfarth aside, took his place in front of the British general. With difficulty, he brought himself under control. "General Stanfield," he said slowly. "I offer you my deepest apologies. I take no part in this contemptuous act which dishonors us both. I intend to get it rectified. Your fellow prisoner *will* be released. I pledge that on my word."

Parnell had tried to follow this exchange, the German words coming so fast. But *Our previous agreement has been altered* kept shooting through his head. They weren't going to let Anabel go! The rotten, stinking *bastards!* He felt his scalp crawl, his blood high and hot. He wanted desperately to open fire on these animals, kill every fucking one of them.

There was a long, silent moment. No one moved. Finally, Stanfield broke the silence, speaking only to Strubeiter. "We are both soldiers, *Generaloberst.* I accept your apology and thank you for your pledge." He came to attention and slowly, deliberately saluted the German general. Moving with the same solemn deliberateness, Strubeiter braced and returned the salute.

Stanfield and Blue Team reboarded the train.

The trip back to Toul was conducted in total silence, save for the pounding rumble of the locomotive and the sequenced clacking of wheels over the track seams. Since they had been unable to turn around, the engineer was now backing his engine all the way.

Parnell sat alone at one end of the car. He was unable to gauge his fury, to find its edges. It enveloped him. Oh, God, how he wanted to charge his weapons, get off this fucking train, and go back there to get her. Fight his way through the whole goddamned German Army if he had to.

His men watched him while General Stanfield sat in

the middle of the car, his face still red, his eyes blazing. Parnell finally glanced up, looked at Bird. Into the weathered young face of a soldier. Wyatt dipped his head. *You say the word, Lieutenant.* Red's gaze moved to the others, studied each man's face, saw in it the same cold, steady look of readiness.

He rose and moved to where the general was seated and braced beside him. "Excuse me, sir. May I have a word?"

Stanfield seemed to rouse himself. He turned, looked up. "Yes, Lieutenant?"

"Was Agent Sinclair at the same prison where they took you, sir?"

Stanfield nodded. "Yes. I saw them put her in some sort of annex building the night we were brought in. Resembled a bloody stable. Early next morning, several dozen women prisoners emerged from it and were trucked off. They returned just before nightfall. Agent Roxanne was not with the group."

"Could she have been moved?"

"I doubt it."

"Have they tortured her?" The word was like a sharp spray of acid in his mouth.

"I don't know."

"Why did they break the agreement?"

Stanfield's face went stiff again. "I smell Himmler's stink in this." He snorted with scorn. "The bloody sick *bastard.*"

"*Can* this Kraut general get her released, sir?"

"I believe he'll try." He paused, then added, "But I don't think he'll be successful."

Parnell looked away, stared at the floor of the car.

"Why the pointed questions, Lieutenant?"

Red came back to him. "Anabel Sinclair is my fiancée."

"Ah, I see." Stanfield inhaled, let it out. "I'm terribly sorry for this unbelievably indecent situation, Lieutenant."

Parnell came right back: "I'd like your permission for my men and me to try a rescue, sir."

The general studied him. "Only the five of you?"

"Yes, sir."

"And if I refuse?"

"Then we'll do it *without* your permission . . . sir."

Stanfield sat back, looked up at him, grunted. His lips moved almost imperceptibly. After a moment, he nodded. "All right, Lieutenant. Tell me what you'll need."

0211 hours
23 September 1944

The rain feathered on the edges of the towing bay. It was icy cold, Parnell and his men and one of the flight crew members squeezed in around the square black opening in the stern of the plane's fuselage. They were aboard a Douglas JD-A26C attack bomber out of Tempsford Airbase.

This particular aircraft had been specially fitted for target-towing. Stanfield suggested using it since it had the open towing bay big enough for all five men to leap out very quickly, and it was also capable of a speed of nearly four hundred miles an hour. Flying at treetop level, it could get to the jump site and out again before the Krauts even knew it had been there.

The towing cable reel and the rack for the disengage rings had been removed back at the base. Now the space was taken up with the men and their weapons and demo packs. Against the forward bulkhead was an intercom and a single white bulb beside it used to signal the tow operator to send one of the big disengage rings down the cable to release the towed target before landing.

Parnell and his men were dressed in U.S. Air Force flight suits, another of General Stanfield's suggestions. He explained the reasoning. Recently Hitler had issued a personal order that stipulated that enemy soldiers, particularly commandos, who had dropped behind German lines could be shot on the spot. If Blue Team did get captured, they'd be able to claim they were part of an air crew and, as such, prisoners of war protected by the Geneva Convention.

As the plans progressed, Stanfield grew more pessimistic over the operation's success. He had aptly code-named it Operation Jeopardy. There were many reasons for his skepticism. The biggest was that it was being mounted too hurriedly, without proper study and lacking in-depth intelligence of the target. But he remained firm on his agreement to let Parnell try it. Although it was flawed, Stanfield had always been a believer in the bold, unexpected stroke in combat. This was certainly that. So the moment they crossed through the Allied lines, he was on the radio to London, pulling up the logistics for Jeopardy.

Among the first things he called for were the most recent aerial recon photos of the Saarbrücken area, particularly those showing Neue Bremm prison and its surroundings. By 2200 hours, he, Parnell, Dunmore, and the two newly arrived A-26 pilots were huddled over maps and those photos working out the mission drop procedure.

In addition, the general also exhibited an amazing ability to remember minute details of the prison. Well enough so that he was able to draw several sketches of it, showing Parnell several aspects of its operation and physical makeup.

The basic plan was essentially simple. Blue Team would be dropped into a craggy forested area a mile east of the prison. The photos showed portions of clear cut, all triangular-shaped meadows that formed open breaks in the trees. The road from the prison was clearly seen as it wound its way into the higher ground.

Stanfield had theorized that the women he'd seen early that morning were daily trucked to the forest to fell trees for firewood. Meanwhile, the male prisoners were sent off in the opposite direction to do the heavier work in the coal mines and steel mills outside Saarbrücken.

Once on the ground, they'd set up an ambush, take out the German truck drivers and guards, and free Sinclair. Then they'd release the women. If she wasn't with the wood crew, they'd drive back to the prison in the commandeered vehicles. The general remembered the trucks had used a small gate on the southern side of the compound with only a single two-man guard post that could easily be breached.

Inside the compound, they'd set up diversionary explosions, using plastique blocks and smoke, concussion and phosphorous grenades. Meanwhile, three men would locate and enter the stable annex and free Sinclair. In the confusion from the explosions, they'd exit through the same gate using a single truck and return to the woods.

For the remainder of the day, they'd go to ground and evade patrols. One thing would be in their favor. If many of the freed women prisoners chose to run off, they'd leave so many scent trails the German's tracker dogs would become confused and unable to follow *any* trail.

At precisely 2130 hours that night, a Lysander Mark

IIIA, its big-bore nine-hundred-horsepower Mercury
XXX engine capable of lifting off with a full load, would
slip in and pick them up at a specific coordinate point in
the potato strip-cropped fields adjacent to the Sarre
River, two miles to the southeast.

Wyatt Bird was already in that place in his head and
body, ready to go, quiet inside, just waiting to do the job.
He was braced over the tow bay hole watching the dark
ground below. Suddenly, light flooded out from the bottom of the plane, the landing lights coming on. It cut
through the rain, illuminating the ground down there.
The tops of pines were silvery in the light, crowded
thickly together maybe a hundred feet away.

According to the air recon photos, the land south of
the prison was on a continuous downslope, the area
folded into shallow meadow vallies fringed with forest.
Now the pilots were coming in low over one of the deepest meadows, spotting out the jump site on the first pass.
Then they'd begin a timed duster turn and come back
on a 180, counting off seconds.

The crewman with them abruptly dipped his head, listened through his earphones. He pointed at Parnell,
held up his right hand, all fingers extended, then made
a zero and pointed at the disengage light: *fifty seconds to
the jump, watch the light.*

Below, the landing lights went out and Wyatt felt the
plane dip first to the right, hold, then swing over into a
left turn, coming around. The engine sound increased
slightly, the pilots putting on more power to offset the
drag of the turn and to climb slightly.

He lifted his legs, squatted, his boot tips on the edge
of the bay hole. Lined around it were the others, every-

body chuted up, weapon and gear bags resting on their laps, looking down as the plane came around and leveled, no longer in a climb. In addition to their standard weapons, each man carried a short-barrel Smith & Wesson .38/200 British Service revolver with a blast suppressor attached.

The crewman hand-signed twenty seconds. Now the engines throttled back as the pilots slowed the aircraft's speed, gliding in, holding close to stall. The white light went on. Wyatt lifted slightly and dropped through the hole.

The turbulence was violent, not like the rush of engine backwash off a C-47, this time the air roiling from the near-stall flow off the wings and lowered flaps. He spun head over heels once, straightened, and yanked the rip cord, felt the drag chute go out and then the main canopy, jolting him in a half swing.

Rain peppered the silk, sounding like pebbles as a gust of wind slammed Bird to the left, his gear bag on its line accentuating the swing. He hauled risers, got straightened out, and there were the treetops. *Shit!* The pilots had slightly mistimed their approach, sent the first jumpers out too early. Overhead, the sound of the plane slowly faded off.

He went down into the trees with a hurtling, driving plunge. Branches whipped at him. He caromed off a large branch, still headed down. Then the canopy caught and he was jerked to a halt. He looked down. Water filtered down in icy streams all around him. He listened to it hitting the ground, a wet, slushy sound. He estimated he was about forty feet in the air. He popped his harness and started down.

* * *

Parnell knelt in the grass and checked heads as the men came in. As the last one out, he'd come down in deep grass, soft as a cushion. Laguna and Wineberg were already with him, rolling chutes.

A moment later, Fountain came limping in, cursing. "I hit a goddamn stump," he mumbled, disgusted. "Sumbitch like to gelded me."

"Where's Wyatt?"

"I seen him go down in them trees, Lieutenant."

"Shit."

Bird already had his chute buried and was emerging from the trees, gear bag over his shoulder, when they found him.

0359 hours

There were two German trucks and a flatbed, the trucks with wooden side panels and canvas tops. About forty women prisoners were crammed into the backs, most standing. The vehicles were old and their engines ground noisily up the steep road among the trees. The rain had stopped but it was still night-dark, the dawn two hours away. The road was rutted and full of rain pools and runoff streams and fog drifted through the trees.

The women all looked exhausted and underfed, their slender female bodies in dark, ragged dresses, no particular uniform. They wore dirty scarves over their heads. It was obvious some had been shaved bald, others wore stringy braids. All had different-colored ID tattoos on their forearms.

The trucks turned onto a smaller logging road, bouncing and jostling. Parnell and his men followed, lying back a few yards and holding to the trees. The vehicles went slowly along for a quarter mile and then stopped beside an area of felled trees. It was shaped like a slice of pie. There were hay wagons among the stumps and fallen trees. Leather breast harnesses hung from the oversized wheels that the women used to haul the wagons full of firewood.

The drivers lowered the truck tailgates and the women trooped out. In their filthy rags, they moved with a dark, hopeless somberness, like the chorus in a Greek tragedy. The flatbed pulled in behind them and the driver and two guards began unloading equipment, hand saws, and crude hatchets. Parnell studied the women's faces as they trudged forward and felt a solid lump form in his throat. Anabel wasn't with them.

There were seven German soldiers in the convoy: the three drivers and four guards. They all wore black greatcoats and had machine pistols draped over their shoulders. Their bean pot helmets glistened in the backglow from their flashlights. The women waited in small clusters, blowing on their hands and hugging themselves, then lined up to pass beside the flatbed to get their tools. The guards carelessly watched, their hands in the pockets of their coats.

Blue Team hit the Krauts in a rush, from both sides of the road, the zipping *thrup* of their silenced Smith & Wessons snapping through the silence, the suppressors throwing blast flames to the side. The Germans leaped up, yelling. Four were dead before they hit the ground. One managed to get his machine pistol swung up. Cowboy put a bullet into his forehead. It struck bone and sheered up through his helmet. The remaining two were instantly cut down.

Stillness, dense as the forest. Fog drifted, smelling of cordite. The women stood openmouthed. Then they began to cluster together again, cowering like tyrannized children.

Smoker and Weesay got into the two paneled trucks, started the engines, and began turning them around while Bird and Fountain stripped off the soldiers' greatcoats and helmets.

Parnell faced the women. "*N'aie pas peur,*" he called, holding his palms out. "Don't be afraid. Does anyone speak English?" No one moved. The hollow-eyed faces looked at him, at the dead Germans, and back again. "English? *Parle vous Anglais?*"

A woman came forward. She was hunched and held her head oddly. She may have been in her thirties but looked sixty. She stared at his uniform, then reached out and touched it hesitantly. "*Je t'en prie,*" she whispered. "*Americaine?*"

"*Oui,*" Red said.

"*Oh, Seigneur Dieu!*" she cried and began to sob.

"*Ecoute, Madam. Anglais dire ici?*"

The woman wiped her eyes. "*Oui,* I am speaking Anga-lais."

"*Bon.*" He waved his arm at the women. "Tell them they are free to leave."

"Is true?" Again the woman shyly touched his uniform. "*Americaines* are come?"

"*Non, non.*" He pointed to himself, the others. "Only us. Understand? But all you can go if you want."

She turned, rattled off a long stream of French. Many women began to weep. Then some of them came forward, stepping cautiously toward the bodies of the dead Germans. They began kicking and spitting on them, their sucked-in faces contorted with hatred.

Wyatt came up. "All set, sir." He looked at the women

for a moment, shook his head. "Them pore ole gals ain't got a snowball chance in hell, have they, Lieutenant?"

"Maybe some will make it. We're close to the French frontier. They could find refuge somewhere. Hell, this could be the only chance they'll ever get." He watched a moment longer, then exhaled through his teeth and said brusquely, "Let's get the hell out of here."

0502 hours

Frederich the Great's hunting lodge *looked* like a prison: high, flat walls of black stone with mansard roofs of rust-colored pipe tile and three tiers of small windows. Most of the walls were overgrown with wild vines. The grounds, once manicured into forest gardens, had not been kept up and were now jungles of thorns and thick clusters of berry vines that had long since overrun the statues of Teutonic gods and fountain pools.

With everyone dressed in greatcoats and helmets, the team quickly and easily killed the two guards on the south gate and then drove into the main compound. Dirt roads crisscrossed each other through the dense undergrowth. They scanned the roofline of the prison but saw no sentry turrets or inner perimeter of guard posts.

They passed two German soldiers walking toward the main building, both men smoking, their collars turned up. Parnell waved at them. They waved back. As the second truck came abreast of the two men, Wineberg shot them both, then stopped the vehicle long enough to shove the bodies into the brush and went on.

Stanfield's sketches turned out to be right on the button. They came to a small bridge across a stream and then a fork in the road. From there they could faintly make out the roofline of the stable annex about seventy-five yards up a slight slope. Its long roof had been formed into straw storage bays and showed above the dense undergrowth. To the right was a large barnlike structure that appeared to be a repair and blacksmith shop. Two trucks were parked near it.

Parnell's heart jammed up as he studied the stables. *She's in there.* He knew it, felt it. He wanted to go charging up there, tear through doors. He inhaled, calmed himself. He ordered Wyatt to stop. The other truck pulled up directly behind them.

They huddled beside the lead vehicle, hunkered down. "Smoker, Cowboy, turn one rig around, then lay trip charges across the road." His breath smoked faintly. "Double line. We'll lay time blocks on the right, behind that barn. When you finish, come up on the left and lay more charges beyond the fork. Set up cover fire positions at the fork. But remember, mark your wires on this side with stones. We'll be coming right back this way."

He checked his watch. "We'll set our charges for 0519. That gives us ten minutes. It's 0509 . . . now." Everyone set their watches. "Questions?" No one had any. "All right," he said. "Get those Kraut coats and helmets off and let's do it."

The dense brushwood was full of rats, good-sized ones, dark shapes darting through the weeds and tangles, squeaking, just ahead of and to the side of Smoker as he crawled through. One crossed over his right leg. Their holes were everywhere, mushy with mud.

"Sons a' bitches," he growled, wanting to take out his Smith & Wesson, blow a few rat heads off. He hated the damned things. He'd seen many varieties during his days on the bum, in close quarters, demon-eyed little shits that would feed on anything that moved or didn't.

He and Cowboy had already set up their trip charges on the road: frag and smoke grenades in tandem. Now they were laying more beyond where the road forked, one side going up to the stables and barn, the other continuing on to the main prison. It had begun to rain again, thick, heavy drops slamming down through the tangles.

He taped his last grenade against a thick vine stalk and quickly connected the wire from the other one he'd laid across the road, pulled the tension tight, and hooked it with pliers to the grenade's pin. He clipped off the other side of the pin so that the slightest pull on the wire would slip it out completely.

He returned to the road. Cowboy had already finished setting his trip charges and was squatted in the rain a few feet away. Even though there was a thick cloud cover, the dawn light was increasing rapidly, the color of slag steel, silhouetting the upper roof and chimneys of the prison and the trees beyond. Smoker crossed the road, crawled to the first grenade and also clipped its pin, then backed out, careful not to rub any of the brush against the now tightly set trip wire.

Behind him a rat poked its head out of a hole, its nose testing the air. After a moment, it scooted out and approached the grenade, smelled it all over. Another rat appeared, then two more. They clustered around the peculiar-shaped object, went along the trip wire, sniffing furiously.

Smoker reached the road, turned, and stood up, staying low. Cowboy rose and came down to him. The rain had slowed somewhat yet still fumed off the ground. They started back toward the fork in the road.

One of the rats tested the wire with its teeth. Another

jumped him, tried to grab hold, too. They tussled, tumbled over the wire, each biting it.

Both men heard the snapping click of a grenade arm flipping up, the soft buzz of its detonator. Then they heard the second safety arm click up. Instantly, they dropped to the ground, arms over their heads. The first went off, then the second. The ground trembled, fragments of metal slashed through the rain, chunks of brush and mud and road dirt lifted into the air. Cowboy's charges immediately exploded, four simultaneous flashes, the blast vibrations from the first two triggering them. Thick debris, smoke, fragments hurled upward.

Parnell's head snapped up at the crack of the first grenade explosion. He swore. *Too soon!* He'd just set the timer on a kilo block of RE 808 plastique, taped to the lintel of a side door to the barn. Wyatt was to his left, on the top corner of the building. Weesay had crossed over to a secondary structure, what looked like a small milking shed that sat between the barn and stable.

The rapidly following explosions jolted through his anger, Smoker's and Cowboy's charges all going off. Something was bad wrong. Wyatt came running down to him, looking to where the expolsion debris was arcing, falling back to earth. They looked at each other, stark-eyed.

"We gotta hit that stable *now!*" he shouted. They raced toward the milk shed, Weesay suddenly there, waiting, half turned. He shouted something, swung up his Thompson, and fired a burst, down past the stable, his muzzle flashes bright in the grayness.

Parnell saw movement down there, shadows, soldiers running up the slope, bullying through the underbrush.

Others came along the road, farther back, running hard. He fired at them, heard Wyatt's weapon start banging away, too. Something began to squeal, high-pitched, terror sounds.

Counterfire came blazing back. Bullets sizzled through the air, exploded into the stone barn. From one of the upper tiers of the main prison, an MG-34 model machine gun opened on them, the peculiar quick rap of its short recoil Solothurn breech mechanism instantly recognizable. Rounds cut a ribbon of dirt eruptions twenty yards downslope.

They reached the cover of the cowshed. Weesay was on his knees near the corner, firing. A fence made of raw logs with a gate had been built into the other side. Behind the shed was a large, stone drying oven shaped like a beehive and racks with deerskins hanging from them. Inside the shed were two large Landrace meat pigs, squealing and hysterically hurling themselves against the fence, their white bodies covered with dried mud.

Soldiers appeared down at the far end of the stable, gray-black uniforms darting, firing. Parnell felt his insides turn over. *Anabel, in there, in there.* He glanced at Bird, saw his cold, dark eyes, deep, emotionless.

"Cover me," he bellowed. Wyatt nodded. He braced his legs. The German fire slowed, stopped. A terrible, terrible silence shattered only by the pig's squeals.

He leaped forward, running.

Anabel had been jolted out of a dark place into another dark place by an explosion. Instantly several more, so close together they were like one. For a confused moment, she couldn't tell from which darkness they had come. She became aware of a heavy drumming. Rain, onto the top of the building. Had it only been thunder?

Then there were three distinct bursts from three automatic weapons, muffled by the stone walls but not far away. She blinked. Thompsons? German counterfire erupted, the faster *thrupppping* of MP-40s and then a machine gun. A full firefight developed, its echoes riffling off as full consciousness swept up into her mind.

Parnell?

She rolled onto her back. Dull pain throbbed through her head, chest, legs, anus. She held herself motionless, listening. The firing stopped. Shouts drifted from the other side of the darkness. They sounded like young men playing football on a nearby summer field.

A door slammed open far down the corridor and the crack of boots, running. She forced herself to sit up. Pain again. A surge of relief: *God, he's here!* Someone was fumbling with the lock on her door. A chain clattered to the floor and the door was kicked open. Two flashlights like small sunbursts appeared, hurting her swollen eyes.

Two guards rushed in. They played the beams over her. Finally, one stepped close, grabbed her arm, and roughly threw her over onto her stomach. She tried to get up. "*Verdammt noch mal, Schlampe,*" the man shouted. He shoved a boot into the base of her spine. Outside, the gunfire started again.

Her face was sideways on the stone floor. One guard told the other, "Turn her head."

She heard the metallic slide and snap of a handgun being cocked. *Oh, God!* The realization was like a scream in her brain. *They're going to kill me!* For a moment, she couldn't breathe.

A hand gripped her forehead, the fingers hooked into her eye sockets. It brutally jerked her head back. She stared at the darkness and tried desperately to free her head, hold it against the floor again, as if she might pull herself through it. The guard's hand was too strong. Her breath returned. For a wild moment every sense in her body went into overload, sounds, smells, touches amplified a thousand times.

She began to pray: "Our Father Who art in Heaven, hallowed be Thy Name." Louder and louder.

"*Um Gottes willen,*" the guard holding her head shouted. "*Tu's doch!*"

"Thy Kingdom come, Thy will be done on Earth as it is in Heaven." Louder still. "Give us this day—"

She didn't hear the discharge of the weapon. There was only a violent sensation of searing heat in her head as the bullet crashed through bone and into her brain. In a transition as rapid as the hurtle of an electron, she was sucked from this place into another where there was neither light nor sound nor dimension.

Parnell blew the stable door off its hinges with a grenade and lunged through the smoke, the echo of the explosion coming back at him from the other end of the corridor. Darkness down the long reach of it, open cell doors like upright coffins diminishing in perspective.

He pressed into shadow against the back wall. A room was to his right. He cautiously looked in. The dawn light coming through the blown door showed harnesses, a glass rack, chairs, a white bathtub. He looked back up the corridor again, squinting into the dimness. His head pounded. Abruptly, a spray of bullets crashed through the blown door, tore stone chips out of the opposite wall.

He saw a flashlight beam suddenly emerge from one of the cells. German voices. A figure stepped through the door. Another light beam jabbed out, silhouetting the first man, a guard in black uniform. Another man appeared. Both turned and broke into a run toward the far end of the building, the sound of their boots cracking like slow castinettes.

He cut them down, the echoes of his fire bounding back and forth. Spent rounds tinkled onto the wet cobblestones. The bullet impacts hurled the guards to the floor where they coiled over onto themselves like gutshot snakes. He fired at them again, moving forward. They finally went still. He scooped up one of the flashlights, turned, and began searching the cells.

She lay on the stone floor in that flat, deflated structure of death. He knelt beside her, for a moment would not touch her for fear of what his fingers would discover. "Oh, God," he murmured. "Oh, dear God." Even with her head shaved, he knew it was her. Gently he reached out, traced his finger along the line of that profile he had come to contain in memory.

The bullet's entry hole was as black and round as a scarab in the base of her skull. Somehow the projectile had been twisted, contorted in its trajectory and had exited through her left temple. It had blown part of it away. In the cold, her blood had already begun to coagulate. It looked like a glistening pool of purple ink.

Outside, the corridor exploded with sound, Thompsons and MP-40s throwing bursts, bullets *whanging* off walls, blowing through wooden doors. He heard Bird's voice, cursing, Weesay's screaming Mexican challenges, Germans bellowing.

Parnell shut down his eyes, put his right hand across his forehead, gripped it as if his fingers were a vise, as if they

could crush the images it had absorbed. For a long, agonizing moment he didn't move. Neither in mind nor body.

At last, he rose, leaned to pick up his Thompson. He
walked to the door and out. Bullets slammed past him,
jolting the air. He lifted his weapon and emptied it into
the two dead German guards, shifting the muzzle from
one to the other and back. The corpses jerked and
bounced.

The receiver locked back. Methodically, with bullets still
hurtling past, he reloaded, stepped over the bodies, and
opened on the other end of the corridor, heard Bird
come up behind him and fire, too, and then Weesay, three
Thompsons going in that slow, steady thundering.

For eighteen minutes, they held off the Germans until
their ammunition and grenades were gone. Then they
fought them with knives and fists and teeth. But there
were too many. Eventually, they went down, knocked unconscious with rifle butts and clubs.

LIONHEART

Chapter Sixteen

23 September 1944

When the first wet mornings of September began, the Allies had the German Army disorganized and whipped, fleeing eastward across France. Their rout had been so sound that people were beginning to believe the entire war would be over by Christmas.

Then things began to go wrong. The biggest problem was maintaining supply lines for the advancing Allied front. Cherbourg was still the main entry point for equipment and unit replacements. Although the Luftwaffe was now far too weak to operate over France, the logistics of transporting such huge quantities of supplies across nearly five hundred miles of central and northern France were extremely complex and time-consuming.

Two of the most critical items in short supply were ammunition and gasoline. In fact, Bradley's reason for holding Patton back during his thrust into Lorraine was to give as much fuel as he could to Montgomery for the ill-fated Market-Garden strike into Holland.

Teams of U.S. Engineers were now working night and day to complete two oil lines from Le Havre and Boulogne in order to relieve the shortage that would become critical once the Brits and Canadians began offensive operations against Antwerp on 16 October.

Now opposing Patton on the Moselle was a brilliant tactician, Generalleutnant Herman Balck. By constantly shifting his forces in what is called an "elastic defense" in the hilly and forested country of Lorraine, he had managed to contain the Third Army at the Moselle River.

His tactics were so effective, in fact, it would take Patton two entire months to cross Lorraine and strike at the southern section of the Siegfried Line, the continuous, thirty-mile-deep barrier of heavy fortifications, minefields, pillboxes, and antitank obstacles that ran along Germany's western frontier from Basel, Switzerland, in the south to Aachen, near the Netherlands' border in the north.

Meanwhile, the U.S. First Army had successfully crossed the Meuse River and entered Belgium. But its forward thrust was quickly slowed, particularly when its forward units began probing the Aachen corridor, which lay between Holland and the dense Hurtgen and Ardennes forests.

Adding to the already entrenched troops along the entire length of the Siegfried were the still formidable divisions that had escaped both the Falaise Pocket and the encirclement of the Lorraine corridor. Once the Allied forward movement stalled, these divisions had ample time to regroup and replenish before going into defensive positions.

The final reason for the stalling of the Allied thrust was the weather. Autumn in northern France, Belgium, and the German frontier is always a time of nearly constant and heavy rains. The land turns to mud and the rivers crest, making them nearly impossible to cross with armor. Under such conditions, Allied air strikes and armor-supported offensives could not be mounted.

Historically, an army in this situation would have gone into winter quarters to replenish and wait for spring

weather to begin new offensive operations. But Eisenhower wouldn't wait. He had good reasons not to: the
heavy V-2 raids on England; the increasing intelligence
concerning the savagery of German concentration
camps; the rapid and foreboding development of new
German weapons, including the atomic bomb; and the
rapid approach of the Russians on the eastern front. He
therefore ordered his armies to continue their thrusts
toward the east and northeast up to and through the
German frontier and its waiting Siegfried Line.

Parnell was naked save for his combat boots. He sat in
a metal chair with his hands cuffed behind the back of
it. He had been waiting for an hour, alone. The room
was large, rough stone walls full of odd angles, like a
room in a Frankenstein movie. In contrast, the floor was
made of neatly placed black and white tiles. There was
a single military type of desk and chair, the only furniture in the room. It was stone cold.

His entire body ached. His face was swollen and there
were dark bruises and abrasions on his shoulders and
neck and along the curves of his thighs. Some of his
teeth felt loose. He could not tell whether it was day or
night. He had awakened in a pitch-dark cell several
hours before. He had been alone there, too.

The door abruptly opened and an SS Hauptsturmfuhrer strode in with two guards in black uniforms and
black berets. The officer went quickly to the desk and
seated himself. He carried a briefcase and wore an odd
green uniform with black and silver collars. He was
stocky with sand-colored hair carefully combed back in
a wave off his forehead. His eyes bulged and were round
and blue and dead-looking, as if they were artificial.

Ignoring Parnell, he lit a slender, yellow-papered cigarette with a silver lighter that carried a swastika. He blew the smoke toward the stone ceiling. It smelled foul, like that from a mosquito punk. He lowered his eyes and fixed them on the American.

"Welcome to Neue Bremm," he said in accented English. "I hope your stay will be comfortable." He smiled. It did not touch his eyes. He opened his briefcase, took out several papers. He studied them a moment, then looked up.

"Why did you come here?" he asked quietly.

"I am an American airman," Red answered brusquely. "First Lieutenant John Parnell, U.S. Army Air Corps, serial number 046441."

"Ah," the German said. He nodded his head. One of the guards stepped forward and laid Parnell's flight suit onto the desk along with his Thompson and Smith & Wesson revolver with its suppressor still attached The guard stepped back, out of Red's vision.

The *Haupsturmfuhrer* casually lifted the Thompson, examined it, laid it down, and picked up the handgun. He turned it over in his hand, studying the silencer tube closely. Finally he laid it down, too, and began probing through the flight suit.

"*Ah, was haben wir denn hier?*" he said as if to himself. He withdrew a piece of paper, unfolded it, spread it out on the desktop. It was one of General Stanfield's sketches of the prison. After scrutinizing it, he looked at Parnell. He smiled again. Then he suddenly lunged to his feet and screamed, "*Lugen!*" He rushed around the desk, glared down at the American. "*Spion, Saboteur, Terrorist!*"

Parnell watched him from under his eyebrows. "I am an American airman. First Lieutenant John Parnell, serial number 046—"

Without warning, the German officer drove his fist into the side of Red's face. A sharp pain exploded in his head, as if he had just plunged it into icy water. One ear rang. He blinked and blinked, tasted the saltiness of blood in his mouth.

The German's face loomed into view, inches from his. "You come here with assault weapons?" he bellowed, spraying Parnell with spit. "Pistols with silencers? Grenades? No, you are *Terrorflieger*, a stinking pig air gangster."

"I'm an American airman," Red repeated, his lips feeling numb. "First Lieutenant John Parnell, U.S. Army Air—"

This time the blow came from behind him. A weighted rubber hose smashed down across the back of his neck, then his shoulders, the end wrapping down over the round curve of his deltoids. A roaring filled his head. Again and again he was struck.

He closed himself down, held tight inside. His mind flashed and leaped each time the blows came and bursts of color raced through the darkness behind his lids. He checked his mind, slowed it, drew up images. *Focus, focus.* An old trick. He thought of a high mountain, snow, wind that buffeted him, sunlight far off silhouetting a distant palisade of trees.

Each time the beating stopped, he'd slowly return to the room, to the chair, to his body, lift his head, panting. "Get fucked, you son of a bitch," he'd croak. "I'm an American airman, Lieutenant John Parnell, U.S. Army Air Corps, ser—"

They never let him finish. The beatings went on and on. Time became meaningless. There was only the pain and the retreat into himself. At last, it did stop. He was uncuffed and taken from the room, half dragged down corridors and steps and more corridors. They reached a series of metal doors. One of the guards unlocked it, pushed it open, and roughly shoved him into a dark cell. He went tumbling to the floor. They tossed his clothes onto him and slammed the door, cutting off all light.

Now he felt the full impact of the pain, like something that had been waiting there for him in the darkness. He put his palms against the stone floor. It was wet. He pushed himself to a sitting position, felt for the wall, touched it. Slimy. The air was dank and sour like a sewer warmed into full essence by the sun. He felt fleas bouncing on and off his bare skin.

His movements made his muscles grip up. It felt as if his bones had been fractured. He heard a soft sound, shuffling, felt someone there with him, approaching. He slid his buttocks on the floor until his back was against the wall, squinted into the blackness, waiting.

"How you doin', Lieutenant?" a voice close by asked quietly. It was Bird.

"Wyatt?" More movement, like animals shifting positions in a deep cave.

"Yes, sir."

"Who else is here?"

"The whole team."

That lifted him. "Smoker and Cowboy, too?"

"Yeah, Lieutenant, we're here," Fountain answered.

"What the hell happened with those charges?"

"I don't rightly know, sir. Either a bad igniter or them rats. Knocked us silly."

"It *was* them fuckin' rats," Wineberg growled. "No-good little bastards tripped the goddamned wire. Like to fuckin' *killed* us."

"Anybody badly injured?"

"No," Wyatt said. "But ever'body's hurtin' some."

Parnell felt for his clothing. "Is everybody else naked, too?"

"No," Laguna piped up. "We *was* bare-ass when them Kraut *lambiosos* work us over, though."

"You know, Lieutenant," Cowboy said, "I don't think they buyin' us as flyboys."

"No, they're not," Red said. "The assault weapons and they found one of the general's sketches in my pocket. I think we can kiss POW status good-bye." He moved his jaw, opened and closed his mouth.

Finally, he lifted himself, holding on to the wall and his flight suit. Hands reached out to help. It hurt like hell, but he finally got dressed. He sat down again, got himself settled. Staring into the darkness, *wham!* there it was, the full memory vision of Anabel's broken corpse rushing at him like an explosion. He felt despair well up in him. With it came a surge of sorrow so powerful he felt a sob rising. But the pain of loss and rage was too great and stopped it cold, leaving him only the darkness and the silence.

He inhaled deeply, expelled. Even that made his mouth hurt. "Christ, I'm thirsty. We got any water?"

"Yeah, Lieutenant, but it ain't hardly fit to drink," Wyatt answered. "I think the sumbitches use the same buckets for water and shit."

He heard a soft metallic tinkle. Something touched his chest, a metal pail scoop. He took it, drank. The water tasted like the cell smelled. It burned his gums. He lowered the scoop, inhaled again. "Okay," he said wearily. "Let's get our shit together here and figure a way to get out of this place."

Major Land enjoyed watching Vaillant Duboudin sweat, the Frenchman so agitated he seemed continually on the verge of leaping up and fleeing. His face was contorted with anxiety, the perspiration shiny on his skin. Fifteen minutes earlier, Land had informed him that, yes, it was true, he *was* being hunted by his own Resistance.

"What can I do?" Duboudin cried. "*Mon Dieu,* their assassins will find me, even here. They won't stop until I'm dead." He shook his head, unbelieving. "I'll die a traitor."

Following the capture of Stanfield and Sinclair, Vaillant had been permitted to cross the border into Germany, to Saarbrücken, where the Gestapo had sequestered him in a small hotel near a refinery. It was a depressing city of gargoyles and soot-blackened stone buildings, many demolished by Allied bombers, an industrial city, a place fit for the dreary gray smoke that constantly hovered above it.

Although he was not certain, Vaillant suspected the Germans were eventually going to either kill him or imprison him. With the Allies knocking on the Siegfried Line, a minor French Maquis captain no longer had much value to them.

He abruptly shoved himself forward. "I think the Gestapo is about to abandon me," he hissed.

Land studied him calmly but made no comment.

The Frenchman's eyes narrowed. "It's true then, isn't it? They're throwing me to the wolves."

"Yes."

Vaillant looked away, squeezed his fingers, came back in a rush. "Then you have to go to them. You owe me. Berlin owes me, *Hitler* owes me. I've risked everything for you Germans. Now I'm lost and you desert me." His gaze darted across the German's face. "Well, will you do this?"

"No."

"*Je m'en fous de ce que tu en penses!*" he blurted angrily. "I've delivered people to you, *key* people. Even a high-ranking enemy general. *Mon Dieu,* what more could I have done? What *more?*"

The accusation hung in the air. They were in a Saar-brücken *Rathskeller* named the *Toller Hengst,* the Great Stallion. It was early evening. The room was cold but stuffy with pipe smoke, a cheap tobacco stench saturated with the muskier odor of workingmen's bodies. All the patrons were coal miners, shingle cutters, or timber drivers, morose creatures who talked in the ancient accents of Alemannic.

The walls were a faded yellow, lined with the workers' hats on pegs and imitation crest shields from ancient Teutonic warrior clans, the logos of old soccer teams and dueling societies. The two *Bardames,* beer-maids, were as stout as brood sows, their heavy breasts stuffed into flowered red vests, their skirts ankle-length and ale-stained.

"Actually General Stanfield is no longer with us," Land said casually. He picked up his beer stein and quietly took a long pull. The vessel was made of dented pewter, its sides as thick as his thumb.

Vaillant's head snapped up. "What? What is that you say?"

"The British general was exchanged."

"*Mon Dieu,* why?"

"Berlin found it expedient."

The Frenchman's face tightened so sharply it quivered. "So my sacrifice was for nothing? Is that it?"

"Apparently."

Vaillant made a sound as if he were about to draw phlegm from his throat. His face flushed. "You Germans!" he blurted loudly. "I should have known. Oh, *God,* I should have known. You're all barbarians, the lot of you. Without honor, without—"

Land struck him across the face, his body and right

arm moving forward as quickly as a snapping spring. Around the room heads turned, steins paused in midair and the murmur of conversation ceased.

Vaillant's head jerked to the side. His eyes looked jolted, then they flashed, like alcohol tossed onto an open fire. He reached up, touched his jaw as if he had just newly discovered it. For a moment the two men's eyes locked. Land's were flat, opaque, as lithic as bedrock. Seconds ticked past. Then Duboudin lost his hold. His eyes darted to the side, came back, a mere fragment of a move. It was enough.

He lowered his head. Softly, he said, "I apologize, Major."

Major Land relaxed. A tiny sardonic smile touched his lips. He lifted his stein, took a drink, watching the Frenchman over the pewter rim.

"What am I to *do*?" Duboudin whined.

"Like me, you'll die for your country. But then, you no longer have a country to die for, do you? Pity."

Vaillant fixed his gaze on the officer's face again, the look like that of a dog that had been cowed yet still carried the dignity of rage in his eyes. "You find this very amusing, don't you, Major? A great joke to share with your comrades?"

Now Land's smile came up bright, clean. "Don't you understand, Duboudin? It's *all* a joke."

"A sick joke."

Land appraised him a moment, then asked, "Do you still possess your driving skills?"

"What?"

"You were an auto racer once, true?"

"Yes."

"How good."

"The best."

"Are you still?"

"Yes . . . but I don't understand."

"You don't have to. For now . . . go back to your hotel. Stay there until I contact you."

"I don't— Why?"

"Your hotel."

"But I have no money."

"I'll see to it."

"When will you come?"

"When it's time. Go, get the hell out of here."

After a long moment, Vaillant rose and went out. The workers darkly watched him go.

6 October 1944

The ceiling of the mine was barely five feet high, Parnell and Cowboy working side by side, having to stoop and lean so as to swing their picks against the coal face that gleamed like a black-brown wall of jewels in their hat lights.

The mine was heavy with heat that sucked the remnants of sweat from their bodies. Their body fluids carried a peculiar smell now, like the clotty odor of sulfur. This was their third day in the mine, killing work, the meager food and prison conditions already sapping strength from their bodies.

The rest of the team had been split up, put into other prison crews. Smoker and Laguna were at the base of the main pithead where they unloaded the shuttle cages from the surface that brought down timbers for the shoring braces. Then big wooden sledges brought the coal out through haulage drifts and they would load the now empty cages, which were then lifted by teams of thin-shanked black oxen. Bird had been assigned to one of the groups pulling the sledges, the men harnessed like animals.

As a University of Colorado graduate engineer, Parnell was very familiar with coal mines. This one disgusted him. Goddamned Krauts were a hundred years behind in technology, still using room-and-pillar techniques, sledges and animal power. And their hand-worked pumps were pathetic, malfunctioning constantly. They left the diggers in ankle-deep water breathing unventilated air thick with coal dust.

This particular mine was outside Saarbrücken, deep in a cedar and fir forest. The entire area, once ancient seas, was rich in lignite and anthracite fields and serviced the steel mills of the Rhur. Germany was desperate to increase its production of war materials, so had mobilized slave labor gangs from the prisons.

Most of the prisoners were thin and emaciated, living on daily rations of watery, maggot-filled soup and tiny loaves of black bread called *Knackebrot*, solid as lumps of coal. Many had died of malnutrition, exhaustion, or diseases like pneumonia, scarlet fever, and diphtheria. There were permanent cremation pyres outside the prisons and near the mine pitheads and mill enclosures. The corpses were always incinerated naked so their meager clothing could be redistributed to new inmates.

Parnell and his men had endured two days of constant interrogations at Neue Bremm; the same sandy-haired *Hauptsturmfuhrer*, the same screamed accusations and brutality. The worst beaten was Wineberg. Cuffed to the interrogation chair, he'd attack the officer and guards, his eyes gone wild, roaring curses and kicking and biting until they beat him into unconsciousness.

Twice they had used electric probes on his testicles

and once hung him from a ceiling beam with his arms
behind his back and then abruptly dropped him six
inches. A man with lesser shoulder and arm muscles
would have had his joints instantly dislocated.

The last time, Parnell angrily scolded him. "Goddammit, Smoker, don't fight the bastards. You hear me?
Don't let them get to you."

Wineberg's voice growled mushily in the darkness, "I
gon' kill them fuckers. I gon' tear they fuckin' hearts out."

"They'll kill you first," Parnell said. "Look, we're getting out of here. When we do, we'll need you."

Abruptly, the interrogations stopped and three days
later they were moved to a large basement room filled
with about a hundred other inmates. The room had
small windows high up with frosted glass. Vomit and
dried blood and excrement veneered the stone floor.

Men paced around or stood in silent clumps, others
sat against walls and tried to sleep. Many had had their
teeth knocked out, some the first joints of their fingers
cut off. They seldom spoke to each other and sometimes
they fought over food, vicious encounters that nobody
stopped. They heard bloodcurdling screams in the night
from other rooms in the prison.

The following evening the guards brought in a powerfully built Frenchman. They had beaten him
mercilessly. He landed on the floor near Red. One of his
front teeth had been knocked out completely and his
mouth and nose were clogged with dried blood. Each
time he breathed, the air would hit the exposed nerves
in his jaw, making him grunt.

At dawn, Parnell woke to thin light coming down
through the windows. The big Frenchman was still beside him but was now sitting against the wall. His face was
darkly bruised, purple as a plum, looked as if it had been

stung by a thousand bees. Both eyes were almost closed completely and resembled knife cuts in dark putty.

He turned his head and looked at Red. Then he reached out and took a pinch of his flight suit, mumbled something.

Parnell said, "What?" The Frenchman dropped his hand to Red's forearm and traced the letters U S with his forefinger, then pointed to the ceiling. Parnell understood. "Yeah, American airman," he said. "*Oui, Americaine aviateur.*"

The Frenchman nodded.

Early the next morning, everyone was rousted. It was pitch-dark. Flashlights sent yellow tunnels of light probing the vast room, guards bellowing, "*Aufstehen. Los, los, ihr Scheisskerle.*" They slammed the inmates with their rifle butts. "*Raus, raus!*"

They were marched through corridors and made to assemble outside in a courtyard in front of the old hunting lodge. It was raining heavily and everyone shivered uncontrollably. Roll was taken. Then they were herded into lorries and driven into Saarbrücken and then up into the forests to the east.

It was dawn by the time they reached the mine. It had stopped raining but thick fog drifted through the trees. They encountered an area where the air carried a foul, sweetish stench. It was cleared of trees and there was a deep pit in the center filled with partially burned logs and hillocks of ash that had been turned into a black mud by the rain. A burial pyre, still seeping little strings of smoke.

The ground around the pithead was also black from tamped coal dust, scarred from truck tires and the metal treads of shovel loaders. The pit itself was thirty feet wide, a dark hole in the ground. There were pulleys and chain and cable leads going down into the pit and a huge pile of coal the size of a three-story building beside it where the shuttle cages were emptied. A half dozen gondola trucks were parked nearby, their drivers sitting in the open cabs, smoking. Two teams of oxen stood among the trees docilely waiting, their breaths smoking in the cold.

Over the next few days, Parnell and the big Frenchman became acquainted. He could speak decent English, despite the air whistling through the gap in his front teeth. His name was Andre Labarre, an architect from Reims before the German takeover. He'd been arrested for Resistance activity in the small border town of Creutzwald.

To Parnell, he neither admitted nor denied the charge. But Red often caught him studying him, and when he'd look, Labarre would grin a puffy grin and say, "Do not abandon hope, *mon ami*. One day, one day . . ."

The bombers came just after dawn, American B-24 Marauders with P-47 Thunderbolts for air cover and cleanup. They first struck targets in Saarbrücken, steel mills and train farms, and then moved over the foothills and hit mines and coal operations in the forests to the east.

Apparently, they'd been waiting for the clear weather. The previous night there had been a light snow and then the stars came out. At 0430 hours when the prisoners were herded out to the roll area, there was a thin film of snow still on the ground and the underbrush and the air had a winter bite to it, the sky cloudless.

The prisoner trucks were a half mile from the pithead when they heard the sudden whine of aircraft engines and bombs exploding down in Saasbrücken. German ack-ack opened up, pom-pom guns and carriage-mounted 37s and 88s sending up a matrix of white and orange fire.

The prisoner convoy stopped immediately. As usual, there was a thin fog layer on the ground and in the trees. Some of the German guards dismounted and went out into a large meadow beside the road to see if they could spot the enemy planes. Then they came back and climbed back onto the trucks and the convoy moved on.

The first Thunderbolts seemed to come out of nowhere, a sudden explosion of sound and there they were, flashing past just above the trees, two of them, silvery, rocketing in leader-wingman formation. They were gone instantly, their engine sound abruptly chopped off.

Seconds later, two more burst into view. These carried wing tanks of napalm. They opened with their .50-caliber wing guns, the rounds sounding like individual grenades when they hit, hurling dirt and meadow grass and slashing through the trees.

The second released both wing tanks, chunky and dull silver, tumbling once, again, and then exploding into double traveling walls of orange and black fire that coiled and billowed into the air eighty yards from the trucks.

Parnell and Cowboy had both hit the floor of the truck the moment the planes appeared. The other prisoners crouched and stared openmouthed at the incoming aircraft. The napalm exploded with a peculiar rolling, *whooshing* sound like a sudden waterfall. Shrapnel whistled past, slammed into the sides of the trucks. First there was a powerful rush of wind that was followed immediately by a blast of intense heat. Men screamed and began to stampede to the back of the trucks. Canvas covers caught fire.

Shielded by the truck side, Red felt the heat wave pass just above him, felt the metal floor of the vehicle instantly get hot enough to burn his hands. A prisoner fell onto his back, his clothes aflame. Parnell slammed his palms against the fire, put it out. Then he was moving, hurling himself between legs, over bodies. He leaped over the tailgate, hit the ground running, pointing toward the trees downslope and bellowing, *"Allons! Allons! Allez le trouver!"*

The meadow to the right of the road was burning fiercely, billows of black smoke boiling into the sky, dimming the dawn light. A guard appeared beside him. His face was ashen and the bottoms of his boots were on fire.

Parnell jumped on him, wrapped his legs around the man's waist. The German cursed and flailed with the muzzle of his MP-40 machine pistol, trying desperately to bring it around. Gripping the rim of his black helmet, Red twisted the man's head sharply to the side. The helmet strap jerked against the guard's chin, snapping his head around. He fell limply to the ground.

Parnell scooped up his weapon and a knife from his harness scabbard. Cowboy came up, slid in on his knees. He also had a guard's knife. The other prisoners, some with clothes burning, were still leaping from the trucks and running hysterically toward the trees. Two guards fired at them with rifles, hitting several, who tumbled into the grass. Red swung the MP-40 around and cut loose, the smooth action of the weapon hardly bucking as the rounds went out in a single *thruuuuuuup.* Both guards went down.

The sounds of machine guns firing and bomb impacts rumbled down from the higher slope, interspersed with the quick splurges of aircraft engines. Smoke and fire seethed up above the treetops.

"Where're the others?" Parnell hollered to Cowboy.

"I seen two of 'em yonder in the last truck, Lieutenant," Fountain shouted back.

"Let's go."

They rose and sprinted back along the line of trucks just as a Marauder twin-engine bomber came over, a hundred feet above them, its fuselage painted in camouflage colors, the exhaust ports of its two engines blowing fire. For a fleeting instant, Parnell saw the head of the plane captain looking down at them, his twenty-mission campaign cap scrunched down under his headphones. Then he was gone.

Wyatt Bird killed his guard ten seconds after the napalm tanks exploded, the German obviously not combat savvy, standing there watching them tumble down and probably thinking that they were merely empty fuel tanks.

Bird and twenty prisoners were in the lead truck of the coal pit convoy. The explosions threw a wave of searing heat in every direction. It hurled the guard and several prisoners on that side to the bed of the vehicle where Wyatt was already lying flat on the corrugated metal. Chunks of the tanks slammed into the sides of the truck, the bed got too hot to touch. Prisoners screamed and began falling out the back.

Wyatt spotted a smoking sliver of debris. Pulling down one sleeve of his flight suit to cover his hands, he picked it up and rammed it into the German's neck. It hit the carotid. A slender, coiling thread of blood shot out, sizzling on the metal sliver.

Scooping up the man's machine pistol, he checked to see if a round was chambered, then grabbed the single cartridge pouch off the guard's belt. A small French prisoner scurried forward. He had only one eye, the other socket empty, a pit in his head as if a thumb had been pressed into soft clay. He followed Bird as he leaped from the now burning truck and ran back along the road.

A pair of guards began firing at the prisoners. They were suddenly knocked down and Bird spotted Parnell and Fountain. He made for them, pausing just long enough to grab up one of the German's rifles and cartridge pouch. The one-eyed Frenchie grabbed the other one.

Parnell was staring at the black napalm cloud, now well above the trees. The Marauder's passage had churned it, thinned it. White smoke was beginning to lift off the meadow grass. He turned as Wyatt approached, hollered to him, "Secure a withdrawal line. The tree line downslope." He then ran father down the road, looking for Smoker and Laguna.

As Cowboy came up, Wyatt tossed him the rifle and spare cartridges. They both went to the ground to set up a fire base. The Frenchie did the same. Bird peered through the grass, the stuff two feet deep. Three more trucks were fully engulfed in fire. He saw a guard suddenly lift from the grass and sprint toward the trees. He killed him. Another rose. Cowboy killed that one, his round tearing out the back of the man's neck. Then counterfire came from somewhere beyond the trucks, the bullets popping as they passed overhead.

Two sharp whistles sounded over the hissing roar of the burning meadow, Parnell calling them in. They immediately rose and ran back down the road, zigzagging, the Frenchie close behind, German bullets snapping and slicing into the grass around them. Parnell, Wineberg, and Laguna opened up with covering fire, the lieutenant and Smoker with MP-40s, Laguna shooting a handgun. The Kraut fire stopped.

Parnell waved them past. They made for the tree line, entered it twenty seconds later, into cool, shadowed light, the sounds of explosions and gunfire immediately

muffled. They turned and began firing as the others
came lunging and dodging through the grass.

Deep in the forest, Parnell called a halt. Now they
numbered seven, the team, the little one-eyed Frenchie,
and Labarre, who had joined them during the firefight.
They took stock of their weapons and ammunition: two
machine pistols with six rounds between them, one rifle
and eight rounds, Laguna's already empty handgun.

Red looked at Labarre. "This is your country," he said.
"Where do we go?"

The closer sounds of explosions and gunfire had
stopped, but they could still hear other, fainter explosions in the direction of Saarbrücken. The sun had risen
above the higher ridges now. Its light, shafting sideways
through the trees, was honey-colored, and the air was
filled with the sweet scent of burning wood.

"Best is Vorbach," the massive Frenchman said. "It has
safe houses there."

"How far?"

"Perhaps three kilometers, southwest."

"Let's go."

Always moving downslope, Smoker on point with one
of the MP-40s, they traveled rapidly. Fifteen minutes
later, they came to a stream that was about twenty-five
feet across. It was rain swollen, the water cloudy with
mud, chest high, and icy cold.

Twenty minutes later, beyond the stream, the air
began to grow smoky, faint at first, then thicker. They
could feel a breeze moving through the trees, going
downslope. It chilled their wet clothing. A moment later,
Wineberg came back.

"We got fire right ahead of us, Lieutenant," he reported.

Charles Ryan

"From the way it's suckin' air down the slope, she's big."
They listened. For the first time, they could hear the
sound of it, directionless, a low, moaning roar.

The one-eyed Frenchie rattled off something to
Labarre. He listened a moment, turned to Parnell. "He
say we must go back to the stream."

"Can't we parallel the front of the fire?"

Labarre asked the little man, who shook his head vig-
orously and said something. Andre translated, "He say
we must reach water before it overruns us."

Parnell glanced at Bird. "What do you think? I hate
like hell to backtrack."

"I don't know, Lieutenant," Wyatt said. He turned and
spat, came back. "Either way, we gonna be cuttin' 'er
tight."

Smoker said, "I think the Frenchie's right, sir. I
worked fire line in Arkansas. When y'all got a downslope
fire suckin' upridge air, that means she's movin' fast."

Red thought a moment, nodded. "Okay, we go for the
stream."

Soon cinders began floating through the trees, drifting
and dipping like black butterflies. The honey light darkened, became hazy, and the roar of the fire was viciously
loud and seemed to be all around them.

They reached the stream and immediately plunged
into it, the swiftness of the current sweeping them
along. The air grew hotter, the smoke choking. Holding their faces just under the surface, they skimmed
along. Images flashed above the water, red and orange
and yellow light shifting and intersecting into convoluted patterns.

They came to a series of small cascades. The water fun-
neled between boulders, going faster, sluicing them over
the smooth stony bottom, foaming, the men tumbling and

caroming, the air so hot it hurt their lungs to breathe. Now and then they caught glimpses of tongues of fire leaping and whirling above the treetops.

At last the stream broached out into a vast meadow. They could see small groups of dark-colored deer fleeing through the grass, leaving trails, and the air hung in a dense white layer just above the ground.

They stayed with the stream, which now branched out into several smaller courses, narrow, grass-banked channels. On the far side of the meadow, they came together again and the main stream curved around a sheer rock promontory that boiled with fire.

Then they were past the fire line, skimming down into burn-off, the trunks of trees like stenciled prints poking into the sky. Some were still afire. The ground was pitch-black and humped with drifts of ash that glowed and pulsed deep inside. The air stank of burnt wood and the acrylic stench of evaporated sap, a dark, unmistakable miasma. Here and there, badly burned smaller animals plunged into the stream, screaming, frantically trying to swim across. Most went under.

Six minutes later, they ran head on into nearly two hundred German soldiers moving up through the burned area, their uniforms and boots and weapons coated with ash. There was a tiny firefight and then they were recaptured.

All through that day and night and then into the following day they and other prisoners were forced to fight the fires in the upper ridges, cutting fire lanes and brush and hauling canisters of kerosene used to set backfires. They were fed nothing. Some men fell from total exhaustion and were shot. Others went insane and were also shot. Two committed suicide by running into the backfires. Finally, the rains came, flooding down the bare slopes. They were trucked back to Neue Bremm, herded into their cells, and finally fed.

Sometime in the night, Labarre woke Parnell. "*Ecoute,*" he whispered. "I have news."

"What?"

"Many are to be moved tomorrow. Especially those who tried to escape."

"Who told you that?"

"One of the *fideicommissaire.*" These were prisoner trustees who worked with the Germans and who were made guard assistants. Many were Resistance fighters, however, who feigned cooperation so as to garner information.

"Where we headed?"

"To a Gestapo *Kozentrationslager*, a concentration camp. It is called Buchenwald."

"Where is it?"

"Weimar, near Leipzig in Thuringia." Labarre bent closer. "Do not despair, *mon ami.* But be very alert from now on." There was a smile in his voice. "These Boche *chatte* have just made a mistake."

Chapter Seventeen

14 October
Wiener Neustadt, Austria

They came at 4:30 in the afternoon, two trucks with sixty-one SS troopers in their black and silver uniforms and polished black helmets. They quickly unloaded and surrounded the neat house among the pines.

The weather was unusually clear, a break in the normal overcast. Snowdrifts were banked along the windward side of the house and there was a foot of snow in the garden. The soldiers stood about, distracted, embarrassed. Even their noncoms appeared uncomfortable at having to perform this particular duty.

An ambulance and a command car drove up and stopped and a young SS colonel got out of the CC. Carrying a slim black briefcase, he headed up the curving walkway that had been shoveled free of snow. The front door of the house held a polished brass stag's head knocker. He tapped it lightly.

The door was instantly opened by Generalfeldmarschall Erwin Rommel, meticulous in the dress gray *Sturmartillerie* uniform of the Panzer Grenadier, the trousers bearing the cardinal field marshal stripe down the legs, the knee-high black boots shining as brightly as if they had just been dipped in hot wax. The colonel snapped to rigid attention, saluted. Rommel returned it, then stepped aside. The visitor strode briskly into the house and the door closed softly.

The colonel's name was Josef von Gyer. He stood in a front hall paneled in rosewood. A stairwell curved upward deeper in the house. The hall smelled of polish and brass cleaner. For a moment, Rommel calmly studied him, then nodded, indicating him to proceed into a side room.

It was a library, the walls lined with bookshelves. Most of the volumes were on military history and tactics and were written in at least eleven different languages. The furniture was spare, leather and oak: a wide, glass-topped desk, lounging chairs with side tables, a coffee table. A large window looked out onto the garden and there was a marble fireplace in which a fire crackled softly.

Gyer remained braced. Rommel offered him coffee. He declined. A single droplet of perspiration slid down the center of the young officer's back and his armpits felt moist. Like his troopers, he did not relish this unsavory business.

Rommel walked to the window and looked out, hands clasped behind his back. Classic posture, head slightly lifted, tilted, as if he studied distant sand dunes shimmering under a North African sun. His color was still slightly sallow, the facial skin tighter than usual across his cheekbones.

Finally, without turning, he said quietly, "Do your duty, *Oberstrichter.*"

"*Yawohl, mein Feldmarshall,*" von Gyer said briskly. He immediately withdrew a single-folded paper from his briefcase. It had a light blue backing. "I am required to read this aloud to you, sir. But I do not—" For a moment, his voice caught. He stopped.

Rommel turned, held out his hand. The colonel

placed the paper into it. The field marshal unfolded it
and glanced quickly at the wording. It said:

OKW/WFSt/(Rommel)
Secret Warrent
14.10.1944

Pursuant to the prescribed administration of
Military Justice and General Courts-Martial proceedings under Sections 1176dd and 1098fd of the
Articles of War, Generalfeldmarschall Erwin Rommel has been found guilty of conspiracy to abet
and facilitate the attempted assassination of the
Leader of the German State, Adolph Hitler. Further, he has also been found guilty of dereliction as
a senior officer of the Third Reich.

In implementation of this warrant, issued by the
designated Court of Honor on this, the fourteenth
day of October, the said Generalfeldmarschall Erwin
Rommel shall be placed under arrest and conveyed
to a facility of military detention. There, he will await
his execution by musketry on a day and time to be
assigned by the Court of Honor. No appeal of this
order and warrant is possible.

However, due to the Generalfeldmarschall's
great and honorable service to our beloved Fatherland, the Führer in his mercy has allowed a
dispensation to be offered. The particulars of said
dispensation will be explained to the Generalfeldmarschall Rommel by the officer in attendance.

It was signed by the chief of staff of the German High
Command, Generalfeldmarschall Wilhelm Keitel.

With no detectable change of expression, Rommel

refolded the letter and handed it back to von Gyer. Only his eyes held something, a darkness, utterly deep, a solidness, a resolution, perhaps a melancholy. He said, "What are the conditions?"

The colonel inhaled before speaking. "The Führer has offered you the opportunity to retain your full military honors by choosing suicide rather than arrest and execution, *mein Feldmarschall*."

Now Rommel's eyes flashed. "What happens to my family?"

"The Führer has ordered that they will be placed directly under his protection."

Rommel nodded. "What means have been offered?"

"Weapon or poison, sir."

"I choose the poison," Rommel said. "I will not dishonor by arms in suicide. What is the poison?"

"Trisulfide of arsenic, sir." Gyer again opened his briefcase, extracted a tiny vial of yellow-brown liquid. In the sudden light, it shimmered with a slight grayness. He handed it over. "It is lethal within fifteen minutes."

Rommel took it into his palm. He stared at it, clasped it, turned, and returned to the window. "How much time am I allowed?"

"Thirty minutes, sir."

"Please send my wife in."

"Yes, sir."

Colonel Gyer remained in the hall. The minutes seemed inert, as if lingering, hesitant to pass out into the cold sunlight. A stiff, polished silence. Yet he sensed the house whispering delicately to him: a creak, the sigh of a breeze along the windowsill, a winter bird outside with a sound like the end note of a chiming.

Lucia Marie Rommel came out of the library, a stout country woman. She did not appear shaken, this woman who had seen her husband off to war so many times, successions of good-byes, now a final one, certain, yet somehow the same. She looked at Colonel Gyer, a steady, cold, unrelenting stare. He could not hold it. She passed along the hall, silent as a ghost, and disappeared into another room.

Hesitantly, he went back into the library. The field marshal was seated in a chair that he had moved to the window. The arsenic vial and a glass of water stood on a side table. He said to the colonel, "What is your name?"

"Von Gyer, sir."

"If you do not mind, I prefer to do this alone."

"Of course, *mein Feldmarschall.* . . . Sir, might I say, I am extremely sorry."

"Thank you."

The younger SS officer withdrew into the hall again. Once more the silence seemed stunning, an unbearable pausing of time. He moved to the door, eased it open. His men stood about looking silently at the house. The sky was achingly blue, a frigid, light blue, the forest below green black, dense.

He heard a sound, an inhalation of breath, like someone surprised. He listened, checked his watch. It had been seventeen minutes since he'd left the library. He went to it and entered.

Rommel was slumped in his chair, his head thrown back against the leather. His eyes were open, yet all aliveness was gone; that studied stare, those eyes which men had once trembled under, vanished. Von Gyer gently touched his carotid. Rommel's fingers trembled, a muscular reaction. Then they lay still.

The Desert Fox was dead.

The young colonel braced, slowly saluted, which he

held for a long moment. Then, his face ashen, he whirled and strode back to the hall and out the front door.

Throughout September, the victorious Allies, fifty-five divisions strong, had swept across France in pursuit of a demoralized, fleeing German Army until October when the rolling momentum of their thrust slackened and finally halted completely all along the western front.

In the northeast, Montgomery's Twenty-first Army Group, badly shaken by the debacle of the Market Garden operation in Holland, wouldn't take Antwerp Estuary until November. Bradley's Twelfth, in the center of the Allied line, would run head-on into the Siegfried Line and fight bloody, useless battles like the taking of Aachen, a key northern terminal of the Siegfried, and the blind attacks in the Hurtgen Forest that chewed up divisions like fodder. Meanwhile, in the southern flank, General Jacob Dever's Sixth AG eventually also stalled along the Strasbourg/Swiss border.

The Siegfried Line was a wonder of modern defensive war. It was composed of mile after mile of deep fortifications, minefields, Dragon's Tooth pads, barbed wire clusters, pillboxes, steel-and-concrete bunkers, artillery gun pits, communication trenches, all with easy access to supply road networks and major autobahns running clear back to Cologne.

Manning this nearly impregnable wall were actually more German divisions than the Allies possessed. However, many were made up of young boys and old men, some even commanded by totally inexperienced and untested Luftwaffe officers who had been pressed into infantry field duty. Other units had been reconstructed from the demoralized but still strong troops who had managed to escape France.

Still, pressure to continue the Allied fall–winter offensive grew more and more intense, Eisenhower and the Combined Chiefs were convinced the war could be ended by Christmas. This mind-set filtered down through the ranks to create an almost fanatical sense of must-do in local field commanders. Against all common sense, they continued hurling themselves and their men into hopeless, tragic attacks against the Siegfried.

Quickly, the situation devolved down into a bloody, stalemated battle of attrition, similar to that of the trench warfare of the First World War. Only this one was being fought during the wettest and coldest autumn and winter central Europe had experienced in decades.

Adolph Hitler, however, had never been one to relish an even successful defensive war. Already sinking deeper and deeper into mental instability, he had nevertheless by mid-October formulated plans for a new, decisive offensive that he believed would drive the Allies back to the coast and into the Channel.

The Führer's headquarters
Rastenburg, East Prussia
17 October 1944

Hauptbannsturmfuhrer Otto Skorzeny stood six-feet-seven, a man who always instantly drew people's attention when making an appearance. He was slender yet broad-shouldered and bore a faint resemblance to the Hollywood movie actor Ray Milland. Although he was now in the presence of the highest brass in the German military, it did not intimidate him. Instead, he stood quietly watching the general officers who were now gathered in the main conference room of the *Wolf-sschanze,* the code name for Hitler's main headquarters.

The facility was deep in a cedar forest, an entire complex of camouflaged bunkers constantly guarded by troops, observation posts, and minefields. Since the attempt on his life, the Führer had become obsessively paranoid. Even his closest friends were held off. At night he would allow no one into his bed chamber except his German shepherd, Blondi.

This particular situation room lay in a deep bunker at the very core of the complex. It was long and rectangular and filled with indirect lighting to eliminate shadows. In the center was a large table on which were numerous general staff situation maps and dozens of colored pencils held in silver beer steins.

A fireplace was in one wall, next to it two small, silver-framed Dürer paintings of mounted fifteenth-century knights. There were no chairs for the officers, only stools for Hitler and his two female secretaries. The bunker had only recently been completed and the walls gave off a damp, warm odor like ozone.

Gathered around the situation table were five of the most powerful military men in the Third Reich. There was Generalfeldmarschall Wilhelm Keitel, chief of staff of the OKW, the German High Command. Beside him stood Generaloberst Alfred Jodl, who was OKW's chief of operations. Both were senior advisers to Hitler and known yes-men. Behind their backs, other officers called them *Nikesels,* nodding donkeys.

Directly across from these two was Generalfeldmarschall Walter Model, Hitler's miracle worker whom he would soon appoint as overall commander of his new offensive plan. To Model's left was Generalfeldmarschall Gerd von Rundstadt and Generaloberst Heinz Guderian. Although von Rundstadt had been relieved by the Führer after the invasion of France, he'd been reappointed to command the field forces for the coming thrust. Guderian had been the master of the blitzkrieg and would be the chief tactician for the armored units.

Skorzeny shifted his glistening boots and hungered for a cigarette, the man a four-pack-a-day addict. He continued taking no part in their conversation, an aura of aloofness about him. At thirty-six, he possessed thick brown hair combed straight back in a tight wave and light blue eyes that always seemed to hold an arrogant yet mischievous smile.

He carried three prominent scars on his face, wounds received as a young man on the dueling floors of the Markomania Dueling Society, the most prestigious fencing club in Vienna. Instead of marring his looks, however, they actually added to the rakish masculinity of his features.

He was Hitler's favorite, known as the *Führer's Kommando*. He and his five-hundred-man unit known as Panzer Brigade 150, all handpicked and highly trained troopers, had accomplished amazing feats. In 1943, they rescued Mussolini from his mountain prison in a daring glider raid. During the chaos after the 20 July attempt on Hitler's life, Skorzeny had immediately taken control of the Ministry of War building in Berlin where, for forty-eight hours, he actually controlled Germany. Only recently, he had forced the dictator of Hungary, Miklos Horthy, to resign after the man threatened to sue for peace with Russia. Again, for a short period, he was the literal head of a country.

The door opened suddenly and Hitler's dog came bounding in. A second later, the Führer himself entered, followed by his two female secretaries, sallow, homely women. Blondi sniffed at the officers' trousers. The men braced stiffly, as the secretaries took their stools. Slightly dragging one leg, Hitler moved to the head of the table and sat down.

Skorseny was shocked by the Führer's appearance. Hitler had deteriorated from the last time he'd seen him only five weeks before. Dressed in his usual gray field jacket over a white shirt and black tie with the Iron Cross First Class and silver wound badge from World War I on his breast, he appeared old-man frail, his skin pale and papery thin.

His right hand trembled so badly he walked with it cupped in his other hand to keep it still. Rumors said he had Parkinson's disease and also suffered from painful chronic stomach disorders, shattered nerves, and insomnia. For these maladies, his doctors prescribed powerful drugs that some said included small amounts of strychnine.

Yet despite his frailty, his eyes had not changed at all. They still had that penetrating, black, mesmerizing stare which seemed to radiate an energy, a light that beamed outward, capturing, demanding, *imprisoning* attention.

Now he stared at his senior commanders for a long, drawn-out moment. At last, he spoke, in that slightly elevated, hysteria-sounding voice: "All right, gentlemen. Now I will show you imbeciles how to win this war."

For the next hour, he went over his entire plan for a major offensive. His memory and grasp of the complex details were astounding. Without notes, he covered complex offensive schedules, attack route allotments, specific unit distributions all the way down to company level, lines of movement, supply networks, types of air cover, hourly mission goals.

Occasionally, one of the officers would utilize a pause

to point out a potential problem, pose a question, or make a suggestion. Mostly it was from either Model or von Rundstadt, who were openly skeptical of the offensive's success. Each time, Hitler savagely launched into a screaming, blistering tirade before returning to his plan.

Essentially it would be a massive surprise offensive that would strike across the Luxembourg and German border from Monschau to Echternach, a front of over forty-three miles. Its main thrust, however, would be through the dense terrain of the Ardennes Forest. Hitler had code-named it Operation *Herbstnebel* or Autumn Mist and had designated its strategic objective as the port of Antwerp. This would split the Allied forces, leaving the British and Canadians isolated in the north, while Bradley's two armies would be scattered in the south.

To execute *Herbstnebel,* he had assigned three of his best armies. The Sixth Panzer Army under the command of the thuggish-looking Oberstgruppenfuhrer Joseph Dietrich would make penetration in the north. At the same time, the hard-drinking, womanizing, sergeant-turned-general Hasso von Manteuffel would command the Fifth Panzer army to the south. A third army, the Seventh, was given the task of protecting von Manteuffel's left flank.

Hitler had gathered every bit of manpower and equipment he could lay his hands on. And he'd done it in total secrecy, keeping it even from many of his own military. The assassination plot, along with the deadly purging of the *Wehrmacht* officer corps afterward, had left him pathologically mistrustful of field commanders.

Dietrich would act as the main spearhead of the offensive, slashing directly into the Ardennes to cross the Maas River, capture Louvain and Malines, and then strike straight for Antwerp. *His* leading unit would be the veteran 1ˢᵗ Panzer Division's elite battle group commanded by Kampfgruppenfuhrer Jochen Peiper, the bold but arrogant hero of the eastern front. Farther north, von Manteuffel's Fifth Army would focus on the cities of Dinant and Brabant, then swing northwest to capture Brussels and link up with Dietrich in his drive for the coast.

Abruptly, Hitler stopped talking, sat scowling down at the scatter of maps and situation reports on the table. His hand shook violently until he angrily slapped at it and pinned it to his chest. The officers exchanged furtive glances. Across the room, Blondi snored loudly.

At last the Führer looked up. "Everyone but Skorzeny out," he shouted. "Go, make my goals reality." The secretaries rose and headed for the door. Behind them came the five senior commanders. Blondi, awakened by the sound of their boots, lifted his head.

Skorzeny stepped briskly to the table and stood at rigid attention. As the door closed, Hitler looked up at him. "You have studied the aerial bridge photos?" he snapped. He was referring to recent air recon pictures of the three bridges over the Meuse River at Huy, Amay, and Engis. These would be key capture points in Dietrich's thrust.

"No, *mein Führer,*" Skorzeny answered. "I never received them from the Luftwaffe."

"What?"

"I requested them three times. They never came."

Hitler hissed. "Dear God, how long must I tolerate such incompetence from Goring's people?" The muscles in his jaw momentarily tightened. Then, inhaling slowly, he calmed himself. "At least how are your *Grief* preparations?" he asked.

"Right on schedule, *mein Führer*. The men are still completing training at Friedenthal. But they are already finely tuned and eager to undertake their missions."

Operation Grief was a personal assignment from Hitler to the commander of Panzer Brigade 150. To carry it out, Skorzeny had reorganized his men into three commando units called *Steinhausen*.

The first would parachute ahead of Dietrich's forces to secure the Meuse bridges. The second would immediately follow so as to create confusion behind the U. S. lines. Dressed as American soldiers and riding captured U.S. jeeps and modified Panther tanks made to look like M4 Shermans, they'd conduct demolition raids, cut communication lines, and misdirect traffic by switching road signs.

Hitler nodded, pleased. "And *Dreifach?*"

"Also on schedule, sir. The infiltration team has been chosen, eight of my finest. Each speaks American dialect perfectly and all are very familiar with France."

"What of the vehicle's driver?"

"He is a French collaborator named Vaillant Duboudin. Before the war he was a race driver in Gran Prix, a champion."

Hitler's eyes narrowed. "Can he be trusted?"

"Yes, sir. He has no choice but to continue working for us. His own people intend to kill him."

Operation *Dreifach*, which meant Triple, was the most secret aspect of the coming offensive. Only three people knew of its very existence and purpose: Hitler, Skorzeny, and General Deitrich. Even the very commandos who would carry it out would not be told of their precise target until the morning of 15 December, the day before the major offensive was scheduled to begin. Operation Triple was Hitler's ace up his sleeve.

Once more the Führer nodded. He was thoughtful for a moment, then straightened up and rose from his stool. "We are at a crucial junction," he said quietly. "You are one of the few men I truly trust, Otto. Do not disappoint me."

"I will not, *mein Führer*," Skorzeny barked, bracing again.

Nothing out of the ordinary happened at Neue Bremm for the next four days. Even those who had tried to escape were not punished. Instead, the prisoners were again put to work in the mines, the trucks passing through stretches of burn where the air stank of wet ash, the snowdrifts black.

Another Allied air raid came the third afternoon. Parnell and his group were underground when the planes attacked three miles to the east near Zweibrücken. When they came out of the pithead that evening, they could see the glow of fires above the mountains, flickering against the overcast.

On the fifth day, the guards roused them at three in the morning and went among the men with flashlights picking out individuals. Fifty-three were taken from Blue Team's cell, including all of Parnell's men and Labarre. They were marched to the assembly area. Over 150 other prisoners from neighboring cell blocks were already there, shivering in the freezing rain.

As they were leaving the building, Labarre had managed to whisper to Red, "Soon now, *mon ami*. Stay together and be ready."

They were counted and recounted, then forced to wait. Soon, several headlights appeared from down the slope, flashing through the trees. Four green-and-yellow buses turned into the prison compound and came forward to park next to the assembled prisoners, their engines idling.

The guards separated the prisoners into four groups. Parnell, Wineberg, Laguna, and Labarre were in one, Bird and Fountain in another. Quickly, they boarded the buses. The vehicles were very old with a high platform at the rear and narrow top windows that had been sealed. The seats were gone so the men sat on the floor. Each bus carried six guards with machine pistols.

Again they waited. Despite the cold, the air in the bus quickly became rank, a dense foulness made up of old sweat and dirt and dysentery excrement like rotted flesh. Finally, they started moving, rattling and lunging down the dirt road that ran down through the forest. The guards sat up near the driver, their weapons on their laps, and smoked and cursed the stench, their helmets silhouetted against the headlights and the orange tail lamps of the bus ahead.

Dawn was already graying the east by the time they reached a town. Someone said it was Saarlouis. There were many demolished buildings in the outskirts. Twice the bus convoy stopped at control points and finally turned onto a narrow side road and soon pulled up in the back of a small train depot.

Two trains sat nearby. One was shut down, sitting off on a small siding with only its tender, coaler and a single gondola hooked on. The second locomotive thumped and hissed steam, which instantly condensed into a thick, perfectly white cloud in the icy gray light. Behind its tender and coal car were twelve boxcars and eight flatbeds with strapped-down tanks aboard, all the armored vehicles badly damaged and battle scarred. Several dozen SS troopers, some with leashed dogs, German shepherds and big-headed rottweilers, milled about beside the tracks, waiting for the prisoners.

The doors of the bus swung open and the guards

began driving the prisoners out, shoving them with their weapons. The SS men hurried over. They had dark green uniforms with red piping and their dogs screeched excitedly at the prisoners and lunged against their leashes.

The men were herded up ramps and into the two boxcars just behind the tender. Going up, Parnell could hear hollow thuds and bangings from the other boxcars, the sounds like cattle shifting position, a heavy, awkward, mindless noise. He figured it came from prisoners who had been taken from other camps.

The boxcars were tiny by American standards, barely ten feet across, twenty feet deep. The SS troopers shoved and kicked the men up the ramp, hollering at them, their eyes darkly vicious under the rims of their swastika helmets. Inside, there was little room and the men were forced to stand shoulder to shoulder like matches in a box. The only air vents were two slits in the wooden sides high up near the overhead, cross-stitched with barbed wire. A metal pail sat at each end of the car. One contained water, the other was to be used as a toilet.

Parnell worked his way over to Smoker and Laguna and whispered to them, "Stay alert. Arm yourselves with whatever you can."

"Already done, Lieutenant," Smoker said.

Before he could show what he had, the train started off, the roar of the locomotive rising, then dropping, only to rise again, steadier, and the sharp cracks of the couplings coming one after another all along the train like sequenced explosions. The boxcar jerked back and then forward. Many of the men fell down on one another, cursing bitterly.

Time disappeared into the press and disjointed agony of the boxcar. Fights broke out. Pale light seeped through the air vents, a sickly radiance as if made gray by the fume of human bodies. They could tell the train was headed up grades from the pound of the locomotive, slow, straining stack bursts.

Parnell once more moved to Smoker and Weesay. "How you hanging?" he shouted over the systematic clack of the wheels crossing rail joints and the creak and shudder of the car.

Laguna was infuriated. "Some goddamn *puro pendejo* jes' shit on my boot," he said.

"What're you carrying?"

Smoker opened his flight suit, showed Red a bracing spike he'd smuggled out of the mine. Then Weesay slipped a foot-long sliver of wood from his sleeve. He'd managed to work it loose from the floor and then wind a piece of cloth from his suit around it to form a handle.

Red said. "Stay as close to the door as you can."

Parnell returned to Labarre, the Frenchman slyly sliding a length of wire into his hand. He'd already fashioned loops at each end so the wire could be used as a garotte. Red took it, shoved it into his suit. "What will you use?" he asked.

"I have a knife. From a *fideicommissaire*."

The scent of cedar and pine kept drifting in through the vents, forest out there. Then it began to rain, quickly turning heavy. The droplets pounded the top of the box-car and a fine mist blew in through the air vents, with it the stronger odor of turpentine. The men held up their faces to feel its coldness.

The light was suddenly cut off and the rumble of the locomotive went deep and hollow. They were passing through a tunnel. Immediately, the powerful smell of soot and smoke came through the vents in the darkness. The air began to warm up.

Now, the train's brakes slammed on with a wild metallic scream. This was followed by a violent blow of steam, the sounds merging, echoing back through the tunnel. Everybody was hurled forward violently, their bodies tumbling, falling, piling up against the front end of the boxcar, men cursing, trying to untangle themselves.

An explosion came from ahead, a loud sharp detonation magnified by the narrowness of the tunnel. Another burst and then a third. The still-moving boxcar shook as couplings crashed together, eased off, crashed again. Gradually, the cars came to a complete halt.

Parnell was already moving, shoving people away, making for the door. *It's here!* It was pitch-black, the oily, smoky stench of soot increasing, the sensation of suffocation starting in the pit of his stomach. The prisoners began to scream and pound on the side of the boxcar.

"Lieutenant?" someone calmly said close by. "Where you at?" It was Weesay.

"Here. Over here."

Arms, legs, bodies pressed against him. He reached the door, put his back against it, waited. It was getting more and more difficult to breathe. His eyes stung. People coughed and gagged all around him in the darkness. Some vomited, others clawed at the side of the car, trying to get their faces up to the narrow vents. Tiny cinders from the engine's stack drifted and bobbed lightly in the darkness like fireflies.

Time extended itself terrifyingly. Vaguely, Red heard the throb of the engine, the screams from the other boxcars. The thought came to him precisely and clearly: *This is how the bastards're going to kill us*. It seemed suddenly an absurdly wasteful way to do it. He heard Laguna near his shoulder cursing in street Mexican.

Then the engine blew its whistle, like a giant woman's

scream rolling back, and began to blow power strokes.
The boxcar jerked back hard, people falling down again.
It held, then jerked in the opposite direction. The couplings cracked like grenades. They began to move
backward along the tracks.

Minutes passed . . . four . . . five. Abruptly, light came
down through the vents again, a smoky, hazy, oily-look-
ing light. Parnell glanced around, Smoker and Weesay
right there, Labarre to the left.

The train stopped and the SS troopers opened the
door. Prisoners erupted out of the cars and fell to the
ground, lay there gasping in the cold, soggy air. Above
them the sky was low, just above the trees, the color of it
like gray mildew. They were in forest, everything wet and
cold, mist drifting through the trees looking like steam
escaping the earth.

Parnell knelt on one knee, eyeing the SS guards. The
Krauts prowled among the men, their machine pistol
straps over their shoulders, weapons at the ready, nervously scanning down the slope and up into the higher
forests. Their dogs for once ignored the prisoners and
sniffed at the air and walked on their toes, their heads
and ears up, eyes excited.

He glanced back at the boxcar behind his, spotted
Bird and Fountain far back. He caught their eye. Both
nodded. He swung back the other way, toward the engine that now sat idling just outside the tunnel entrance.
As he watched, two Germans hurriedly set up an MG-34
machine gun on the coaler. It was pointed straight down
at the prisoners.

Labarre shifted his buttocks until he was near him. He
leaned in. "It comes," he whispered, a hot grin in his
eyes. "*Bonne chance, ami.*"

Parnell slid his hand into his suit, gripped the garotte.

He picked out one of the SS troopers, a stocky man with beefy hands, his eyes scowling beneath the rim of his helmet as he looked down the slope. He stood ten feet from him.

Red fixed his mind on him, everything else fusing off into periphery. He visualized his moves, calculated distance, his leap, the placing of the garotte, first out enough to clear the man's helmet, then down, and the snapping pull, putting all his weight in it so the wire would cut deep into the man's Adam's apple. His fingers tingled, adrenaline triggering nerve circuits now, filling muscle, bringing his heart up into that loping rhythm of kill mode. He waited.

Nothing happened.

They kept them outside the train for an hour. Twice officers came along the side of the train, regular *Wehrmacht* soldiers in their gray field uniforms, slipping in the embankment gravel, and disappeared into the tunnel. After a while, they came out again, looking grim. It began to rain, a light, misty fall, and the faint rumble of artillery came like the soft, almost imperceptible growl of a distant sea squall beyond the horizon.

A senior SS officer finally came down along the track. He brought a platoon of regular *Wehrmacht* troopers who had apparently been hurriedly trucked in to assist the SS guards. He ordered them to assemble the prisoners into a column, three abreast. Then he spoke to the captives in French, saying that they were being detoured around the tunnel and that if anyone attempted to escape, the entire column would be shot.

They trudged along the track and down a narrow, muddy, rain-rutted road that took them immediately into dense forest. The regulars and the guards with their dogs took up positions at the front and rear of the column. The prisoners were made to march with their right hands gripping the shoulders of the ones directly in front of them, everybody bunched up and stumbling on the slippery ground.

The woods were quiet and dark with undergrowth. In the deeper shadows, the snow looked very white and here and there contained the tracks of foxes and small deer. They soon reached a mountain hamlet, a dozen tightly clustered houses made of barked logs and mud plastering. People came out to watch, a dark, somber collection. Several spat at the prisoners and threw stones. The soldiers laughed.

The road began to climb up through the trees, curving back and forth. In places it was steep enough to make men fall. One emaciated prisoner slipped and rolled down into a ravine, two guards instantly after him, kicking him about the head until he scrambled to his feet and climbed back to the column. It started to rain again.

Parnell was disappointed and disgusted. Back there he'd been ready, anticipating freedom. Labarre had seemed so confident a strike was in the works. Then why hadn't they hit? A perfect ambush position, the train stopped, soldiers milling. He turned, looked back. Weesay and Smoker were six ranks behind him, and there was Labarre, his pounded face and massive frame standing out. The Frenchman winked at him.

Shit.

They came to a narrow bridge. The water was high and dimpled by the rain, and cattails bobbed in the current. Beyond the bridge, the road turned and headed northeast, back toward where the rail track was. Thirty minutes later, they reached the track on the other side of the tunnel. A half mile down the rails they could see the mouth of the tunnel. It had been blown apart and was completely blocked with boulders and broken timbers.

The first sniper's bullet killed one of the SS guards, exploding his jaw apart. Now a crackling fusillade of small arms broke out from the woods. Everybody hit the ground. Bullets slammed into the tracks. Two more guards were hit. By now the *Wehrmacht* troopers were laying in counterfire. Some of the SS guards joined in, the prisoners scrambling out of the way, crawling over the tracks and running up into the woods on the other side.

Parnell and his men were already moving into attack. Red retrieved the weapon off the first guard shot. Weesay and Smoker jumped another guard, stabbed him to death, and took his MP-40. Labarre had also attacked a guard, nearly slicing his head off.

Suddenly a *Wehrmacht* sergeant leaped up, bellowing orders, and his men rose, formed a skirmish line, and went plunging down the embankment into the woods, firing as they ran. Several SS men got up and followed them. As he observed the charge, a side of Red's mind thought clinically: *correct tactical maneuver against ambush: attack head-on into the center of it.*

Bird and Fountain came running up. Both had automatic weapons. Cowboy cut down another SS guard. The two with him immediately threw down their guns and raised their hands but were instantly swarmed by prisoners who began beating them savagely with rocks and sticks.

Down in the woods a vicious battle was going on, men bellowing, going at it hand-to-hand. Gradually, the clamor began to taper off until there were only scattered shots, then silence. Several minutes passed. Then men began emerging from the undergrowth, walking slowly up the slope, some carrying their wounded. Prisoners along the track rose cautiously, staring at these men coming up.

They looked like mountain men, dressed in motley combinations of animals skins and clothing, bandoleers lashed across their chests. Their weapons were French and German and American and all carried long knives. Some even had short swords like buccaneer cutlasses slipped under their belts, and two men carried horn bows with wooden quivers and cedar-shaft arrows.

A tall man in a black leather Gestapo coat came out of the shadows under the trees and started up the hill. A British Sten gun was slung over his shoulder. He wore a gray beret with a red feather cockade and his face was terribly disfigured.

The left side of it looked as if it had been blown in by a powerful burst of wind, the skin pressed tightly back against the underlying bone. His left eye was merely a grotesque, pitted bulge in its socket, like a lizard's eye, while the lower part of his left cheek appeared waxy, streaked with tiny blood vessels like black pen lines, the ridges of his teeth showing through the skin giving him a half skeletal look.

Labarre immediately went down to greet him, the two men hugging. Then they came back up and the huge Frenchman introduced the man. His name was Paul Laznec. He was the leader of this band and Labarre's brother-in-law.

Laznec's good eye studied the Americans expressionlessly, up, down, the socket of the other one visibly moving under its mound of scarring. Finally, he nodded briskly, spoke rapidly to Labarre in an odd patois, half French, half something else, then turned and went back down the slope.

Labarre said to Parnell, "There is another train coming. Two miles away. We must leave. You and your men come with us. The others will remain here."

Red frowned. "He's leaving the prisoners?"

"*Oui.*" The Frenchman shrugged his massive shoulders. "It can not be altered, *mon ami.* They would merely make us slow."

Two minutes later, Blue Team and Laznec's raiders melted off into the woods.

At that precise moment, eighty-seven miles to the northwest in the Hunsrück Range near Bad Kreuznach, Vaillain Duboudin jammed the Porsche into second gear and sent it screaming around a steep, 180 mountain turn.

He felt the car begin to skid off the road, the sensation coming up through the wheel, centrifugal force sucking at his body. Instinctively he countered it, the vehicle nearing the apex of the curve. By overcorrecting the wheel, he sent the Porsche into a counterskid, its momentum carrying it right around the turn in a controlled reverse slide.

As it began to drift off in the opposite direction, he stomped down hard on the throttle, felt the tires grab traction, and neatly cleared around the turn sideways, straightened, and brought the car back into perfect balance as he started climbing back through the gears.

"*Superbe! Superbe!*" he shouted out of pure joy, thinking happily, *Mon Dieu! how good it is again.* The thrill of pure speed, the mastery of such power, he and the vehicle one entity, the machine sending a constant stream of messages to his senses through metal and rubber, his body reacting on instinct, *click, click,* so rapidly the actions were already completed even before his conscious mind had time to issue orders.

For the last nine days he'd been making these against-the-clock runs through the snow and sleet in rugged mountain country; sometimes across stretches of meadow and farmland, startling hell out of field workers and German patrols. At first, he'd had a terrible rustiness, a missing of the car's subtle clues. It frustrated him beyond belief. But then his old skills returned in a rush. Now it was as if it had been only yesterday that he had conquered the Gran Prix circuits.

The car was a Porsche TYP 356, one of two prototypes Dr. Ferdinand Porsche had built in his small shed in Gmünd, Austria, in 1937. Now they had been honed into perfectly balanced, powerful racing machines, sleek two-seaters, aerodynamically designed and constructed of aluminum alloy. Powered by rear-mounted, supercharged four-cylinder engines capable of 190 horsepower and 230 foot-pounds of torque, they could reach flat-track speeds of well over 130 miles an hour, each using close-ratio five-speed gearboxes and studded Finnish Hakaapelitaa winter tires.

Only one addition had been made to the driver-car dynamic before each run, two sandbags placed into the left mechanic's seat. These weighed precisely 163 pounds, which was the known weight of the passenger Duboudin would be carrying when he made his ultimate run.

On Vaillant sped, now through gloomy, mist-filled corridors, the walls of pine trees flashing past in a light snowfall, screaming into and out of cutbacks and hairpins and cross-overs, running right on that thin edge before control loss.

During his racing years, he had always preferred mountain rallies to circuit track racing, winning such ones as the Tour de Corse, called the Devil of Ten Thousand Turns, in Corsica, the Stuttgart-Lyon-Charbonnieres Rally, or the grueling Swiss Post National. These mountain runs always forced a driver to do constant battle with the course, keep him in a place where split-second decisions made the difference between disaster and triumph. A contest of concentrated will against the road. They always exhilarated him, rendered a sweet, hot sense of true vanquishment.

Nine minutes later he exited the forest, executed a final turn, and went racing along the last quarter mile of the course that paralleled the crest of the main ridge. Directly ahead, down in a small grassy meadow, were two large Alpine-camouflaged tents, his maintenance pits, his crew mechanics waving as he flew past.

A half mile away, Obersturmmfuhrer Skorzeny lowered his binoculars and shook his head, impressed. "This Frenchman is truly *good*," he said. He held up his stopwatch. "Look, he cut two whole minutes from yesterday's run."

Standing with him on a bare granite dome that gave an unobstructed view of the entire race course was Major Freidrich Land, who now nodded and said, "Yes, the Frenchie turncoat drives well."

"Well?" Skorzeny chuckled. "No, Freidrich, not just well. He's exceptional. Now I see why he was a champion." Land made no further comment. This drew the superior officer's attention. "You don't like this man, do you?" he said.

"I dislike traitors, sir."

Skorzeny's eyes went flat. "But now he's our comrade, is he not?"

"Of course, sir."

Again Skorzeny chuckled, a cynical dryness to the

sound. He enjoyed baiting his new intelligence officer a bit. He'd met Land back in 1943 when he and his commandos trained with Freidrich's Panzer Division in northern Italy in preparations for raids into Greece.

Actually, he was quite fond of him. An outstanding officer and leader, the quintessential German soldier. That was why he had had him recently transferred to his own Panzer Brigade 150 as intelligence adjutant. That and the fact that Land still had many contacts with German sympathizers in France, which would play a major role in Operation *Dreifach*.

Still, he found the younger officer a bit stiff-backed. For instance, his reaction to Skorzeny's decision to use American uniforms and vehicles to cross through enemy lines. Although Land had not openly said so, he knew the man considered the practice a breach of honor. Unchivalrous. Apparently, to Land war was a field of honor where gallant knights did battle bearing their own colors, where the nobility of victor and defeated exchanged one, final salute as the proper climax to combat.

All very pretty and cinematically heart-tugging, Skorzeny knew, but in reality a dangerous sham. Such delusions punctured a soldier's armor, made him vulnerable. Simply because they were predicated on passion and passion was a weakness. He himself never allowed such sentimentality to be part of any operation's equation or execution. *That* approach freed his mind of maudlin morality, made the only essential component of an operation the achievement of it.

As here with Operation *Dreifach*, a stunning coup with a rich prize. Essentially it was simple but extremely risky, a commando strike into the very heart of the Allied fortress. On the morning of 15 December, the day before the great German offensive, they would execute a lightning raid against a designated target for the purpose of kidnapping a key Allied figure.

The victim would then be transported to a remote railroad siding on the outskirts of Paris where Duboudin waited in one of the Porsches. With the captive drugged and strapped into the passenger's seat, he would race across country roads to northern France and on to Belgium's Ardennes Forest. There he would go to ground in the ruins of an abandoned abby and wait for advance units of Dietrich's Sixth Panzer Army to reach him as they struck through the Ardennes.

Over the last few minutes, the snowfall had changed to a freezing, sleety rain that swept up over the side of the granite dome. Skorzeny and Land worked their way back down to level ground and then headed along the ridge to the maintenance tents.

The identity of the important captive was known only to him and Hitler. In a twist of irony, the Führer had given the captive the code name Lionheart, after another great leader, Richard, King of England, who had also been kidnapped back in the eleventh century.

This leader's name, however, was Dwight D. Eisenhower.

Chapter Eighteen

Schnee Eifel Mountains, Germany
10 December 1944

Cowboy Fountain was freezing off his testicles, suspended up there by a line on the face of a granite wall, the wind filled with ice droplets slamming him in the back as it swept up out of the Prumgrat Pass below him. His hands were numb in their fox skin gloves, made it hard to set his charges, lay out his timer wires.

For nearly a month, Blue Team had operated with Laznec's band. They weren't French Resistance fighters at all, but actually bandits, Slavic by blood, called Wends. At the beginning of the First World War, the Germans had driven them out of their ancestral homeland in the Bohemian Forest of western Czechoslovakia.

They resettled in the rugged mountains of the Schnee Eifel along the eastern Luxembourg border northwest of Trier. Excellent mountain guerillas, they continued to wage war against anything German. In 1931, Labarre's older sister, Berthe, had voluntarily gone into the mountains as a nurse-missionary to the Wends. She eventually married Paul Laznec and bore him nine children.

Parnell and his men had accompanied the band on several raids: against a meteorological station, a train depot, and a supply train from which they'd obtained fresh ammunition, engineering explosives, and weapons. They also recovered three *Raketenpanzerbuchse,* or German bazookas, two MG-34 machine guns, and crates of bagged flares with launch guns.

In the past they had always left behind such weapons simply because they didn't know how to operate them. Blue Team, with Labarre translating, gave instructions on their use, along with some advice on better ways to set up ambush attacks against heavier enemy concentrations. The band was now preparing to strike again, this time against a German supply train that periodically ran through the Prumgrat. It would be initiated by blowing part of the mountain down onto the tracks.

"Wire comin' down," a voice called from above. A second later, a spool of copper wire came sailing over the granite overhang. Cowboy caught it, then squeezed back into the narrow split in the rock face from which he'd been working.

He, Bird, and Smoker were laying German demolition charges all along the underside of a massive overhang, strings of cup-shaped, fourteen-ounce penthrite units called *Hohlladungen.* Each unit had twin copper electric blasting caps that were connected to a main runout line, which then fed up to a single, small Gluhzundapparat C-40 exploder. Since they had no stone drills, they'd placed the charges into splits in the stone and then braced them with climbing pins.

It was difficult work, connecting up the caps, crimping them home with fingers numbed by the cold, the gloves bulky as mittens and the stronger gusts burrowing down into his double-layered deerskin coat. But what was more bothersome were the constant sour-tasting belches that had lately dogged everybody in Blue Team. They were caused by the biscuits the Wend bandits lived on while on the move. They called them *chattes,* a French slang for cunt since a fold in each biscuit resembled the lips of a vagina. They were hard as rocks and made from a dried mountain berry and bark flour.

Yet despite such food, Parnell and his men had quickly regained their garrison weight along with stamina from constantly climbing up and down steep, densely forested mountains. Only once had the band returned to their main village, deep in a remote part of the Schnee Eifel to rest, distribute booty among the clan, and tend to their wounded.

The village was composed of cave dwellings carved out of the granite base of the mountain. The Wend women were sullen, round-faced, and sturdy as Russian peasants, wearing long, checkered skirts and Mennonite-type babushkas. That night they held a funeral feast for those who had been killed. Everyone, even some of the children, got roaring drunk on stolen wine and schnapps and some of the young men ran barefooted over hot coals. Afterward Blue Team could hear the women moaning and crying out as they fornicated in their caves.

Fountain laid in his last charge, hooked into the main outrun, and called out, "Climbing." The line went taut as he began to ascend and it hummed in the wind. Clearing the overhang, he crawled the last few feet to solid ground where Weesay sat against a tree with a deerskin blanket wrapped around him.

Cowboy flopped down nearby. "Jee-sus H Christ," he said, hugging himself. "It's colder'n a whore on Sunday mornin' out there. I swear, I got *cajones* the size of raisins."

Laguna looked at him, shook his head. "Shit, *meng,* chu sound like a goddamn pussy."

"Gimme that blanket," Cowboy said, wrenching it away.

* * *

They waited two days for the Kraut train to come through the pass. It intermittently rained and then snowed and thunder boomed along the high ridges. The temperature fell below zero.

Parnell and his men constantly worked on their weapons, cleaning and recleaning them, keeping them cased in animal skin bags so the sears, operating rods, and bolt lugs wouldn't turn brittle and crack. They also replaced the regular gun oil with high-viscosity lens oil they'd found during the raid on the meteorological station, this to prevent jamming, and they kept the batteries for their C4 exploders wrapped in skins to maintain charge.

Laznec had deployed his men on both sides of the track where they figured the train would stop. There the rails had been laid about three hundred feet above the bottom of the pass. The Wends would be using one of the machine guns and a bazooka.

Parnell had also split his team, sending Bird and Smoker up to the exploder above the overhang. They carried the second *Raketenpanzerbuche* and were accompanied by three bandits who would be the fire team for the other MG. Now the entire attacking force was in scattered but good defiladed positions with clear fields registered on the tracks.

Only Cowboy and Weesay were farther out, set up at a point closer to where the explosion debris would smash down onto the track. They were armed with the last bazooka and two bags of flares.

Red himself had already laid track charges closer in, tandem loads of rigged grenades taped up under the rail flanges and hooked to spark-gap electric blasting caps.

He intended to derail any boxcars that escaped the initial explosion avalanche.

They continued to wait. At night they withdrew from ambush positions and retired into the lime caves that pockmarked the area to get out of the cold. The caves were dry and the men warmed themselves with deer dung fires fed with cedar branches that made the rock caverns smell like cabinet shops.

At three o'clock in the morning of the third day, Red was awakened by Labarre. "The train is here, *mon ami*," he said. Parnell instantly sat up. His fire had worked itself down into a pile of gray ash that pulsed with coals.

He wakened Weesay and Cowboy in a nearby cave. They quickly unbagged their weapons and checked loads. Parnell had a German MP-40 machine pistol. He slammed in a round, flicked it on safety, then shouldered into his exploder harness.

Outside, the cold was sharp and solid and made their breaths form into bursts of smoke. The was no wind, a Christmas-night stillness with billions of stars splashed across the firmament like incandescent salt crystals, their faint light etching the treetops and giving a soft, grayish glow to the open fields of snow.

At first Parnell didn't hear the train but then abruptly he caught the distant locomotive sound, its engine pounding sequentially, the echoes of it coming and then disappearing only to come again. Down the slope, Laznec was shouting final orders to his men and there was the crunch of snow and the clicking and metallic slam of weapon bolts.

For a moment, Laguna and Fountain huddled with him. Weesay carried the *Raketenpanzerbuchse* and two flare bags, Cowboy lugging the rocket cases. "Pop flares as soon as the ridge charges go so we can see what the damage is and be able to pick targets," Red told them. "I figure the Krauts'll probably be running armored cars in this chain. If so, put rockets into the bastards damn quick. One other thing, keep an eye on that Wend MG team up near you. I know damn well they're gonna long-burst and jam the son of a bitch."

"We'll handle it, Lieutenant," Cowboy said. He and Weesay ran off.

He worked his way down to the tracks and began hooking the charge wires onto his main runout line, spooling it backward toward a low barrier of rocks about fifty yards up the slope from the rails. Embankment gravel kept getting kicked up under his boots as he moved, pinging tinnily as it struck the frozen steel of the tracks.

Reaching the barrier, he braced his exploder bag between two rocks and ran a check of its battery, using a small neon test tube that had come with it. The tube registered a perfect operating level of one ampere at eighty volts. He quickly hooked up the runout leads to its terminals, rebagged it, and began pacing to keep warm.

Stillness again. The cold was like a weight that pressed down through the darkness. He lifted his head, scanned along the ridge where Wyatt, Smoker, and the machine-gun team were located, up where the stars were abruptly blotted out by the higher forest line. Below it the ridges were in pure darkness.

The picture drew up a sudden memory, his first winter hunt with his father in the Colorado Rockies when he was eight years old, camping for the night way up in the high country, snug in his new sleeping bag, slowly discovering for the first time as night came in the scary reality of how *totally* dark a forest could be once the campfire died away.

He continued pacing, thinking about the possibility

this train would have armored cars with strong guard units. It abruptly occurred to him that it was downright idiotic to go up against such opposition with men as untrained as these Wend bandits. They were great fighters, savage and fearless, but really warriors with feet still planted in the nineteenth century. Bows and arrows and swords, for God's sake?

In the previous raids they'd been on, the Wends had hit small, isolated enemy units and tiny shuttle trains. But this track was a main thoroughfare through this section of the Schnee Eifel. He couldn't believe the Krauts would be stupid enough to send it through unprotected.

The train came steadily on, its rumble and huffing bursts growing ever louder. Under them he could hear the hiss and clank of the wheels now. But he couldn't see anything yet, the engineer obviously running without headlights through this portion of forest. The sound increased even more and then echoes began appearing, bouncing off the steeper ridges to cross and recross over each other before fading.

A dim red glow appeared far to the left, tinting the tops of trees that were then swallowed back into the darkness as the locomotive passed them. It burst into sight about half mile away, twin red lights that were canted down onto the track. The front side of the engine's boiling smoke bursts were tinged with red like the upsurge from a small but deep volcanic fissure.

He quickly unbagged the exploder and checked the play in the firing handle. To send the electrical surge through the circuit, he knew, it would have to be jammed all the way to the *Notbehelf* or stopcock line. Through the cold, his skin tingled with hot adrenaline.

He glanced up at the ridge. *Good, good, Wyatt'll be able to see the train from up there with those lights.* He heard the crunch of snow again, some of Laznec's men shifting positions.

When the ridge charges went off, he felt the ground shake violently. A massive outcast of rocks and snow and tree parts blew out sideways into the air. There was a pause, the sound of the train merging with the reverberations of the explosions, both riffling and rebounding together between the ridges.

There was the banshee scream of brakes and colliding couplings. At the same moment two streaks of scratchy flame arched into the sky. They exploded into twin bursts of light that hung up there, flooding the entire scene with a hot, white brilliance. Sparks streamed off the train's wheels and the cars slammed and jolted from side to side.

Parnell cursed, seeing that there were at least three armored cars, easy to spot with their heavy metal sheeting that extended above their rooflines, the sides filled with firing slits. Outside guards had been posted on the rear platform of each car. Several had been hurled off when the engineer hit his brakes. Now the others dangled over the couplings, desperately trying to climb back aboard.

The rumbling of the rock slide quickly deepened in volume until it was a thunderous roaring. The air being pushed ahead of it made the flare chutes oscillate wildly, their light jumping back and forth on the ground, casting shifting shadows. Within seconds, a great cloud of snow boiled into view, huge rocks and ripped tree trunks falling through it, the light creating purple and orange rainbows in the snow's mist.

The avalanche smashed into the train like a tsunami, instantly engulfing the locomotive and at least half the cars. For a moment, Red caught sight of the engine and coaler turning upside down and then watched them go tumbling out of sight below the embankment, crashing down toward the floor of the pass. Three seconds later the locomotive's boiler exploded in a huge ball of orange-reddish flame, which immediately turned into a fuming white cloud as its superheated steam hit the snow.

Parnell rammed the firing handle all the way to the right, hit the stop. The linked grenades went off all at once, a single explosion made up of smaller explosions. It threw the tracks upward, hurled the last two cars up into the air, snapping their couplings. They landed on their sides just below the rail embankment.

Machine-gun fire opened up from the high ridge and from the forest on the upside of the tracks. The one up on the ridge fired in short bursts, but the one near the tracks had opened with one long, sustained train of bullets. Parnell let out a curse and bellowed, "You dumb sons a' bitches! *Quick* bursts!" It was too late. He heard the unmistakable slam of a weapon jamming. "*Shit!*"

By now everything was going, the *thruuuuuping* of MP-40s and the deeper *cracks* of rifles joining in. But their bullets *whanged* and ricocheted harmlessly off the armored cars. One had been turned onto its top by the avalanche. The other two were still upright and on the tracks, motionless now.

From inside both, German counterfire began, flashes of automatic weapons through the armor slits. At least one machine gun was firing, too, its gunners laying in short bursts but traversing rapidly, reconnaissance-by-fire, trying to probe out the enemy positions by the returning muzzle flashes.

Weesay's first *Raketenpanserbuchse* rocket struck one of the armored cars dead center, the first impact of the seven-pound armor-piercing projectile making a cracking, metallic sound as it punched through the steel plating and then it exploded with a muffled roar inside the car. Fire shot through the punch hole and the firing slits. The blast lifted the armored car off the rails and slammed it down again onto embankment upright but with its wheels off the rails.

The *whooshing* back-blast of another bazooka came, this one fired by the bandit team up the slope. The projectile shot high over the train. Trailing a twisting streak of smoke, it exploded uselessly in the forest three hundred yards away.

Parnell now opened with a short burst, then ducked. Instantly his position was taken under machine-gun fire. The bullets hurled rock chips. The firing paused and he quickly shifted position, cautiously peered out.

There were German soldiers lying on the opposite bank firing into the woods. Farther back, several more soldiers had jumped out of the armored car Weesay had hit and were sprinting along the embankment toward the others. Close above them, the flares were now near the ground, the perimeter of their light collapsing. But in that lessening light, he counted at least twenty Krauts already deploying and more still dropping from other partially damaged boxcars.

He lifted his face and hollered at the top of his lungs, "Hit 'em! Hit 'em! Don't let the bastards form a defensive line!" Then realized only his own men and Labarre were able to understand what the hell he was saying.

Two more flare streaks went up and burst into fresh hot light. Seconds later, another rocket round came streaking out of the trees, Weesay firing again. It struck one of the armored cars slightly aft of center. When it blew up, it threw the roof of the car completely off, the explosion sharp and filled with fire and bodies and parts of bodies, all twirling disjointedly into the air.

Through the racket of firing and explosions, Parnell's ear caught a familiar, deadly sound: the hollow, tinny barrel rush of a Granatenwerfer 50mm mortar. Two more came. He hit the ground. Seconds later the three 2.2-pound rounds exploded along the upslope about sixty yards from the tracks, the Krauts firing with nearly ninety-degree elevation.

There were three more hollow, ringing *whomps* from the mortars and then the agonizing pause as the projectiles arched to be followed by the dull quick explosions as the enemy mortarmen walked their rounds along the slope.

Parnell felt the hair on the back of his neck rise. *This ambush is deteriorating,* he thought angrily. A deploying enemy with mortar and machine-gun support against a single MG, one accurate rocket team, and scattered small arms fire. *Jesus!*

As if to counter that, Wyatt's MG again began banging away from the ridge, this time laying in grazing fire, long bursts since the weapon was now warm. The round impacts made a line of exploding gravel, traversing, cutting right into the exposed Germans. Far to his right, Weesay and Cowboy continued hurling in rockets one after another, firing and moving, getting off at least eight a minute.

The Wends directly up the slope from Parnell again fired their *Raketenpanzerbucshe.* This time the rocket went straight up in the air and its back-blast blew right into the chest of the loader, flung him off his feet, his clothing afire.

That's it, Parnell decided. He leaped up and, zigzagging through the trees, made for the bandit's position. When he reached it, he ripped the weapon out of the firer's hands and shoved him back toward his fallen comrade. Scooping up the rocket case, he hurried to a new position, self-loaded, the weapon barrel hot, took aim through the protective shield slit, and fired. He didn't wait to see where the round hit, but was already moving to a new firing position.

For the next several minutes, Blue Team and the one bandit-manned machine gun carried the weight of the battle. Small fires had broken out in the forest with one larger conflagration going down the far slope where the locomotive had exploded.

The new flares were now closing with the ground. Laguna fired off two more. As they burst into full light, Laznec launched a head-on charge up the lower slope, his men looking like medieval peasants as they broke from the trees, screaming and firing, pouring up the incline. The remaining Germans laid in a fusillade that cut down the front line of the charge. But the Wends came on. Within two minutes, they had overrun the thinned German defense line, which now erupted into a wild, hand-to-hand fight.

Parnell and his men stopped firing and started down toward the tracks to help. Suddenly, three fleeing Germans lunged out from under one of the cars and broke into a run back along the rails. They were cut down.

By the time Red reached the far side of the track, the fighting was all over. The few surviving Germans had thrown down their weapons. All were young boys. But the Wends rushed these few, knocked them down, and then shot each one in the forehead, the men pleading for their lives. Other bandits prowled among the wounded, decapitating them with their short swords.

Weesay and Cowboy came running up to Red, stopped short. "God-*damn*," Cowboy said, shocked. "Look what them boys is *doin'!*"

Labarre ran by. In the brittle light from the flares, his big face appeared ashen, his eyes shadowed holes. Parnell grabbed at him, wrenched him to a stop. "Goddammit," he yelled into the Frenchman's face. "Stop this! This is butchery."

Labarre kept shaking his head numbly. "I can not, I can not," he sobbed. "This is blood feud."

"Fuck blood feud. This is *wrong*."

"I can not."

"Then *we* will."

But before he and his men could intervene, the last of the wounded Germans had been dispatched. Now Laznec and his lieutenants strode among the dead, kicking corpses and rolling heads with their boots. There were pools of blood on the embankment. They shone gray black and the eyes of the dead, even those in the severed heads, glistened emptily in the harsh light.

Bird and Smoker approached, panting from their rapid descent down the main ridge. They saw the German dead, their condition. Wyatt shook his head, turned, spat, turned back. Neither he nor Smoker commented.

Parnell looked toward the east and tried to quell his rage. The new flares were less than a hundred feet above them now, like alien things come to hover and observe, sizzling and popping. Beyond their light, the stars had been swallowed by the radiant glare.

Finally he said evenly, "We'd best get the hell out of here. Kraut lookout posts up in those eastern ridges must have seen this. We could have heavy ordnance coming in damn quick. They might even dispatch another train load of troops."

He sought out Labarre again, tightly, disgustedly told him about the possibility of German artillery. The

Frenchman was unusually quiet. He went to talk to Laznec, returned to say that the bandits intended to bury their dead before leaving.

It took them over an hour to dig graves in the frozen ground. They wouldn't let the Americans or Labarre help. There were thirteen bandit bodies. No artillery came, but they did see small, flashing lights up on the ridgelines to the east. By the time the graves were dug, the surging sound of another approaching locomotive drifted faintly through the darkness.

Smoker approached Parnell. He and Cowboy had been probing through the boxcars, looking for weapons. "Lieutenant," he said, "y'all gotta see what me and Cowboy found in one of them cars."

It was a racing automobile, camouflaged green and brown, sleek, the metal polished to a fine brightness, which sparkled and danced under Red's small flashlight. The boxcar itself smelled of cordite and shellac and polished metal and new leather. There were cases of spare parts, snow tires, and tools chained to the walls.

"What in hell would the Krauts be haulin' one a' *these* things around for?" Smoker asked. "In the middle of a fuckin' war?"

Parnell didn't comment. He played his light over the automobile again. A beautiful piece of machinery and workmanship, he saw. He checked the interior. There were twin seats of soft white leather, one with two sandbags in it. The dashboard was made of highly polished wood, the dials gleaming like silver, and there the name *Porsche* was written in silver in the hub of the steering wheel.

He could hear the dead bandits being lowered into their graves, the frozen dirt and stones hitting the corpses. No prayers were said. He leaned in and opened the automobile's glove compartment.

It contained a Luger handgun, two spare clips, a tire pressure tester, and a slim leather map case. In it were papers written in German and a military battle map of northern France. Twin red lines had been drawn onto it. The lines ran from near Paris to a point just west of the Luxembourg border in the Ardennes Forest.

There were also several colored photos. Red flipped through them. The first showed several Germans dressed in white coveralls, grinning at the camera. The second was of two German officers, one an extremely tall, dark-haired man, an *Obersturmbannfuhrer,* the other a blond, handsome major. The third photo stopped him dead.

There, standing between the same two officers with a wide smile, was Vaillant Duboudin.

Maizieres, France
13 December 1944

It was close.

They'd been waiting three hours in the boxcar, a *vehicule du coffret,* made to haul automobiles, with a rear door and sliding ramp for unloading. There were Vaillant Duboudin, Major Land, and two of Skorzeny's Triple commandos, standing around inside with the Porsche, the men cupping their hands over small cans of American Sterno to keep warm. Now and then came the surge and fade of a switching engine working, coming close, then receding. Twice highballing freights had rumbled past, the wind of their passing shaking the boxcar. It was now seven in the morning.

Vaillant and Land were dressed as French officers, their shoulder patches indicating they were attached to the French 2nd Armored division, which was currently operating as part of Montgomery's Twenty-First Army Group northeast of Brussels.

The two commandos were strong, boyish-looking men, one named Steckel, the other Luttichgau. They had on American uniforms with the letters MP on their helmets and armbands. Both spoke fluent American dialect. Steckel actually had a southern accent developed in Nashville, Tennessee, where he'd been raised by an uncle until he was thirteen.

A vehicle pulled up beside the boxcar, the tiny squeal of brakes. Boots crunched on the gravel, American voices, the metallic *chunk* of a weapon bolt. A moment later, the boxcar door noisily slid open and two U.S. military police sergeants looked in. One had a Thompson submachine gun, its butt nestled in the crook of his elbow, the other a drawn Colt .45 pistol.

Land stepped forward. Realizing he was an officer, both Yanks braced, snapped salutes. But their eyes were narrowed, suspicious. "Excuse me, sir," the one with the Colt said. "But what are ya'all doin' out here?" The other leaned through the door to peer into the flickering interior of the boxcar.

Land rattled off something in French. The American shook his head. "*No parle vous francais*. You speak *Anglaise?*" Land said, "*Non.*" The American glanced at the two commandos dressed as American soldiers. "Hey, y'all understand what this officer's sayin'?"

Steckel came forward, squatted down, giving the Yank a broad grin. "Hell no, Mac," he said. "The asshole's been barkin' at us in Frenchie ever' since we left Metz."

"Asshole?" the American said. "Y'all better be damn' sure he *don't* understand English, buddy."

"He don't understand shit," Luttichgau said.

"What outfit ya'all with?"

"The two-oh-third MP Battalion, Ninety-ninth Division."

The second American MP looked sharply at him. "Is Major O'Donnell still CO?" he snapped.

Steckel nodded. "It ain't O'Donnel, it's O'Sullivan. Yeah, ole Kickass is still there. 'Cept now he's a light colonel."

The Yank MP grunted. He climbed up into the boxcar, began looking around. The first one said to Steckel, "So you want to tell us what you all're doing settin' out here with a goddamned race car?"

"Waitin' on a through train. They're sending the sumbitch to Paris. It's a gift from General Montgomery to DeGaulle. We was sent along to guard her, make sure some hotshot GI don't hook it." He turned, looked at the Porsche, turned back. "Slick, ain't she?"

"How come it to be camouflaged?"

"Beats hell outta me. If I owned her, she sure as hell wouldn't be."

"Where'd it come from?"

Steckel shrugged. "Some Kraut museum up north. Around Aachen, I think."

The night before, Duboudin had driven the remaining Porsche from the German town of Merzig in Saarland, crossing the French border and then following the Nied River to rendezvous with Land and the two commandos in Maizieres. They had parachuted into France the night before. Meanwhile, the rest of Skorzeny's strike team had also chuted in just north of Paris, coming down in pairs and then linking in the rail town of Meaux from which Operation Triple would be launched.

Major Land's pro-German Frenchmen had arranged for the empty boxcar to be waiting at the Maizieres siding. When Vaillant arrived, the Porsche was quickly ramped aboard. Now the men were merely waiting for other French collaborators who worked for the rail line to get them hooked up to a Paris-bound freight.

The first Yank MP said, "Well, I'm gonna have to see some ID papers and orders of transit."

Steckel pulled out his SHAEF identification card, handed it down. The Yank MP studied it, handed it back. Steckel stood up and spoke to Major Land, speaking English but sticking in mispronounced French words and making hand signs. Land finally nodded. He picked up a briefcase near the door and produced several sheets of paper, handed them down to the American.

The MP paged through them. They were written in French but signed by Brigadier General Basil McCourt of the British Twenty-First Army Group's Transportation Command.

The second Yank MP returned to the door. "They check out?" he asked his partner.

"Damn things're in Frenchie."

"So what do you think?"

"I dunno."

"I don't like this," the second Yank said and swung down the muzzle of his Thompson, put it on Steckel and Land. "Okay, all of you, *out.*"

Steckel shot a quick glance toward his fellow commando, then turned on a wide grin for the American. "Hey, come on, guys," he said. "What's the problem?" Unseen, his right hand curled slightly, touched the haft of a stiletto that was strapped upside down on his forearm beneath his field jacket sleeve. Major Land, his eyes holding on the closer American, shifted subtly to his right, positioning himself for attack.

"I said *move* it, goddammit," the Yank MP growled.

The first American said, "Hey, wait a minute, Frank. If

these jokers're telling the truth, we're gonna be in some deep shit when that goddamn Limey general finds out."

"Then radio the CP and check 'em out."

Instead, the first MP swung back to Steckel. "Where y'all from?"

"You mean back home?"

"Yeah."

"Nashville, *Tenn*-e-ssee."

"How come the Gran' Ole Opree to bounce Hank Williams?"

"Shit," Steckel said, holding the grin. "They din't boot *him*, he quit *them*. Ole Hank told them boys to flat stick it."

The American thought about that for a moment, then nodded. "Come on down, Frank," he said. "They're okay."

Two hours later the switch engine came to move the boxcar onto a second siding where it was hooked onto a late morning freight headed for Paris.

The bandits and Blue Team kept moving until nearly dawn when they were far from the site of the train attack and finally stopped in dense forest to eat breakfast, no fires, and properly administer to their wounded. One had died on the trail. The others sat looking pale in their bloody clothes, the blood frozen so that it crackled like squeezed cellophane whenever they moved. The other men, including Parnell's, searched out hollows beneath trees, made pine needle beds, and went to sleep.

But Red sat on a rock and smoked a German cigarette. He felt no weariness. Instead, a hot rage burned inside him that was focused like a beam through a lens on Duboudin. That traitorous *bastard*. The whole time he'd worked with them in Normandy, the son of a bitch had been working both sides of the fence, setting them up, getting good men killed.

But there was something else, much, much deeper. He sensed it, felt it, dark and monstrous. Yet he would not let himself look directly at it, see it fully, all the time knowing that sooner or later he would have to.

The only other person he'd told about the photo was Bird, showed it to him. Wyatt took it into his gloved hand and studied it a long time before handing it back. His eyes had gone flat and deadly hard. He didn't say anything, just shook his head and walked away.

Parnell finished his cigarette, got up, and went over to where Labarre was sleeping under a fir tree. He parted the branches and shook the big Frenchman awake, Labarre quickly coming up, grabbing for his machine pistol cradled between his legs. Seeing it was Parnell, he relaxed, rubbed one meaty hand over his scarred face.

"What is it, *mon ami?*" he asked. He noticed the tightness of the lieutenant's face and sat forward anxiously. "Something is wrong?"

Parnell took the photo from his jacket and held it out. "Do you know this man?"

The instant Labarre's gaze fell on it, his eyes narrowed. "*Traitre!*" he blurted and cursed, then glanced at Parnell. "From where you obtain this?"

"From a race car that was on the train."

"A racing machine?"

"Yes. You *do* know the man in the middle, then?"

"*Oui,* I know this pig. This *worse* than a pig. An Iscariot. His name is Duboudin. You too are familiar with this one?"

"He operated with us in Normandy."

"You should have killed him."

"How did you know he was a traitor?"

"Before the *Bosche* captured me, I received orders from Paris that this Duboudin was to be killed on sight. He had led a British general into a Gestapo trap near Rastatt."

Parnell felt the skin of his back grip up, then seem to crawl and shift over his bones. He heard his voice ask, "Was this general named Stanfield?"

"*Ah, oui,*" Labarre cried.

There it was, the dark thing come to full life. *Duboudin had set up Anabel's capture and murder!* The knowledge swept through him, sucked his rage into a boiling-hot sphere in the center of his belly. Another formed in his head. He felt as if things had pierced his heart. He looked into Labarre's eyes, then turned away and stared at the snow.

After a moment, the Frenchman gently touched his arm. "*Leftenant?*"

Parnell swung back. "I want this man."

Labarre shrugged. "*Ah, je ne sais,*" he said. "All the Resistance tries to find him but can not."

"I *want* this fucking animal," Red said very softly.

Labarre saw his eyes. He blinked, then frowned, thought a moment. "All right. But we will have to cross back into France."

"We go *now.*"

"*Tres bien, mon ami,*" Labarre said.

Eight minutes later, Blue Team, carrying fresh ammunition, grenades, and food and with Labarre guiding, moved off, headed southwest toward the French border.

In northern France and eastern Belgium, early December had dragged past in an endless procession of rain- and snowstorms, the sky a horizon-to-horizon blanket of low, gray-black cloud cover.

Each day the German forces, utilizing the bad weather that had kept out U.S. recon flights, continued massing their Autumn Mist forces in secret assembly areas all along the eastern fringes of the Ardennes Forest and the Schnee Eifel Mountains.

Meanwhile, on the Allied side of the front, things had become static. On 7 December, Eisenhower met with his senior commanders to reevaluate his stalled winter offensive. Montgomery continued pushing for a direct attack into the German Ruhr, but Bradley adamantly disagreed, proposed instead to mount another Normandy-like breakout north of the Ardennes, which could send U.S. divisions directly into Germany. Monty had lost much of his power after his debacle in Holland, so Ike eventually sided with Bradley. A renewed Allied offensive was set to begin shortly before Christmas.

During the nine days before it would kick off, a key target, the great German dam works of the Roer River, which sat on the northern flank of the coming attack, could be destroyed. The Brits had already sent in air strikes against the dams but failed to take them out. So now Eisenhower okayed a ground attack.

On 10 December, two corps of the U.S. First Army struck at the dam works. They immediately ran head-on into the 12th SS Panzer Division, part of the northern shoulder of the coming German offensive through the Ardennes. The two corps were stopped immediately.

Most of that same sector controlled by First Army also included the Ardennes Forest, which was, in total contrast, the quietest area on the entire Allied line. In fact, it was so inactive, they called it the "ghost front" and used it as a replenishment area for the divisions that had been badly mauled in the earlier Hurtgen Forest fighting. It also processed green, untested units like the 99th and 106th Infantry Divisions, which had just come in from the States.

In addition to this, the defenses throughout this area were extremely weak. The biggest reason was the mind-set among senior commanders who believed the Germans would *never* launch offensive action through this particular sector in winter. Moreover, during the last two months there had been a pronounced breakdown in Allied signal intelligence. The German buildup in the mountainous Schnee Eifel area east of the German frontier had been completely missed, particularly since the Krauts had managed to execute their massive repositioning for attack in nearly total secrecy.

The Allied top brass were actually feeling cocky and confidently secure from enemy attack. Hell, they said, the vaunted German Army was already whipped and demoralized, totally unable to mount anything but defensive war in the Siegfried Line. By 14 December, many senior commanders actually departed for short leaves, well away from their commands.

General Bradley and Lieutenant General William Simpson, commander of Ninth Army, had departed for Versailles together. They were to attend a meeting of senior officers of SHAEF there, then head south to Chartres to attend a USO show featuring Bob Hope on 15 December. Meanwhile, British Field Marshall Montgomery had already arrived in Paris where he planned to play a few days of golf with old naval friends.

On 15 December, Eisenhower's schedule claimed he would be touring the World War 1 memorial at Chateau-

Thierry and later visit the 101ˢᵗ Airborne Division, which
was refitting near the city of Reims.

But there was another item not covered in his official
schedule. Ike was notorious for ditching his security
teams. He was going to do it again in Reims. A favorite
enlisted man, his driver Corporal Peter McKeogh, was
getting married there, in the early evening at the famous
rose-windowed Cathedrale Notre Dame d'Riems. Eisenhower intended to be present.

The coded message came through at 6:31 the morning of the fifteenth, a shortwave broadcast from Radio
Berlin, the station still putting out regular commen-
tary and propaganda from a basement bunker in
Berlin. The announcer's voice came muffled through
the speaker of the commando's small Feldverrstarker
KwE.a unit, sounding like Hitler only slower, as if the
Führer's speech were being run at the wrong speed on
a turntable.

The whole Triple strike force was now sequestered in
the loft of a safe house in Meaux, twelve miles north of
Paris. It was owned by a doctor at the city's Hopital
d'Sante Gertrude, a devout Nazi supporter who hated
de Gaulle. There were twelve now: eight Skorzeny commandos, Major Land, Duboudin, and two *citoyenne,* the
word the French Nazi sympathizers used for themselves.
It meant *freemen.*

The house had originally been a flour mill in the
thirteenth century but then was converted into living
quarters during the Renaissance. An upper loft was
added that stuck out over a narrow, stair-steep alley,
and an enclosed cylindrical "conspirator's" staircase
to the loft was built on an outside wall. The rest of the

building was made of ancient timber the centuries had turned gray as granite. The building squatted beside a polluted stream called the Chope two blocks from Meaux's main train-switching yard.

The radio message was quickly deciphered by the commando team-leader, an *Oberjagerfeldwebel* or staff sergeant of paratroopers named Gerhard Statz. He stood six feet two and was built as solidly as a tree trunk. His almost Mongol face never seemed to wear expression and it carried numerous scars attesting to multiple close combats.

He shook Land awake. The major had been asleep on a window seat. "Excuse me, sir," Statz said. "A message from Berlin."

Freidrich swung his legs off the seat and Statz handed him the decode. He scanned it. It was from *Abwehr*, German Military Intelligence. Eisenhower's schedule had suddenly been changed, it said. He was now expected to remain in Reims overnight of the fifteenth in order to attend an early evening wedding at the Cathedral Notre Dame d'Reims.

It added a shocking note: the target would be there *without* a regular security team.

When Ike's headquarters had first been moved from England to France, the *Abwehr* had actually managed to deep-plant an agent inside his staff secretarial pool, an Englishwoman who then supplied them with a continuous stream of secret data, first sent to French contacts who then sent it on to Berlin.

She was the one who had supplied the information about Eisenhower returning from Reims on the evening of the fifteenth. Based on that, the Triple strike team had planned to kidnap the Allied general inside the Meaux switching yard when his train came through.

It would have to stop for at least six minutes to be rerouted onto a Metro line into Paris.

According to the agent, the general always traveled in his own passenger car while his security teams were located in the ones in front and back of it. The Germans had decided to hit his car as the train went into transition, striking swiftly, killing anyone accompanying him with silencers and knives. Eisenhower would then be drugged, taken off the car, and put aboard the Porsche now sitting in a toolshed in the switching matrix. Vaillant Duboudin would then begin his wild race to the Ardennes' abbey while the commando team faded off into the night.

"So," Land said quietly. "We have a complication."

"Apparently, sir," Statz said without emotion.

"But there's also a fantastic opportunity as well."

"I agree, sir."

Duboudin had been listening. He walked over. From outside the house came the sounds of children laughing and shouting as they played *boules*, a kind of lawn bowling, in the alley beside the house. "Is something wrong?" he asked the major.

Land handed him the decode. He read it, cursed in German. "You are canceling the run?" Land looked at him, said nothing, his mind obviously working. "Well?" Vaillant demanded. "After all our work, we do not do it?"

Still Land said nothing.

Duboudin pressed. "We can shift the raid to Reims, can't we? I'll take the car there now."

"No."

"Why not?"

"Day traffic here is too heavy in the daylight," Land said. "You'd be spotted and stopped before you got out of town."

"*Ah, merde!*" Vaillant growled disgustedly, switching back to French.

Land turned, waved the two French *citoyenne* over, both men like twins, bearded, in workman caps and dark rough-woolen jackets. The other commandos watched, pausing in their cleaning of weapons and knives. All were in American battle dress, some bare-chested, well muscled, graceful-moving young Germans wearing U.S. Army dog tags stolen from POWs or corpses, their combat fatigues bloused into paratrooper jump boots.

"The racing machine *must* be in Reims before evening," Land said quietly in French to the two men. "You will have to move it in the boxcar immediately."

The two men frowned, softly questioned each other for a moment. Finally, the taller one said, "*Je ne sais, Commandant.* It would be too difficult."

"But not impossible."

"*Eh bien. . . .*" The man shrugged, held out his palms.

Land stared threateningly into the man's eyes. "You *will* do it, *m'sieur. Non?*"

The Frenchman blinked, twice, then shrugged once more. "*Oui, c'est possible.*"

"Then get on with it." Both men nodded, exchanged looks, and started to turn away. "One of you stay with us," Land added. The shorter one remained.

The major and Sergeant Statz discussed the logistics of the changed attack. Duboudin was left out, staring, frowning. At last, Land turned to the remaining *citoyenne.* "You have agents and a safe house in Reims, of course?"

"Yes."

"Choose one near the Cathedral Notre Dame. Also have someone there who can thoroughly describe the church interior to me."

The *citoyenne* nodded.

"We'll also need an American military vehicle here immediately. I think an ambulance would be preferable."

"*Tres bien,* I see no problem."

"You must make certain there is space enough at the safe house to conceal the ambulance. Last, I want three monks' habits."

The man looked surprised. "*Un moine! Pourquoi?*"

"Just get them."

"What kind of monk do you wish?"

"That doesn't matter."

The Frenchman sighed. He had a bulbous nose and bulging eyes. They made him look clownish. "*Oui, mon Commandant,*" he said resignedly and hurried away.

Duboudin asked, "We're going through with it, then?"

"Yes."

"How?"

Land ignored the question. He said to Statz, "Get the men ready. We'll leave as soon as that ambulance arrives."

"*Jawohl, Major,*" the sergeant said.

Chapter Nineteen

Bleialf, Belgium
15 December 1944
1003 hours

Parnell paused before the farmhouse door to knock mud from his newly issued boots. It was pouring rain, windy, the sleety drops slamming into his back. The building, with foot-wide walls of stone and a high-peaked timbered roof, was now headquarters for the 392nd Regiment, 2nd Infantry Division.

He pushed the door open and stepped inside, pulling the German map case he'd found in the Porsche from under his coat. The room had a low ceiling and a large stone fireplace but no fire in it. It was very cold despite the powerful stench of kerosene heaters. Newly set up, the place was crammed with unopened crates of communication equipment. But one radio unit was already working along with a teletype machine and a mobile telephone switchboard.

He approached the switchboard operator. "Who's your G-2 officer?"

The young man looked up. His lips were badly chapped from the cold. "Captain Swanson, Lieutenant."

"Where's he at?"

"Just stepped out to take a crap, sir."

Four hours earlier, Parnell and his men with Labarre had crossed through the American lines outside the small road junction town of Buchef. After leaving Laznec's band, they'd headed due west, moving quickly down through the deeply forested Schnee Eifel Mountains, avoiding villages and dodging German patrols. Twice they'd paused to rest and eat at remote safe houses where the civilians told them they'd seen extensive German activity all along the frontier over the last week.

Last night, they finally crossed the Belgium border, the forests different from those in Germany. Here the trees were planted in neat rows and the ground brush was cleared away. The Belgians harvested their forests for firewood and charcoal production.

Just before dawn, they made contact with a patrol from C Company, 2nd Division. Young, jumpy troopers who nearly shot Bird, who was on point. He managed to identify himself as an American by showing them his tattered USAAF flight suit under the animal-skin coat. Back at the company CP, they were fed and issued new clothing and weapons. At 9:30 in the morning, Parnell was ordered to report to the regimental intelligence officer for debriefing.

Captain Frank Swanson looked too old to be in combat. He had a round, red face, tiny blue eyes, a built-in scowl. He came stomping in, his fur-lined parka and Jeep cap drenched. Spotting Parnell, he snapped, "You the guy just come through our lines?"

"Yes, sir."

"How long were you out?"

"Over two months. We've been operating with a group of Wend bandits in the Eifel."

"Bandits?" Swanson grunted and nodded Parnell into a side room that was being used for his office. It had previously been the farmhouse's kitchen. Cooking utensils still hung from beams and there was a baking oven and ancient wood stove. His desk was made from a door placed across two wooden horses, his chair an artillery ammo box.

Swanson plunked himself down onto his box and said, "All right, let's have details."

Red quickly summarized Blue Team's capture, their escape, and time with the Wends. Swanson listened without interrupting, his eyes even narrower than before. When Parnell finished, he asked sharply, "What kind of Kraut movement?"

"We saw a lot of patrol activity and lights at night. But not any major repositioning. Still, the civilians living near the border claimed they'd seen heavy troop movements along with mobile artillery and even some armor."

"I knew it!" the captain cried. "God-*damn* it, I knew it."

"Something big's in the wind, right?"

"Hell yes, there is, for chrissakes," Swanson growled. "But try and get those dumb sons of bitches back at division to believe you." He nodded toward a pile of folders on his desk. "See that? Patrol reports up the kazoo about possible Kraut concentrations east of us." He leaned forward, his eyes suddenly full of light. "I'll tell you something. When those sons a' bitches're *done* concentrating, they're gonna come right through *here.*"

"Can we stop them?"

The captain scoffed bitterly. "In a pig's asshole. Our defensive depth's one-goddamn-*third* of what DS manuals consider baseline. And what we've got are mostly replacements, green as bird shit, totally untested. Most of *them* are down with dysentery or trench foot. Do you know that our gun crews haven't even fired a round in six goddamn weeks? There's not one single fieldpiece in the whole damn Ardennes preregistered on attack lines through the Gap."

"Jesus Christ," Parnell said, shocked.

"Jesus Christ is right. He's gonna be the only one who can save our sorry asses once those Kraut bastards come across." He put his head down, agitatedly scratched at his forehead. "All right, enough of that. . . . Look, you and your men report to one of the line companies. Pick any one you want, they can all use you."

Red said quickly, "Captain, I'd like to request we remain temporarily unattached. We're on the track of a French collaborator, a Maquis leader who got a helluva lot of people killed. He was even responsible for the capture of a British general who was Churchill's emissary to Rommel."

Swanson tilted his head. "You mean General Stanfield?"

"Yes, sir."

The captain stared at him. "Then you must be the guys who went in to rescue that British agent who was with him."

Parnell's face went stiff. "Yes, sir."

"You get her out?"

"No, sir, we didn't," Parnell said.

The way he said it caused Swanson to give him a quick glance. "I hit a nerve?"

"Yes, sir."

The captain shifted on his box. "Sorry. . . . So what makes you think this turncoat Frog's in our sector?"

"We're not sure he is." He took out the map case and placed it on the door-desk. "But there's something here that makes us think he might be."

Swanson emptied out the contents and slowly went through the items. He paused at the picture of Duboudin and the two German officers. His eyes widened. "Holy shit, one of these guys is Skorzeny?"

"Who?"

"Hauptbannsturmfuhrer Otto Skorzeny. The Führer's *Kommando*. Hitler thinks the guy shits gold." His eyes shifted. "This the Frenchie prick?"

"Yeah. His name's Vaillant Duboudin, code-named Lucas."

"Where'd you get all this stuff?"

"From that train we hit in the Eifel. It was in the glove compartment of a Kraut race car they were transporting in a boxcar."

"A what? A race car?"

"Yes, sir. A Porsche."

Swanson grunted. He moved on to the papers written in German, then unfolded the map and laid it out, leaning in to get a closer look. "This is a standard Kraut SS-15 theater officer's battle map. But what in hell do these red lines mean?"

"I don't know, sir."

"They're too damned simplistic and overextended to indicate an operational movement." He leaned back on his box, thoughtful for a moment. "This was a regular race car?"

Red nodded. "Yeah, a Porsche, painted woodland camouflage."

"Camouflaged? What the hell're they going to do, have a secret race?" Swanson sucked air through his teeth, then hollered into the outer room, "Carrazelli, get your ass in here."

A short, balding corporal hurried in. "Sir?"

"Didn't I hear you telling somebody about a race car recently?" Swanson asked.

"Yeah, Captain, was Scarnes. He's crazy about racing, use to dirt track on sickles."

"Fuck the sickles. What about this race car?"

"I seen an attached post note about it in our daily DIS supplemental yestiddy," Carrazelli said. "A couple MPs found it in a boxcar on a siding outside Maizieres. It was just sitting there with these two French officers and two GIs. They said they was takin' it to Paris and it was going to be a gift from General Montgomery to de Gaulle."

"What make of car was it?"

"A Porsche, sir. But Scarnes never heard of that make."

Swanson slid his eyes to Parnell, went back to the corporal. "Anybody follow up on the report?"

"I don't know, Captain."

"Then find out, goddammit." The corporal dashed out. Swanson said, "This couldn't be the same car you saw, could it?"

Parnell shook his head. "Not possible, sir."

The captain frowned, distractedly scratched his chin. "Something doesn't wash here. Old Monty giving de Gaulle a personal gift? No way. Those two egotistical sons a' bitches hate each other. And now with Skorzeny in it? What the hell're we looking at here?"

The corporal returned. "Metz MP headquarters said they sent it up to Corps with their daily summary, Captain. But no follow-up on it's come back."

"Well, now, ain't that just fucking par for the course?" Swanson snorted. To Carrazelli: "Contact Corps and ask for details about this incident. And notify Army, while you're at it." He picked up the German papers, handed them to the corporal. "Also, have Teller translate these, stat."

"He's gone down to G Company, Captain."

"Then get his ass back here, for God's sake. I want that translation *yesterday*."

"Yes, sir." Carrazelli left.

Parnell had been staring down at the map. Upside

down, the red lines looked different. Swanson noted his concentration, asked, "What?"

"From this angle," Red said, "those lines look like what a tourist would draw to show a vacation route he intended to take. To and from some place."

The G-2 officer turned the map around. "Yeah, they do, don't they?" He glanced up from under his brows. "You know what? I think this is the track line for a quick in and a quick out. Now, what the hell does *that* tell you?"

"A sabotage team?"

"Bingo."

"Its deepest penetration point west is Meaux. What's there?"

"A fair-sized rail-switching yard just outside Paris. But, hell, there're far more strategic depots all over northern France. If the Jerries're willing to risk a team going in this deep just to disrupt a supply network, why wouldn't they hit something a damn sight bigger?"

"Maybe it's not sabotage," Red suggested. "What about an assassination squad? Maybe gunning for de Gaulle?"

Swanson considered that, nodded. "With the hotshot *Kommando* involved, that could just be it. Still, I can't see why they'd want to take de Gaulle out. That wouldn't slow anything down. As far as the war's concerned, that arrogant Frog bastard's nobody."

"How about Montgomery?"

Swanson stared at the ceiling, old beams and spiderwebs up there. After a moment, he shouted for Carrazelli again. The corporal stuck his head around the door frame. "Sir?"

"Find out exactly where Montgomery and de Gaulle are right now. And where they're likely to be over, say, the next forty-eight hours." As he finished, his eyes met

Parnell's. A dark specter passed between them. "You think?" he said.

Red tilted his head. "I don't know. But *that* sure as hell would slow things down."

"Christ, yes," Swanson said. He looked at Carrazelli again. "Run a check on Ike, too. And red-tag the request."

"Right, Captain," Carrazelli said and disappeared.

Colonel James Dunmore could hardly believe his ears. "My God, John, you're actually alive!" he cried through the secure phone. "I thought you men were goners for sure this time. Where the hell are you?"

It had taken one of Swanson's harried clerks nearly an hour to locate Dunmore, who was currently deputy G-2 for Patton's Third Army at its headquarters at Nancy in Lorraine. "With the 2nd Infantry in the Ardennes," Parnell answered.

"The whole team make it out okay?"

"Yes, sir."

"Good, good. And Sinclair?"

The mention of her name, the actual voicing of it, its specific sound, was like a trigger that instantly brought forward the full image of Anabel Sinclair in Parnell's mind. It was as if she were suddenly right there with him at that moment. The sensation sent a cold, hard tightness surging deep into his belly.

"She was dead when we got to the prison," he said quietly.

Silence. Then, "Lord, I'm sorry, John. I'm deeply sorry."

"Thank you, sir."

Another pause that stretched uncomfortably until Dunmore said, "Well, fill me in on where you've been all this time."

Red hurriedly recounted what had happened after their capture. When he told about the German concentrations in the Schnee Eifel, Dunmore interrupted him, asked how things looked in the Ardennes.

"Not good, Colonel," Red said. "They're thin as paper up here. Lots of green replacements with most of them down sick. Even their artillery's been static for six weeks."

Dunmore swore softly. "It's just like George said. He's been trying to convince the top dogs at E-TOHQ the Krauts're returning to the offensive. He believes they'll come through the Ardennes Gap. Even General Strong agrees with him. But nobody else seems to want to listen." General Karl Strong was Eisenhower's intelligence chief.

Parnell waited till Dunmore had finished, then continued, ending with, "There's one other thing, Colonel. I found some recent photos of Vaillant Duboudin with German officers. One of the Krauts is Otto Skorzeny."

"What?"

"Colonel Skorzeny. Swanson says he's Hitler's fair-haired boy."

"Oh, Jesus, that he is. *He* was with this Duboudin?"

"Yes, sir. And some panzer major."

"So the son of a bitch really *did* set up Stanfield's party."

Red went on to tell about the Porsche and the map case and its papers, and the report of a second Porsche spotted on a rail car outside Maizieres. When he finished, Dunmore silently mulled the information over for a few moments. At last he said the whole damned thing looked like either a sabotage or an assassination team about to enter France somehow using a high-speed vehicle.

"This could be really bad, John," he concluded somberly.

"I fully agree, sir."

"I want you to stay right on this. Understand? As of now, I'm attaching you and your men to Third Army's intelligence section. I'll call Robertston as soon as I get off the line and see you get full cooperation." Major General Walter Robertston was commander of the 2nd Infantry Division. "What about this regimental G-2 officer? Swanson, was it? Is he fast on his feet?"

"He looks pretty good, sir."

"Okay, we'll set up liaison through him. First thing I want you to do is send me all the material you found in that car. Use a Piper observation plane to get it down here if you can. Otherwise, go with a runner."

"Yes, sir."

"About this map. You say it has two *eastern* terminuses?"

"Yes, sir. One's at Merzig across the German border, the other's at Esch on the river Sure in the Ardennes."

"Okay. I'll have our units west of Merzig set up roadblocks on any route that crosses the border. Robertston'll do the same on the roads coming into Esch from the west. That material you send I'll have analyzed, see if anything jumps out. Keep in constant contact with Swanson and I'll relay updates through him." He thought a moment. "Might as well use our old football code system, just in case."

"Yes, sir."

Another pause, then, "And, John, when and if you find this Duboudin, kill the son of a bitch."

"I intend to, Colonel."

"Good luck." And he was gone.

The American MP was out there beside the road just outside Meaux, Highway SP-3, which ran from Paris to Reims and then northwest, becoming SP-15 to the Belgium border, the man with his uniform muddy and snow-wet, pumping his right arm up and down, saying, "Everybody move ass!" pissed off at the world for the duty he'd pulled in this shitty weather.

A particularly nasty cold front that had been sitting out there in the North Sea for the last eight hours had finally moved inland, thrusting a salient through western Holland and Belgium and due south across France as far as Normandy. It was now four minutes after twelve in the afternoon and it had been snowing heavily since nine.

Steckel was at the wheel of the U.S. Army ambulance, a heavy Ford MTP 1.8 field vehicle with six stretcher racks in back, which were now filled with sitting commandos in their American GI uniforms. This time they had medic armbands instead of MP designations, and there were newly painted red crosses in white circles on their helmets. Major Land was up front in the passenger seat, Duboudin directly behind him.

Steckel stopped the vehicle back a ways from the edge of the highway, a convoy of military trucks rumbling past one after another endlessly, big two-and-a-halfs stacked with cargo under canvas, their exhausts smoking in the snowfall, big tires hissing on the pavement. The American MP turned and glared at them, then walked over.

Steckel rolled down the window as the American stepped up on the running board and peered in. He spotted Land's and Duboudin's French officer uniforms, made a halfhearted salute, and pointedly asked Steckel, "Where the hell are *you* headed, Mac?"

"We're medic replacements for the 4th Infantry Division."

"That ain't what I asked you."

"Our AD's a repo-depo in Bouillon."

The MP nodded his head at the two French officers. "Them, too?"

"Naw, we're jes' given them a lift. They're headed for the Frenchie 2nd Armored at Eindhoven."

The American peered into the back of the ambulance, the German commandos watching, a couple smoking Lucky Strike cigarettes, their medical bags at their feet.

He finally nodded. "Okay, I'll make a break for you," he growled. "Expect delays you get farther north. This fucking snow."

He walked back to the highway and stood watching for a gap in the endless line of trucks. Finally one came. He stepped out and stopped the oncoming vehicle, then turned and angrily waved Steckel into the line, his mouth going, "Move it! Move it!"

The German commando geared and hurriedly pulled out into the convoy line and closed with the truck ahead. It contained crates marked with green-and-black stencils: ammunition. Glancing over at Land, he grinned. "*Verdammter Dummkopf, eh, herr Major.*"

"Turn on your wipers," Land said.

Trois Ponts, Belgium
1251 hours

Major Wes Colley had a bad cold. His long, slender nose was red, he had a hacking cough, and his black eyes were watery. He stood before a large wall map, saying, "That about covers every road, footpath, and cow trail for five miles on either side of Esch, Lieutenant."

"Are they already posted, sir?" Parnell asked.

"They will be by 1330."

"Thank you, sir."

Colley was 2nd Division's G-2 head, a thin man with a

stalk neck, rounded shoulders, and a radio announcer's deep bass voice. The division's commander, General Robertston, had gone to visit his old comrades in the 4th Infantry Division located farther north. After talking with Dunmore, however, he had immediately started back for his own headquarters and was now still in transit.

The HQ was located in Trois Ponts, twenty miles due west of the U.S. front line, in a white, two-story building that had been a convent school. All its classrooms, still pungent with the cloistered scent of chalk and habit wool, had been cleared of students' desks and were now stacked with all the paraphernalia of a divisional command center.

Colley took out a damp handkerchief, blew his nose into it, stared at what had exited, then replaced it into his field jacket pocket. He sighed tiredly and said, "Tell me, do you really think it's Ike these people are after?"

"We're not sure yet, sir," Parnell said. "But I think it's pretty certain *somebody* high up is a target."

"And they're using a race car?" He shook his head. "Sounds to me like they intend to kidnap rather than kill whoever that happens to be."

"We think so, too."

"Tell me, how do you intend stopping this high-speed vehicle if it's spotted? Even if you're able to ground-fire it off the road, the passenger could get killed. If that passenger happens to be General Eisenhower, we'll all go down in history as king killers." He added: "After the American people burn us at the stake, of course."

"I'll be honest, sir. I don't know *what* we'll do. I figure we'll just have to play it by feel."

"Damned dangerous business, that."

"We don't have any choice. One thing, be absolutely certain your men understand they are *not* to fire *at* this car. Lob ordnance ahead of it, okay, try and tear up the road. But no rounds directly at it. Also, they're to radio its position to Captain Swanson so he can forward the information to whatever CP is closest to the sighting."

"All of that's already done," Colley said. "Incidentally, did Swanson get anything concrete from the translation of those German papers?"

"His people weren't able to break the code. Apparently it's something new, some sort of highly convoluted number system. We're hoping Colonel Dunmore has better luck."

A roll of thunder came faintly to them from the higher peaks to the east, the sound rising slowly like a distant artillery battalion laying in saturation fire. It reached its trembling crescendo close by and rumbled past, eventually fading off into after echoes.

Colley poured himself a cup of coffee, glanced questioningly at Parnell. "Cup?"

"Yes, sir. Thank you."

They drank in silence for a while. Finally, Colley said, "This may be a silly question, but I assume Dunmore's alerted Eisenhower's people?"

"I would certainly think so, sir."

"Well, I contacted Army myself, right after I talked with General Robertston. Didn't get very far, though. Finally managed a senior intel watch officer who said he'd pass the word on to Eisenhower's security people. He said the general was scheduled to visit the 101st in Reims today."

Parnell's head came up. "Reims?"

"That's what they said." Frown lines formed around Colley's watery eyes. "Something about that?"

"Reims was one of the towns marked in red on the Porsche map."

"Oh, my Lord," Colley said softly.

* * *

Dunmore's alert hadn't gotten much further than Colley's. He'd initially called First Army headquarters at La Roche, which was command center for the Ardennes sector. The place was in a frenzy. It had been First Army's V and VIII Corps that had launched the stalled attack against the Roer dams only five days before, getting themselves badly blooded in the process.

The battle was still raging and the First's commander, Lieutenant General Courtney Hodges, and his staff were working feverishly to shore up the Roer thrust by shifting reserve divisions through other units on the line to replace the badly mangled spearhead corps.

A staff G-2 captain told Dunmore, "I'm sorry, Colonel, the general's been all over hell in the last forty-eight hours. We're having difficulty raising him ourselves, what with the weather."

"Have you received anything about a possible assassination or kidnap attempt on Eisenhower or Montgomery?" Dunmore asked sharply.

The captain laughed. "Oh, sure, sir. We get rumors like that all the time."

"This one's got some damn tight evidence to back it up, Captain. And I want it followed up on. You got that?"

"All right, sir. I'll pass it on to General Hodges as soon as I can. Until then, there really isn't much I can do."

"Bullshit!" Dunmore shouted. "You can forward my conversation *verbatim* to AG as soon as I get off your line." AG stood for the Twelfth Army Group, General Omar Bradley's command. "I'll expect confirmation from both AG and General Hodges within the next thirty minutes. Is *that* goddamn clear?"

"Yes, sir."

He immediately put a call through to 12th Army Group himself, couldn't wait for other people to plow through levels. But he, too, got shuffled around the AG staff, the place full of colonels and majors passing the buck, wasting time.

He finally got to Bradley's deputy intelligence chief, Colonel Niles Heller, who had just come in from the line. Heller said, "Well, hello, Sticks, long time no see."

"Goddammit, Niles, what the hell are you running up there?"

"What's that?" The friendly tone was instantly gone.

"I've been trying to raise somebody on your staff with some bloody juice. I keep getting booted to somebody else."

Heller's good humor returned. "And you're surprised?"

"Look, I've got pretty strong evidence that either Ike or Montgomery might be kidnapped or assassinated some time very soon. There's even an outside chance the target's de Gaulle."

Heller's tone again changed, *click*, serious now, saying, "What evidence?"

Dunmore ran through it. When he finished, Heller was silent. Then he said, "A race car," and grunted. "Looks like a kidnap." He grunted again. "Crazy but ingenious. . . . Well, I think we can scratch de Gaulle. If this involved only Frenchmen, it could be possible. But with Germans, and particularly with Skorzeny, that's not likely."

"Where's Ike now?"

"I think he's scheduled to review Taylor's unit at Reims today. He's probably there right now."

"Where does he go afterward?"

"Back to Paris, I assume."

"How about Monty?"

"He's in Paris already."

"According to the map," Dunmore said, "a terminus point is marked just outside Paris, at Meaux. I've got a strong gut feeling that if there's anything to this, the hit'll come at Meaux. Or between it and Reims. Today or tonight."

"That makes sense. All right, I'll notify the 101st to alert Ike's security team. I'll also contact Monty's Twenty-first AG. I think it'll be a lot easier for me to punch through than for you."

"Hallelujah!"

"What kind of security have you set up on the other end?"

"I tried to reach Hodges. No luck. But I did speak with Robertston. We're liaisoning through one of his regimental G-2 officers. They're placing roadblocks all around the map's eastern terminus at Esch, and also this side of the frontier farther south."

Now both men grew silent, neither wanting to put into words the thoughts each was thinking, that what if this crazy plan *was* real and the Krauts actually got the supreme commander into a high-speed race car headed for the border? How in God's name would they stop it? Worse, what if they actually got him into Germany? Or even killed him?

Heller finally sucked air in, let it out, audible through the secure phone. "I hope to Christ this is a false alarm, Jim."

"I'm praying like hell for that, too."

"Have you told Patton yet?"

"No, he's in transit. But I notified Frank." Brigadier Frank Metzler was Third Army chief of staff. "He's on pins and needles, too."

"Okay, I'll keep you apprised," Heller said. "But you keep us in your loop, too."

"Of course. Thanks, Niles."

He rang off, glanced at his watch. It was 3:31 in the afternoon. He swiveled his chair around and called to one of his radio operators, "When was Captain Swanson's last report on Parnell?"

"Thirteen-thirty, Colonel."

"Raise him."

"Yes, sir."

Dunmore swiveled back, sat there tapping his pen against the edge of his desk, tiny, spaced hits. He felt cold, knotted up inside. The feeling of a man staring up at a ridge full of snow, watching the wind feather its edges, and then seeing the first, small slides begin, the surface of the snow shifting with gravity, making streaks and shallow pockets that kept getting bigger and bigger, and all the time he knew that once it all got moving, it would be impossible to hold back the downward rush.

Damn!

Monsieur Jean Pierre de Beauvoir looked like a diplomat, sleek in a dark suit with a vest and glistening black shoes that showed no sign of slush smear. He carried a slender cane with a golden eagle's head and seemed a man particularly at ease in the gilded splendors and tapestries of the Salle du Tau. He was Land's new *Citoyenne* contact in Reims.

The Triple team and Duboudin had arrived in the city at 3:30, coming up Boulevard Louis Reoderer past the war-damaged arcades and statues of Square Corbert now deep in snow. Both Land and Vaillant were familiar with the city, the place looking different now with American soldiers and army vehicles on the streets and the buildings bomb damaged. They swung onto Rue Libergier, which would take them right to the Cathredal Notre Dame.

The Salle was in the Palais du Tau, which sat in the same square as the cathedral, only a hundred yards from the church's southern wall. The Palais had been the seventeenth-century residence of an archbishop but had long since been made into a museum containing splendid artifacts from the cathedral.

Vaillant and Land approached Beauvoir. Despite its natural brilliance, the room was dim from the snowfall outside. A few U.S. servicemen in their starched field fatigues wandered aimlessly among the huge paintings and statues.

"Pardon, Monsieur," Duboudin said. "You possess a beautiful cane there. Its head reminds me of the eagle on the banner of Richard the Lionheart."

Beauvoir turned, nodded. "Ah, *merci*. You are a student of English kings?" Coded chitchat, establishing identities.

"*Oui*. And of eagles. They are the symbol of strength."

Beauvoir again nodded, a mere dip of his slightly balding head. "There is a lovely tapestry in another room that depicts Richard on Crusade. Allow me to show it to you gentlemen."

"*Je vous en prie,*" Vaillant said.

He led them down a hall of gilded half-pillars and circular paintings in the high ceiling. They passed through a side door into a smaller, less ostentatious room, then through another door. From somewhere came the sound of hammering, the thud of timbers.

Beauvoir abruptly paused, his voice dropping. "All is

prepared. The vehicle arrived thirty minutes ago. It sits on a siding at the south end of the train yard."

"You have the monk's habits?" Land asked.

"*Oui*. They are of the Cistercian order."

"Where can we hide the American ambulance until it's needed?"

Beauvoir turned his head, lifted his chin to indicate the rear of the Palais. "Right here, among the construction work."

"What?"

"A portion of the building is being rebuilt." He glanced at his gold wristwatch, noted it was now 3:51. "The workmen will leave at four o'clock. You can place the *ambulance* among the equipment after they've gone. No one will see you and the museum guards will not venture out into the snow. Come, this way."

They went downstairs to a large basement with stone arches and banks of crates containing art objects. The air smelled of stone dust and old books. A final door opened onto a cargo ramp. To the left were scaffolds and canvas-covered wooden pallets of uncut stone, lumber, steel reinforcing bars, and bags of cement, everything coated with a few inches of snow. Several workmen in heavy coats and carrying their tools moved up the cargo ramp headed toward Rue Voltaire.

"The monk's habits are in that wooden crate marked *Acajou*. It's mahogany paneling." Beauvoir turned to Duboudin. "Will this be adequate?"

Land pointedly answered, "For now. Who instructs us on the interior of the cathedral?"

"Ah, of course." Beauvoir took an envelope from his inside coat pocket and handed it to the major. "Here are the schematics for the cathedral. They're copies of the original 1937 blueprints of the building when it was reconstructed. They show all rooms and passages, including those rarely used and those that were secret."

Land extracted the bundle of miniaturized blueprints, thumbed through them, then replaced them into the envelope and put it in his tunic.

Beauvoir said, "I think it best we leave now. The museum closes in twenty minutes. It would not be advisable if we are the last to depart."

They went back through the building.

At precisely 4:45, Supreme Commander Dwight D. Eisenhower sat down to dine with the officers and troopers of the 101st Airborne Division in the main mess hall of its refit base two miles east of Reims. The place was noisy with chatter and the metallic clink of utensils and mess gear. Whenever he inspected a unit, Ike always opted to eat with all his troops and was served the same fare.

Twelve minutes later, he was interrupted by a young captain from his security team. Ike listened as the man said something quietly into his ear, then excused himself, rose, everyone at the table doing the same, and followed the junior officer out. The division commander, General Maxwell Taylor, also left.

After several minutes, both men returned. Eisenhower now became unusually quiet. The other officers exchanged discreet glances and, following normal table protocol, also maintained silence. The dinner ended at 5:32, at which time the supreme commander and General Taylor were driven back to the base headquarters.

Winter nights in the mountains of Belgium and western Germany come swiftly. On the Sure River in

Luxembourg, ten miles southeast of Bastogne, it had
rained all day. But the wind died by midafternoon and
then there was a momentary break in the cloud cover,
which extended into early evening. Now it was clear
enough to see stars, but the temperature had begun
dropping rapidly, turning the muddy thoroughfares icy.

Parnell and his team had taken up positions outside
Esch, on the western side of the river and above the approaches to the small forest town. From Esch, main
roads ran to Bastogne in the northwest, Neufchâteau, fifteen miles due west, and to Vianden and Diekirch,
which lay between the Sure and Our Rivers that marked
the border between Luxembourg and Germany. The
railhead of Ettlebruck lay eight miles to the south.

Parnell gave one last scan to the Neufchâteau road,
now nearly invisible out there, and settled back on his
haunches. He checked his watch: 6:13. He, Smoker,
and Weesay were in an M-2 half-track parked on the
lip of the upper mountain road, unbroken forest all
around them save for a single break where the ruins
of an ancient abbey, the Abbaye St. Mathieu, stood
about a half mile up the slope.

The monastery was visible for long distances, particularly from the west. In the past, American artillery crews
had used it as a triangulation base and reference point
during practice barrages. It bore the firing-map grid reference of TR-3356, the numbers indicating its elevation.
As the last rays of the evening sun had faded, the tumbled parapets and truncated spires had glowed softly
yellow, stark amid the deep black green of the forest.

Their half-track carried a swivel-mounted .50-caliber
machine gun and the pedestal for a small pack howitzer.
Besides these guns and their own personal weapons, the
three men had also brought along a bazooka, now

packed in woolen blankets to keep its battery charged, and two M1-Garand rifles with grenade charges.

"Chu know what?" Weesay now said from the fur-lined folds of his heavy jacket. "That shit Frenchie come up here, he gonna be slippin' and sliddin' bad on that road, baby."

"No way," Wineberg scoffed. "Running on them snow and mud tires? He'll be *flying*, man. And lemme tell you, it's gon' be a bitch puttin' a stovepipe round just ahead of him without you taking out ole Ike, too."

Laguna snorted. "Chu jes' load for me, baby. I'll lay that rocket in like it was a fixed charge."

"Shit, you won't even be able to *see* the goddamn road. Hell, you can't see it now."

"No problem. I got bat eyes."

Wineberg chuckled derisively. "What you all got, Zorro, is a fuckin' bat brain."

"Hey, *hombre, no me friegues*," Weesay came back. "Or I have to bust you up, *meng*."

"*Besa me cola, Chihuahua*," Smoker said.

Parnell idly listened to the good-natured banter, but he knew Smoker was making a solid point. Like Major Colley had said, it *was* going to be dicey getting that race car stopped without killing its passenger. Maybe, he thought, they *should* have laid demo charges on all the approach roads. But, no, that would have been foolish. The kidnap scenario was still just an assumption, after all. To destroy the use of an entire road system across at least ten miles of front simply from speculation would have been tactically and strategically insane.

He looked up at the sky, stars still up there but dark shadows beginning to cross over again. *Come on*, he said to the sky in his mind, *rain again, hard. Turn those roads into goddamn rivers of mud. Even that knob-tired Porsche wouldn't be able to handle too much of that.* He leaned back, closed his eyes.

All through the afternoon he'd received updates from Dunmore, using the code name Knute Rockne. He'd give the data to Captain Swanson by secure telephone and then the regimental G-2 officer would relay it up to Red by walkie-talkie. So far, there hadn't been anything particularly unexpected to report. But at least Dunmore had things rolling, had alerted the proper people.

In the Ardennes, the roadblocks had all been ready when Colley said they would be. They were spotted all along both sides of the Sure River and on every fair-sized road in the entire Esch sector. Also, Colley had emphasized again, without actually telling the platoon leaders and company officers specifically about Eisenhower, the utter importance of being *ultra*-cautious about stopping and approaching this particular automobile.

Parnell sat forward again, picked up his walkie-talkie, and compressed the Transmit switch. "Blue One to Blue Two," he said.

Bird came right back: "Go ahead, Blue One." He and Cowboy were about two hundred yards down and away from the half-track, in a prepared position on the other side of the Neufchâteau road.

"How's your visibility there? Over."

"Not good. Looks like we might get some more snow, though. It'll give us silhouette sighting."

"Yeah, clouds *are* moving in right now. Keep your ears open. If Duboudin comes this way, the whine of that high-powered engine'll sound like a goddamned mill saw up here."

"Right." Bird always refrained from using any references to rank when he spoke with an officer, just in case enemy listening posts were ranging the area.

"Blue One, clear," Parnell said.

He settled in. The increasing cold was turning sharper, the feel of frigid wetness slipping from it. The darkness was complete now, nothing here, not even the glimmer off weapons. He listened to the dry, whistling sound the air made moving through his nostrils, felt his cheeks stiffening.

And the image of Vaillant Duboudin suddenly took his mind, rushing and tumultuous. He watched it, a dark deviltry moving through remembered moments, recalled words, phrases, all insidiously fraudulent.

Anabel's face emerged then, coming with the full re-creation of that first moment he'd seen her in the dark landscape of Normandy. The vision drew into him an ache so profound and complex it seemed to stupefy him. He closed his eyes and forced it away, gently, gently, back into the silence, leaving only the cold and the night and the misting stars.

Thirty-one minutes earlier, U.S. Military Police units, acting in conjunction with officers from de Gaulle's newly instituted Deuxieme Bureau de Securite, had initiated a citywide sweep through Meaux. They rousted suspected Nazi sympathizers and collaborators, particularly those who were known to be affiliates of the *Citoyenne*. The city's switching yard was also thoroughly searched. Nothing was found.

At the same time, roadblocks were thrown up on all the western approaches to the city of Reims. Within the town, American patrols prowled the snowy streets, randomly stopping civilians and U.S soldiers to closely examine their identification papers.

By now, all Allied security units in the immediate area

had been informed of a possible kidnapping of either
Eisenhower or Montgomery. The Brits, playing it safe,
had already whisked Monty away from Paris. But no one
knew precisely where Eisenhower was.

Since his security team and the senior intelligence officers of the 101st had been told of the potential danger
Ike was in, it was assumed he too had been secretly transported to safety following his visit to the division.
Unfortunately, they didn't know about his intention to
slip away from his own security team to attend his driver's wedding in the Cathredal Notre Dame du Reims.

The footsteps crunched in the snow outside the boxcar, moving around it once, then again, Vaillant and
Commando Steckel inside, freezing in position to listen.

Earlier, Duboudin had started up the Porsche, running it a few minutes to warm the engine for the big
show. At first, it had been sluggish from the cold. But
it finally got going after he pulled the cleaner rings
and injected starter fluid directly into the fuel injec-
tor ports. He didn't rev it but just let it go on a fast idle
with the door open to disperse the exhaust fumes.
Meanwhile, Steckel had disconnected the racer's bolt-
down chains, unlocked the sliding rear door, and
moved up the off-loading ramps so they'd be in position for a quick deployment.

Beauvoir had driven them over to the boxcar from the
museum, the train car sitting on a siding far back in the
yard. The area was hidden behind a line of tall sycamore
trees and an equipment yard was nearby, full of rusted
train wheels and axles and boiler tanks. The matrix of
the main tracks lay about two hundred yards away.

Coming over, they had seen military patrols stopping

cars. Beauvoir commented that the military security seemed tighter than usual. He figured that perhaps the American division based nearby was preparing to move out. By staying on backstreets, he had avoided being stopped.

It was only a few minutes after they shut down the engine, just long enough to clear out the fumes and reshut the door, that the footsteps came. Now Steckel eased the door open again, just a crack, and peered out.

It was pitch-black out there, snow still coming down in that silent sifting. He spotted the glow of a flashlight moving around the forward end of the car. Then a man appeared, walking with his light playing on the numbers of the train car. His upper body was in a heavy coat that was silhouetted against the back reflection of the beam. He carried what looked like a metal clipboard.

Steckel turned around, whispered, "I think it's the tallyman taking night inventory of the yard." He slipped a Luger from his belt, affixed a noise supressor to the end of the barrel.

"What are you going to do?" Duboudin asked anxiously.

"Kill him, of course."

"No, wait. There could be others."

They listened. The man came to the door again. They could hear him sniffing at the opening, obviously picking up the last residue of exhaust fumes. Without a word, Duboudin grabbed the door and shoved it open, the bottom wheels sounding hollowly in their slid track.

Startled, the tallyman jumped back. Recovering, he put his light on Vaillant. "*Oh, Seigneur Dieu, Capitaine!*" he gasped. "You scare the shit from me." He had an old man's voice. He played the light into the boxcar now, saw the Porsche. "What is *that*?" The light returned to Duboudin's face. "*Pardon, Monsieur,* but what are you doing here?"

Vaillant squatted down. In his friendliest tone, he said, "I did not mean to frighten you, *mon ami.* We're here guarding this vehicle. It's being shipped to General de Gaulle."

"Ah?" The tallyman frowned. "But I don't have the number of this *vehicule du coffret* on my yard list. No one informed me of its arrival."

"It's being transported secretly," Vaillant said. "Would you want someone to find out and spoil the general's surprise?"

"*Oh, non, non.*"

"Of course not. . . . Perhaps you would like to see it up close? It is a magnificent machine."

"But I think it is better that—"

"Come on, *mon ami.*" He held up a forefinger, as if instructing a child. "But you must promise to tell no one?"

"No, *Capitaine,* I won't tell anyone."

"Is there anybody else with you? They can see it, too."

"I am alone."

He helped him aboard. The man felt light in his big jacket and smelled of tobacco and musty clothing. While he stared at the vehicle, its polished metal bouncing his light beam, Vaillant killed him with a knife into his liver, the tallyman crumbling soundlessly to the floor of the boxcar.

They dragged his body to the rear and propped him against the bulkhead. Returning to the door, they pulled it shut, leaving a crack through which they could watch the back entry road just beyond the trees, waiting.

The tiny phosphorescent dials of Major Land's wristwatch showed it was 7:01. He and two commandos, Statz and an *Unteroffizier* or corporal named Halke, were hiding near the outside wall of a partially completed room in the back of the Palais du Tau. The place was filled with stacks of cut stone and pieces of two-by-fours, smelling of masonry paste and iron reinforcement rods. All three were dressed in the white habits of Cistercian monks of the Fraternite de Clairvaux

From their position, they had a direct view of the back and southern side of the cathedral, sitting out there huge and Gothic-solid. Its two entrance towers and the two-hundred-foot-high apse spire were lost in the snowfall. On this side, the building's flying buttresses were topped by needle spires that made them appear like rockets lined up beside the wall.

Between the buttresses were colored-glass tracery windows, their brilliance now darkened. The only lights on in the church came from the front of the building and from this side of the transept where a panel of five sharply arched lancet windows cast vivid pools of color out onto the snow.

Several secondary buildings were scattered around the rear of the cathedral grounds. They included a long, narrow chapter or council house, a beautifully constructed chapel, a two-story dormitory and dining hall, and a line of maintenance shops. Occasionally, a priest would cross between the buildings, scurrying along in his dark robes.

Moments before, Land had placed three of his men in positions along the upper side of the museum from which they could lay in covering cross fire homed to the rear of the cathedral. The remaining commando waited in the ambulance, which was now sequestered among the piles of building material on the museum's loading ramp.

The German major had his plan of attack all worked

out in his head, everything visualized mentally, just as he had always done before tank battles in Italy. Seeing the movements and countermovements playing themselves out on the screen of his brain, then executing them in reality, the whole thing unfolding like a movie.

"*Herr Major*," Statz called softly. "Cars, out front."

Land swung around. Three automobiles had just pulled up before the cathedral. Men and women in evening clothes got out and hurried up the main steps, a priest standing out there with an umbrella. Obviously, members and guests of the wedding party.

A few moments later, three more cars stopped, a little line formed now. One was a long, black American limousine. From it stepped the bride, a coat thrown over her flowing white gown. There were sparkles in the material of her dress and when she ran, she held up her hem.

"Stand ready," Land ordered quietly. He reached under his habit to check his armaments by feel: a paratrooper's folding-stock MP-38 machine pistol strapped to his right thigh, a holstered Luger with a silencer attached, and three thirty-two-round clips in a chest bandoleer that also held a commando stiletto. The others were doing the same. Besides the weapons, Statz had a pair of long-handled bolt cutters. No one carried explosives. This job would have to be delicate, soundless, and swift.

Land now withdrew a medical kit, opened it to examine the contents with his tiny vest light. It had a felt lining and held a syringe, two spare needles, and four tiny phials of sodium pentathol. He tilted it, jiggled the liquid to see it had not solidified, then snapped the kit shut and returned it to his inner pocket.

They waited. The snowfall muffled sounds, distorted distance. The crinkly whisper of tires as two more automobiles stopped out front, laughter, the clang of an ambulance, the honk of a horn. Then abruptly came the throb of the cathedral's organ rising up in a sprightly hymn. Merging with these sounds now came the rich scent of cooking food that drifted across from the dining hall.

The jeep appeared suddenly, swinging sharply off the Rue Guillaume de Marchault and down between the dormitory and dining hall. Two American officers were in it, the visors of their caps gleaming with reflected light, their heavy winter coat collars pulled up.

The vehicle was by itself. Its tires crunched, left narrow lines in the new snow cover. It crossed the parking lot and stopped near a stairway that led into the back of the cathedral's apse. The men dismounted. One paused at the foot of the stairs, waiting for his companion to come around. He glanced to his left, the movement fully exposing his face for an instant. It was faintly etched in red and blue from light pouring through the transept's windows.

The officer was General Dwight Eisenhower.

"You guys get some sleep," Parnell said. "I'll take first watch."

It had begun snowing again, so they'd stretched a canvas tarp across the open back and over the driver's seat of the half-track. They had dinner under it, C-rations of frankfurters and beans, crackers, strawberry jam, and Nescafe coffee powder, heating snowmelt over the tiny paraffin heaters that came in the ration boxes.

Smoker and Weesay crawled into the back of the vehicle and stretched out on ammo boxes and a spare tarp. Red scrunched down in the driver's seat and looked out at the snowfall. Despite the increasing sharpness of the cold, he felt comfortable and warm. Even as a boy, he'd always liked cold weather, mountain weather and snow, the stuff so soft and silent and carrying with it the feel of Christmas, the sweet headiness of pines.

Now and then he'd have to shove accumulating snow off the tarp, the things sounding like cow pies hitting the ground beside the half-track. That and the clothy whisper of his coat when he moved were the only sounds in the vast stillness of the night. To him, it seemed impossible that thousands of men and guns and equipment were scattered out there in the darkness, the silence so pure and complete, as if nothing were alive for a long way out. Almost like a graveyard at night.

Graveyard . . . death.

The words, like a jolt of adrenaline, instantly called Anabel into his mind again, flashing in out of the darkness like a homing round to strike his belly and chest. Desperate, he forced it away. It leaped back at him. He focused his mind on the night, the quiet, the soft breathing of his men, anything that would hold off the pictures in his head.

He took out a cigarette from the Chesterfield minipack from his ration box and lit up, cupping his gloved hands over the Zippo flame, pulling the smoke down deep, feeling a slight menthol-like sting from the cold.

Under the dashboard, the tiny red receiver light of the half-track's radio abruptly came on. A moment later, the speaker crackled to life: "Blue One, this is Ticket Booth, over." It was Captain Swanson.

He unhooked the mike, keyed. "Go ahead, Ticket Booth."

"Message from Rockne as follows: *West Stadium groundskeepers have swept west arena for ticket scalpers. None located. Further sweeps possible. Unable to read playbook . . . stop.* Do you copy, over?"

"Roger that."

"Have you sighted anything?"

"Negative."

"Heads up, Blue One," Swanson shot right back. "Indications here wind might be shifting to the east. *Comprende?* Over."

Parnell hesitated. He'd understood Dunmore's message, which said there had been police sweeps in Meaux without results and further sweeps were possible, and that the German papers from the Porsche were still undeciphered. But what the hell was that last?

He keyed. "Say last again."

The G-2 officer repeated, this time finishing with, "As per our recent chalk talk, over."

He thought a moment, then got it. His first conversation with Swanson had covered the German buildup along the SchneeWald. He keyed. "Message understood."

"Report anything unusual your sector, over," Swanson said.

"Roger that. Blue One, out."

He immediately called up Bird, told him to be extra alert for anything east of his position. Then he sat back, thoughtful. What specifically had prompted Swanson's warning? New patrol reports? Sightings of German movements?

He reached back and slapped Weesay on the leg. "Look alive, guys," he called. "We're maybe gonna get some German company soon."

* * *

They trooped across the parking lot in single file, their hoods up, three monks moving fast enough to get out of the snow but not running, Sergeant Statz in the lead. They left a single trail in the snow.

They passed the rear stairs into the apse where Eisenhower and his companion had gone, the American jeep already gathering a thin coverlet of snow, then turned to the right and went between the chapel and the rear of the chapter house, passing close enough to the former to see the intricately sculptured friezes of saints and martyrs that circled the chapel, all chiseled in sacred parade.

The back of the chapter house had stone steps that led up to a back door. On either side of the steps were cement alcoves, each containing a smaller door. Without a word, two of the commandos dropped down into them, Statz to the right, Halke to the left. Land moved up the steps, paused long enough to be sure the others were ready, then opened the door and stepped through.

He was in a narrow hallway, the floor made of highly polished wood. A room halfway down the hall cast the only light. It gleamed off the floor, making a bright pool. He hurried to the room and ducked in.

A man in a white, short-sleeved shirt and black trousers was seated at a desk. Hearing Land enter, he turned in his chair, frowned. His glasses reflected the glow from the table lamp. Around him, the room was filled with metal cabinets and bookcases containing what looked like bound financial records. The room's air smelled like the inside of a suitcase taken from an old attic.

Land went straight at him. The man's frown disppeared, another look coming, one of sudden apprehension. He started to rise. As Land came up, his right hand slipped from his habit, holding his stiletto. With a straight, thrusting lunge, he plunged it into the center of the man's throat, twisted the handle, and drove it upward through mouth and into brain. Clutching at the haft, the man fell back onto the desk, sent books and pens thudding and clattering to the floor. Behind his glasses, his eyes were stark with shock.

Land returned to the hall. From the main council room at the far end of the hall, Statz appeared. There was a large blotch of blood on the front of his habit. Halke came up right behind him. Land paused for a second to orient himself.

Earlier, he had meticulously studied Beauvoir's architectural schematics of the cathedral and the outbuildings renovated in the thirties. Mentally reviewing them now, he realized the entrance to the tunnel that linked the chapter house to the cathedral was down and to the right. He instantly broke into a sprint, headed to the council room, the others on his heels, their boots pounding loudly on the wooden floor.

The council room was as spacious as a dance floor. Dozens of wooden folding chairs lined the walls, which were completely windowless, like a fortress. The walls were made of a dark brown wood and had inverted arches carved into them. Several doorless openings branched off to right and left.

Land chose the last one on the right. Just inside the doorway was a spiral stone stairwell to the basement. Using their flashlights, the tiny beams darting, they descended to the basement. It had arched bracings of gray stone that gave the space a feel of largeness. Land followed the eastern wall, noting there were metal rings in the stone, like those to hold prisoners, and small patches of fungus that sparkled when the light hit them.

The door to the tunnel had been made from raw ingot iron, thick as the space between a man's knuckle joints and rough-surfaced as solidified lava. It had a sliding bar with two stock-and-barrel locks hooked through the ends to prevent it from opening. Statz immediately moved forward and cut the bolt extensions, the jaws of the cutter making sharp, hollow cracks in the darkness.

The door slid open with surprising ease, exposing a dark, low tunnel three feet wide that disappeared beyond the flashlight beams. But Land knew it led to the cathedral's vestry. On the schematics, it was called the *passage d'pourchasson*, an escape tunnel for those who had sought sanctuary in the main church during its seven hundred years.

They moved quickly through it, hunched over, the trapped, ancient air thick as a mist, spiderwebs like sprays of water white in the light. On the low ceiling there was a dark line of soot from centuries-old torches. Soon they reached another stone stairs. At the top was a similarly rough-hewn iron door. Statz pushed against it.

It was locked from the other side.

The organ was playing again, the *Marche Nuptial du Handel*, its deep, sonorous vibrations majestically rumbling through the building, seeping into the tunnel from around the door, impressing themselves into the air and making the sounds more hollow. Land cursed. He recognized the song, knowing the bride was already making her walk toward the wedding altar. Within minutes, the ceremony would be over.

Statz had been closely examining the door. He turned and said, "I think a bullet will shatter such iron, *herr Major*."

Land added his own light. This metal looked dull. He felt it: wrought iron. He knew that such iron was very brittle and couldn't withstand sudden shock. But dare they chance making noise? He considered that a moment, shrugged. There was no other option.

He fired off two 9mm rounds from his Luger, so swiftly,

their muffled *ffiiitt-ffiiitt* merged into a single snapping
rush as tiny flames blew back through the suppressor slits.
The muted sound was instantly swallowed by the compacted air of the escape tunnel. Not so with the bullet's
impacts. They literally made the door ring and blew a
chunk of metal the size of a man's fist into the vestry.

They froze, listening intensely as the throbbing boom
of the cathedral organ suddenly grew louder, the organist
reaching for his crescendo. Small metal utensils on the
other side of the door tinkled, responding to the increasing vibrations. Abruptly, the music stopped, left the entire
cathedral filled with echoes of the song that gradually
faded off.

Nothing happened. Nobody had heard the door blow.

Reaching through the hole, Statz was able to slide the
bar back far enough to shove the door open. The room
was dim. Shelves containing vestments and altar linens
and sacred vessels lined one wall. On the other were more
shelves of blessed wine in glass decanters shaped like balls.
The room carried the odor of candle wax and incense.

They crossed a hall that had black and white, dia-
mond-shaped tiles. It opened onto the north side of the
transept, the walls covered with sculptured insets por-
traying the phases of Judgment Day, and half columns
channeled in spiral chevrons and trellis patterns.

The nuptial altar sat squarely in the intersection of
transept and nave, up on a two-step platform like a
catafalque. The main altar, set squarely below the soaring
apse dome farther in, was out of sight to their left. Sear-
gent McKeogh, in full dress blouse, and his bride knelt
before the smaller altar. The officiating priest was in white
and gold vestments and a small gathering of relatives and
friends sat in the choir section, partially visible to the right.

There, standing quietly with their hats in hand beside

a tall statue of a bowing saint on this side of the transept, was Allied Supreme Commander General Eisenhower and his companion.

Land and the two commandos withdrew back up the hall. It was lined with full-sized statues in alcoves, the back portion of it in dim light. At the far end was the door through which the Americans had entered. Just inside the door was a small reception room furnished in baroque style with a thick blue rug covering the floor.

Using hand signals, Land ordered Statz and Halke to take up positions in the nearer alcoves. He himself stepped back into the reception room. He took out his medical kit, quickly drew up a shot of pentathol, squirted a few droplets, then eased back against the inside of the door frame to wait.

Six complete minutes passed.

Then the organ began to play again, a joyous song, something by Bach. Under its powerful reverberations came the small clicks of shoes on tile. And then the two American officers were there, walking with their heads down, murmuring, pulling on their heavy coats.

There was a quick, shadowy movement from an alcove. It caught their eyes and both officers turned. Eisenhower's companion was immediately set upon by Statz, who rammed a knife into his side. The officer crumpled silently to the floor.

Eisenhower's mouth opened to shout, his right hand clawing for the small officer's .45 automatic pistol he always carried in a clip-on holster at his hip. But Halke was on him before he could either draw the weapon or yell, the commando flinging one arm around his throat, the other cupping his mouth. The two men struggled, the general surprisingly strong. His cap fell off.

Land rushed up in front of Eisenhower. For a second, Ike's eyes glared at him, then they cut to the side, saw Land lifting his syringe, the needle aiming straight for the general's throat. It went in, a full shot.

Eisenhower continued to struggle, his eyes blinking rapidly. Then they went blank and rolled. Before he could fall, Land ducked slightly, pulled the limp body onto his shoulders in a fireman's carry, turned, and headed for the back door.

The two American sharpshooters' bullets struck Statz and Halke at the exact same instant. The back of the sergeant's head literally blew apart, the shooters using rounds with noses that had been cross-filed to expand on impact. Statz dropped.

Halke was hit between the shoulders. His monk's white habit instantly bloomed with a blood spot and he was hurled forward into the snow. He thrashed, bowing his back and trying to twist his arm to reach the entry point. Then he simply fell forward onto his face and quit moving.

Land had stopped dead at the crack of the high-powered rifles, the shock of the sudden attack jolting through his mind. One—two—three seconds went slamming past in snowfall silence. Then the sharp, vicious bedlam of a full firefight erupted. Muzzle bursts flashed from all around the cathedral parking lot and rounds went slamming into the rear of the Palais du Tau museum. Instantly, counterfire from the German commandos came back. Bullets snapped and popped through the falling snow.

Before his thoughts could actually coalesce into a decision for reaction, Land was already moving, Eisenhower's dead weight across his shoulders no longer even felt. He sprinted to the jeep, literally threw the general into the backseat, and dove behind the wheel. Flipping the ignition switch, he stomped down on the small starter. The engine immediately kicked into life.

Ramming in the gearshift, he hurled the jeep around in a tight turn and went barreling between the chapel and charter house, the vehicle's little four-cylinder M38 Willys-Overland screaming.

Crossing the Rue Guillaume de Mauchalt, he headed northwest toward Place Royale two blocks away, intending to work his way across the town to the train yard by using backstreets. From behind him, he could hear the firefight already beginning to dwindle in volume.

The sound of the gunfire came faintly but clearly into the boxcar, the snow giving it no direction. Duboudin and Steckel were quickly on their feet. Vaillant felt his heart leap inside his chest, felt the adrenaline explode into his blood.

Here they come!

The commando was already swinging up the rear door, the thing made of steel slats that rolled up over a barrel block, and then slid back under the overhead. It made a terrible racket moving, the sides of the train car magnifying the sound like thunder. The two men quickly shoved down the off-load ramps, Steckel locking them in while Duboudin leaped into the Porsche and started the engine. To the east, the raucous *wah-wah* of police horns began to sound from all over the city.

Duboudin was gunning the Porsche beside the boxcar when Land's jeep appeared, tearing past the empty, snow-trimmed Ferris wheel and circus rides of Le Cirque at the southern end of Square Colbert, then crossing the Bouvelard Louis Roederer and down into the train yard. He skidded to a stop beside the racer.

His face was grim, yet he moved with cool precision, hefting Eisenhower's body from the jeep with Steckel helping. They carried him around the Porsche, hand-cuffed his wrists together, and strapped him into the passenger seat, Eisenhower still totally limp.

Straightening, Land tossed the small medical kit to Duboudin, stared at him for a long moment, his gaze dark and deep and still. Then the edge of his mouth curved up slightly, his eyes picking it up, a soldier's smile, devilish and cool. "Don't fuck it up, Frenchman," he said.

Then he was sprinting back to the jeep, flicking his hand for Steckel to join him. They climbed into the little vehicle. He spun it around and they dashed away, back across the boulevard toward the city. A few seconds later, they disappeared into the snowfall.

Vaillant looked over at Eisenhower, that famous face. He couldn't believe it, the supreme commander of all the Allies in Europe right there beside him, himself taking him to Hitler. And, perhaps, to the end of the war and his salvation.

He drew in a deep breath, snugged up his gloves, geared, and stomped down on the accelerator. The Porsche leaped ahead, wheels skidding then gripping solidly. He felt the old, familiar, delicious pull of inertia suck him back into the seat as the screaming big-bore engine hurled the racer past the rusty train axles and discarded boilers. Rocketing over the tracks, he snapped the wheel hard over and shot up Rue Edouard Mignot, headed northeast for the forests of the Ardennes a hundred miles away.

Chapter Twenty

Adolph Hitler's vision of the great Ardennes offensive was vast, the crucial point of which was to completely reverse the tenuous position of the Third Reich in the war. As he had told his generals, "The world thinks Germany is already dead. Only its funeral is left. They are wrong. *This* corpse will rise up and hurl itself at the West."

Originally code-named *Wacht am Rein*, Watch on the Rhine, but now designated *Herbstnebel*, the offensive had been postponed several times to take advantage of the worst winter weather possible. This would hold down Allied counterattacks by air.

All along the Shnee Eifel, the assault units of the German offensive were in the last hours of waiting in their staging areas and assembly depots. Jump-off time had been set for 0300 hours on 16 December, about six hours away.

In the north, General Joseph Dietrich's Sixth Panzer Army would be striking the U.S. 99th and 2nd Divisions and the 14th Cavalry Group. The center, consisting of von Manteuffel's Fifth Army, would drive straight into sectors defended by the American 106th and 28th Divisions, the latter units badly wounded from the Heurtgen. Finally, to the south was the Wehrmacht's Seventh Army, which would take on the U.S. 4th Division and the 9th Armored.

One of the main spearheads of the attack was *Kampf-gruppe Peiper* or Task Force Peiper, commanded by the onetime aide-de-damp to Gestapo chief Himmler and the hero of the Don and Donets Rivers in Soviet Russia, Lieutenant Colonel Jochen Peiper, now attached to Dietrich's 6th Panzer Army.

By direct order from Hitler, Colonel Skorzeny would accompany his thrust. The *Kampfgruppe* made up a force of nearly twenty-thousand assault troops, tanks, and mobile artillery. They were to attack directly into the forward elements of General Robertston's 2nd Division along the Sure River on a line from the mountain town of Esch to Clervaux and St-Vith, in the middle and the southern shoulder of Dietrich's Sixth Panzer Army.

Now, amid the stillness of the mountain snowfall and the increasing fog, the troops of nine full German infantry divisions, nearly 140,000 soldiers, and three armored divisions nervously counted off the time before they would hurl themselves into the Ardennes Gap.

Swanson's message from Dunmore about the capture of General Eisenhower reached Parnell at 0923 hours, the G-2 captain's voice shaky through the radio. "Quarterback taken," he read solemnly. "Transport headed northeast. God help us."

Parnell glanced over at Smoker and Weesay, their eyes wide in the tiny glow from the receiver light. Fog now seeped in under the tarp. Over the last hour it had begun moving in, thickening, a sharp, bone-chilling fog.

"Holy *shit*," Laguna murmured.

Swanson went on, "I can't believe the bastards pulled it off. *Christ!* All right, listen up, Parnell. I expect we're in some deep shit here. And I think it's about to get deeper. I want you to coordinate with the units on your flanks so you can merge if necessary." He quickly relayed the call signs and frequencies for the line companies on either side of Blue One's position. He continued: "We're in full red condition, as of now. Watch both your approaches. And, by God, stop that fucking Porsche. Ticket Booth, out."

When Red informed Wyatt, there was a short pause, then Bird said, "So the sumbitch actually done it, huh?"

Parnell keyed. "Affirmative. Ticket Booth thinks this could be part of something bigger. I agree. Keep a tight eye on both slopes. You see anything you don't like, open on it."

Bird came right back: "Do we still attempt to stop that race car or go ahead an' take her out?"

Parnell put his head down to think. *Jesus Christ.* And in that precise moment, he knew, honed combat instincts coming up, the sense in the gut rarely wrong, that Vaillant Duboudin and his prized passenger were heading here, straight to him.

He keyed, "He's coming at us," he said quietly. "Soldier's gut, Wyatt. Don't let him pass. Go double-check your firing stakes while there's time."

"Right," Bird said and was gone. Parnell hadn't specifically answered his question.

Vaillant felt powerful, invincible. He was in total control of the Porsche and the road. That awareness of supremacy symbolized an even greater governance: here in his hands was the single man so crucial to the Allied war effort that without him its very direction and momentum would be altered.

He hurled the racer through the darkness like a fired

shell, eating up the miles. The snow wasn't deep enough or icy enough to create a skidding problem that his knobbed tires couldn't handle. His headlights threw a fan of orange light far ahead of him. Especially designed to operate in fog and falling snow, they had been mounted low on the front bumper and cast their illumination down low to the ground.

He stayed on secondary country roads mostly, crossing main thoroughfares only when necessary. Usually he passed through snow-covered landscapes filled with open fields and pastureland and small farm hamlets that were all dark as he sped through.

He hadn't seen any military patrols at first. Then, as he drew farther away from Reims, they began appearing: the lights of emergency vehicles and roadblocks in the snowfall. Twice he was spotted and police and military personnel took out after him. But he easily outdistanced them. He also noticed that they consistently refrained from firing at him. *But of course,* he realized. They couldn't chance injuring the general. Knowing that made Vaillant feel even more unassailable.

Now he was into territory he knew well. In addition, he spent many hours studying recent German aerial recon maps of the precise country he would be traversing. The photos had been magnified so much they actually showed things as tiny as footbridges, barn hedges, walls, even small road signs.

He had memorized the entire course so thoroughly he could have actually completed it as a timed run, using only reference points to establish his position and thereby know precisely what lay ahead of him. The mark of a champion racer, Duboudin had long ago learned, was to always be mentally far ahead of your vehicle.

He reached Vouziers and turned farther east. Within

forty minutes, he sped through Buzancy, crossed the Meuse River over a farmer's bridge outside Stenay, passed through Montmedy, and finally turned due north for Avioth on the Belgium border around 10:45.

That's when he ran into trouble.

He'd just entered a long, curving turn, trees along the side of the road, fences, when *Mon Dieu!* there they were, two cows in the road. One was slightly ahead of the other, both heads turned, the headlights making their cream-colored bodies look orange, their eyes gleaming like jack-o'-lanterns.

Reacting instinctively, Vaillant jacked the wheel and hit the brake. The Porsche immediately went into a skid, the rear snapping sideways to the right. He instantly threw the wheel in the opposite direction, steering into the skid. Out there in front of him, the cows had stopped. They were on the periphery of his headlights since he was now sideways to them, twin dark frames closing fast.

In his head, Duboudin ticked off the parts of seconds as they rushed past, holding off further reaction, waiting until he felt the car load up the suspension and take a new set. *There!* Now, he recovered, unwinding the steering wheel. The rear end slid back into place and the headlights swerved back to the road, the two cows illuminated in full glare again, less than twenty feet away.

He struck the first one with his right fender, saw the animal get violently turned around, the thick weight of its body dragging all along the side of the vehicle. The Porsche bounced and veered crazily. In the passenger seat, General Eisenhower's limp body snapped and jerked against his seat harness. Three seconds later, the racer plowed deeply into a snowbank and came to a complete stop.

Cursing, Duboudin climbed out. The racer's hood was covered with snow. Back down the road, the struck cow was down on the ground, bawling pitifully, the snow around it darkly stained. The other animal had run off, but was now cautiously coming back to sniff at its wounded companion.

Dragging snow off the vehicle, Vaillant checked the damage to the fender. It had been bent back onto the tire. He pulled and kicked at it, finally managed to get it out enough so it wouldn't rub against the wheel.

Returning to the driver's seat, he stopped abruptly, sniffed at the air. Raw gasoline! *"Ach, merde alors!"* he bellowed, realizing he had probably punctured at least one of his three tanks.

Furiously, he again dug away snow until he could slide under the carriage. He checked each tank by running his fingers across their bottoms and smelling his fingers for gasoline. He found that the left secondary tank had a hairline crack in it. The gas was seeping out slowly. He jury-rigged a seal with heavy winter axle grease, but knew it wasn't going to be adequate for the whole trip. He'd just have to find fuel somewhere.

By rocking the car, he finally got it free of the snowbank and back on his way, climbing up through the gears while his hands and body assessed the car's motion damage. It felt slightly heavy, he realized, a bit unstable and obviously pulling to the right. He relaxed. That wasn't too serious, he'd counteract such balance and alignment problems by simply overcorrecting when necessary.

He checked his watch. It was 11:12. He'd lost eighteen minutes.

* * *

Colonel Shelby "Gabby" Hayes had been an ex-oil-field roughneck with a barrel chest and a baleful stare. Now he was U.S. Provost Marshal for the District of Champagne with his headquarters at Reims.

At the moment, he was seated in the back of the U.S. ambulance that the German commandos had used to come to the city. It was shot full of holes and there was blood on the driver's seat. With him was his deputy PM, Major Gerald Mytinger, a slight, pale officer with a habit of occasionally pinching his lower lip. Seated between the two men was German Major Freidrick Land.

Land listened quietly to Mytinger as he read the charges against him. The German officer had been wounded in the left arm. An American medic had sprinkled sulfa powder and bound it, but now it was bleeding through the gauze. Mytinger droned on, his breath making bursts of frosty clouds. Now he was reading directly from the Fourth Hague Convention of 18 October, 1907, specifically Article 23 (f), which prohibited the wearing of an enemy's uniform to conduct warfare.

After leaving Duboudin, Land and Steckel had sped back to the cathedral in the jeep. They could no longer hear firing. The young commando sat in the passenger seat, one boot resting on the side. He looked over at the major. Land said nothing. Steckel turned back to his weapon, checked it and his spare ammunition.

For only a fleeting moment the thought of withdrawing had come to Land's mind, he and Steckel going to ground among his *Citoyenne* contacts, then working their way back to the French frontier. He immediately dismissed it. In all his years in combat, he had never abandoned men on the field of battle. He would not do it now.

Working his way across town, seeing Allied military vehicles and French police cars up long blocks, Land

crossed Rue Seres, swung left, then a sharp right onto
Rue Voltaire. This would bring him to the east side of the
Palais du Tau museum.

He stopped a block from it. The snow was coming down
heavily. There were lights all around the museum and
cathedral. He knew his men were dead or captured, knew
it would be utterly hopeless to proceed, to rush right into
a holocaust. But did it really matter? he wondered. From
that moment when he first donned a German soldier's
uniform so long ago, he'd always known this specific moment would come. Sometime. Somewhere. As with any
warrior, death was always preordained. So, why not here?

He glanced at Steckel. "You are free to leave, Corporal. If you so desire."

Steckel grinned back at him. "I believe I'll stay, *herr
Major.*"

Land nodded. He pulled off his monk's habit, cast it
aside. Swinging up his MP-38, he checked its load. Then
he geared and they roared ahead.

The first fusillade killed Steckel immediately, two
rounds striking his head, slamming it back as if it had
suddenly been caught by a taut wire. Land leaned out
the side of the jeep and opened up with his machine pistol, firing left-handed at muzzle bursts, the spent
cartridges flipping against his shoulder, his face, hotly.

The windshield blew out. He heard the bullets go by
him like angry wasps, tearing the back of the jeep's canvas cover to shreds. A bullet hit him in the left arm,
between elbow and shoulder. The MP-38 went somer-
saulting out of his hand.

Knocked backward, he lost the wheel and the jeep
swerved sharply to the right. He tried to recover but the
little vehicle fishtailed wildly across the road, jumped a
stretch of sidewalk, and smashed into the corner of a

building. It flipped over, pinning him beneath it. Before he could bring his Luger into action, hands were roughly dragging him out, American curses filling the night. . . .

Now Mytinger read the provost marshal's statement: "Acting as legal representative for the military and civilian authorities duly established within this district, and following the decrees recognized to be in effect under the Articles for Conducting Civilized Warfare codified by International Agreement at the Hague Convention; and, furthermore, abiding by the rules governing Class-C Trial, Sentencing and Execution procedure as prescribed by Section 31(s) of the established Military Justice Protocol, I hereby order that you be immediately executed at a place designated by the commanding military officer of this provost district."

Mytinger stopped and Hayes immediately barked, "Draw up an execution squad, Major."

"Where will it take place, sir?"

"Right here, beside this vehicle."

"Yes, sir." Mytinger moved to the rear of the ambulance and jumped to the ground.

Hayes and Land held each other's eyes. Finally, the colonel said, "You're a cool son of a bitch, ain't you?"

"What purpose would be served to be otherwise?" Land said pleasantly.

"You figure you done it, don't you?"

"Yes."

"Well, you *ain't*," Hayes hissed. "We'll stop that goddamned Frenchie. You can make book on that, buddy boy."

"I sincerely hope you are wrong, Colonel."

"Well, you can stick your hope up your fucking Kraut ass, shit-face."

Land smiled.

They stood him up against the ambulance. The firing squad was made up of MPs, firing M1-Garand rifles. They stood in a somber line, seven soldiers. A lieutenant was in charge. He approached Land. "Is there anything you wish to say?" he asked. His voice quaked slightly.

"No," Land said.

"A cigarette?"

"No. Thank you."

He looked up at the snow falling. It was so utterly silent and soft. He inhaled deeply, relishing the sharp sting of the cold in his lungs. The slam of the Garands' bolts made a discordant, metallic cracking in the silence. Land looked at the soldiers. They were merely shadows standing motionless against the whiteness of the snow. The voice of the lieutenant came then, abrupt, throaty. The firing squad's rifles came up snappily, their muzzles all at the same level.

Land braced himself, felt his muscles going tight, tighter, felt his jaw muscles gripping, teeth on teeth. "*Fire!*" There was a voluminous explosion, separate bursts merged together. He felt the bullets go into his body with violent impacts and he was slammed against the ambulance. There was a moment of unbelievable pain, so excruciating it seemed too powerful for his senses to register its hugeness. Then he was crumbling downward, his legs going useless, his body enveloped in the pain, dropping, dropping. But there was no bottom.

The fog was so thick Cowboy could hardly see Wyatt less than ten feet ahead of him. They were triple-checking their firing stakes, walking the road as it curved slightly up the slope from their position. Ordinarily, they'd register fire onto real markers, a peculiar-shaped stone or a stump, which were always referred to as firing stakes. Then they'd lay in the first bazooka round and key off its explosion for the rest, saturate the target.

But now that the fog was obliterating even a hazy visual, they'd have to depend on *estimated* angles and paced-off distances. Goddamned blind ranging, with a fast-moving vehicle between them and the hit zone.

From their position, they'd be firing over the vehicle and slightly to the right of it in order to take out the road ahead, yet far enough out to give Duboudin time enough to stop before he hit the explosion crater. All in all, Fountain decided, it was going to be a piss-poor shoot.

He called out to Wyatt, "I still think we shoulda laid in charges." The sudden sound of his voice seemed abruptly intrusive in the forest silence.

Bird shook his head. "We might could blow ole Ike to hell and gone, too."

"Shit, we might still."

Bird halted and began walking back and forth across the road. It was frozen, rock-hard ruts that made a harsh sound beneath their boots. He paused and looked toward the east, everything seamlessly white around them. Now and then there was the soft, stealthy *plop* of snow falling from branches. Cowboy thought they sounded like dead birds hitting swamp water.

Up close now, he could see Bird's face, stolid as usual, yet with a darkness in the eyes. "What?" he asked.

"Ya'all hear it?" Wyatt said quietly.

"I don't hear nothin'."

"Exactly. It's *too* goddamned quiet." He turned, looked at Cowboy. "We about to get our nuts busted, partner. Them Krauts is up beyond that ridge east of us and flat fixin' to come down here pretty damn quick."

"Shit all, I know that. That's another reason we shoulda laid charges, get this shit over with fast."

Again Wyatt shook his head. "Division'll need this goddamned road. Along with every trail and cow path to reposition forward units."

Fountain sighed, blew out a stream of vapor. "So, when ya'll figure the sausage-eaters'll come?"

"Before daylight," Bird answered. Without another word, he turned and started back down the road.

Fountain followed, thinking, *Jesus Christ, it's too goddamned cold to fight a war here.*

"*Idiotsehan!*" Skorzeny shouted, furiously tore off his earphones, and threw them and the radio mike back at the radioman. "Request verification of that message. Immediately!"

He sat back into his seat, almost trembling with rage. Seated beside him was Lieutenant Colonel Peiper, commanding the *Kamfgruppe*. They were in a Mercedes Benz M-136 command vehicle parked near a country road junction on the western side of the Our River.

The snow was still coming down heavily, deepening the cover of the unseen fields around them, which were usually planted in winter wheat but were now fallow. This stretch of comparative flatness went as far as the Sure River. There, the ground rose into low forested mountains that continued on to the small towns of Esch and Wiltz and what would be the first primary target of *Kampfgruppe Peiper*, Bastogne.

"What is it, Colonel?" Peiper asked. He was a short man yet carried himself with a swaggering arrogance. Well liked by Hitler for his audacity on the battlefield and his brutality in crushing partisan cells, he was referred to by his own soldiers as "Blow Torch Jochen" since he had often tortured captured resistance fighters with such a tool.

"Someone forgot to send trucks to take my men to their airfield," Skorzeny growled venomously.

"Ah?"

"They *forgot! Mein Gott,* how can there be such stupidity?"

"Is it too late to recover?"

"Of *course* it's too late. They should have been in the *air* by now."

He was speaking of the twelve-hundred-man contingent from his Brigade 150, which was assigned the preoffensive jump onto the three key bridges of the Meuse in an operation code-named *Hohes Venn* or Auk. Now he had to scrap that extremely important mission. He felt betrayed, by his own men. Worse, the *Führer* would sure as hell feel betrayed, by *him.*

"It does not matter, Colonel," Peiper said nonchalantly. "We'll take the Meuse so quickly the Americans will have no chance to destroy those crossings."

Skorzeny's eyes went gelid. "It does matter, *Oberstleutnant,*" he hissed.

Peiper shrugged as if unaware or disregardful of the colonel's tone.

For a moment, Skorzeny wanted to strike the little bastard. He'd always had a thorough dislike for this particular man, considering him an insolent phony whose daring in combat was too often reckless and done merely for show. Unfortunately, Hitler liked him and that was always that.

Invisibly spread out around the command vehicle were the *Kampfgruppe's* tanks and mobile units: King Tigers and Panthers in their yellow-and-green camouflage, along with half-tracks and 105mm and 15cm mobile assault howitzers. For the last half hour, the two officers could hear the muffled crunch of boots moving between the silent vehicles, infantry units passing through the armor to take up assault positions farther ahead.

The radio operator turned in the forward seat. "I've checked the message, *herr Oberst,*" he said. "It has been verified by Major Heydte." Major Friedrich von der Haydte was a veteran paratrooper who now commanded the Auk jumpers. "Do you have a return message, sir?"

"Yes. Shoot the son of a bitch who forgot to bring us the trucks."

"Yes, sir," the operator said, turned away.

"*Schisse!*" Skorzeny said. He looked at his watch. It was one minute after 1:00 in the morning, 16 December.

The Porsche just died, without warning, no stutter, no choking, the fuel injectors pressure keeping it going till the very last drop of gasoline. Vaillant coasted to a stop. A low stone wall paralleled the road, capped with snow like one continuous ice-cream cone.

He climbed out of the racer and scanned the countryside, swinging in a complete circle, looking for lights. He knew his exact position: two miles north of Martelange, an agricultural railhead that lay on the Sure River. Twenty-one minutes before, he'd crossed the main highway between Luxembourg and Brussels. There had been a lot of traffic on it, but he'd managed to slip across at the junction of N-825.

He spotted a single light about a quarter mile away. The snowfall had eased off somewhat, but there was still enough to make the light dance and shiver. He could smell cattle, the distinctive rust odor from the wire used in vineyards, the sour stench of a wine-crushing yard somewhere nearby.

He returned to the car for a flashlight. Eisenhower grunted, shifted in his seat. His head came up and fell back onto the rear of the seat. He was coming out of the pentathol. Duboudin put the light onto his face. The supreme commander's eyes were half-lidded, his pupils narrowed down tightly. He tried to say something but it was only a mumble. He drooled. Vaillant drew up another shot and gave it to him in the top of his left hand. Ike went back to sleep.

It took him nearly twenty minutes to cross a field, stumbling over ruts hidden beneath the snow. The time was now 1:27. The light came from a pale-colored farmhouse, almost invisible against the backdrop of white. Two mongrel dogs rushed at him suddenly. He hollered at them and they scurried off into the darkness, still barking.

A second light came on in the farmhouse, then a door opened, silhouetting a man. He had a cane. Parked beside the house was an old roofless truck "Who is out there?" the man called in Belgian French.

"A French officer," Vaillant shouted back. He walked directly to the house and up onto the porch. The house was made of stone and timbers.

The owner stepped aside slightly to let the inside light show the intruder. He wore a nightcap and long gown. He studied Duboudin's uniform. "Has there been an accident?"

"No, I have merely run out of fuel. Do you have gasoline?"

"Yes, of course. . . . You will pay?"

"Certainly."

"One moment, I must dress," the farmer said and

closed the door. The dogs came and sniffed along the edge of the porch and one urinated on the step.

The man sold him two dekaliters, about five and a half gallons, which he siphoned from his truck, drawing it into a spouted can and using a kerosene lantern for light. Then he drove Vaillant back to the Porsche. He tried to engage the French officer in conversation, but Vaillant merely shook his head.

When the man saw the racer, it astounded him. While Duboudin put the gas into his main tank, the farmer walked around and around the vehicle. Then he leaned down and looked inside, holding up his lantern. He saw Eisenhower, drew back, looked again, and then swung toward Duboudin. "*Sacre Mere!*" he gasped. "This is the American general of generals!"

Vaillant shot him, twice, his silenced Walther making harsh spitting sounds in the night. The man hugged his chest, seemed to be choking, then fell down. Duboudin left him lying in the road, his old truck idling noisily.

He had to prime the Porsche's injectors to get the engine started again. At first it ran rough, missing. Vaillant cursed, gunning it. Gradually the engine began to smooth out, yet he could still detect a slight hesitation in its sound. The farmer's gasoline was obviously contaminated, probably with water.

Finally, he geared and roared away. His exhaust left a thick cloud of vapor drifting over the farmer's rapidly stiffening body, the stuff slowly dissipating until it was gone.

The Germans began jamming American radios. It caught Parnell in the middle of an update message from Captain Swanson, a sudden burst of earsplitting sound blowing through the half-track's radio speaker, a high-pitched screeching that warbled, faded, and then rushed in again.

Parnell could faintly hear the G-2 officer's voice down under the sound but not clear enough to understand what he said. He turned down the volume, waited. Each time he tuned it back up, the screeching was still there. He began swinging channels, finally caught one that was open.

"Ticket Booth," he called, "this is Blue One transmitting on 137.7. Can you read, over?" Again and again he tried, nothing coming back except bits and pieces of distant transmissions. Then the jam hit that frequency, too, blew it out of the air.

This is bad, he thought. He knew the Germans always jammed enemy radios just before an attack. They also sometimes did it randomly. But now they were blocking nearly *all* frequencies, something they didn't do when they were just harassing. No, this meant an attack was definitely coming very soon.

He raised Bird easily on the walkie-talkie. As a rule, the Krauts didn't bother jamming these low, short-ranged frequencies. He told him about the jamming. The sergeant grunted, said, "That about puts shit in the well, don' it?"

"Exactly. When it starts, you get your asses up here. On a dime. If that Frenchie fuck hasn't shown by then, we'll go back down this road till we find him."

"Will do," Bird said.

Red clicked off, turned to Weesay scrunched down beside him. "You guys go recheck our fire lines."

"Right, Lieutenant," Laguna said. He and Smoker slipped from under the tarp and disappeared into the snowfall.

Parnell pulled out the operational map Swanson had

given him and opened it across his knees. Using a flash-light, he followed the probable route Duboudin might take, from Reims to where he now was. Before the Kraut jam, Swanson had managed to tell him the Porsche had been spotted at two roadblocks, one at Monthois, the second at Stenay. The captain gave the times of the sightings. In both cases, the Frenchman had simply outrun his pursuers.

By using the distance and time data, Red quickly ex-trapolated Duboudin's possible arrival time at Esch. The figures indicated he should have been here already. He reworked them, came up with the same answer. Okay, he thought, this had him on a straight line, no delays, no detours. Impossible. So how could you foresee such things? He went back over the map, meticulously tracing a route, checking off each area that might present a problem for Duboudin. He came up with a new TO: somewhere between 0240 to 0255 hours. The whole thing was a guess, a shot in the dark. But then, what the hell, it *felt* right.

He checked his watch: 1:48.

0200 hours

Along the entire one-hundred-mile-long German front, from Julich on the Roer River and Düren in the north, from Stadtkyll and Prum to Lutzkampen and Das-burg in the middle, and finally to Vianden/Diekirch in the south, Operation *Herbstnebel* entered its final moments before jump-off.

Radios crackled throughout assault companies, ar-mored battalions, and artillery regiments of the 1st SS-Panzer Corps and Division, the 12th Volksgrenadier and SS-Panzer Divisions, the 277th Volksgrenadier and 3rd Fallshirmjager Divisions with last-minute orders. Also deeper south at the forward CPs of 66th Army Corps, the 18th and 62nd Volksgrenadier Divisions, the 116th Panzer Division, the *Kampfgruppe Peiper*, and the Führer Begleit Brigade.

The massed German troops now did their final weapon checks. The engines of tanks, armored cars, half-tracks, mobile field guns started warming up in the falling snow and fog as runners dashed between units delivering last-minute assault orders. Senior commanders held their final prestrike briefings with staff and junior field officers, while platoon leaders issued their squad men specific route allotments, target schedules, and barrage sequences.

Yet, despite all this hectic activity, the deep gorges and valleys of the Schnee Eifel Mountains, aided by the dense snowfall and fog, hid and muffled the sounds of these two armies in their last stages of preattack. But here and there along the Allied line, scattered American patrols were only now beginning to detect the presence of something massive just over the next ridgelines.

Vaillant had just completed his final detour and crossed the Luxembourg border at the ferry landing of Alzey and was steadily climbing now into lowland forest. Holding to the Sure River road, he made good time, his fog lights giving astounding visibility for at least thirty yards ahead of him.

He knew he was within five or six miles of Esch and had chosen to remain on the river road since it skirted the town. Just beyond lay the higher ridges and hairpin turns of the Ettlebruck Forest, a branch of the Ardennes that lay between the Sure and Our Rivers. He grinned to himself. It was only a matter of minutes before he reached his target sanctuary, the ruins of Abbaye St. Mathieu.

The American rocket round came out of the fog like a streaking meteor, from off his right, slamming past to impact to the left of the road in a sudden orange-red flash. The sound of its back-blow came with it, Duboudin hearing it clear and violent over the roar of the Porsche's engine. For a split second, he was startled into confusion. He'd been riding speed so easily and then *wham!* this out of nowhere.

He quickly recovered, flew past the explosion site, the acrylic stink of explosives coming in through his vents. Another rocket flashed by. This one struck the road slightly off center. Even before its burst light disappeared, he was reacting, slinging the racer to the right, feeling it drift slightly. Dark smoke and debris flared, spattered his vehicle, and then he was past the second blast hole, swinging back to the road again, running.

He went immediately into a curve to the left. The road ahead raced toward him in an orange haze, the snow smooth and cloud-soft-looking, his tires making their peculiar mushy sizzling sound faint below the thunder of the engine.

Another curve and he was gone back into the night and the fog.

"Blue One— is Cobra Four-Zero— back."

The walkie-talkie's signal was very weak, filled with static and fading in and out, the transmission from somewhere on the edge of the little SCR-300's four-mile range. Parnell, outside the half-track, leaned under the tarp, picked it up, and keyed: "Cobra One-Zero, this is Blue One. Go ahead."

"Watch vehicle—one-two our position. Map refer— one. Headed yo—Two tennis balls—negative, over."

"Cobra, this is Blue One, say again."

"—vehicle spotte—zero-two-one-two. Headed your sector. My MR is three-three-one. Two tennis—negative hit. Over."

"Roger that," Red called back. *I knew it!* "Stand by, Cobra." He hurriedly opened his map to check precisely where position three-three-one was. There, less than five miles down this road. He keyed: "What was estimated speed?"

"—burning road for these con—Estimated five-zero miles an hour."

"Is there anything else between us?"

"Negative."

"Can you relay CP?"

"Negative."

"Watch yourself. East wind full up watch here."

"Roger that, Blue—bra Four-Zer—" Cobra was gone.

Parnell raised Bird, Wyatt's signal coming back with so much power he had to turn down the volume, something acoustically boosting it. He keyed, "The Frenchie's coming up. Approximate five minutes. If you stop, do not approach until we come down."

"Right."

"If he passes, converge on me immediately."

"Got—" Bird's signal suddenly exploded with a roaring burst of static that immediately devolved into a steady, shrill screech.

"God-*damn* it," Parnell roared. The Krauts had just dropped their jamming signals down into the walkie-talkie's forty- to forty-eight-megacycle range, blowing communications down to platoon level.

He swung around to Smoker and Laguna, who had been listening. "Set up in your fire positions." For a moment, he considered ordering his men to fire directly at the car if Duboudin got by Wyatt. *No, can't do that. Stop him, just stop him.* "Tear that fucking road up."

"Right, Lieutenant," Wineberg said. He and Weesay darted away.

Shit!

Bird shoved the three-and-a-half-pound projectile into the rear of the bazooka, Fountain down on one knee already dead-sighting his target. The round clicked into place, activating the electrical charge circuit.

He tapped Cowboy on the shoulder, picked up his M1-Garand rifle, and quickly moved several yards to his right. Kneeling, he shoved his left arm through the rifle sling and snugged up, his movements practiced and smooth. He took two M3-A rifle grenades from his belt pouch, six-inch-long cylinders, and attached one to a fitting below the muzzle of the rifle. He held the other between his little and ring fingers for a fast reload.

They waited. The cold was forgotten. The gentle touch of snowflakes on their faces went unnoticed. The silence gave the impression that they were on a high ridge where there was no wind, only the feel of distance that stretched out into the whiteness forever.

The sound came so faintly it might have been imagined. It was like the last whirring of a winding-down toy. Then it rose, coming through the snow clearly, going higher, only to fade off once more. When it returned again, it was closer, the powerful, full-throated scream of a high-performance engine, dropping, then throttling up again as it came flying up the slope, traversing cutbacks.

Cowboy glanced at Wyatt. "That sumbitch is flat haulin' ass, ain't he?"

Bird turned slightly, spat, came back. "Yeah, the prick's eatin' up too much road too fast. We can't delay any. Fire as soon as he passes us."

"You got it."

The racer's headlights made a fume of orange light in the fog, the roar of the engine now so close it bounced and echoed through the corridors of unseen trees. The fume of light became two distinct ovals of orange that illuminated the edges of the road, tree branches, trunks, everything tinted with orange as if it was being coated by the first coppery rays of a still unrisen sun.

The Porsche hurtled past, the orange light fume heralding its way, its velocity sucking fog after it, which coiled, forming spirals that danced across the momentarily cleared space where the racer's exhaust had burned off the fog.

Cowboy's bazooka blew a huge candle flame of fire out the back of the weapon as it fired off with a hissing rush. The projectile slammed through the snowfall, made the frigid air sunder with a loud *crack*. Merging with it came the hard *boom* of the M1's grenade launcher as Wyatt fired.

The rocket impacted out there in the darkness, a sharp flash and then the hollower burst of the grenade, both detonations riffling off through the forest. Bird already had the second grenade fitted. He fired. This time, the explosion was deep in the echoes of the others, all of them fading.

Both men leaned forward, their heads tilted, listening.

They heard the Porsche's engine suddenly drop away, then come right back up again into full throttle. Below the engine was a heavy thud, as if something large had struck the road. The engine screamed for a moment, then its volume dropped abruptly back down into driving-speed range as the vehicle pulled away, its sound folding back into the night.

"*Fuck!*" Cowboy cried. "The sumbitch is still *movin'.*"

The Porsche was there so quickly, roaring, first a vague orange brightness in the fog, and then it blew straight out of it, the lights twin spots coming directly at the half-track. They shifted slightly and a second later the racer went flashing past, the dark curve of roof and fender-line gleaming orange for a split second.

"Fire! Fire!" Parnell bellowed. He lowered his cheek to the stock of the M1, his finger already squeezing off. Smoker's bazooka went out with a slamming rush to his left, then his and Weesay's Garands fired at the same instant. The rifle stock bucked hard against Red's shoulder.

The string of three explosions came nearly at once. Flashes, their reverberations bounding away. There was a slight pause, his ears ringing loud enough to hide other sounds. Then there was a soft *whooshing* burst and another flash out there, misty and diffused through the falling snow. It lingered, its light fractured, dancing. Flames!

"Jesus Christ!" Red shouted. *They'd just hit the car.* He was up and lunging back toward the half-track. "Let's go, let's go."

He dove into the driver's seat, flipped the ignition switch, and hit the starter. The engine turned over sluggishly. He heard Wineberg and Laguna come vaulting over the side of the vehicle. There was another sound then. *What?* It was the Porsche's engine, running rough but still going. A wave of relief swept through him.

He hit the starter again. The engine again cranked over slowly, the small starter motor straining. "Come *on*, you son of a bitch," he growled through clenched teeth. It finally caught, sputtered, then came up into full life. He geared and started to swing around, flicking on the blue headlights.

Wyatt and Cowboy, loaded with gear, suddenly appeared in the glow, running up the road. They passed through the light. He heard their weapons clatter on the floor of the half-track, their boots on steel, and Bird yelling, "Go, go."

He completed the hard swing to the right and put on throttle, the vehicle's tracks clanking metallically and incongruously in the forest stillness as he headed up the road.

Duboudin had acted on pure instinct when the third rocket struck the road ahead of him, the Porsche just going into a gradual curve. It hit dead center, orange-tinted snow and road debris erupting, looking like a colored film of a lava tube blowout. His mind registered it, but his hands were already moving to counter the onrushing situation.

He flung the wheel hard to the right. The racer instantly darted that way. Vaillant felt the rear end begin to slide sideways. Correcting smoothly, he shot past the rocket crater and regained the road's center, just as he had done with the earlier rocket round. Debris slammed into the vehicle, sounding like rocks hurled into an empty barrel. Then he was beyond the outthrow.

He whooped and triumphantly, arrogantly shouted, *"Quand les poules auront des dents, cochon Americaine!"*

The two rifle fragmentation grenades exploded side by side thirty feet from him, so close he was already unable to see the craters in the road, only the quick bursts like photographers' flashbulbs. They were too near to avoid.

Again instinct took over. Vaillant's foot rammed down on the brake, all the way. The car instantly locked up, began to swing around. He and Eisenhower were shoved violently against their harnesses as the sudden braking caused a massive shift of the car's weight onto its front wheels. He continued to hold on full brake until his instincts, somehow estimating the distance to the burst craters, told him *Now*.

His foot leaped from the brake pedal to the accelerator and he jammed it to the floor. The engine screamed up. This sudden counter to the braking force immediately shifted the car's weight back onto its rear wheels. The whole front actually lifted off the ground just ahead of the first crater. The Porsche literally jumped the hole, the rear portion following the arc of its forward trajectory. Debris and rocks crashed into the bottom with a loud clattering.

The second crater loomed. *Too late, too late.* He tried to handle this one by flinging the wheel hard to the right again so the car's whipping momentum might slide it straight across the top of the hole. There was a shuddering jolt. The car snapped back hard, kept going, out of control. It wirled around in two rapid 180s before Duboudin was able to regain control and get the front once again pointing straight up the road.

He hit the accelerator and the car leaped forward. He began climbing again, everything feeling solid, tight. He started to grin. There was a peculiar rushing sound, like air blown through a narrow tunnel. A blue flash came from under the car. It quickly erupted into the color of flame. He jerked his head around. *Merde!* The rear of the Porsche was on fire. One of his tanks had been ruptured, the escaping fuel ignited by a hot fragment.

He slowed. The fire was quickly growing more intense, tongues of flame flickering and snapping along the edge of the hood. He stopped, heard the fire seethe and hiss below him. Heat was fuming up through the floorboards, quickly getting unbearable.

Still, he paused, his gloved fingers on the door handle. A sudden, overwhelming sense of exhaustion, of defeat, took him. He looked at his watch. The crystal reflected the fire, formed a small, shimmering yellow circle on his wrist. It read 2:19.

So goddamned close.

Anger rushed through him then, hurled away the tiredness, the sense of defeat. *Not yet, you bastards.* Resettling back into his seat, he engaged the clutch and stomped down on the accelerator. The engine roared up and tire knobs skidded for a moment, then gripped snow, hurling it sideways as the Porsche leaped forward and he went barreling up the slope, trailing flames, headed straight for the Abbaye St. Mathieu now only a quarter mile away.

0220 hours

They were forced to go slowly, past their own blast craters with Wineberg sitting up there on the hood of the half-track yelling back directions to Parnell. They were following the darkened-snow track left by the burning Porsche. The fog had thickened so much it was now nearly impossible to see anything beyond a couple of feet. They couldn't even hear the high-pitched rap of the racer's engine over their own motor and the clatter and rattle of the M-2's treads.

On they went, taking curves like a crippled animal, inching along. The smell of the burning racer had saturated the fog and now it stank of burned grease and roasting metal. Suddenly Smoker pounded on the hood, shouting, "Hold it, Lieutenant. Flames ahead."

Red eased off the throttle and the half-track drifted to a complete stop, the engine idling, everybody thrust forward, squinting out into the fog. There was a yellow glow up ahead, like the sheen of candlelight seen through a frosted window. They caught the crackle and snap of fire.

Red tapped Bird's shoulder. "You and Cowboy move up on the left," he said quietly. "Weesay and Smoker on the right. Set up a perimeter. I'll go straight in. But, Christ, watch out for Ike."

The sharp clicks of Thompson bolts sounded and the men jumped from the half-track. Their boots crunched in the snow as they moved off. Parnell checked his .45 pistol, picked up his Thompson, and slid from the driver's seat. He waited a few moments for the others to get into position, then he headed straight for the glow in the fog.

He approached hunched over, darting and going to one knee to listen. The air felt achingly cold after the engine warmth of the M-2. It made his finger bones ache. Ahead, the flames created a high dome of yellow that grew, its warmth beginning to filter through the fog, increasing.

He saw the Porsche. It was totally engulfed in flames and burning fiercely. Moving quickly, he went to his belly, crawled into the full light from the fire. The heat grew intense as he went forward, at first feeling good in the cold, then moving beyond comfort.

He got to within twelve feet of the racer, shielding his face. He could see the tops of the seats, the leather and harnesses already burned away, only the charred metal backs left. The camo paint had all burned off and billows of black smoke poured from the Porsche windows and out of the hood seams. It smelled like burning linoleum. He raised himself up enough so he could see the entire interior.

There were no bodies.

Wyatt materialized out of the fog, his Thompson's butt in the crook of his arm. He knelt beside him. "Lieutenant, there's tracks up yonder along the road," he said. "Looks like two men, one draggin' the other. The Frenchie's makin' for them old monastery ruins."

He led Red around the fire to show him the tracks. The snow had been badly disturbed close to the wreck, the occupants crawling out. Then a single track led off up the road, the print of a body, two legs spread, creating twin lines in the snow that nearly obliterated the forward set of footprints.

Parnell squatted and played his flashlight on the tracks, the light making delicate shadows. "Look at that," he said, pointed to one clear boot print. "The walker's wearing French boots. That means the other one's Eisenhower." He shook his head. "Ike must be unconscious. At least he isn't dead. Duboudin wouldn't be dragging a dead body."

He whistled, two short bursts. In a moment, the others appeared out of the flame-colored fog, coming to the sound. Parnell quickly positioned them into a tight night patrol formation, Wyatt on point with a flashlight, the others spread out behind him but staying in sight of his light.

"If the son of a bitch opens on you, he'll be firing blind" Parnell said. "Hit ground and try to pinpoint his muzzle flashes. Then we converge on him. But, Christ, don't fire unless you've got an absolutely clear shot." Everybody nodded, the men in a circle, snow on their shoulders and Jeep caps. "All right, let's go."

Vaillant Duboudin struggled through the snow, driven by wild panic. He knew the American soldiers would be coming soon, trailing him in the snow. He had lost all sense of direction, yet he managed to remain on the road by turning back to it each time his boots hit the berm along the side.

Dragging Eisenhower's deadweight had rapidly sucked energy and wind from him. He gasped in the sharp, icy air, his heart pounded, the sweat on his face froze. He squinted into the fog, afraid to use his flashlight.

Mon Dieu, how far is it?

He had visited the ruins of the Abbaye St. Mathieu as a boy. Built in the twelfth century on the site of a Roman fort constructed to guard against wild Germanic incursions from the Schnee Eiffel, it had been a hospice for over six hundred years but was then abandoned just before Napoleon's time.

Duboudin had to stop to rest. In frustration, he turned and kicked Eisenhower in the shoulder. The general didn't move. "*Salope!*" he hissed. He spat on him. He should leave the *batard* to freeze. Or shoot him right through the head, end it all here. But gradually he calmed himself. He couldn't do that. This single man was now his only salvation.

He grabbed the general's collar and started off again. After several minutes, a ruined wall suddenly loomed out of the fog, so quickly he ran into it, stumbled, and fell. He reached out and explored it with his hand: rough stone, brush and grass growing from crevices.

He stood up. Dragging Eisenhower with one hand, he felt his way to his left until he came to a doorway. He entered and immediately stumbled over fallen rocks, nearly fell down again. Recovering, he stood there, trying to decide whether to use his light.

He finally did, found himself in a small stone room, the space godlessly cold, holding faint traces of fog that made the light beam look solid. Two doorways were cut in the wall, their sills quite low. He put the light through one. A corridor with an arched ceiling led downward. The slanted floor had bevels chiseled into it to prevent slipping.

He rested again. The stone silence suddenly seemed eerie, himself in deep isolation. To distract his mind, he scanned the light about the room. There were drifts of broken stone and pottery shards and damp dirt along the bottoms, rusty food cans and condom rings. Higher up, Roman words and strange runes had been chiseled into the stone. A single line of English graffiti was scribbled near the door. It said: *Had good French pussy here—Corporal Billy Way, 11-24-44.*

He started forward again, down the inclined corridor. The heavy sound of his panting and the drag of Eisenhower's boots along the floor bounced off the walls. The air smelled of decay like graveyard soil.

He came to a series of rooms, tiny cells lining both sides of the corridor. Inside several were animal skeletons, gray-white rib cages like huge, grotesque Victorian combs. Beyond the cells he reached a dead end. When he turned to step back over Eisenhower, he noticed the general was awake.

"Ah, so you are awake at last, Monsieur General," Duboudin said contemptuously. "Good. Get on your feet." He reached down and roughly pulled the general up, Ike silently staring at him as he came, that famous forehead gleaming in the flashlight's beam, his eyes lit with a cold hostility beneath their sleepy appearance.

They returned up the corridor, left the ruins of this particular structure, and crossed what probably had been a fountain area. They came to a second building and went inside. This one had no roof. Snow filled with small animal tracks covered the stone floor. Winter-dead weeds and grass, their blades a dried-out yellow, protruded from cracks in the remnants of the walls. The back of the building had fallen in, creating a scrabble field of shattered rock and brickstone.

Something suddenly leaped from the right and went bounding through the side glow of the flashlight. Vaillant swung the beam to it, his heart leaping, his hand frantically clawing for his holstered Walther PP pistol. He caught a fleeting glimpse of pale brown hindquarters as a large buck deer leaped through the hole in one wall. In a second, it had disappeared into the snowfall.

The shock had put a tremble into his hands. He inhaled, trying to settle himself. Ahead of him, Eisenhower turned, glared back at him. Vaillant viciously slapped him across the face with the back of his hand. "Do not *look* at me, *souteneur Americaine*," he growled throatily in French. "*Move.* Or I will kill you where you stand."

They proceeded slowly, the light off, the general stumbling, feeling his way with his boots. They came to a high wall and then the edge of forest. Vaillant grabbed the back of Ike's jacket, stopped him. He stood a moment, his thoughts hurtling through his mind. Should he hide in the ruins or go back into forest?

He lifted his arm, flicked the light on for a second so he could see his watch. It was 2:40. He chose the woods. The ruins would only have trapped him. He pushed Eisenhower ahead, hissing, "Into the trees. Quickly, quickly."

It was astounding how Wyatt Bird could always sense his immediate surroundings, even in pitch-dark night or in fog, like Wineberg, possessing an added sense that registered his position in space. For the past minute, he'd been following Duboudin's track without his flashlight, in white darkness, going on that extra *feel.*

Now he stopped, aware that something big was right in front of him. He backtracked until he was beside Parnell. "Structures ahead, Lieutenant," he informed him quietly.

"Hold up," Red ordered. The men held position. "Ruins ahead. Cowboy, Smoker, spread into deeper flank and set up security. Weesay, you, Wyatt, and me'll go straight in."

Within a minute, they reached part of a wall, slowly followed it to the right, where it broke off into tumble rock, then back to the left. After a few yards, Bird stopped abruptly. Parnell nearly bumped into him. Wyatt was running his hands along the wall. After a moment, he knelt, pulled off a glove, and felt the snow cover with his exposed fingers. Rising, he moved in a half circle and again knelt to touch the snow.

He came back. "Doorway, Lieutenant," he said softly. "Tracks go in."

"Regular insertion procedure," Parnell said. He stepped around Wyatt and ducked through the entrance, took two steps, and dropped to one knee. Bird and Weesay came in right behind him, spreading and then going to a knee, weapons fixed on different areas of the darkness.

They remained motionless, listening. The air seemed more intensely cold inside. Finally, Parnell took out his flashlight, cupped it under his Thompson's barrel guard, and flicked it on. Its beam drilled a misty hole into the darkness as he swept the room.

Weesay said, "Corridor on the left, Lieutenant. Wet tracks goin' down."

Parnell went down first. The walls of the corridor were stained, coppery-colored patches that ran to the beveled floor. They reached twin lines of cells. Quickly, using room-insertion procedure, they checked out each one. They were all empty save for animal remains.

Back in the upper room, Parnell whistled the others in. For the next several minutes, they thoroughly probed the ruins, peering into hollows and empty rooms, ducking among sundered stone arches and truncated cantilevers, exploring partial stairways that went up to half-destroyed rooms.

There were mosaics on many of the walls, saints and dragons so faint and devoid of color they appeared to be seen through gauze. French and German graffiti was scribbled all over, and there were thick blankets of moss on the exposed stonework. As they moved, their boots disturbed the ancient silence.

It was Bird who finally found the tracks that led away from the building. The boot prints of *two* men. He and Parnell knelt to examine them closely. "At least we know Ike's still alive," he said.

He let his gaze follow the tracks out into the fog and felt his chest tighten, instincts rising suddenly. He looked up at the snowflakes drifting gently through his light. The night suddenly became rife with a dark, nameless omen.

Like the soundless sounds and vibrations beyond hearing that animals sense. A feeling, perhaps primeval, that something deadly lay just beyond the horizon.

Without even being aware of it, Red pushed up the sleeve of his jacket and glanced down at the dials of his watch. In the back-glow from his light, they showed 2:59.

Once more in tight patrol formation, they started across the stretch of open snow. They had gone about thirty yards when the quick, sharp crack of a breaking branch punched a tiny round hole into the silence. Everyone dropped, weapons homing to the sound.

The stillness settled again. Seconds seeped away. Finally Parnell pushed himself to his feet, the others coming up with him. They started ahead again. Red was aware of the steady, even pump of his heart, felt the cold as it layered a frigid mask across his cheeks and nose. He planted his right boot, shifted weight, started to plant the other.

Before he got it down, the whole world exploded apart with light and sound.

At precisely 0300 hours, the great German offensive into the Ardennes Forest Gap began with a horrendous thundering of barrage fire all along its hundred-mile front: V-1 rockets, field howitzers, 88s, 155s, mobile 105s, heavy mortars and Nebelwerfer racks hurling a tremendous hail of steel ordnance into the forward units of the Allied frontline.

Adding to the shock and confusion in the U.S. ranks was the sudden appearance of thousands of German searchlights that flared up through the fog. As their beams bounced off the low overcast, the entire landscape was immediately drenched in an eerie, glowing false dawn.

Fifteen minutes after the start of the massive barrage, the German gunners began moving their points-of-impact deeper into the enemy's lines with pinpoint accuracy, focusing on bivouacs, transportation depots, ammunition dumps, and communication centers.

At the same time, whistles blew all along the assault front and the German infantry assault units surged forward, some in marching columns where there were passable roads, others in wild screaming charges across fields and through woodlands. Forging ahead right along with the advancing infantry, using specific route allotments designated *Rollbahnen,* rumbled massed echelon-formationed German tanks followed by Panzerwerfer 42s, self-propelled 88s, and half-tracked antitank vehicles.

Due east of Esch, Peiper's spearhead units immediately slammed into the scattered elements of the 14th Cavalry Group, the 801st Tank Destroyer Battalion, and remnants of the 245th Engineers. Within minutes, American unit integrity disintegrated and the troopers were driven into isolated pockets, many quickly killed or wounded. Some were overrun, captured and murdered on the spot.

By 0316 hours, Peiper's more advanced units reached the eastern slopes of the Ettlebruck Ridge and entered forest. With their blood raging, the assault platoons and squads actually raced each other to be first over the ridgeline and down the long slope toward the key towns of Neufchâteau and Bastogne.

Accompanying the farthest advanced of the units, riding high in the turret command seat of a Mark VI Tiger, was Colonel Skorzeny, his low-light binoculars to his eyes. Less than two miles due west lay the ruins of Abbaye St. Mathieu.

Blue Team moved through a phantasmagoria, a glowing yellow-white plasma where their bodies cast faint, intertwined shadows down onto the snow, every man feeling that first-contact surge of adrenaline and fear blowing through him, knowing precisely what was happening: the big German offensive was under way and coming straight at them.

The ground beneath the snow shook continually from explosions, the impacts seeming to come from all directions. They could hear the distinctive sound of artillery air bursts deeper in the forest. Yet here there was only the light, themselves suddenly appearing pale in it, like mannequins come alive in the snow.

Then they were sprinting, Parnell bellowing, "Get to cover! Get to cover!"

In the peculiar light, the abbey ruins looked stagelike, something concocted by wild imagination. They made the second building, dove in among the shattered rock and partial walls, their weapons traversing, Bird and Parnell moving, setting up fire positions.

They waited, the world around them motionless, encapsulated within an enveloping thunder. Now small animals began dashing in panic across and between the ruins, huge rabbits with elongated legs that flew over the snow, a small, Corsican red doe, its fawn, and a half-grown chamois, their eyes wild, leaping in long, graceful arcs before disappearing downslope.

Parnell swung his gaze across the landscape, right to left, back. His eyes picked out Duboudin's track, little hillocks in the misty yellow light. It went to a half wall to his left, then turned and moved directly to a finger of woods that had grown down among the ruins.

He signaled Bird. Wyatt crawled over. "He's in the woods," Red said.

"Yeah, I seen his track."

"We have to take back Eisenhower *now*. In thirty minutes, there'll be Kraut infantry pouring down that ridge."

"Frontal?"

"Yes. First we work around to the left as far as we can. Then go right at him in a rush."

They slipped through the jagged eruptions of rock, through half windows, and finally set up in a line behind a low stone parapet rampant with new-growth pine trees. A rabbit came blindly down the top of the parapet and dove over Cowboy's head, the terrified animal emitting a tiny, hysterical squeak.

Vaillant had almost killed Eisenhower when he broke the stick, making a loud, sound-carrying snap, knowing, *convinced* this general pig had done it deliberately to pinpoint their position. He had shoved the muzzle of his Walther right up against the supreme commander's head, just above the ear, his finger already tightening while his mind hesitated, caught between rage and reason.

He heard the stealthy crunch of snow again, the American soldiers moving once more. His reason won out. He slipped the Walther safety on, shoved the weapon back into his holster. He was about to move farther back among the trees, feeling his way, when the fog lit up into a great ocean of white-yellow light and the crescendo of German artillery tore the silence to shreds.

He felt a spasm of joy and relief come up out of his chest that was so powerful, emotional, he felt his cheeks quiver with the intensity of it. *They're coming!* All around him, the misty light infiltrated down through the trees, creating a misty chiaroscuro of yellow and shadow.

He remained motionless for only a moment. Then, knowing the racket of the barrage would conceal his sounds, he grabbed Eisenhower and pulled him along, plunging through brush, dark branches slapping across his face, no matter, hardly feeling it, just moving away from the Americans.

Mon Dieu, they're coming!

There was a shattering of the play of half-shadowed light. Even amid the pounding thunder of the explosions, he caught the quick snap of brush, the outburst of air through nostrils. He turned to look along his back trail. He saw Eisenhower's face staring at him. And then the general was closer, suddenly, coming at him, his cuffed hands shooting upward through the yellow light, lunging for his throat.

"Here," Ike bellowed. "Over here."

He got Duboudin by the neck. The two men wrestled to the floor of the forest. Duboudin punched at the general, struck him in the side of the neck. He felt his hands loosen for an instant, then reclasp, but with less strength. He twisted, trying to draw his pistol. He finally got it out, began lifting it.

There was the crash of brush close by. Shadows jumped and twisted beyond the general's bald forehead. Dark figures loomed, faces partially lit like Greek play masks. He aimed at the closest one and pulled the trigger. He had forgotten to click off the safety.

Before he could recover, he was being hauled upward, Eisenhower's hands falling away, other, much more powerful hands physically lifting him off the ground, a voice near his face inhuman in its roaring. He was flung to the left, sailed for a second, then crashed into a tree trunk. His Walther was gone.

Parnell had been the first one among the trees, brambles catching around his legs, branches slapping back. As the others plunged into the forest, he heard someone holler, "Here! Over here."

Eisenhower.

He turned toward the sound, crossed through a low wall of brush, Wyatt to his left, someone else to the right. All three lunged over pine seedlings, past snow-laden branches, the snow flying up in a yellow sparkle. He saw shadows, two men. He saw a bald head, the other turned upward, stretching away.

Duboudin.

He hurled himself at the Frenchman, Eisenhower momentarily forgotten, got two handfuls of jacket. Growling like a cornered animal, he lifted Duboudin into the air, turned, shifting weight, and threw him with all his might against a tree, then instantly dove after him.

But Vaillant was very fast, up onto his feet again, hands outstretched. Extending from his right hand was the soft glint of a knife blade. Red's momentum had brought him too close. He tried to divert his weight, twisting to the side. The knife came straight in, the point going through cloth to viciously slice across his hip. He felt the blade, almost painless in its sharpness, felt the wide gash it created, felt the warm blood pump out before he could disengage.

Duboudin, bent at the waist, was slashing at the air like

a man cutting weeds, his eyes in the yellow light wild, himself now truly the cornered one, fighting for his life.

"Kill the fucker!" voices shouted. "Shoot him."

Parnell flung away his Thompson, drew his boot knife. He stared across the small, shadowed space between them. "I'm gonna cut your fucking heart out, Duboudin," he bellowed under the thunder of the barrage.

They circled. The Frenchman feinted and then lunged. Parnell sucked his stomach back, easily avoided the blade. But as Duboudin's arm went past, he leaned over it like a matador leaning over a bull's horns and cut the opposite arm high on the biceps. When Duboudin drew back, cupping the wound, blood sifted through the fingers of his knife hand.

They circled again. Just for an instant, Parnell caught the distant sound of armored vehicles in a break in the artillery. Again. Then it was lost once more in the explosions. Apparently, Duboudin had heard it, too. It seemed to renew his ferocity. He lunged, drew back, and quickly lunged again.

This time Red was waiting. Blocking the second lunge, he whipped his left arm under and then up over the Frenchman's knife arm, locking it in against his side. Duboudin tried to recover, falling back. It was too late. Parnell moved in and drove his knife deep into the man's chest, hit solid bone, the blade going deeper, all Red's shoulder and body weight behind it.

The Frenchman was furiously trying to break free, little wordless sounds deep in his throat. The guard of Parnell's knife hit jacket material. Parnell twisted the blade, ripping upward, cutting through cloth, flesh. Duboudin screamed in agony and clawed and trembled like a dancing rag doll, tried to bite Red's skull. Up and then down the blade continued, sundering heart.

Red felt the Frenchman's weight go suddenly dead. Withdrawing his knife and stepping back, he let Duboudin fall to the ground. Vaillant screamed again, this one a stifled cry. He murmured something and then made no further sounds.

Parnell stared down at the body, merely a dark clump among the shadows. It did not evoke thoughts of Anabel Sinclair. It was merely a dead man. He inhaled deeply, felt nothing, then remembered Eisenhower.

He turned, his men making dark silhouettes, Ike's bald head gleaming. "Sir, are you all right?" he shouted over the noise.

"I'm fine," Ike shouted back, grinning. "Neat kill, Lieutenant. But might I suggest we get the fuck out of here?"

"Of course, sir."

"Not sir, Lieutenant," the man corrected. "Sergeant . . . Sergeant Joe Webster, Forty-fifth Evac Hospital Battalion, Eighty-fourth Division. But originally from Kansas City, Missoura. Which I'm hoping to get back to . . . sir."

"What?" Parnell said, shocked.

Webster chuckled. "I ain't Ike, sir. I'm just one of his doubles."

The men of Blue Team could do nothing but stare. Finally, Cowboy said, "I'll be goddamned to hell."

"Sir?" Webster said.

Parnell roused himself. "Yeah, right. Let's move."

They left the forest and went sprinting through the yellow mist back to the road and the half-track.

Aftermath

Operation *Wacht am Rheim/Herbstnebel* almost succeeded. For six viciously fought days, the outcome hung in the balance. But the gallant stands at Bastogne and St-Vith threw the German offensive schedule into turmoil. Although St-Vith would finally fall, it held out long enough to delay the commitment of the powerful 2nd SS-Panzer Corps, which, in turn, stalled the entire thrust of the Sixth Panzer Army's lunge toward Liège until it was too late.

Southward, the holding of Bastogne by the 101st Airborne Division prevented the German Sixth Army from utilizing alternate routes to their western targets. It also led to the entrapment and destruction of Peiper's *Kampfgruppe*, the strongest spearhead of the offensive, at La Gleize.

There were numerous other battles in the vast Ardennes in which U.S. soldiers showed their fighting ability, tenacity, and courage by stopping the Nazis in their tracks. Places like Krinkelt-Rocherath and Dom Butgenbach, Houffalize, Büllingen, Roberville, and Second Malmédy. Yet even then, the Germans might have reached the Meuse River at Dinant on Christmas Day if their armored units hadn't run out of fuel.

Hitler's great illusion of splitting the Allied forces and driving them back into the Channel completely dissolved, just as the autumn mists would eventually disappear. The Third Reich was now in the last throes of its existence. There was still fighting ahead, but by May 1945 it would all be over.

Bastogne, Belgium
28 December 1944
1123 hours

Colonel Dunmore idled his jeep through the town, dodging explosion holes and tall piles of shattered concrete and brick. Bastogne had been almost completely destroyed. Wrecked and blackened vehicles lay among all the intricate, ruined refuse of war. The human corpses had already been taken away for burial, but there remained the bloated carcasses of cows and dogs and donkeys that gave off the deep, full stink of rot, the aftermath stench of war that coiled the stomach.

Riding with Dunmore was Tech Sergeant Sol "Horse" Kaamanui, the sixth member of Blue Team. He had been badly wounded in Italy and had sat out the invasion of western Europe recuperating at a hospital in Tunbridge Wells, England. Now he was back to rejoin the team.

They approached a rubble field that had once been the town square. Passing it was an endless line of military trucks hauling equipment and replacements up to the Main Line of Resistance to the east. A statue of Saint Godula, patron saint of the town, was the only thing still upright in the square.

Across the street was the Le Brun Hotel, partially destroyed but with its facade of gray-and-white stone and half its steep, red-tiled roof still intact. Dunmore pulled up in front and he and Kaamanui got out. As they approached the hotel porch, they caught sight of a large steel barrel that was burning beside the building, pouring out black smoke. Down inside, they could see the remnants of amputated arms and legs, the flesh turned black as coal. The smoke smelled putrid, like burning hair.

The Le Brun had been turned into a field hospital. The main dining room was crammed with hotel beds, army cots, and litters containing wounded soldiers. Behind tarps along one wall surgeons operated under jury-rigged klieg lights. Medics and nuns in bloody white habits hustled among the wounded, the air thick with the odor of blood and iodine and vomit and that cloying, sweetish stench of death.

They found Lieutenant Parnell in the basement. It had been the hotel's wine cellar, laundry, and storage area. Now there were beds and litters here, too. Red was sitting on a five-gallon Jerry gasoline can, shirtless, while a thin, shriveled-faced nun sewed up a wound on his right side just above his hip.

He gave them a tired grin as they came up. "Hello, Colonel," he said. He looked at Kaamanui and his smile brightened, something warm coming up into his eyes. "Well, by God, Horse, you old son of a bitch." They shook hands warmly.

"You look like shit, Lieutenant," Sol said, still grinning.

"I expect so." He jerked his head. "The team's out back. Go say hello."

"Everybody okay?"

"Yeah." Sol braced, thanked the colonel for the ride, and withdrew back upstairs.

Dunmore leaned against a stone pillar, crossed his arms. He studied Parnell, his eyes occasionally sliding over to watch the nun at her stitching. "Seems like we've gone through this routine before, doesn't it?" he finally said.

"Yeah, we have, sir."

"It got rough as hell up here, didn't it?"

"Yeah, Colonel, it did."

"At least the team got through."

Red nodded.

The nun finished her job. She sprinkled the wound with sulfa powder, wound a bandage around Parnell's body, castigated him in Belgium Waloon, and moved off to perform other duties.

Dunmore waited while Parnell dressed, pulling on his filthy woolen blouse, field jacket, muffler, and heavy overcoat. They went back upstairs and out to the porch. A platoon of Sherman tanks was passing, clattering, the smell of exhaust drifting in the frigid air.

They lit cigarettes and sat down on the hotel step. Dunmore asked Red for details of Blue Team's sojourn following Eisenhower's kidnapping. Red told about their failed attempts to stop Duboudin and about the final recovery of Ike's double.

The colonel interrupted, chuckling. "His security people certainly pulled a slick one there, all right. *Nobody* knew they'd made a switch in Reims."

Parnell went on. After leaving the abbey, he said, they'd tried to reach Esch in the half-track but kept running into rapidly advancing patrols of German assault troops. They were in sporadic firefights all that day and into the night. Around dawn, they ran into a battalion of Mark V Panzers and damned near got blown all to hell.

Just after daylight, the half-track got mired down in a muddy flax field, but they managed to slip across the Sure River and head northwest toward Bastogne. On the eighteenth, they finally linked with the 2nd Battalion of the 506th PIR, part of the 101st Airborne Division, which had been hurriedly brought into Bastogne to set up a ring defense around the town. For the next two days they fought with the unit and Team Desobry of the 10th Armored as they took on the 2nd Panzer Division at Noville.

But by the twentieth, the 506th had withdrawn back behind the MDL around Bastogne. Blue Team was then assigned to 3rd Battalion's Dog Company, running night combat recon patrols behind Kraut lines. For five days they and the rest of the 101st fought off continual attacks by seven full German divisions, withstanding nearly constant artillery and mortar barrages that the German gunners put high in the trees. The blistering rain of shrapnel even forced them to use the frozen bodies of dead Krauts to cover their foxholes from the overhead bursts.

There was little food and the troopers quickly ran low on ammunition, eventually getting down to only one round for each of their 105 and 155mm field guns. They were totally out of mortar shells by then, and each rifleman had only two clips left. The entire time, day and night, German loudspeakers blared threats and demands for surrender.

The weather continued getting more and more bitter as the temperature fell far below zero. At last, on Christmas Eve afternoon, the fog lifted enough to allow American C-47s to drop supplies into the town. Two days later, Patton's Third Army, spearheaded by the 37th Tank Battalion under Lieutenant Colonel Creighton Abrams, broke through the German lines to relieve the Screaming Eagles.

Dunmore shook his head, quietly field-stripped his butt. "At least the Germans are pretty much finished now," he said. "This was their last real bolt. SHAEF believes they'll pack it in within four months. I agree."

Parnell finished his cigarette silently, making no comment. Such a possibility didn't seem possible to him. The war actually over?

Dunmore continued, "And that brings up a decision you and your men'll have to make."

Red turned. "Decision? What decision?"

"The Mohawkers are being disbanded. Orders from Washington, since force reductions are already being implemented. In fact, it's already a done deal for us. Except for you and Blue Team."

"Where will we go?"

"That's your choice. Members of the other teams are either being rotated back to old outfits or going into detached duty as instructors, Stateside."

Parnell grunted. *Jesus.* He wondered what the hell it would be like not commanding his team, this particular group of men. Strange, unnatural even.

"You all have enough combat points to go straight home, right now," the colonel added. "So I'll leave it up to you and your men, rotation or instructor slots."

The States. Home.

Parnell tried to reach back, bring forth what that meant. It seemed so unbelievably far away, in time, in place, now even in memory. What the hell was home now? Simply a place where there was no fighting.

"Is there any way we can stay together, as a team?" he asked.

"Only if you remain an active unit in the field."

"Is that possible?"

"Yes."

Parnell eyed him. "You're holding on to something, aren't you?"

"Yes, there *is* a mission. But frankly, John, I don't think you're up to it. Christ, you're bone tired, right on the edge. I see it in your eyes. I suspect your men are the same."

"What's the mission?" Red asked, knowing he shouldn't, knowing he would.

"A rescue of American POWs in the Philippines."

"The Pacific Theater?"

"Yes."

"Tell me about it."

"You'd ship back to Hawaii first for 10 days, rest, then be flown to Leyte for a week of jungle training with an Australian outfit. It's called Operation Forty-niner."

"What's this rescue?"

"There're a hundred or so prisoners at a labor camp in the central Luzon highlands. Used to be owned by a British gold-mining company up until the war. Since their capture in '42, these prisoners have been working the main mines. Treated like slaves. I've seen aerial recon photos of them."

"Why didn't the Rangers pull this duty? They're the ones know jungle. Or maybe send in an Aussie team."

Dunmore shook his head. "Can't. Most of the Sixth Ranger Battalion's already been committed to do preinvasion insertion tasks on Luzon and the island of Okinawa. As for the Aussies, MacArthur insists an American unit be the first ones into the camp. He feels it's a point of honor. I can understand that. Most of these men were with him on Corregidor."

Parnell lit another cigarette and thoughtfully smoked it in silence. At last, he stood up. "Let me talk it over with my men."

"Wait a minute, John. If you people do decide to take this on, *can* you handle it?"

"We wouldn't take it if we couldn't, Colonel."

"Fair enough."

They huddled behind the hotel. Just beyond them, two old women probed a hillock of debris. It was snowing again, a fine, dry fall. Red quickly outlined the situation, pointed out their choices: Operation Forty-niner or become instructors back in the States.

The men listened silently, smoking, Kaamanui's spic-and-span battle dress looking out of place amid the combat-filthy overcoats and jump smocks of the others. Parnell finished with: "However you people decide, the States or the Pacific, I'll go along with it."

Nobody said anything at first. Then Weesay said, "Hey, it don' never snow in them Philippines, right?"

"Right," Red said.

"We go there, we unfreeze." No one laughed.

Bird spat in the snow, then said, "Here's wot I'm thinkin', Lieutenant. We all come a long ways together, seen a helluva lotta shit together." He looked at the other troopers. "I know I'm a thirty-year man and y'all ain't. Maybe that makes a difference, I don' know. But I *do* know a soldier sticks with his unit unless he cain't no more." He shrugged. "That's what *I'm* thinkin', anyways."

"I go with Wyatt," Kaamanui said immediately. "Like back in Africa, we started together, we end it together."

"That's by God right," Smoker growled. "Me, I'm for stickin'."

"Fuckin' A," Weesay piped up.

Cowboy looked around, then shrugged and gave everybody a lopsided grin. "Well, hell," he said. "I guess I wouldn't mind gettin' some Filipino pussy."

"Shit," Laguna scoffed. "All you can handle is rodeo slit, *meng*. Filipino cunt gonna make you puke."

Red said, "You're all sure about this?" Everybody nodded. He walked back around the building and sat down beside Dunmore again. "We're sticking as Blue Team, Colonel."

"I'm not surprised."

"Me neither," Parnell said.

TYPHOON

BY
CHARLES RYAN

Chapter One

Honolulu, Hawaii
14 January 1945
0355 hours

They looked like a squad of Marine Marauders, sitting on their battle gear in the dark, everyone in new jungle-camo fatigues, soft-soled jungle boots, and sandpounder boonie caps. Close by were the darkened Quonsets of the 109th Air/Sea Rescue Squadron. The only lights came from the unit's operations building and from the string of red and white bulbs on the facility's landing wharf.

The wharf protruded out into Kiehi Lagoon, a shallow-water bay located slightly north of the city of Honolulu. Tied up to it was an old Elco PT boat, its guns and upgear under canvas, and a recommissioned Coast Guard MTF cutter named USS *Piute*. Anchored out in the channel were two PBY Catalina patrol sea-planes, their hulls painted blue white.

Back of the station stretched the matrix of runways and taxi lanes of Hickam Air Force Base, their multicolored side lights and tower strobes looking oddly lonely out there in the darkness, like distant campfires on a plain. Across the lagoon were the dimmer lights of Fort Armstrong, nearly lost in the brighter glow from Kapalama Basin and the city beyond.

Lieutenant John "Red" Parnell, team leader of a small commando unit designated Blue Team, settled himself back against his pack and lit a cigarette. A cool onshore breeze drifted in off the channel, smelling of ocean and the sourness of mudflats. The others had already fallen back to sleep, curled on their gear bags, everybody badly hungover.

He'd rousted them from bed at 0200 hours. They were all staying at the EM quarters in Fort DeRussy, a military recreational facility near Waikiki. Afterward, the team was driven to the 109th by Lieutenant Commander Sam "Woody" Chestnut, a Naval Intelligence officer who had acted as their liaison during their seven-day leave in Honolulu. He'd also invited Parnell to stay with him and his family in their home in Kahala, an upscale, beachside neighborhood located at the eastern foot of famous Diamond Head Crater.

Blue Team was part of an elite army unit officially known as the Mohawkers. Created by Colonel James Dunmore, a senior officer with General George Patton's staff, it had originally been composed of eight separate teams, all volunteers and highly trained in reconnaissance and commando tactics for conducting operations behind enemy lines in the Mediterranean and Europe.

But in late 1944, Army Command Headquarters in Washington had ordered Dunmore to disband the Mohawkers. It was part of a military force reduction since it was obvious Germany was near unconditional surrender. All the other teams had already been recycled back to the States, each member returning to his old unit or being assigned to a new one.

Still, Parnell and his men had always been the colonel's favorites. He hated to see them separate now. Blue Team was the first Mohawker unit to see combat. They'd fought in Morocco, Algeria, and Tunisia, and had performed so admirably, they won official recognition for the entire Mohawker unit. After Africa, they were sent into Sicily and Italy and then dropped into France ahead of the D day invasion, fighting all the way across Normandy and eventually in the great Battle of the Bulge in Belgium.

Just after Christmas, Dunmore came to offer them the choice of remaining intact as an operational team or getting reassigned to other units as instructors back in the States. All of them voted to remain as members of Blue Team. With Patton's help, the colonel got ACHQ's clearance for them to be kept in the official logs as an active operational unit of the United States Army. Now they were headed for the Philippines to go into jungle training for a highly secret operation on the island of Luzon.

Parnell quietly smoked, listening to the surge and fade of aircraft engines as military planes transited in and out of Hickam and watching the light reflections dance and shimmer on the surface of the lagoon. He was still half drunk, his head throbbing, his stomach sour and noisy. He and Beth Jennings had tied a heavy one on earlier that night.

Beth was Woody Chestnut's sister-in-law, temporarily living with them while she waited for employment with the Hawaiian Board of Health as a testing nurse for VD among the brothel prostitutes of Honolulu and the outer islands. She was twenty-four with a nursing degree from Stanford, a vivacious blonde who resembled Carole Lombard.

She and Parnell had hit it off immediately, spent all their time together covering ground in Beth's beat-up '39 Ford coupe: bodysurfing at Makapuu or skin diving off Kaena Point where the water was as clear as gin and they could see the shadowy shapes of sharks moving just at the blue-green edge of their vision. They often slept on the beach and got roaring drunk on Primo beer and once even hiked up to Sacred Falls and went swimming naked in the dark, frigid water.

Red enjoyed Beth's bright, funny, adventurous personality. And she found his quiet, combat-vet lethality heroically attractive, his big-shouldered physicality deliciously arousing. From the first, she had blatantly tempted him into bed. Yet Parnell found himself uncomfortable at having another women just yet. It was too soon. He tactfully managed to hold her off.

Until last night. Recalling it now, he chuckled to himself. A bittersweet thing. They'd started out the evening with an early dinner at Lau Yee Chai's in Waikiki, then walked down to the Moana Hotel to see its Banyan Court floor show. Afterward, they hit the Waikiki Tavern and then the Aloha Lounge. By eleven o'clock both were decently sozzled.

They headed back for Kahala, drunkenly singing football fight songs as they skirted Diamond Head. On a sudden whim, Beth swung the Ford down onto a side road that branched off to a coast guard lighthouse and also down to a tiny strip of beach lined with Samoan dwarf palms and wild mangroves.

They sat on a stone water break and Beth pointed to the tiny blue lights that formed a slanted line up a nearby cliff face. "You know where those go?" she asked him.

"Where?"

"To Doris Duke's summer house."

"Who the hell's Doris Duke?"

"You know, the tobacco heiress? You should see it. Damn thing looks like an Arabian palace. But she only

uses it, like, one weekend a year. . . . You know what?
Let's sneak in and go skinny-dipping in her pool."

"What?"

"Come on, she isn't there now. And the caretaker lives
far down the slope."

They skirted the shore to the base of the cliff. A cement dock stood out in the water with a stone bathhouse
shaped like a desert tent. Two hundred yards farther
out, reef surf hissed and tumbled, looking like rows of
cotton in the light of a waning half moon. The tiny blue
lights were bulbs embedded into the steps that climbed
up the cliff face.

The main grounds had a long stretch of perfectly
groomed lawn bordered with bougainvillea, hibiscus, and
white-petal oleander. There were statues and small foun-
tains scattered among cement lawn chairs. A large,
free-form pool curved around an open patio that looked
out over the sea. The edge of the pool had been built so
the water seemed to roll right off into space. Its tiling was
exquisite, forming arabesque patterns that gleamed like
jewels in the moonlight.

The main house had damascene screens and alabaster
domes and spires. The patio itself was floored with white
marble and had an oval mirror pool in the center and
there were delicately slender pilasters carved with silver-
plated spiderweb filigree. The furniture was crystal-topped
tables and, oddly, common wicker chaise lounges and
chairs with embroidered pillows.

They went swimming naked, the water like melted
silk, like air, and Beth wrapped her legs around him and
they kissed hungrily and then went up onto the patio
and began to make love on one of the chaise lounges,
Beth already aroused to roughness, whimpering and in-
sistent and groaning obscenities.

Their foreplay was short, both wanting it badly. Parnell quickly mounted her and lunged furiously into her body, felt her nipples hard as little thumbs against his chest, her nails clawing his back. On and on until his loins began to tremble as orgasm rushed at him. He let it come, heard himself moaning as if he were lifting great weights. There was a sense of white sunlight behind his lids. Then the ecstasy was receding away and he heard his voice cursing, the sound like a sob, as a powerful surge of guilt exploded in him. He roughly disengaged himself and slid off the chaise lounge.

"What's the matter?" Beth hissed. "God, don't stop!"

He walked to the pool's edge and sat down, his legs dangling in the water. His erection was already flaccid. The distant surf murmured beyond the cliff edge and the moonlight made blue-white rings on the pool's surface, the air thick with the perfume of gardenias and mock orange.

After a while, Beth came and quietly sat beside him. He glanced at her. "I'm sorry," he said and felt cold sober. She didn't say anything, instead slowly twirled her feet, making the moon circles merge and sunder apart to reform in segmented matrices.

"Jesus, I'm really sorry, Beth," he repeated.

"You remembered someone, didn't you?"

"Yes."

"Tell me?"

"No."

"Please?"

He did, slowly. About Anabel Sinclair and about England and France and about finding her dead body in a stinking cell in a stinking stable in western Germany. She listened, her legs slowly stopping their twirling. The night became still and remote. When he finished, neither said anything for a long time.

Finally, she pushed her arm through his, tenderly kissed his cheek, and stood up. "We'd better go, John. It's probably near one. We can pick up your gear and then I'll drive you over to DeRussy."

The sound of an aircraft abruptly punched through his thoughts, coming in low, its engines powering back. He glanced out toward the channel. The wing and landing lights of a seaplane were out there against the darkness over the ocean, appearing motionless. Then they grew very bright and a moment later, the aircraft flashed in silhouette against the fort's lights and touched down, water hurling off its hull chines, the big engine rumble dropping off instantly.

A moment later, a jeep pulled up beside the team and the driver called out, "Time to load up, Lieutenant."

Wyatt was saying, "I tell ya, Hoss, that ole gal has a jelly roll'll make your nuts shoot through your asshole." He and Kaamanui were comparing Honolulu prostitutes and their specialties.

"What, at the Golden Pagoda? The one with a tattoo of a snake on her tit?"

"No, this 'un ain't got no tattoo. She's over to the Silver Slipper."

"Naw, I'm talking about Jo Ann at the Pagoda. Blond, little plump, got eyes on her like a Chinaman?"

"Oh, yeah, I know that one," Bird said, sitting sideways on the steel seat, his back to the window showing all that ocean down there far below the gull wing of the PBM Mariner 3R flying boat. "But she all's gettin' a mite long in the fang, ain't she? I use to do her over to the old

White House back in '40. Had red hair then, always use to shave her pussy."

"She don't no more," Sol said. "But, damn, she can *work* it. Me, I don't like bare pussy. Feels like you screwin' your palm."

They'd been in the air for nearly four hours now, the deep-bodied Mariner part of the Naval Air Transport Service, her twin heavy-duty Scott-Allison engines roaring steadily, not missing a beat. There were a dozen metal seats and about three tons of cargo under netting aft the radar/radio compartment, the air at twelve thousand feet nippy. The other men were still asleep.

For six days Blue Team had hit the bars and brothels in downtown Honolulu, first coming in by taxi from Schofield Barracks where they'd been processed and given all their overseas shots after arriving from Europe, riding in the humid Hawaiian afternoon with the January Kona Wind blowing heavy moisture in from the south. And pulling up in town across from the Army YMCA and making a quick stop for that first cold one at the old Black Cat Café.

Afterward, strolling down through the seedy honky-tonks and massage parlors and photo shops and upstairs dance halls along Hotel and Beretania and River Streets with shit-kicking music pouring out into the street and the air rife with the stink of greasy hot dogs and cheap-meat hamburgers and sour sweat coming off the parade of soldiers and sailors and marines that streamed endlessly, aimlessly, drunkenly along the sidewalks.

Inevitably homing to the whorehouses with their color-names like Paradise Blue and the Red Robin, which always seemed located up two flights of stairs and through doors with little viewing holes like speakeasies, and inside the door pay cages eternally overseen by bored old Chinese women and dilapidated jukeboxes full of "San Antonio Rose" and "Pistol Packin' Mama" and the bull-pens where the whores worked the cheap lays, rotating around a four-stall booth, *bing-bang-bong* and you were gone. Those who had sufficient money could rent a private screwing room for thirty minutes: old and musty places with wainscoted walls and the medicinal odor of disinfectant and pubis and cock buckets long since impressed into the wood.

And finally, at long last, feeling again that old, anxious, tight-groin tension rising to explosive release within the smooth, moist-slippery warmth of female flesh that had only been fantasized about and masturbated over during those long days and nights between furlough.

For Bird it had been a homecoming from his prewar days when he was with the 25th Infantry, the old Tropical Lightning Division stationed at Schofield. That first day back at the Barracks, he walked the main company quads again, wandered through empty day rooms smelling of that familiar garrison odor of gun oil and leather and polished cement. He visited the payday gambling shacks still out there and had a few icy cold cans of 3.2 in the deserted garden of the EM Club, the place still owned by the same Chinese couple named Lum, who immediately recognized him.

It had brought up a wash of tender sadness in him, a peculiar thing for Wyatt Bird, the stolid thirty-year man, the quintessential soldier used to shifting posts. Yet there was something indefinably rich and poignant in this particular place. Perhaps it was the remnants of his youth, perhaps the scenes of old discoveries of manhood. But more, it was the memory of old friends, squad and platoon mates all gone now, most buried in sandy graves on countless, peculiarly named islands that lay scattered across the southwestern Pacific.

Still, standing in the midafternoon quiet of Quad 3, with only the distant, sporadic rattle of rifle fire from a basic training company going through its qualifying shoots disturbing the humming stillness, he had allowed himself to remember. . . .

Weesay sat up and sleepily asked, "Where the hell we at?"

"Over the ocean," Sol answered. "Where the hell you *think* we at?"

"What, still?" Laguna said. "Jesus, how long we been flyin'?"

"Six hours."

"I gotta take a crap."

"Use your tin hat," Wyatt said.

"Bullshit. Where the hell's them crewmen?" He stood up, whistled over the steady rumble of the engines. A corporal poked his head around the door of the radar/radio compartment. Laguna pointed to his butt, hollered, "I gotta use the head. Where's it at?"

The crewman pointed to the rear of the aircraft and shouted back, "Remember she's a pneumatic unit, mack. You gotta bring up pressure before takin' a dump."

Kaamunui and Bird chuckled. "Yeah, it's a pressure crapper, Chihuahua," Wyatt said to Laguna. "Jes' be sure you blow the shit *outta* the plane, not *into* it."

"*No me jodas, pendejos,*" Weesay said sourly and stumbled off over cargo tie-down belts.

* * *

The first stop on their six-thousand-mile island-hopping journey was at Johnson Island, a thousand miles southwest of the Hawaiians, the time 11:00 in the morning as the big seaplane swept in low over coral reefs, the water shifting from deep blue to green and then white green as the aircraft settled down onto the surface of the main lagoon that was enclosed by a rim of beach as white as toothpaste in the sunlight.

They refueled off an old Dutch Kazbek-class tanker that was now part of the U.S. Pacific Fleet, anchored in the roadstead. The entire ship was painted in red lead. The Mariner's chief pilot, Navy Lieutenant Josh Paraguirre, went aboard the auxiliary and returned with sandwiches and two gallons of steaming coffee. They lifted off again at 1400 hours, continuing west-south-westward for the next stop, which would be Kwajalein in the Marhalls.

Through the long afternoon, the men played cards or cleaned their weapons or dozed, watching the endless expanse of ocean far below them. Around five o'clock, they passed an American submarine recharging its batteries on the surface, cutting a slowly dissipating V in the sea.

It was well after dark when they reached Kwajalein, another atoll, very large with a completely enclosed lagoon and shaped like a lopsided rectangle. The naval seaplane base was on Lib Island, which sat in the middle of the lagoon like the pupil of an eye. On the southern side of the atoll was a long military runway edged with Quonsets. Everything was blacked out except for the tiny red channel markers near the island and the far-off runway lights that came on only when an aircraft approached for a landing.

Apparently, the Mariner had been having slight fuel line problems in its starboard engine. While a crew of motor-mechs towed the big aircraft up onto a repair ramp, Paraguirre and his men and Blue Team had dinner at the navy mess: thick T-bone steaks and Pacific lobster and skillet biscuits.

Afterward, the air crew went off to transit quarters to grab a few hours of sleep. Parnell and the others chose to bunk out on the beach. They bought beer from the EM Club, a buck a case, and went down to a stretch of beach near the maintenance hangars, sat out there on the sand that was cool and as white and fine as processed sugar, and watched the tilted half moon slowly drop toward the western sea, listening to the rustle of surf on the outer reef and the clicking of sand crabs that scurried along the tidal line.

They took off again at 4:00 in the morning, lifting up into a slight overcast that had moved in during the night. Their next fueling stop was Truk in the Carolines, thirteen hundred miles due west. Bucking headwinds, they took nearly six hours to arrive, flying in over two-thousand-foot-high peaks misty and covered with green-black jungle.

While their aircraft was being refueled, Smoker and Cowboy scrounged up lunch for the team and the plane's crew from a small marine jungle-training base near the landing ramp: boxes of cold fried chicken and cans of peaches and potato salad. They also got hold of two bottles of torpedo juice, made from torpedo propellant filtered through loaves of bread and mixed with pineapple juice. It was nearly 190 proof and carried a helluva wallop.

Just before noon, they took off again in a heavy rain. This would be the final and longest air leg of their trip, nineteen hundred miles to the tiny island of Cabugan Chico off the southeastern coast of Leyte.

Leyte had been invaded on 20 October 1944 by the X and XIV Corps of the American Sixth Army, which was led by Major General Walter Kreuger. For two months intense combat operations had been conducted against stiff opposition by the Japanese 16th Division, part of the famous crack Fourteenth Army of General Tomoyuki Yamashita, the brutal "Tiger of Malaya" who was now overall commander of all Japanese forces in the Philippines.

By Christmas, most of the island was secured. Still, strong pockets of Japanese soldiers had fled into the mountain jungles of the south-central highlands and remained active. By the first of the new year, Kreuger's forces were rotated back to Australia for rest and replenishment for the coming assault on Luzon, replaced by elements of the U.S. Eighth Army commanded by Major General Robert Eichelberger.

On Cabugan Chico, an Australian Commando FTC or Forward Training Camp had been set up in early November to instruct Filipino guerrilla cadres on the use of modern weaponry and demolitions, along with small Allied units in the techniques of jungle warfare.

So far, they'd processed a company of the 6th Ranger Battalion, a scout team from the 5217th Recon Battalion, and an incursion group from MacArthur's Allied Intelligence Bureau, which he had personally created because of his hatred of the OSS. At present, a six-man cadre from the Philippine 114th Guerrilla Regiment was being run through the training cycle. Now it would include Blue Team.

* * *

They picked up the radar blips of two Japanese aircraft fifteen miles to the west, following a vector directly toward them. The radar operator, calculating from blip configuration and speed, concluded they were probably A6M2-N Mitsubishi Zero floatplane fighters on an air reconnaissance of American fleet operations off Leyte Gulf. It was a little after 7:00 in the evening, an hour from Cabugan Chico, the sky still glowing with the fading yellows and deep crimsons of sunset.

At the first blip sighting, Lieutenant Paraguirre quickly dumped altitude, got right down there on the deck, thirty feet over the ocean to make themselves hard to spot from above in the tricky, gradually diminishing light as he raced for darkness. Meanwhile, his gunners came scrambling astern, pulling themselves hand-over-hand along the metal overhead spine beam in the steep incline of the aircraft's deck.

This particular variant of the Mariner had originally been designed as a sub-chaser but was then switched to a service transport. It was only lightly armed with a single dorsal power-operated .50-caliber machine gun and two hand-operated .50s in beam positions. By the time they reached the ocean, the gunners had their weapons uncased and were scanning the sky above them, looking for glints.

They almost made it. Right below, the sea slowly shifted into deeper shades of blue black and then black etched with whitecaps. But then one of the enemy floatplanes came right at them from off the ocean, up the bucket on the port side twin fin, the thing invisible in the radar bounce until it was there, bursting onto the screen full blown.

The dorsal gunner opened on it, his spent casings flying down hot and whirling. A few seconds later there was a loud, slamming crash and the Mariner's machine gun went silent. At the same moment, a perfectly round hole appeared in the port wind inboard the engine, one of the Jap wing-mounted 20mm rounds going right through it but fortunately failing to fuse off.

Now the starboard gunner started firing, then stopped as the enemy floatplane flashed by and up. Far out but swinging in was other plane, also skimming the ocean. For a tiny second its windshield reflected the vanishing glow of the sunset, flashing red. Then its weapons let loose, the cannon rounds arching as slow as Roman candles toward them and the 7.7mm nose gun throwing tracer lines. All of them missed, the pilot undershooting. In a moment, he roared right over them and was gone.

Blood dripped down the ladder up to the dorsal turret. Smoke and Parnell, the closest to it, immediately scrambled up. The gunner had been hit, part of his left shoulder gone. He was wild-eyed. Through gritted teeth, he kept saying, "Oh, Jesus! Oh, Jesus!"

They got him down onto the upper deck, ripped open his flight coveralls. Blood was everywhere. The young man had light blond hair. There were chunks of his own flesh in it. He stopped talking, but his eyes were still wide open, frenzied, and his skin was pale and clammy.

Parnell and Bird got out their medical kits, hit him with a shot of morphine, and began putting compression pads onto the gaping wound. The others pulled out blankets and got him covered. By now, Cowboy had taken his place in the dorsal turret. They could hear the slipstream hissing through the shattered bubble, Fountain cursing. Then he was firing, the cracking muzzle bursts clear and powerful under the engine roar.

The dimness inside the big seaplane steadily increased as they flew straight into the deepening evening. The

Japanese fighters made one more pass, then broke off the attack. A moment later, Paraguirre came back, squatted beside his wounded crewman.

The young man looked at him. His name was Corporal Robert T. Peeke. The morphine had begun working, his eye lids quivering. "You gonna be okay, Bobby," Paraguirre said and brushed the bloody hair from his forehead. "Take it easy now. You gonna be fine."

He turned, leaned close to Parnell. "You're combat vets, John," he said close to Red's ear. "How bad is it?"

"He's lost a lot of blood. Have you got any plasma aboard?"

"No."

Parnell shook his head. "Not good. He's already in shock."

"God-*dammit*," Paraguierre said. He turned to look at the young gunner once more, then went forward again.

Sixteen minutes later, Bobby Peeke died.

Forward Training Camp Hannon lay just inland of a thick mangrove swamp that rimmed a lagoon on the north side of Cabugan Chico. The big Mariner had come in a little before nine o'clock, homing to an intermittent frequency signal from the FTC and setting down on the surface of the lagoon with only the glow of the already risen half moon.

There were no lights visible anywhere, everything merely black silhouettes, even the great mountainous bulk of Southern Leyte, which rose up off the dark sea five miles to the west. The lagoon was choppy with a stiff northern breeze, but Paraguierre brought the aircraft in perfectly by the shimmer of moonlight off the water.

An ANZAC sergeant in a large rubber surf-runner met

them, the Mariner bobbing with her engines in idle, filling the night with the smell of hot metal and cylinder
oil. Blue Team hurriedly loaded their gear into the rubber boat, a small Evinrude outboard on a wooden
bracket at its stern.

Paraguirre watched, squatted in the cargo doorway.
Parnell was the last man off. He paused a moment to
shake the pilot's hand. "Thanks for the lift, Josh. Sorry
about your crewman."

Paraguirre nodded. "Yeah. He's the first one I ever
lost." He straightened up. "Well, good luck to you boys."

"Thanks," Parnell said and jumped into the boat.

Before they reached the mangroves, the big, gull-
winged seaplane, running without lights, lifted off into
the moonlight and soon her engine sound faded off into
the night's silence.

Australian Special Service Force Captain William
"Bush" Hannon, head training officer of the FTC, whose
name was also the code reference for the camp, looked
like a Melbourne waterfront thug, big shouldered and
thick legged with a broad, rough-hewn face, standing in
the moon shadows in front of his jungle hut dressed in
a dirty khaki shirt, jungle shorts called "stubbies," and a
crumpled Aussie campaign hat brimmed up on the left
side atop his head. A cigarette dangled from his mouth.

Parnell snapped to attention, saluted. "U.S. Army Lieutenant John Parnell and his team reporting for duty, sir."

Hannon returned the salute. "Welcome to the bleedin'
jungle, Lef-tenant," he barked without withdrawing his cigarette, his accent heavy Digger. He jerked his head toward
his hut. "Come on inside," he said, then turned to the
sergeant who had brought them in and ordered, "Tommy,
show the Yanks where they can stow their kit."

His hut was made of bamboo with mud-and-grass

caulking, the roof covered with bundles of nipa grass. It was built off the ground on three-foot four-by-fours with little pools of oil at each base to keep the ants out. Where the moonlight hit the oil, it shone like metal.

The single room reeked of mosquito repellant and the crotch-odor of mud- and-sweat impregnated clothing. British weapons and jungle packs hung from the walls. There was a bamboo table and two bamboo chairs, all held together with knotted strands of vine. A kerosene storm lantern and a British Hallicraft SCT-2000 transceiver were on the table. In the rear of the structure was a cot with a tentlike mosquito net draped over it.

Hannon indicated for Parnell to sit and lowered himself into his own chair. He chain-lit another cigarette and tossed his pack across the table to Red, who extracted one and fired it up with his Zippo.

The Aussie captain leaned back and studied him. Two large, pale beetles banged and fluttering around the lamp. In its disturbed glow, his eyes were the gray color molten steel turns when tempered in oil. "I understand you gents're fresh from the Ardennes," he said.

"Yes, sir," Parnell answered. From the jungle came the sudden cries of a clan of monkeys, the sounds like those of women in distress.

"Quite a fight, that," Hannon said. "Bluddy Huns nearly pulled it through, aye?"

"It was very close."

The captain continued appraising Parnell. Finally, he said, "Are you and your mates up to this business? So soon after that?"

"Yes, sir," Parnell snapped.

Hannon nodded. "All right, bluddy good-oh." He stood up, retrieved a bottle of Victoria gin from one of his jungle packs, came back, and sat down again. He took a long pull of the liquor, then handed it across the bamboo table to Red. He drank. It was hot but smooth.

"Well," the captain said, "I think we best introduce you gents to the bush straightaway."

"Very good, sir."

"I just received a signal from KK-2." KK-2 was the code name for ASSF's northern headquarters located at Kola Kola on Fergussen Island in the D'Etre Castenauix group off the northeast tip of New Guinea. "They're sending up a shipment of signals gear for guerrilla units on Samar. I'll be taking it in myself. At Giporlos. You can come along. Only be a couple of days instructing the *Mangs*. That's Tagalog nick for the guerrillas. Give you blokes a look at their operation." He glanced at his watch. It was 9:20. "The pickup boat'll be here at 0100. Bring only your weapons."

Parnell rose. "Yes, sir."

"If you're hungry, Tommy'll roust som'ing from the mess hut. And, oh, the dunny's the last hut in line."

"Thank you, sir." He braced and left.

The monkey clan had quieted, the moonlight casting deep shadows and the air thick with humidity. Parnell moved along between the silent huts. From the lagoon suddenly drifted the cry of a hornbill, its repeated *callao, callao* sounding melancholy in the night.

DON'T MISS CHARLES RYAN'S RECON FORCE THRILLERS

LIGHTNING STRIKE
ISBN 0-7860-1564-0

For their inaugural mission, the Mohawkers are sent to the African coast ahead of the Allied invasion to take out a battery of railroad-mounted artillery. Led by the relentless Lieutenant "Iron John" Parnell, the misfit unit of soldiers must fight their way past a corps of hardened French foreign legionnaires who are out for their blood, outwit an enraged Luftwaffe colonel, and grab the guns. Surrounded by enemies who'd gladly end their first mission before it begins, the boys know there's no room for mistakes—and they'll have no mercy for anyone who gets in their way.

THUNDERBOLT
ISBN 0-7860-1565-9

Two days before the Allied invasion of Sicily, Lieutenant John "Red" Parnell and his Blue Team are put ashore for a high-risk mission—to find and rescue a powerful Mafia *capo* who can aid the Allies in taking the island. But a bloody war erupts between Mob strongmen and Blue Team is sucked into it, fighting against bloodthirsty *mafiosi* armed to the teeth by a brutal German Waffen-SS officer, Captain Karl Keppler. Obsessed by his hatred for Blue Team and their partisan guides, Keppler grimly continues hunting them throughout the invasion of Salerno, through the bloody guerilla fighting on the Volturno River and the great Liri Valley, to the final, deadliest event of the Italian campaign, the assault on Monte Cassino.

ABOUT THE AUTHOR

Charles Ryan served in the United States Air Force, as a senior airman and munitions system specialist in the armament section of the 199th Fighter Squadron based at Hickam AFB, Honolulu. He attended the Universities of Hawaii and Washington, and has worked at numerous occupations, including judo instructor, commercial pilot, and salvage diver. He's written for newspapers and magazines in Honolulu and San Francisco, as well as being the author of eight novels. Ryan currently lives in northern California.

More Books From Your Favorite Thriller Authors

More Nail-Biting Suspense From Your Favorite Thriller Authors

More Thrilling Suspense From
Your Favorite Thriller Authors